Praise for *The Prague Sonata*

"Twining music history with the political tumults of the 20th century . . . a sophisticated, engrossing intellectual mystery . . . [Morrow's] captivating, hopeful book presents a vision of the broken past, restored."
—Sam Sacks, *Wall Street Journal*

"An enthralling epic quest of a novel . . . *The Prague Sonata* is without doubt Bradford Morrow's magnum opus . . . Musical passages are conveyed with lyrical grace. Regular doses of surprise and suspense keep us immersed and involved . . . Compulsively enjoyable."
—Malcolm Forbes, *Minneapolis Star Tribune*

"Morrow stages an academic mystery with real historical sweep . . . [*The Prague Sonata*] is plotted and scored like a golden-age film, and its triumphant ending will rouse you to applause."   —*Weekly Standard*

"A highlight of the year for me . . . [A] wonderful, vast novel."
—Bill Goldstein, "Bill's Books," NBC

"Music and war come to a crescendo in Bradford Morrow's *The Prague Sonata*."   —*Vanity Fair*, "Hot Type"

"[A] textured, style-rich historical novel . . . enjoyable for anyone who loves a symphony of words."   —*Booklist* (starred review)

"Music infuses Morrow's descriptions of war, revolution, peace, love, friendship, and betrayal. Finely crafted storytelling . . . The reading pleasure comes from both Meta's pursuit and the prose, which brims with musical, historical, and cultural detail."   —*Publishers Weekly*

"A musical mystery set against the backdrop of a nation shattered by war and loss . . . sonically rich . . . an elegant foray into music and memory."   —*Kirkus Reviews*

"*The Prague Sonata* is a sweeping narrative, through 200 years and across two continents, that examines the relationship of music to people and their cultural landscapes."   —*Lincoln Journal-Star*

THE PRAGUE SONATA

A NOVEL

BRADFORD MORROW

Grove Press

New York

Published simultaneously in Canada
Printed in the United States of America

First Grove Atlantic hardcover edition: October 2017
First Grove Atlantic paperback edition: September 2018

ISBN 978-0-8021-2868-3
eISBN 978-0-8021-8923-3

Library of Congress Cataloging-in-Publication data is available for this title.

Grove Press
an imprint of Grove Atlantic
154 West 14th Street
New York, NY 10011

Distributed by Publishers Group West

groveatlantic.com

18 19 20 21   10 9 8 7 6 5 4 3 2 1

For Cara

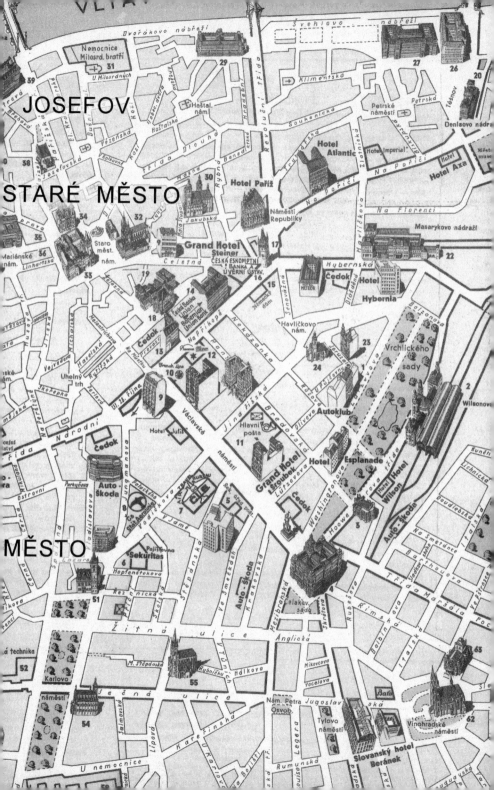

I

We are in the situation of travelers in a train that has met with an accident in a tunnel, and this at a place where the light at the beginning can no longer be seen, and the light at the end is so very small a glimmer that the gaze must continually search for it and is always losing it again, and furthermore, both the beginning and the end are not even certainties.

—Franz Kafka, *The Blue Octavo Notebooks*, 1917

· 1 ·

ALL WARS BEGIN WITH MUSIC. Her father told her that when she was nine years old. The fife and drum. The marching songs, sung to the rhythm of boots tramping their way to battle. The bugle's call for an infantry to charge. Even the wailing bassoon sirens that precede bombardment and the piccolo whistles of the falling bombs themselves. War is music and music is war, he said, breath strong from his evening stew and mulled wine.

The girl looked up from her pillow and said nothing. This soldier father of hers, in peacetime a piano teacher at the local conservatory, the man under whose strict instruction she practiced until her fingers ached, was all she had left. She had no siblings. Her mother, already suffering from tuberculosis, had just succumbed to the influenza that was beginning to cut like a scythe across Europe. She knew she needed to remember what he said even if she didn't really understand. She did her best to focus on him, a raving blur in her candlelit bedroom, more a delirious dream than a man, his voice melodic if a little slurred.

Not just the outset but the end of war is music, he continued with a sweep of his arm as if conducting an invisible orchestra. Screams of the fallen will always play counterpoint to the crack of gunshots, just as dirges of the defeated are the closing theme in any symphony opened by the fanfare of victors. Think of it as God's duet of tears and triumph, from the day war is declared to the day the surrenders are signed.

Why do people fight wars? the girl asked.

Because God lets them, he answered, suddenly quieter.

But why does he let them?

Her father thought for a moment, tucking the wool blanket under her chin, before saying, Because God loves music and so he must abide war.

Don't go back, she pleaded in a voice so faint she herself hardly heard the words.

He traced his fingers over her forehead, moving her fine brown hair away from her face so he might see his daughter better. When he kissed her cheek, she could smell the vanilla and cinnamon she'd mixed in with his wine. And that was how she would always remember him, there where he stood by her bed, her papa, whispering his good nights, this wiry wisp of a man in his tattered uniform and thin boots, with coal-dark eyes and a rich tenor voice that never failed to convince the girl of whatever puddings came into his head. She fell asleep lullabied in the arms of a beautiful tune he often hummed to her.

The following day, Jaromir Láska's furlough was up—his commanding officer had granted him a brief week to bury his wife and make arrangements for his daughter—and he was gone before she woke, leaving her in the care of a widow neighbor. Under her pillow he had tucked what she knew was his most prized possession, a music manuscript he kept protected in a hart-skin satchel. She did not take this as a good sign.

Within a month of his drunken evening rhapsody he was dead, one of the unfortunate last to fall in the war that was supposed to end all wars. Barraged, as she pictured him, in some muddy trench as the tanks rolled through and mustard gas settled over the ruined land like clouds of ghosts, leaving her another orphan of the Great War.

She was packed off to live with a Bohemian aunt in the Vyšehrad district of Prague, capital of what was now to become the independent state of Czechoslovakia. On the crowded train out of Olomouc, clutching a valise containing her few clothes, a photograph of her parents on their wedding day, and that antique manuscript her father had acquired in Vienna long before hostilities began, Otylie made a pact with herself. She would never again listen to men who talked war. And she would never sing or play music as long as she lived.

When war came raging into her life once more on a gray morning, the fifteenth of March, 1939, she thought of her doomed father's last words. She heard no fife and drum. No bugle blared. The timpani of gunfire didn't shatter the air. But music was there on the first day just as he had promised. Voices rose up together as masses of Czechs crowded Wenceslas Square to protest the German troops marching into Prague.

Otylie, now thirty, saw the unfolding nightmare from behind the sheer curtains of her third-floor apartment window as a wan sun struggled to peek through the clouds. Many thousands of men and women bundled in overcoats and scarves were pushed aside by the advancing soldiers, shoved against the facades of buildings as they defiantly sang the Czech national anthem. A frigid wind blew across the cobblestones under a sky dim as an eclipse. Crisp snow fell over the spires and statuary while the crowds sang with patriotic anger at the occupiers, *Kde domov můj* . . . Where is my homeland? The opening line of the anthem had never before made such poignant sense, Otylie thought. A requiem for the dead had begun and, look, the first shot hadn't even been fired.

Her immediate concern was for her husband. Jakub had gone to work early. Would he get back home before the inevitable violence broke out? So many of Prague's narrow, serpentine streets would be dangerous to negotiate if a throng were to stampede or the troops began making arrests. His shop was near the river by the university, in Josefov. There he sold antiquarian artifacts, religious objects, some musical instruments, a miscellany of collectibles.

If he had any knowledge of what was happening, he would right now be spiriting the most precious items to his back-room safe so he could lock up the shop and return to the flat on Wenceslas Square that his family had inhabited for generations. First he would move the finger-polished ivory mezuzot, ornate menorahs, and old siddurim out of the display window. Next would come the early violins and rare wind instruments. Under an old horse blanket he would hide the harpsichord with its cracked soundboard, dating back to the year Mozart completed *Don Giovanni* here and conducted it over at the Estates Theater. Some first editions and manuscripts by lesser composers—Franz Christoph Neubauer, for one; or cellist Anton Kraft, who worked closely with Haydn— would be locked in the bottom drawer of his desk along with a clutch of letters from Karel Čapek, who had coined the word *robot*. Jakub Bartoš's shop was a mishmash of culture, Jewish and Czech, his twin birthrights. It wouldn't be so much a matter of salvaging inventory, Otylie knew, as protecting heritage.

Whispers and shouts echoed in the hallway of the apartment building. Someone asked what in the world was happening and another answered, Didn't you hear the radio this morning? Our army's under German command now.

I don't understand.

The Führer ordered President Hácha to an emergency meeting last night, the first woman rasped as Otylie pressed her ear to the door. Dragged him up to Berlin without notice, sick as the old man is. They're saying Hitler threatened to bomb Prague into rubble if Hácha didn't hand us over to the Reich's protection. So he signed in the middle of the night.

Doesn't sound like he had much of a choice, the other voice responded.

No, and besides, the Germans had already overrun our army in Moravská Ostrava. The radio said Prague would be occupied this morning, but I didn't believe it until I saw the troops with my own eyes. Leibstandarte SS Adolf Hitler they're called.

I call them monsters. *Ježíš Maria*, what are we supposed to do?

Stay calm, the radio told us, and go about our business as if today were any other day of the week. Imagine!

Otylie heard more shouting. The conversation came to an abrupt halt. Hands quaking, she sat at the kitchen table and tried to gather her wits. They needed to escape. Jakub was too well known in intellectual circles here to hope the invaders would ignore him. She and her husband had read about the bloody pogroms in Austria just the year before and understood what Hitler had in mind despite his public assurances to the contrary. Maybe the train station hadn't been secured yet. Perhaps they could get to France or England. Or even from there to America, where Czech immigrant communities, they'd heard, thrived both in its cities and out in the countryside.

Her husband would scoff at such a plan. I may not be the most courageous man, he would say, but I'm no runner.

The problem was, as she well understood, that an important difference separated her from Jakub. She had been devastated by war once, lost nearly everything. He hadn't. *Kubíčku*, my Jakub, she thought, panic rising like some flaring ember caught in her chest.

Another neighbor, an émigré named Franz Bittner who had recently moved into the next flat, knocked on her door to see if she was all right. No one in Prague is all right, she managed to say. He shook his head and handed her his marmalade cat, asking if she wouldn't mind taking care of it until he came back. He'd been outside and said the Germans were advancing in continuous columns across the Charles Bridge. Shaven, grim, disciplined boys in uniform and helmets, each with a jaw set as square as a marionette's, they marched with rifles bayoneted, past the statues of the Madonna and John the Baptist and the rest. Not one of them glanced up at the sculpted figures mounted on the bridge pillars. All stared ahead toward the towers of the Týn Church as if they already owned the city.

Where are you going? she asked him, holding the poor squirming beast in her arms. No time to explain other than that he'd been a Social Democrat before he fled Sudetenland, was known to the Gestapo as an anti-Nazi, and was going to seek asylum at the American legation. She wished him luck and, after locking the door behind him, set out a bowl of milk for the cat, realizing that in the confusion of the moment she'd forgotten to ask its name.

Her eyes darted around the room before settling on the wedding photograph of her father and mother, posing before a Rhinelandish painted backdrop. She took the silver print down from where it hung and sat at the kitchen table, studying their steadfast if nervous faces, longing to embrace them and ask what she should do.

So many different tones of fear, she thought. Chromatic scales of terror, dissonant chords of dread. Her parents' was simply the newlyweds fear of somehow failing to make life work out perfectly, to draw the dream toward them as if it were tethered on a golden string and all they needed to do was gently, tenderly pull. She too had felt that fear, though she and Jakub shared a golden-dream life, despite not having had any children. Love's early anxieties now seemed so innocent. For the first time she fully comprehended her father's panic at returning to the fields of battle; his wine-inspired lecture about music and war was a heroic, misguided attempt to meld what he most loved and hated.

Otylie rose and peered out the tall window that overlooked the square. More Germans down there now than Czechs. Some in long open-air staff cars carrying officers, flanked by heavily armed SS Guard Battalions. Others, motorcycle troops with sidecars two by two in perfect parallel. Marching men hoisted banners emblazoned with the swastika. It was a brazen show of organization and supremacy.

Maybe Emil Hácha understood what was best for his country, Otylie tried to convince herself. Maybe this wasn't an aggressors' invasion, but instead was a way of defending Prague against the depravities of other forces. As she watched the surging masses, she couldn't help but wonder about those young soldiers marching in tight ranks down alien streets, hearing outraged mobs sing words that were not welcoming. Were they, too, frightened behind their fresh, pink-cheeked military reserve? She saw tussling between day laborers and the German columns along the periphery, beneath the unleafed trees. Several heavy pounding sounds in the distance and a roar went up from the crowd. A drumbeat, also far away. And did she hear the strains of an ambulance or was that the cat crying?

Several hours had passed since the first troops made their appearance. Jakub would surely have left the shop in Josefov by now. The *antikva* was small, just a narrow cavern with high ornate ceilings, its facade a door and display window. Otylie had to believe he'd finished hiding the valuables, shut off the lights, closed, and locked up. This meant he was either delayed by the growing crowds of townspeople and Nazis flooding the squares and streets or that he had been detained.

Without further thought, she pulled out a suitcase from the back of their bedroom closet and began to pack. Some shirts of his, underclothing, a pair of flannel trousers, and a jacket. His favorite cravat, the black silk one he wore to graduation exercises at engineering school, before he left that trade for the shop inherited from his father. For herself, she folded a few dresses, a sweater, toiletries, a pair of lace gloves her mother had passed down to her. Lace gloves, she reflected, wincing, and set them aside. The silly things we cherish.

She also packed the photograph of her parents. Her chest was heaving although no tears filled her eyes. The room reeled as she tried to catch her breath. With effort, she got the overstuffed suitcase closed and buckled its leather straps in place.

Then there was the matter of the manuscript, a piano sonata in three movements, its staves scored with musical notes in sepia ink by an anonymous hand sometime in the late eighteenth or early nineteenth century. It had been her birthright and burden for these two decades since her father's death. Birthright because it constituted her father's most treasured bequest to his daughter. Burden because it never failed to remind Otylie of how that last war stranded her in the world, alone with a child's memories of a man whose mad and maddening words on their last night together had turned her against the thing.

Guard it as if it were your own child, he'd told her when she was still a child herself. One day this will bring you great fortune.

I don't want it, she had said, remembering how bitterly her parents argued over the manuscript. Even years later, her mother considered what he had done an outrage, spending three months' wages to acquire it.

Otylie's father, like her husband, had always been an aficionado of antique things. But whereas Jakub knew what he was doing, her father, who worked so hard as a musician and instructor and who loved his small collection of old hymnals and early printed music scores, was an easy mark for an unsavory dealer with a trunk full of fake illuminated medieval psalters and supposedly original drafts by a famous composer. When Otylie's mother contracted tuberculosis, he sold off his precious scores, for a fraction of what he'd spent on them, to pay her medical expenses. The only jewel he kept from his hoard was this one, although he never told his dying wife that he'd hidden it in a corner of the attic reachable only by a ladder she'd become too weak to climb.

In melancholy moments over the years Otylie wondered if this manuscript with its haunted history ought to be destroyed. What reason did she have to believe it was any more authentic than the rest of her poor delusional father's stash? But sentiment, and maybe faith, always got the better of her. Besides, her father had personally inscribed it to her at the top of the first leaf in the language of his favorite composers, *Engelsmusik für mein Engelchen, Alles Liebe, Papa*—Angel-music for my little angel, Love, Papa—and still it lay protected in its well-worn satchel. Though reluctantly, she too loved passages of the sonata, remembered how much her father used to adore playing it for her or singing its sweet-sad melody to her as a bedtime lullaby. Once in a while, despite her resolutions, she caught herself humming one of its themes when walking along the river or nodding off to sleep at night.

The fact was, she knew the manuscript was probably important. Jakub himself had done some research once she finally told him about its existence. He had shown it to a pianist friend named

Tomáš, who expressed great excitement about the possibilities of its origins. This was several years into their marriage. One would have thought it a dirty secret, the way she had kept the sonata hidden from Jakub for so long. Puzzled but also curious about the manuscript's history, he tried probing Otylie's girlhood remembrances. Where and how had her father obtained it? What was its provenance? After several outbursts the likes of which he'd never seen from her, Jakub understood that the personal, emotional connection between the document and her father's death finally wasn't his business, so he never delved further into the matter.

The artifact itself, however, fascinated, even obsessed him a little. Its fleur-de-lis within a crowned shield and the name H BLUM in the watermark, he told Otylie, suggested that the paper might have been fabricated in Germany or Austria, but it wasn't a watermark he recognized. The brown ink, the stitching holes down the left side of the leaves that indicated it had once been bound, even the pagination in a dark russet crayon from a later period—the more he learned, the more everything about the object only underscored its authenticity.

Questions preoccupied him. When was the sonata composed? Where? Was this a copyist's hand or the composer's own? Why had someone set down staves of hastily penned music in yet another hand on the unused paper at the end of the first movement, notes toward what appeared to be a completely different composition? And who had written these three enlightened movements?

What an unforgettable evening it had been when Tomáš was finally allowed to perform the piece in his atelier in Malá Strana, on an honest if aging Bösendorfer grand piano, before an audience of a dozen acquaintances, including Otylie's best friend, Irena Svobodová, who had long urged her to make peace with the manuscript and what it represented.

Three sonatas were performed that night on Šporkova, a short elbow of a street that curves from the bottom of Jánská around to a square where the Lobkowicz Palace stands. The private concert began with the last of Joseph Haydn's piano works, Sonata no. 52 in E-flat Major, followed by Beethoven's F Minor, his audacious first, a work the younger composer dedicated to Haydn, who had been his teacher in Vienna. Both might well have been performed in their own time at the palace just down the way. After these came Otylie's nameless sonata.

The mood in the room was uneasy, hopeful, doubtful. Otylie and Jakub's friends were excited by the chance to hear the mysterious manuscript played. And yet everyone wondered what would drive Tomáš to premiere this untried work in the wake of such obvious glories. It seemed somehow unfair to the unknown composer.

He performed the first two compositions with real panache. Then, after the clapping ceased, he nodded to Jakub, who brought the manuscript to the piano. Tomáš began to play, his friend carefully turning the pages for him. What unfolded in the first movement was energetic and pleasing, if standard and rather Mozartian. The small audience nodded approval when this classic sonata-form movement reached its satisfying final chord. What transpired in the second movement, however, was unexpected. Melodious descending scales concluded in lyrical eddies, pools of euphony, that defied all laws of spiritual gravity when the waterfall of notes cascaded upward again. The music conveyed joyous esprit that mesmerized its unwary listeners. Then, abrupt as water hitting stone, its rich, poignant tapestries of sound ceased. What followed, without foreshadowing, without warning, was a passage of unspeakable darkness. While Tomáš edged forward through this unsettling soundscape of purest dejection, Otylie found herself hearing the differences between his execution and the way her father used to play these very notes. As dark as Tomáš painted these musical phrases, her father's interpretation, which she related to her mother's death, was more tragic yet. Fighting back tears, she shifted in her seat through the third movement, a lovely traditional rondo that brought the sonata to its graceful conclusion.

Silence hung in the parlor after the last note resounded and died away, but then the reaction was spontaneous and overwhelming. A collective gasp and a sudden burst of applause filled the room. Hobbled as the sonata had been by the fact that its performer was playing the work without benefit of much rehearsal, not to mention the unsympathetic acoustics, it was clear even to the most unmusical ear in attendance that here was something significant.

You absolutely must allow this to be studied and published, Tomáš exclaimed.

But Otylie would have none of it. She refused to say why. Even Irena, who knew that the middle movement was deeply painful for her friend to hear, was unable to persuade her to listen to reason. As trays of wine and beer were brought around, Otylie Bartošová thanked Tomáš for his memorable performance. Then, unnoticed, she carefully slid the manuscript back into its satchel, and there it had remained ever since.

Now she could do nothing but wait. Though the sky hadn't grown brighter, she left the lights turned off and the curtains mostly drawn. The passageway outside her door had fallen quiet. Others had taken to the streets to watch the spectacle or else were cowering at home just as she was. She would never leave without Jakub. At this moment she oddly remembered a joke of her father's about two barristers who walk into a pub eating baguettes. When they order their beers, the waiter warns them they're not permitted to eat their own food here. The barristers shrug, trade baguettes, and calmly continue to eat. The thing was, Hitler had pulled a sleight of hand on Hácha. He now held both baguettes and had usurped the pub too. Otylie frowned, wondering if she wasn't losing her sanity.

Not until sometime past noon did her husband manage to send word to her through an emissary. A rail-thin young man named Marek appeared at her door, a first-year university student who swept the floor at the shop, made deliveries, did odd jobs in his spare time. She let him in, stood with her fists clenched together against her mouth, unable to speak, believing she was about to learn that her husband had been arrested or killed.

But he wasn't dead. He had vanished into the fledgling underground resistance that had begun organizing as the first rumors of a possible invasion circulated, and was making arrangements for Otylie to leave Prague. Shaken, Otylie was at the same time unsurprised by Jakub's sudden conversion from shopkeeper to partisan. She knew that though her husband was Jewish, he was driven by a love not just of religion or culture or antiquities, but of country. For Jakub to have so quickly coordinated with like-minded Praguers meant, of course, that he must already have been in contact with them about the growing threat and had kept it from her in deference to her loathing of talk about war. So many people passed through his shop. It had been a meeting place, a microcosm of Prague's intellectual society. Yet just because she was not caught off guard by his decision didn't mean she had to agree with it. She glared at this kid with his curly dark blond hair and large soft eyes, exhibiting such rage that he took a couple of awkward steps back toward the door.

You tell my husband, she said, her voice hushed but firm, that I'll do nothing of the kind and that he must come home. *Hned, hned ted'!* she suddenly shouted, startling both of them. Immediately, now!

I can tell him, Marek said. But I'm not sure he'll listen.

Do your mother and father live in Prague?

Marek nodded, a bit sheepish for one his age.

Once you've told my husband what I said, go to them, make sure they're all right. Leave the underground to gravediggers.

Somebody's got to fight these jackals.

Only fools fight the inevitable, she said, but even as these words came out of her mouth she felt the stinging shame of them, the embarrassment of defeat without a struggle.

After Marek left, she passed an excruciating hour stealing back and forth from chair to window like some hapless spy before finally putting on her coat and scarf and going outside into the mayhem to search for her husband. Things were more desperate in the streets than they had appeared to be from her aerie. Men and women freely wept, many of them shouting obscenities at the Germans, who either couldn't understand them or were indifferent to what they were saying. Dejected Czech soldiers in drab khaki uniforms looked on in disbelief. Some people threw themselves from windows. A couple of boys from the farmers' market lobbed square cobbles at an armored truck and then ducked away into the swarm of protesters; otherwise the occupation proceeded almost entirely without overt resistance.

Yet the people continued to sing. Singing was their sole salvo against this tyranny. They sang as if music were a kind of fusillade, as if their voices rising together could meet in battle against the clatter of tank treads and jackboots.

She threaded her way across the city toward Josefov, shoving forward while herself being shoved from every side. On reaching Staroměstské náměstí, Otylie paused, looked at the Old Town Hall clock and the cathedral spires, the pastel facades of the buildings lining the square, and, farther along, glimpsed the fairy-tale castle atop the hill in Hradčany that had towered above Prague for many centuries. What washed over her despair like baptismal water was the belief, the certainty, that all this would survive every soldier in the streets. The politics and plunderers of any given day eventually fade into a dust of unreality, she thought, but the best of what people forge with their imagination persists. More than persists, thrives. Otylie clung to this idea, found in it the strength to continue pressing ahead. It was a simple enough epiphany, perhaps overly hopeful, but the extremity of the moment made the idea seem immense.

When she reached the shop and saw that the lights were off, the curtain on the door was drawn, the door locked, she stood staring for a moment at the handwritten sign Jakub had affixed to the display window.

Odmítám, it read. I refuse.

At that moment Otylie understood that Jakub's impulses were right. And she realized she might never see her husband again.

Not that she didn't spend the rest of that freezing, frenetic day looking for him. She knocked on the door of every friend they had, forced her way through the surging multitudes past ranks of soldiers and more soldiers, questioning whether the Reich really needed to send so many to secure the peace among an already defeated people. After spending an hour with Irena, who rued the fact that she was alone with her ten-year-old daughter in the midst of all this chaos while her own husband was off in Brno on business, Otylie arrived home just as the first curfews were announced, in both Czech and German, on wall posters and traffic boxes. Loudspeakers blared in the dusk, ordering people to clear the squares and curbs. That night, alone in bed for the first time since she had been married, she cried until her eyes ran dry. It gave her no solace to know that thousands of others were doing the same.

THIRTY FLICKERING CANDLES lit Meta Taverner's narrow brownstone apartment in the East Village. Its walls trembled with the light of tiny flames. Candles crowded her bookshelves and windowsills. They adorned her baby grand piano. She held one aloft, a bristling little flag of fire at its crown, between her fingertips. It was well past midnight on a Sunday in late July, the first July of the new millennium, and Meta's birthday. What better way to celebrate than by turning her whole home into a birthday cake?

All the party guests having finally left, her boyfriend now followed her with their two glasses of champagne as she walked from candle to candle—living room, kitchen, corridor—blowing them out, making a wish at every stop. Soon, her railroad flat was scented with sweet smoke and bathed in urban darkness, glowing with the pale amber of ambient street light.

The last candle sputtered in her cupped hands in the bedroom at the end of the hallway. She sat on the bed, still wide awake despite having partied since late afternoon with a dozen or so friends—fellow former Columbia and Juilliard students, a couple of professors, a few of Jonathan's colleagues—who had brought presents, food, bottles of wine, beer, vodka. Her final wish, like the others, was difficult, maybe even impossible. But what good were wishes if not to stretch beyond the possible? She blew out the remaining candle and set it on the lip of her bedside table before reaching into the spinning darkness to wrap her strong, lean arms around Jonathan's hips and pull him down, as if in slow motion, on top of her. They lay in a warm, dampening mesh of limbs, mouths locked in a kiss, writhing out of their clothes. When he finally entered her, she couldn't tell whether she was giggling or sobbing or both.

When she woke midmorning, Jonathan had left. For the past month, he'd been working seven-day weeks along with others at his firm, fighting the biggest judicial case he had yet been involved in. Antitrust suit; marquee business names. A positive outcome meant a probable turning point in his life, a promotion at the least, but he still found time to make her a pot of fresh-ground coffee. There it sat on the counter next to her favorite cup, with its portrait of Erik Satie wearing John Lennon sunglasses.

Jonathan was a thoughtful guy, always patient with her and her cloistered, quirky crew of friends and colleagues who, she knew, tolerated more than embraced him. They were monomaniacs every last one—tunnel visionaries who breathed, ate, and drank nothing but music, music, music. How did he manage to stay sane when talking with her musical pals, to whom the Iberian Peninsula was less a spot to take a pleasant vacation than the hallowed ground where Domenico Scarlatti composed? How did he tolerate, bored though hiding it well, listening to them argue at the top of their lungs about Hermann Keller's claim that Scarlatti was, finally, behind his times because he failed to return in his later movements to primary themes as Bach had done, yet didn't rate as a Preclassic innovator because he introduced nothing to pave the way for Haydn, Mozart, and Beethoven? Lunatics all of them, her friends, she knew. Lovable, but nuts.

And those were just the musicologists. The pianists were in another league altogether. One of her pianist friends just last night, tipsy on martinis, had explained to Jonathan, "You need to understand that all great pianists are heliocentric. They're both the sun and what the sun shines on. The world is divided right down their center. Their left hand is one hemisphere, and their right is the other. Nothing exists outside this sunlit world when they are playing, moving the notes of the universe back and forth, through and through them, keeping the supreme center intact while the sperm flies."

"Sperm?" Jonathan asked with a laugh.

"Of course, sperm! And lots of it, oceans. Bach had twenty children, if you count the ones who didn't survive birth. He's not a composer who wrote the B Minor Mass sitting at the keyboard and staring out the window for inspiration. Bach was nothing but a human musical orgasm. The music came and came out of the man. You know the one about why he had so many children?"

"No. Why?"

"Because he didn't have any stops on his organ."

While all this was bandied about, a favorite CD spun in the stereo. The speakers strained with each word of one of Frank Zappa's anti-establishment anthems. When a neighbor came to the door and asked Jonathan, who answered, if they could turn it down, he went over to the stereo to comply.

"Don't touch that dial," warned a lanky man standing at his shoulder.

"Why not?" Jonathan asked, ignoring him as he lowered the volume.

"Because the only way to listen to an insurrectionist like Zappa is cranked up all the way. Anything less is a sacrilege."

Jonathan was a sweetheart, Meta thought, to put up with all this. She'd met him the summer before when he'd moved back from Boston, where he had gone to college and law school, to take a job at a New York firm. He had stayed for a few weeks with his younger sister, Meta's best friend Gillian, who was more surprised than anyone to see Jonathan and Meta falling for each other. "You know he doesn't have a musical bone in his body," Jonathan's sister warned Meta, "but that might not be a bad thing. Get you out of your head."

"I'm already out of my head."

"Very funny," Gillian said. "My sole proviso is that you keep me away from the flames if everything goes up in smoke."

Their first time alone together was when they met for lunch in Washington Square Park. Jonathan brought homemade sandwiches. Meta showed up with pastries from her favorite Italian bakery on LaGuardia Place. Late spring, the blue sky daubed with shape-shifting clouds headed out toward the harbor and ocean beyond. The day was as perfect as an opera set staged by Zeffirelli. They sat on a bench under a plane tree and traded notes about his sister, since what else did they have to talk about, until Meta commented on the distant song playing on a kid's boom box, saying how much she liked "Crosstown Traffic."

"You've got to be the only person in New York who does."

"No," she laughed. "Listen, hear that? Hendrix."

Jonathan, a little embarrassed, laughed at himself.

"You know," she continued, head tilted to the side, "I don't think I ever understood the war in Vietnam until I really paid attention to Jimi Hendrix. It was all words in textbooks and horrible images on the movie screen, but when I heard the Woodstock recording of him playing 'The Star-Spangled Banner' it just clicked. Know what I mean?"

He did, he said, although he only kind of did. Still, it wasn't hard to imagine electric guitar feedback replicating jets. The drums and cymbals, bombs. The throbbing bass, maybe copters spiraling down into an orange inferno.

"Even that song over there?" Meta nodded across the fountain toward where the distorted music was coming from. "There's machine-gun fire in that syncopated riff right before the chorus. Hear it? *Duh*-dah. Duh-*dah*, duh-*dah*, dud-*dah-dahdah*."

"Now I do," he said, hearing it in fact.

The two sat for a moment, listening. Children screeched as they ran beneath the fountain geyser. Somewhere a dog barked without letup while skateboarders clattered on. Pigeons cooed, pecking at bread crumbs thrown by an old, bent woman wrapped in shawls.

"You still have room for dessert, I hope." Meta pulled out the goodies she had brought with her. "They had cannoli, profiteroles, and napoleons. I wasn't sure which you'd like, so I got all three."

He watched her with a sudden giddy desire, as the daylight caught in her long brown eyelashes and paved smooth panels across the translucent skin of her cheeks and chin. Her wide, porcelain brow had a two-inch-long crescent scar on it, which in his eyes only made her more desirable. Her silk-straight brown hair that fell to her shoulders was parted in an unkempt zigzag down the middle. She repeatedly hooked stray strands of it behind her ear with a flick of the skittish fingers of her right hand. When she did this, her hand took on a curious clawlike shape, somewhat deformed and yet at the same time loose and elegant. At first he thought it might be a tic, but as he began to pay closer attention, he noticed there was something decidedly, physiologically wrong with her hand. Muscle spasm from playing too much? Injury, maybe? He wanted to ask but figured that the story, if there was one, would come out of its own accord. Pointing at an imperfection was hardly the best move to make during what amounted to a first date. Besides, her hair tucking was a mannerism Jonathan found endearing, maybe because it relieved him to think that she too was nervous.

Meta wasn't classically beautiful, but she was striking, someone who often drew a second glance from strangers. She looked, it occurred to Jonathan, like a person one had known for a lifetime. The simplicity of what she wore—a black-and-white-striped tank top, faded blue jeans just starting to go at the knees, a pair of pumpkin canvas espadrilles—only added to his feeling of warm

familiarity. Later that night, he confessed to Gillian that the al-
fresco lunch had shaken him to the quick. He was convinced he
had, that afternoon in the park, fallen in love with his little sister's
friend Meta Taverner.

By Christmas they were inseparable. They traded books, recordings, photographs from when they were younger. They went
out dancing. They hit as many heavy-metal rock concerts as classical, from Slayer to Stravinsky, Testament to Telemann—Jonathan
gamely teased her, "Meta the Metalhead"—not to mention jazz in
sacred cellars on Seventh Avenue. Now and then they discussed
moving in together, but for one reason or another this hadn't come
to pass. What was the rush anyway, Meta pointed out, reasoning
that the studio Jonathan had found on Tompkins Square was right
nearby. They were comfortable enough with things as they were.

The one barrier to absolute openness between them, at least
by Jonathan's lights, was Meta's reticence about her hand. Seeing
that she was never going to broach the subject, he finally gathered up the courage to ask her what was wrong.

"Long story," she said, her words all of a sudden staccato.

"I have plenty of time."

Despite herself, unconscious of putting the hand on display,
she whisked a bundle of hair behind her reddening ear and said,
"Car accident. My father driving too fast. I was in the passenger
seat. That's all, that's it."

"Sounds like there's a lot more."

"Much as I adore you, Jonathan, it's baggage I'd rather not
unpack," her voice unwontedly pinched.

"If you ever want to talk—"

"One day maybe. Just not today," she said with a tight-lipped
smile. "I hope you understand."

He didn't, but told her he did.

*

The day after Meta's party, Gillian called to wish her a happy birthday, apologizing again for missing the bash. "I always feel guilty when I get sick," she said, coughing. "A hospice nurse really can't afford to be felled by mere bronchitis."

"We're all allowed to get colds once in a while, nurses included," said Meta.

"Maybe so, but that's not why I'm calling. I still want to give you your birthday present."

"It can wait. Let me bring over some matzo ball soup."

"Thanks, but actually, no, it can't wait. You have a pen and paper?"

Struck by the sharp, serious tone of her friend's words, Meta reached for a pad. "All right, shoot."

"You remember that elderly Eastern European woman, the cancer patient at your recital at the outpatient facility?"

"Hard to forget her. She was a real ball of light, despite her illness. I hope she's still hanging in there."

"She is, tells me she can't believe she's lived to see the year 2000. I'm not supposed to get involved in these people's personal lives, but it's not always possible to avoid. So I went last weekend to visit her in Queens. She's all alone, refuses to consider inpatient care. I took her a goodie basket, some halvah, nectarines, fresh sesame bagels."

"You went uninvited?"

"I got her address off the insurance records in the database, did everything contrary to hospital regulations. Something told me I needed to go see her and so I did."

"You're too much," Meta said admiringly, her pencil still hovering over the scratch pad, ready to write down whatever would make it clear how any of this constituted a birthday present.

"Here's the deal. She's been asking after you, so I want you to take down her address."

As Meta wrote, she asked, "You want me to go keep her company?"

"No, listen. She showed me something I think you'd better have a look at. After your recital, she mentioned it every time I saw her, but I didn't really take it seriously until I was there at her home. She pulled it out of a hiding place under the base of this old trunk, what do you call those—"

"False bottom?"

"Right, and showed me one of the most beautiful things I've ever laid eyes on. Like something you'd only see in a museum. A music manuscript. She claims it's from the eighteenth century. Unknown, unpublished, has a whole saga behind it. When she asked about what you did, I told her how, since the accident, you've spent your life studying this kind of stuff."

"You told her about my hand?"

"It only seemed right since she hardly talked about anything besides you. She liked the way you played, liked that you volunteer to perform for people who are too sick to go to any Carnegie Hall. The upshot is, she seems almost frantic for you to see this thing. Can you go?"

"Of course I will. Just so you know, though, the chances are good her manuscript's a little more recent than all that. But I'm happy to have a look. When are you free?"

"Meta, you need to see her now. Don't wait for me. I can't risk infecting her, and she could well be in her last weeks."

"I'll go right away. Do I call first?"

"She's expecting you. Just when you ring her bell, you have to be patient. It takes her a while to get to the door. Happy birthday."

"Well, Gillie, as birthday gifts go, this has got to be one of the weirdest."

"You know me."

"I'm lucky to. Thanks for this. Feel better," and they hung up.

One of the partygoers had given Meta a large box of Polish chocolate in a bright red-and-gold wrapper—Maestria, it was called, with a card saying *Maestria for la maestra*. She packed it into her shoulder bag, threw on her jacket, and headed out.

Seated on the subway, she realized her thoughts were as scattered as the newspaper pages on the seat and floor beside her. She was at once tired from having stayed up so late and unnerved by this foray into a neighborhood she didn't know to see a dying woman she had met only once in passing. As the lights in the tunnel shot by, a small radiant burst caught the corner of her eye and she glanced down at her lap. There on her finger was the ring Jonathan had given her after they made love. He had left the bed and retrieved a small leather box from the pocket of his sport coat.

"I almost forgot," he said, handing it to her where she lay propped on an elbow, naked in the tangle of sheets and disarray of pillows, then laughed uneasily. "Don't worry. Not an engagement band."

She opened it to find an antique silver ring set with an oval of dark green malachite. "It's beautiful," she said, and thanked him with another kiss after slipping it onto her index finger since it didn't fit any of her others.

"Next week we can get it resized," he said, before turning off the bedside lamp and falling asleep.

The ring kept her awake for a while before she too drifted off. Despite Jonathan's disclaimer, she knew—they both knew—that he cherished the idea of marriage and family. He and Gillian had grown up in a big, fairly happy clan, and that was, to him, an ideal as steady and present as the rule of law itself.

She had never worn jewelry on her fingers or hands, not even a wristwatch, since she got serious about playing piano as a child. The chafing, the constriction, the slight weight bothered her just enough that it never seemed worth the fuss. But now that she was officially out of contention for the concert circuit, reduced to playing for the love of it at hospitals or for public school children or at institutes for the blind, what good was an old habit that prevented her from wearing a ring?

It had taken her some long, grueling years to come back as far as she had from near paralysis. She'd urged herself through thousands of hours of grinding, arthritic, torturous scales. Several surgeries and intense physical therapy got her to a place where she could perform with quite wonderful competence. But for one whose sole desire from an early age had been to achieve not competence but incandescence, even transcendence, each of Meta's triumphs during her long recovery was tempered by the inevitable unspoken question, What would this have sounded like if the accident hadn't happened? Thanks to one of her mentors, she did experience a single, glorious night performing Maurice Ravel's *Piano Concerto for the Left Hand* at a gala benefit concert for the Juilliard School at Lincoln Center's Alice Tully Hall. The reviews lauding her pianistic dynamism and artistry spent more space on the personal tragedy that had interrupted a potentially major career. As much as being back onstage with an orchestra exhilarated her, she hated the idea of being a curiosity. It was best, she believed, that she limit herself to charitable recitals and teaching young prodigies such as she'd once been. Beyond that she would put all of her knowledge and energy into musicological work.

No, she thought as the subway jostled around a bend, strange as the ring felt on her finger, there wasn't any rational reason to beg Jonathan's forgiveness and take it off. She firmly folded her hands in her lap, closed her eyes, returned to the present. Was she really about to find an important unpublished score in Queens, of all places? The prospects were slim to nil, she knew. Still, it couldn't hurt her karma to comfort a dying stranger.

Gillie's birthday gift was a chance to give, she thought as the train pulled into her station.

Yet there was an infinitesimal chance something might come of it. Hadn't those chorale works of Bach, the Neumeister Collection, only surfaced in the pop-rock eighties? And in the disco seventies wasn't Bach's masterpiece, his personal revised copy of the *Goldberg Variations*, discovered in Strasbourg like some living, breathing unicorn that had stepped out of a mythical forest? Just the decade before, when the British Invasion was at its peak, weren't two lost Chopin waltzes, tied together with blue ribbon, unearthed in the composer's great-grandmother's trunk in a château outside Paris?

Sure, life was brief, art long. But the life of art on paper was notoriously vulnerable, unless it happened to be a drawing by Rembrandt or Renoir. Even the manuscripts of writers and statesmen had a better survival rate than music scores, it seemed. Meta wondered, as she walked down the tree-lined streets of Queens toward Kalmia Avenue, if it wasn't because people could understand and therefore treasure pictures and words. To many, the notes and staves of a music manuscript might as well be an army of ants carrying sticks and flags down a four-lane highway. Either way, she could have been spending the first day of her new decade on lesser pursuits than chasing a unicorn.

MORE QUICKLY THAN OTYLIE or anyone else imagined it possible, the Nazis reinvented Prague. They reassigned each street and square a German name. The river Vltava, which flowed through the center of the city, became the Moldau for the first time since the Hapsburg rule in the prior century. Czechs, accustomed to driving on the left-hand side of the road, were forced to drive on the right in accordance with German custom. *In Prag wird Rechts gefahren!* Political parties were abolished, radio and newspapers censored. A torture chamber was established by the Gestapo at Petschek Palace. Jewish businesses were Aryanized even before the deportations began.

Other things changed too, as the new order crystallized. Concealing weapons was strictly unlawful. Possessing a broadcasting set ensured an appearance before a firing squad. Whenever SS troops paraded down streets, passersby were expected to halt, remove their hats, and stand at attention as a sign of respect for the swastika banners or marching band playing "Deutschland über alles" or the "Horst Wessel Song," anthem of the Nazi Party. The world Otylie had known since she was nine years old was being annihilated.

Every day, as the eerie, seething quiet of vanquishment settled over Prague, Otylie walked to Josefov to see what, if anything, was happening at the shop. Not that she expected to find Jakub there sitting on the stool behind his counter reading, as had been his habit before this nightmare began. She had no idea what to expect. More than once she'd taken the key to the *antikva* with her, intending at least to remove the provocative sign in the window. But sentries were posted on every corner of the Jewish quarter, and she dared not expose herself as being in any way affiliated with the place. Intuition told her not to pause in front of the store lest her interest be noticed and she be taken in for questioning.

On the fifth day of the Protectorate's occupation, she side-glanced at the shop facade and saw that the door window had been smashed and boarded up. Jakub's brave *Odmítám* sign had been removed and replaced with a poster printed in red and black stating that this establishment was closed until further notice.

Otylie knew that it wouldn't be long before they came knocking on her apartment door.

She hastily returned home, bracing herself for ransacked rooms. After unlocking the door to find everything undisturbed, she grabbed her suitcase and satchel. Tucking the nameless cat inside her coat—his owner, she'd learned, had committed suicide after being turned away by the Americans—she left the building hoping to make it to Irena's without being accosted. Doing her best not to appear nervous, she gave a submissive nod to a group of German soldiers who stood on a corner, smoking and chatting. One of them beckoned her over, but only wanted to pet the cat before waving her on. After that, she nimbly kept to deserted alleys and back streets when she could, then made a daring dash across a bridge upriver from the Charles, which was blocked by troops. Otylie was welcomed by Irena inside her courtyard flat, where Jánský vršek terminated at Vlašská.

Jakub's wife left no note for him that might lead the Gestapo to her. She knew he would find her hiding place without her laying down crumbs for the rats to follow.

Within a week of sleepless nights and interminable days her guess was proved correct. But it wasn't Jakub who knocked tentatively on Irena's door. Instead it was Marek who turned up again, bearing fresh news, bringing her letters and money. He became their go-between and the one left to plead with her on Jakub's behalf to emigrate immediately, before the noose was entirely closed, and take Irena with her. No longer in Prague himself but hiding on its outskirts with a small, growing group of resisters preparing ways to mount an armed insurrection, Jakub had a plan in place for her, for them both. He had even made arrangements for her to work with the Czech resistance once she was safely resettled abroad. Her sedate, educated, humble Jakub, who loved nothing better than to hike with her to the top of Petřín Hill to picnic on

Sundays or go to the Municipal House in the evening to hear a string quartet, was now a conspirator against the Reich.

Bitterness and uneasy pride were what she felt. The confounding part was that her pride made her unhappy with herself and bitterness left her feeling hollow. The anger she'd always felt toward her father for not having stayed with her now began to form like a wicked storm cloud against Jakub.

What was he thinking? Not of her. Not of them. She sensed her heart was turning on itself, growing black and ugly. Irena reminded her that Jakub had exiled himself from Prague, his birthplace, sending an emissary rather than coming to her himself, because he was trying to protect her from guilt by association. She knew her friend was right.

Irena's husband returned from Brno, and although he was a generous man, Otylie could see that harboring the wife of a fugitive—for by then the Gestapo were openly looking for Jakub—made him sick with worry. Marek brought her rumors that summer of England's and France's impending clash with Germany. The news was sent by Jakub, whose colleagues monitored the situation on their contraband radios in secret safe houses dotting the forests and farmlands surrounding Prague.

Jakub says it is now or never, Marek told her. He says you must listen to him if you love him.

If I love him? she exclaimed. He knows I love him.

Then you must do as he insists. This is what he says.

Otylie Bartošová fled occupied Prague in mid-August that year, not two weeks before Hitler invaded Poland, and Britain and France finally declared war on Germany. Marek was to escort her to a safe house in the woods east of the city, where, if things worked out, her hosts would bring her to say goodbye to Jakub. Travel light, bring little or nothing with you, her husband instructed her. And be prepared to abandon the plan to see each other if the situation becomes too risky. More lives than just theirs were now at stake.

She was giddy with excitement at the chance to see him again. Her own life was largely spent indoors, off the streets, out of sight. She traded her valise for a small traveling bag of Irena's that was just large enough to carry a spare dress, some clean clothes for Jakub, her parents' wedding photograph, which she'd removed from its frame, and her winter coat.

What to do with the manuscript had preoccupied her for months. The Germans had already decreed in June that Jews were forbidden to participate in the economic life of the Protectorate. All assets were to be registered and valuables confiscated. She could only imagine how empty the *antikva* must now be. Though she herself was a lapsed Catholic married to a secular Jew, the Nazis would not see their way clear to such nice distinctions were they to find her. Her heirloom, her troubling sonata, if recognized for what it might be, could be a great prize for the Treuhänder, the Reich's ministry of exemplary thieves. Her father, Jaromir, had boasted that it was the lost manuscript of a great master. Tomáš and Jakub believed her father's theory might not be so far-fetched. But Otylie doubted all of it, as a nonbeliever might doubt the existence of angels. Either way, to her it was of little consequence who wrote the sonata. What did matter was that the SS not confiscate her father's dream, or if they did, that they not have the work in its entirety.

No, she would save it by ruining it. She would split it up into three parts, giving Jakub the final movement, on which she wrote a brief, loving inscription, either directly if she managed to reach him or through Marek if not. The second movement, which made her so sad she preferred never to hear it again, she would entrust to Irena with instructions that if Eichmann's SS larcenists got anywhere near the pages she should burn them. All the better, she thought, that this second movement ended several staves above the bottom of the page's verso, where the opening of Jakub's movement began. More frustrating for the warmongers should it fall into their hands. The first movement with its paternal inscription she would take abroad with her, if she was able to get that far.

If and if and if, she thought. Still, she believed the heirloom would have no more value broken into pieces than some shattered Grecian urn whose mythic narrative could only be rightly read by turning it all the way around in one's hands. If war destroyed her or her husband or her dearest friend, it would also destroy the music the manuscript mapped.

Otylie never did manage to speak with Jakub, but was able to see him standing alone at the far end of a field in a blue-gray copse of trees flooded with morning mist some long miles east of Prague. Sitting in the back of a horse-drawn milk wagon driven by a farmer sympathetic to the underground, she had planned to alight and pick flowers with his wife for them to sell at the market. Under this ruse, it was hoped, she might be able to cross the field and spend a few moments with her husband. As it happened, a Reich convoy came rumbling down the road in the opposite direction, scuttling their scheme. While the farmer continued to drive on without stopping, Otylie spotted Jakub's leaf-dappled figure just within the forest's edge. She didn't dare wave. Looking intently at her, guardedly raising a hand in farewell before disappearing again, he was unable to cross the dangerous expanse that lay between them for fear of being seen by the soldiers. Even as a silhouette he appeared gaunt, pale as skimmed cream, and exhausted. She would have jumped down and run across the meadow of flowers to embrace him but for the urgent whispered warning of the farmer's wife that by doing so she would jeopardize everything Jakub was doing, forfeit both their lives as well as their envoys'.

This reunion, such as it was, lasted less than a minute but would sustain itself in Otylie's memory for the rest of her life.

Before setting out on a clandestine journey that dragged on for days into weeks, she entrusted the sonata manuscript movement to the farmer's wife, asking her to have Marek deliver it to Jakub. Having hidden in wagons, trunks of cars, the closed compartment of a train, and steerage of a boat in rough waters, she finally arrived in London, where she began work with the exile government of Edvard Beneš, whom she and her husband considered the true president of their homeland. That fall, the great vortex began to swallow Prague whole. Many thousands were carried off, never to be heard from again.

After the Allies' triumph over Germany several years later, the Beneš government returned to power with the help of Stalin's Red Army. Otylie, already wary of the Soviets, who were moving swiftly to consolidate control in Prague, went back to look for Jakub and Irena. Stunned by the devastation she witnessed everywhere, she knocked on doors in the old Wenceslas Square building but found no one who knew a thing about her husband's whereabouts or fate. Walking through Old Town Square, she saw that the clock tower, the municipal building, and nearly all the once sumptuous houses that bounded the heart of the city had been damaged. The *antikva* in Josefov was fire-gutted, a shadowy shaft where mice and homeless indigents nested these days. In Malá Strana across the river, she could locate only one person who had heard that Irena Svobodová had returned from a camp, possibly with her daughter.

Please, please, where is she? Otylie begged.

The woman wasn't sure. She had heard Irena had left Prague for parts unknown.

Depression hung in the air like the black fumes of burning coal that poured forth from chimneys across the city. Little of the exuberant hope for the future that marked the end of Hitler and Hirohito in other countries surfaced in the Czech world. Stalin and Communist totalitarianism hovered on the eastern horizon like a toxic red sun. Living in a rented room—their homey apartment on Wenceslas Square was occupied now by others who claimed ownership—Otylie continued her search for months, working part-time for the Beneš government.

One morning, as she walked along the river past workers refit-ting the roads with cobbles that had been removed to build street barricades during the uprising, she caught sight of a mateless swan adrift on the brown water. At that moment, Otylie understood she was alone, a war widow.

Jakub had told her once, through Marek, that if they lost con-tact she should either stay in London or get to America. If he survived, he would find her. Because Prague was no longer bear-able, she returned to England, where she worked hard for half a year to save money. She then booked passage to the States. At least there, she told herself, the ocean would help protect her from any new evils that might arise in Europe. When she packed her few belongings, including the sole sonata movement, Otylie was quite sure that its companion manuscripts were as lost as she was herself.

After a voyage across the Atlantic that passed like dreamless sleep, she arrived at Ellis Island on a brisk, wind-buffeted day in November 1946. Her first impression, as she stood on the ship deck with a throng of other immigrants, was that in Manhat-tan's harbor Lady Liberty bore not a sword, as Franz Kafka had written, but a torch. Her second, once she disembarked from the ferry in New York proper, was of what she heard everywhere she walked in this teeming city of skyscrapers. Jazz, blues, classical, gospel, all manner of other styles and sounds utterly unfamiliar to her. The variety was endless, and these Americans seemed to have an unquenchable thirst for it. Even the promised land, she mused with dawning chagrin and unwelcome excitement, was awash in music.

WHEN IRENA DORFMAN OPENED the door to her modest home, she studied the face of the young woman standing on her stoop. She was aware that her perceptions were warped by the vicissitudes of time, illness, nostalgia, faulty memory. But for a fleeting instant, no longer than the wingbeat of one of the birds on her backyard feeder, she felt as if she were looking into the eyes of her daughter.

"Are you all right?" Meta asked, apologizing for disturbing the woman, who was leaning on a walker, even frailer than she remembered from that Sunday afternoon at the facility.

"Yes. I just thought you are somebody else. But I see you are the glorious pianist."

Meta began to say she was the pianist though not so glorious, but before she could finish, Irena took her by the arm saying, "Come, come," and welcomed her inside.

Everything was snug and spruce. The homey front room was carefully arranged with antique furniture, which, to its resident, probably didn't seem all that antique. An ornate Bavarian cuckoo clock hung on the patterned-paper wall, and on the mantel were photographs from an earlier era. The only concession to modernity was a television on a metal stand in a corner next to the fireplace, but even that appliance, with its rabbit ears, clung to a different day.

The kitchen, where the two of them sat at a round table, seemed more lived-in. The smell of soup—canned tomato, Meta guessed—warmed the room. Its linoleum floors, its old Frigidaire, vintage electric stove, and collection of cut-glass bowls and chalices in a walnut breakfront, sustained the time-capsule feel of Irena's refuge.

"I enjoyed meeting you that day," Meta said, unsure how to begin.

"Your concert was lovely."

"Too bad the piano was so out of tune, but what can you expect of a poor old upright that gets rolled around from ward to ward?"

"You made it sound beautiful. Like an angel of piano," Irena said, Czenglish still teasing the edges of her words even after so many years in America.

"I brought you this," and Meta handed her the chocolate.

"You girls are going to turn me fat," she said, and thanked her.

They chatted for a while, the clock ticking in the other room. Meta described her work as a piano instructor and an aspiring musicologist. She talked about where she lived and how she knew Gillian. But Meta understood that her story wasn't the priority. She didn't find it hard to draw out Irena's past, how she and her daughter and husband had been living in Prague when the Germans took over the country. How their lives were cast into disarray by the Nazis, over the course of a few days followed by a few months that stretched into years—which made Meta wonder if this wasn't why her home was so preternaturally tidy, everything in its ordered place.

Leaning forward, Irena asked if she was boring the girl, and Meta shook her head. "No, not in the least."

"You see, I never talk about this," the woman said, her voice low. "But for you to understand what I am to show you, for part of my past to have some future, I must tell you things hard for me to discuss."

The woman meticulously opened the box of chocolate and, selecting a piece for herself and another for her visitor, said, "It is a long time ago, yes, but still I feel it like today."

Meta took the chocolate but didn't eat, just waited.

"First it was the students," Irena began, "who were arrested for daring to protest."

She told Meta how over a thousand of them were forcibly taken by train to Oranienburg, a camp not far from Berlin. Then, after Hitler's top man in Czechoslovakia, Reinhard Heydrich, was assassinated in 1942, thousands more Czechs were deported to Dachau, Auschwitz, and elsewhere. Mostly Jews disappeared but also gentiles who were friendly with Jews, as well as children who didn't know what a Jew was.

"We didn't learn the details until much later, of course, but we knew people were being sent away and never coming back. Hell's gates were wide opened," she said, going on to tell Meta how the entire village of Lidice, not far from Prague, where Irena had an uncle and cousins, was burned to the ground. How even before the town was torched, all of Lidice's men were rounded up and murdered by a firing squad. How its women were packed off to the concentration camp in Ravensbrück. And how of the eighty or ninety children who were removed to the Gneisenau camp, only a tiny handful were deemed sufficiently Aryan to be spared for adoption into German families, where they would be reeducated. The rest of the boys and girls, she finished, were either left to languish in the stockades or gassed.

Meta, unblinking and barely breathing, set her uneaten piece of chocolate on the foil wrapper that lay open on the table.

"They say Hitler wants that one of every ten Czechs to be slaughtered like lambs for revenge. Many people, they start taking

German lessons. They buy German newspapers and speak up in favor of the Reich."

"But why?"

Because, Irena explained, they were crushed. They capitulated in order to save their lives. A quarter of a million turned out in Wenceslas Square to honor the martyred Heydrich. Shamefully, but seeing no alternative, they sang the German national anthem and offered the Hitler salute. Spirits shattered, so many of them terrorized into submission, the people of her country hit bottom. Informers abounded. Anyone even slightly suspected of collaboration with the resistance was rounded up. During the day each person looked over his shoulder and at night slept with one eye open.

"They come into the house," she went on in her disarming present tense. "They arrest my husband and take him down to the courtyard and without asking a word shoot him dead. Me and my child they leave alone for two days but I know they're coming back. My friend, her name was Otylie Bartošová, her husband, Jakub, is in the underground. She had the score which she give me part, to protect it, you see. Make it worthless to the Nazis because it is broken. Well, I hide it under the floor where there's a loose board, before they come back and take me and my girl to Terezín."

Meta listened, stunned by the raw immediacy of this woman's past. The intimacy of it, nothing varnished or padded, was surely the result of Irena's sense of urgency. Still, when she heard the name Otylie, she wondered if Irena's friend had been named in honor of Dvořák's daughter Otilie, who had married another Czech composer, Josef Suk. Probably not. It wasn't as if the whole world revolved around music.

Irena was one of the fortunate survivors of the camp. At war's end, she returned to Prague with her daughter—it was even rarer for a child to have made it through alive—to try to pick up the broken bits of her life. She heard conflicting reports about Otylie. One acquaintance swore she saw her walking the streets, glassy-eyed and speechless, like a lost ghost. Another was certain she'd refused to return from London, where she had worked with the exile government against the Nazis, once she learned poor Jakub had been killed. It was a time of considerable chaos in the capital city, Irena explained. Maybe she'd returned briefly, seen the devastation, and left, heartbroken.

Irena's flat had been appropriated by Germans who fled when the Allies liberated Prague. Aside from a tottery armchair and chipped china, she recognized none of the belongings left behind by the Nazi occupiers. Nauseated by their abandoned possessions and the foul aura of depredation in her onetime home, she slept on the floor for a week until she found work as a waitress and chambermaid in a hotel in exchange for room, board, and a small wage. To her amazement, no one had ferreted out her hiding place for the sonata movement, so she was able at least to have kept one promise. She'd failed to protect everything else dear to her—including her daughter, who had cruelly suffered—but this one artifact remained.

Life in postwar Prague was a demoralizing grind. Spiritual lethargy spread itself like a low-grade fever over the city, and Irena worried for herself and her daughter. The family who owned the hotel where she worked worried too. They had distant relatives who had left the old country for the United States in earlier decades of the century, and they made plans to join them as soon as possible, along with other Bohemian families in search of a new start.

With nothing to hold her in Czechoslovakia, Irena asked if she and her daughter could accompany them. When they arrived aboard an overcrowded passenger ship in Manhattan, the group dispersed in a host of directions. Some stayed in Astoria, Forest Hills, Flushing, the varied hinterlands of New York City. Others truly went to the hinterlands to farm the prairies of exotic places with names like Nebraska and Oklahoma. Irena told Meta that after all she had been through she didn't have the intestinal fortitude to go west, so she stayed on in New York.

She asked everywhere if anybody knew what had happened to Otylie Bartošová who fled to England during the occupation, but no one did. She found work in a haberdashery that specialized in wares for well-heeled immigrants. After a year or two, she met an Austrian man who'd also emigrated following the war, and remarried. Her daughter grew into a fine young lady, went to college on a scholarship, married, and moved out to Minneapolis, where there was a small, thriving Czech community.

"Is that where she's living still?" Meta asked, immediately regretting the question. Otherwise, why wouldn't she be here now with her mother?

Her intuition proved right. Irena's daughter had died of a heart attack a decade ago. Meta did a quick mental calculation. The woman would have been in her sixties. Too young by far; what a crime after all she had survived as a girl. Not wanting to pry further, she didn't ask if Irena had any grandchildren. The old woman, with her withered face and bluish-white hair done up in an old-fashioned beehive, gave off such a complete air of aloneness that it was breathtaking.

She had outlived her husband, outlived her daughter, outlived nearly all of the friends she'd made here. In many ways, she had outlived herself, she said. She'd had years to straighten out any affairs that were left undone, finish what there was left to finish. The only matter that remained in limbo was the manuscript.

"Do you believe in God?" Irena asked.

Broadsided, Meta said, "Sure." Her answer was little more than an expedient white lie, as transparent as holy water.

"Neither do I," Irena said, looking her guest hard in the eye. "I hope he is there on the other side waiting and all is good after we die, but I don't know and nobody else knows either. But I do believe in responsibility."

"There we're in full agreement," said Meta, aware of the inherent promise she was making. This woman who had carried the manuscript so far needed now to pass it along to someone else.

Their unwritten contract in place, Irena reached for her walker and slowly rose. Meta followed her back into the living room. Beneath the bay window that overlooked the street sat a steamer trunk. At Irena's direction, Meta opened it and removed several quilts, placing them neatly on a stuffed chair. Irena herself tugged out the lightweight false bottom of the trunk and retrieved the manuscript, which was housed in a modest and somewhat scuffed portfolio of dark burgundy goatskin.

"Otylie, her complete original," she said, walking to a nearby sofa and patting the cushion beside her, "it used to be in a leather pouch from the turn of last century. So when I get myself to America, I have a neighborhood cobbler make this to protect it."

Two other passages of music had originally accompanied the manuscript. She was pretty sure hers was the middle movement, adding, however, that Meta had "best not rely on an old lady's foggy memory." Nor could she remember which one had been entrusted to Jakub and which Otylie kept herself. She did recollect an evening long ago when the work had its only performance, at least in her lifetime. A friend of Jakub's played it, Tomáš, she thought his name was—yes, she was nearly certain that had been his name. Meta assured her host that she would probably be able to confirm where this piece of the puzzle fitted with the other movements through an analysis of the music.

"That will be relatively easy," she told Irena. "More difficult and more essential, I think, will be to try to locate those lost parts. To restore the manuscript to wholeness, if it's even possible."

"You will do this?" clutching the artifact in shaking hands. Assured that the young woman would try, Irena passed the satchel over.

"May I?" At Irena's nod, Meta unstrung the thong that was wound around a bone button, pulling an oblong sheaf of pages out into the afternoon light. Edges were yapped and frayed here and there, some smudges and stains obscured notations on the top leaf, but without any shadow of doubt what she held in her hands was not contemporary. Meta had studied quite a few nineteenth-century manuscripts, and even a cursory glance suggested this document was earlier than that. The cursive, the manner of hand-scribing the staves, the weight of the deckled paper, the whole appearance and feel of the document. In the silence of the room, ignoring the ticking metronome on the wall, she read the first dozen measures and heard the music in her head, and that was that. She was galvanized. If it proved to be a fake, it would be an exceptional fake, one of historical interest.

Irena gently placed her hand on Meta's forearm. "There is one more thing," she said. "Look in the pouch. You will find a letter there."

Meta peered inside and indeed there was an envelope at the bottom of the portfolio. She pulled it out and handed it to the old woman, who withdrew and unfolded a sheet of pale blue paper. Someone had hurriedly written a few lines on the front, Meta assumed in Czech since she couldn't read a word of it.

"This is from Otylie. It says my responsibility is to take care of this until it can be put back with the other parts. Says I own it until that is possible, but I never think of it that way. Says too that I destroy it if the Nazis try to take it, but"—and here she smiled— "it is good I never had to do this."

She retrieved a pen from her purse, which was lying on the kitchen table, turned the letter over, and wrote on the back in a meticulous if somewhat shaky hand, *This manuscript now the property of Meta*—"How are you spelling your family name?"— *Taverner until such time she is able to return this to Otylie Bartošová or heir, with agreed that she try to recover entire manuscript as were Otylie Bartošová's stated wishes.* Irena signed and dated the letter and handed it to Meta, who was speechless.

The two sat for a moment in silence before the older woman said, "I'm tired now, dear." She walked Meta to the door, where her jacket was hung on a coat tree. There they embraced like kinswomen.

"I'll come back to visit you in a few days, as soon as Gillian's feeling better. Would you like that? We'll bring you some more sweets to make you fat. Meantime, I will take good care of this, I promise."

Irena lingered on her front stoop, watching Meta walk away down the sidewalk under the shadow-puppeting shade trees with the portfolio cradled under her arm.

· 2 ·

B ACK IN HER OWN NEIGHBORHOOD, Meta felt
disoriented. As if Queens were a fairy-tale dream from
which she hadn't fully awakened. Yet here was this satchel
in her arms. She double-locked her door, cleared her desk, wiped
it down with a dry cloth, and set the portfolio in the middle of this
empty space. Then she went to the bathroom, washed her hands,
and toweled them dry. Pushing up the sleeves of her blouse like
a midwife about to assist in a birth, she carefully drew out the
manuscript and set the leather folder to one side. On her face
swam a look of mingled wonderment, focus, even fear.

With reverent delicacy, she turned the pages one by one, eyes
traveling across the busy staves that filled each leaf. This wasn't
going to be easy to play. Unaware she was doing so, she hummed
an occasional phrase, tapped her toe gently on the floor. Meta
might have sat down with the manuscript at her piano and performed it then and there. But she didn't want to listen to it until

she'd had time to study the piece, learn what its composer was saying.

This was not your everyday second movement of a sonata, despite Irena's recollecting that's what it probably was. Brazen in its initial runs, the music settled now and again, only to move away into knotty clusters of sixteenth notes, like an impish acrobat who pretends to teeter off his tightrope high above the crowd, flails his arms as if he's about to fall, until, nimbly, in slow motion, he moves on.

Then, a plunge off a cliff—everything shifted to blacker registers. Gone was the acrobat. Gone were the playful, bucolic pace and tone of the earlier passage, which was, it now occurred to Meta, a feint, a dramatic setup. The meat, the soul of the dolorous passage had such a rich, slow sadness to it that, surprised, she turned back to the opening and reread the movement up to this radical shift in mood.

With its moments of staggering power and slyness, the music seemed as fresh that day, to this young woman in her barbell flat, as it must have sounded when it was conceived. Who was the conceiver, though? And where were the fore and aft of this noteworthy craft? Halfway down the last page, the movement reached its resolution, its finale.

There was more. Half a dozen measures, clearly the tantalizing first notes of the next movement, which ran to the last measure on the bottom of the verso, then simply dropped off into silence. A very different mood, a different texture, was hinted at here. Could it be a rondo theme gestating in these few measures? Whatever form the next movement took, it promised joy in the wake of the quasi-requiem tones of the adagio.

What was most dumbfounding, she realized, sitting back on her wobbly oak chair in a state somewhere between grace and shock, was that she had never heard a single note of this work before.

There were resonances with other music from the final important decades of the eighteenth century, when she suspected it might have been composed. But she had never encountered this particular series of notes and chord progressions. She couldn't begin to claim to have heard all the piano music written during those years—that would be a lifetime's endeavor—but this was one of her fields of expertise. Yet *expert* and *expertise* were terms she always distrusted because somehow they seemed so very dead. So terminal. As if once you were an expert, your life was essentially concluded because your trials and discoveries lay behind you.

Expert or no, Meta understood that the manuscript was potentially a discovery of a high order. It was, at least, an important moment in her life. If her own thirty years constituted a first movement of a sonata, she sensed in her gut that she was right now living the opening notes of the second.

At dinner with Jonathan that evening at their favorite Japanese restaurant, Meta found herself struggling to concentrate. The case his law firm was involved with had been inching its way toward the front pages of the newspapers. The alleged offenses were nothing new, but to anyone who read the tabloids, the corporate players were becoming household names. Jonathan had been assisting one of his firm's partners from day one of the litigation, and that afternoon the judge had thrown out the tampering charge and expressed concerns about the viability of the entire case. This major victory for the defense team resulted in no small measure from some of Jonathan's own fieldwork.

Meta had been following his progress with interest. But as he launched into a detailed account of how the wheels and cogs of justice turned, her mind ventured back to Irena. Those piercing blue eyes. The woman's strength. The trust, the faith she had placed in Meta.

"You look tired," Jonathan said, interrupting her thoughts.

"Me?" She glanced up from the wooden platter of yellowtail and tuna sushi, as guilty as if she'd been caught stealing. "I'm sorry. Guess I am."

"So tell me what you did with the first day of the rest of your life."

"Nothing special," she hedged, knowing she wasn't ready to share the magic of it with him yet. Not until she'd fully absorbed the day's events. She couldn't risk listening to Jonathan comment on possible legalities regarding ownership, rights, anything that would unsettle her quiet euphoria. But the next day, she telephoned Gillian. No way could she keep this from the one who had acted as catalyst.

"It's real," Meta said, without preliminaries.

"You're sure?" Gillian asked.

"Real as you or me."

"So what are you going to do?"

"I don't know yet but I didn't sleep last night thinking about it." She glanced toward her desk, where the leather satchel still lay, and confessed she'd been too unsettled to play it out loud yet. Needed to study it more before committing it to the air. "But even slow sight-reads tell me volumes. Gillie, it's magnificent, overwhelming."

"Irena's going to be thrilled." Gillian coughed, excused herself. "Have you told your guru yet?"

"Mandelbaum's my next call, but Gillie, I'm bringing you chicken soup today and won't take no for an answer."

"This cough isn't as bad as it sounds. So how old do you think it is?"

Meta said it was far too early to offer anything beyond speculation, but she sensed it was a transitional work. "There are hints of late Mozart, stylistically traditional for the time but with some very weird, totally idiosyncratic stuff going on too. I'm not saying it couldn't be later, written by someone fluent in the language and tropes of that era. But the paper looks to be period. I don't know. I can tell you this. If it's some sort of counterfeit, the person who did it was a genius in his own right. It doesn't feel fake to me, though."

"Based on what?" She coughed again, said, "Okay, maybe I will take you up on that soup."

"Thank you. How can I put it? The musical decisions are just too strange to be fake. If you're creating a fraud, you want it to conform, not revolt. This thing breaks the rules too much to blend into the crowd. Either way, Mandelbaum's the only one I can trust to think it through with me."

"What did Jonathan say about it?"

Here Meta hesitated. Then, guiltily, she said, "I haven't told him yet."

"Why not?"

She took a deep breath. "It's hard to explain, Gillie. I just don't think he'd get it, and I'm not even sure myself what I have on my hands. Please don't say anything to him. I need time to figure out what to do."

The beat of silence at the other end of the line gave Meta a sinking feeling. But had she been asked by a dying mother to assume the responsibility of raising her crippled child, it wouldn't have been a more serious commitment. Through every crisis she had suffered, music had been the lifeline that got her through. Neither love nor friendship, prayer nor sex, nature nor art, other than this one made up of noises produced on what were finally quite quirky machines—violin, oboe, French horn, double bass, the whole quaint graybeard crew that constituted an orchestra— had ever given her a deeper purpose. Music was a form of worship for Meta, and somehow Irena's manuscript seemed destined to be

her charge. She never talked with others in such overwrought, romantic terms about this core part of her life. But its centrality was
never far from her mind. Much as she knew her friend's brother
loved her, she also knew he didn't truly understand this about her.

Gillian was speaking. "Well, I'm sure you'll sort things out. I
wouldn't have sent you to her if I hadn't thought you'd look after
her wishes."

"I hope I can live up to your gift."

"You already have."

Paul Mandelbaum was the most lively minded music scholar
Meta had ever met. Professor emeritus of the department of music
at Columbia, and with a stack of honors and awards he'd never
bothered to hang on any wall, Mandelbaum had recently retired
with his wife to her childhood hometown, Lawrenceville, just outside Princeton, where he continued to write and publish and attend symposia at which he was accorded star treatment. Meta
had been a darling of his while she was taking his classes as a
visiting student from Juilliard, and he saw to it she was admitted
to the Columbia musicology program with a full-ride fellowship
once it was clear her performing days were over. She worked as
his research assistant for several years before he rusticated to the
Jersey flats, where he jokingly planned "to molder merrily away." If
she loved anyone unconditionally besides her mother, it was Paul
Mandelbaum.

"Hello? Me here. So, look, when do you have to be in the city
next?"

He shook his head at the voice on the receiver. That was his Meta.
A curious, and to him endearing, counterpoint of impulsiveness and

gravity. They hadn't seen each other for months and this was how she began their conversation?

"You forget. I'm retired, put out to pasture. I have no need to be in the city. Life's already too exhausting."

"Oh, stop," she scoffed. "You begged off my birthday, which was fine. But this is way more important than a birthday party. I have to show you something."

"And what would that be?"

"You just have to see it and tell me what you think."

"What's to prevent you from getting on the train and bringing this thing, whatever it is, out to Princeton? We can have lunch on Nassau Street and then come back to our place. You can see your future as a retired musicologist living in a small stone house surrounded by people living in big stone houses."

"I'd rather not take it anywhere."

"Very Conan Doyle of you, Meta. Very foggy heaths and dripping grottoes. I hope no one's been murdered."

"I'm serious, Paul. Let me show you what I'm talking about, get your opinion on it, and I'll take you to lunch afterward. T-bone for two at that restaurant you like on University Place, with the half-moon booths and Hirschfeld drawings. Creamed spinach, onion rings, a dry martini or two, the works."

"The Knick?"

"You got it."

"Well, all right then. I can't very well turn down a chance at free creamed spinach, can I?" he mock-sighed.

That night, as Jonathan slept, she knelt beside him, watching him breathe in and out, and tried to think. When they had made love earlier, he had shown unusual ferocity. After entering her, his belly to her back, he ungently rolled her facedown and began to thrust. Involuntarily, feeling oddly alone, she clenched her fists. It didn't hurt, but there wasn't pleasure in it either. After he came with a soundless shudder, Jonathan stretched himself out beside her, stared into the murky light of the room, and breathed heavily, whispering, "I love you" before falling asleep.

Seeing him dream, twitching in his sleep, she pulled the sheet over his shoulders, realizing that Jonathan did, after all, have the instincts of a raptor. He must have felt an invisible tether, one of many that bound them together, come loose on her birthday and slip its cinch. Without so much as a harsh word exchanged between them, he had sensed her deception. What he communicated to her in bed that night, aside from his reassuring words, was that he was afraid. Afraid as a falcon might be, wary and aggressive at the same time. She slid her head under her pillow, feeling herself to blame.

After Jonathan had left the next morning, she went to her own trunk, opened it, and drew out the satchel containing the manuscript. The battered footlocker, with its broken lock, was one of the very few possessions given to her by her father. He pawned it off on his daughter, she figured, because in his rush to leave his family for another woman and a fresh start in Los Angeles, he hadn't wanted to be bothered with such a cumbersome piece of junk. She kept spare linens in it. Winter clothes during summer. Summer clothes during winter. An unlikely repository for something precious, but hadn't a worse-for-wear steamer trunk sufficed for Irena all those years?

The time had come to play. To hear the fragment freed from the page.

Meta sat at her piano, positioned the music on its stand, and placed her fingers on the keys, walking them through the first notes. The music sounded even more passionate than it had in her imagination, in her intuitive and highly trained inner ear. Its first tones were saturated with happiness, even joy. If music were colors, the opening refrain was painted in the primary red of a roulette wheel, the gold-leaf halo of a Renaissance Madonna, the blue of oceans seen from space. Brilliant, heartening colors done up in the circular forms of sacred things and things that spin. Then, as she had noticed the day before, came the brusque, precipitous descent into raw despair. A radical twilight settled over this round aural world. Blues became black. Blacks exploded like slow-motion blossoming flowers into shades of violet and dark orange. How odd to be thinking more in terms of some psychedelic rock-and-roll light show than a classical sonata. But the music merited such imaginative abandon.

Replaying the movement at half tempo, careful of her right hand, which was already a bit sore, Meta now heard, in the tragic middle section, a deep, subterranean coherence and vision at work here. And through a sharp, sly contrast of the two moods, the brief final section combined rising and falling arpeggios like a sorcerer's game of ladders and slides, moving steadily toward a resolution that proved to be no definitive resolution at all.

It was powerful, inspired work. Now joyous. Now chancy and tense. Mortifying, heartbreaking. Finally, uplifting and confounding.

Mandelbaum couldn't arrive fast enough. He might, she suspected, be able to identify the composer instantly. Might even recognize it as a work already known to the rarefied world of specialists. He was, after all, something of a walking, talking *New Grove Dictionary of Music and Musicians*, a living, breathing *Die Musik in Geschichte und Gegenwart*. Sure, his identification might come as an anticlimax, even a letdown, her mentor wiping away the great mystery with a mortal name. But he would no doubt burst her bubble with a mentor's dose of charity.

Maybe not, though. Maybe the manuscript she had come to think of as the Prague Sonata would prove to be a significant musical discovery. Either way, she decided, she would be able to travel back to Queens with Mandelbaum's opinion in place and inform her benefactor what she'd been protecting all these decades.

THE PALI WORD FOR unconditional loving-kindness is pronounced *meta*, but is spelled *metta*. The word *maitri* is its Sanskrit equivalent. Meta, whose parents had been young sixties idealists, named their only child with this high in mind. From the Greek μετά, her name also means *with*, or *after*, or *beyond*, something Meta had found curious when she looked it up, since how could a single word mean both *with* and *beyond* at the same time? In English usage, *meta* is a prefix signifying a concept that is an abstraction of another concept. In epistemology the prefix gets a little more complicated. Here it modifies words in such a way that they become about what they are about. Language as a mirror in which the letters are reflected not backward, but inside out. Metacognition, for instance, is thinking about thinking.

In the days since the score had come into her hands, Meta had been trying to think about how she was thinking, but with mixed results. She felt deep loving-kindness toward Jonathan, and yet it seemed to her that something she had no words for was amiss. Curiously both with and beyond him, she had to wonder, as well, if her remoteness, an inward-gazing reverie, was because of her birthday. The *Big Three Oh-oh* she'd called it, when planning her party. She, who always loved holding soirées and making elaborate dinners for friends, had even wondered out loud whether thirty wasn't too old for a birthday celebration.

"Maybe I'm a little long in the tooth for tooth fairies anymore," she had told Jonathan, mixing vanilla into her cupcake batter the night before the bash.

And hadn't Jonathan himself been inordinately wrapped up in this trial? It had been pretty heady for him to see his picture in the newspapers, walking into and out of the columned courthouse downtown. Granted, his face was not at the center of these photos, any more than he himself was at the center of the case. But his job certainly was at the center of his life these days, much as the manuscript was at the center of hers. They were just going through a phase, she told herself, not altogether convinced.

The morning of Mandelbaum's trip into New York to see her, Meta got up with Jonathan and made him breakfast.

"What's the occasion?" he asked, leaning against the wall of the galley kitchen with a towel wrapped around his waist, his hair still wet from the shower.

"Isn't there supposed to be a ruling today on your motion to dismiss?"

He clearly hadn't realized she'd been tracking the case that closely. "So we're hoping."

"Then you need to go into battle with a decent meal under your belt, right?"

"I appreciate it," he said, waiting for her to tell him the real reason she was up early.

He didn't have to wait long. Pouring two cups of coffee, she continued, "I also wanted to show you something before you took off."

Jonathan dressed, and while they ate Meta finally filled him in about the manuscript, quickly sketching its background. Wrapped up as he was, she knew he wouldn't be any more able to listen to her next week or the week thereafter. May as well be now.

He leafed through a few pages while at the same time guilt-ily glancing at his wristwatch. "I was wondering what had you so distracted," he said with a relieved smile.

"More possessed than distracted. This manuscript and music are unlike anything I've ever encountered," Meta said, an anxious edge in her voice. "It may sound a little nuts but this feels like destiny that it's come into my hands."

"Extreme, maybe. Not nuts. I remember when I turned thirty I felt discombobulated for a while."

She shook her head. Discombobulated was not how she felt. The opposite. Very focused, very much alive.

"I have zero knowledge about these things, but it looks authentic."

"Oh, it's authentic all right. But authentically what and by whom I don't know."

"I want to hear more but I've got to get to work," he said, then noticed the letter tucked into the back of the sheaf. "What's this?"

"A note from Irena. She wrote that the manuscript is temporar-ily mine until I find Otylie Bartošová, the original owner, and give it back to her."

"Temporarily yours?" he asked. "So it's not clear who exactly owns this thing? You want me to have a look at the note, see if it's legally binding? Check on proprietary issues?"

The questions made her cringe. She couldn't have predicted his precise words, but they were just as she had feared. "Pro-prietary issues? That's not necessary, Jonathan. It's music. The world owns it."

He took one last sip of coffee, straightened his tie. "I can't wait to hear you play it, but I've got to run. If you want, I'll talk to one of our deeds and rights people. Just let me know." He kissed her goodbye and left.

Meta carefully rewrapped the score in tissue paper that was left over from one of her birthday presents and slipped it back into its satchel, willing herself not to be angry. Law was Jonathan's life, as music was hers. It was only natural he would see the manuscript through that lens.

The balance of the morning she spent in seesawing emotions. Would Mandelbaum's reaction be as uninterested as Jonathan's? Had she simply been swept away by Irena's story and the beauty of the work? Was it no more than a curiosity, a secondary scrap floating along on the clogged river of human ideas already overflowing with culture's castoffs? She couldn't help but feel a tinge of shame about the melodramatic thoughts chasing around in her head.

Paul Mandelbaum was on time, as always. Over the intercom she told him to come upstairs. While he climbed the four flights, she found herself breathing quickly. She hadn't felt this nervous since her first piano competition.

They embraced warmly at the door and Mandelbaum kissed her on both cheeks. It was a habit from his years in Paris, Vienna, and Prague, where, as a young scholar with a burgeoning knowledge of music history, he had produced a well-received book and a cluster of articles before he reached Meta's current age. His hair, once black as a clarinet, was now a silver mane, his face narrow as the Flatiron Building and just as craggy. As always, no matter what the weather, he was dressed in an oversize black cable-knit pullover and loose-fitting black corduroys. Had he been made to stand behind a Japanese screen and read a few names and numbers out of the phone book, anyone listening would have guessed his age to be as many as three decades younger than his seventy-one years.

"I figured it out on the train," he said. "You discovered that Mahler did in fact finish his Tenth Symphony and you've got the missing manuscript to prove it."

Crazy, she thought. Wrong era, right idea. Startled but smiling, she grabbed his hand and led him into the front room.

There, alone on her desk, lay the manuscript. She had decided sometime in the middle of her latest sleepless night that the best way to introduce it to Mandelbaum was without offering a single cue beyond simply placing him in its presence. He was the one who had taught her that the musical term *clef* derives from *clavis*, the Latin term for *key* or *clue*. Let it speak for itself, be its own clue.

Speak it did. So powerfully that it reduced him to a glance at the young woman who lingered at his side, more high-strung than he had ever seen her, then a look back at the page before him.

"What museum did you steal this from?" he asked, putting on glasses—a prescription magnification that he used specifically for close scrutiny of similar musical artifacts—and examining it more closely.

"Please."

He sat at her desk and journeyed through the manuscript from its first note to its last with a deft, delicate respect for the music he read. From the opening measures of the work he perfectly understood what his former student and amanuensis was so excited about. Every so often he hummed involuntarily, lightly groaned, crabbed his head to left or right. She saw his right heel lift rhythmically and his knee nudge up and down until he reached the abyss in the score, at which time he went as still as a seated statue. Reading over his shoulder, Meta noted that he took about as long to go through the music as she did. Though she was the rare one who possessed an all but perfect inner ear, could literally hear music right off the score—*notational audiation* was Mandelbaum's technical term for it—he and she were always strangely in sync.

When he reached the end, he set the pages back down exactly where they had been. He folded his hands, said nothing. Sat for a time thinking. Meta stood next to him, not daring to move, listening to a baleful distant siren somewhere out there in the city.

"All right," Mandelbaum said finally. Removing his glasses, he pushed the chair away from the table before standing with the kind of rich slowness that follows a lavish holiday meal. "In all seriousness. At the end of what rainbow, pray tell, did you find this marvel?"

For the second time that day, Meta recounted her stunning, brief encounter with Irena Svobodová Dorfman. "Do you recognize the hand?"

"I don't make any immediate connection with the bigger players, but anyway I'm pretty sure this is a copyist's script. Not the most polished or professional I've ever seen. Legible, relatively neat, meant for performance reading."

"That's what I thought too. None of the hurried notations that usually characterize a composition score. What about the music itself? Ready for me to play it?"

"More than ready," he said. "Please."

As Meta performed the movement once, then a second time, Mandelbaum strayed over to a window that faced buildings across the street. Hard white sunlight poured into the room.

When she finished, Meta asked, "Do you recognize it?"

Absentmindedly, he traced with his forefinger on the windowpane the zigzag of one of the adjacent fire escapes. "Off the top of my head, no. A-flat major modulating to C minor doesn't tell me much, but it seems to be the slow movement, or slow movement substitute, of the sonata. Could be a middle movement if it's a three-part sonata."

"That corroborates what Irena remembered. Three movements, not four."

"All right, good. I'd venture to agree with you that it's late eighteenth century."

"Are you hearing a touch of Haydn?"

Mandelbaum turned away from the window, walked back to the piano. "Maybe, the second movement of his E-flat Major, come to think of it—that abrupt transition, the darkness of the central section. But Haydn's too polite for a lot of this. And that flurry of demisemiquavers, if you'll pardon my Latin—not that Haydn didn't use them, just that there's a bit of the barbaric yawp going on through a few of those initial measures. Could you run through those measures again where the transition happens?"

She did, and seeing that Mandelbaum was searching for a response, she asked, "What about Dussek?"

"Jan Ladislav Dussek. That's a plausible idea," he said, brightening. "For one, like your benefactor, he's Czech. Plus, he did favor juxtaposing passages of lyricism with sudden shifts toward the dramatic. There's definitely some Romanticism here, nothing genteel or *galant*, more in the *Sturm und Drang* spirit, I'd say. Spohr's another possibility from the era, but I think of him more in terms of violin than piano. Probably not Wölfl, though I couldn't tell you why off the top of my head. Another Czech possibility could be Beethoven's friend Anton Reicha, but I think there's something stirring in the depths of this piece that's more original than anything Reicha wrote."

"You mention *Sturm und Drang*. What about C. P. E. Bach?"

Mandelbaum crossed his arms as he exhaled, "C. P. E. Isn't that a tantalizing idea." Meta knew that Johann Sebastian Bach's second son was, in the eighteenth century, a far more famous and influential composer than his father, whom he affectionately referred to as "the old wig." Closely studied by Haydn, Mozart, and Beethoven, among others, his treatise *Versuch über die wahre Art das Clavier zu spielen—Essay on the True Art of Playing Keyboard Instruments*—was widely considered the foundation of modern keyboard technique, and he was an ardent pioneer in the development of the classical sonata. Mozart himself said of Emanuel Bach: He is the father and we are the children.

"No question his *Empfindsamkeit* style is here in spades," her mentor continued. "There's a rhetorical quality to it—"

"'*Redendes Prinzip.*'"

"Very good, Meta." Glancing at her, he hoped his comment didn't sound too avuncular. "But, yes. Passionate, agitated, dramatic."

"You might even say impetuous, what with that abrupt shift."

Squinting, her mentor concluded, "Problem is, I kind of feel this is later than C. P. E. Bach, probably just before or at the turn of the century, I'm guessing."

"Don't forget that he published that big collection of sonatas and other keyboard works during the 1780s, a lot of it pretty experimental for the day."

It never failed to impress him how far Meta had come after her crash and burn as a concert pianist hopeful. Not that many manage to make the crossover from musician to musicologist, as the disciplines are more different than one might imagine. She had a way to go, but she was nothing if not persistent.

"Right when Mozart was flying high and Beethoven was just getting started."

"What about Beethoven?" Meta said, the idea coming out of her mouth before she'd given it much forethought.

"Beethoven?"

"More Bonn than early-Vienna Beethoven. Plus, at the same time, don't you hear some of Opus 81a here, that first passage? The adagio allegro's reversed to allegro adagio—"

"I'm sorry, but that sonata is much later than this, whatever it is."

"I know, I know. I'm just saying it may possibly prefigure 81a. It's not like he wasn't constantly revisiting and reshaping early ideas."

"Sorry again, Meta, but Beethoven's Vienna stuff from the Opus 2 Sonata on is all well documented."

"Another WoO, maybe?"

Beethoven had written three sonatas that preceded the first of his famous others, works he hadn't deemed worthy of assigning opus numbers. Meta offered the idea, though she knew it was impossible she had stumbled on another Beethoven *Werke ohne Opuszahl* in deepest, darkest Queens.

"Oh, come on," Mandelbaum said.

Undeterred, she took one last shot.

"Listen. It's probably too sophisticated for the early teen Beethoven but it has some of his personality, some of that unpredictability, like a wildfire in a crosswind. But I suppose this might be a little too revolutionary even for the teenage Ludwig."

"We agree." His mood grew more serious now. "People don't realize just how rough, how derivative some of his early stuff can be. Nobody would guess some of that work was by the genius who'd eventually write the Ninth Symphony or those final string quartets. I don't know, Meta. I do think I recognize similarities to C. P. E. Bach. Stray hints of Mozart and Haydn. Steibelt, Weber. Dussek, as you said. But bottom line? Have I ever heard it before? No way. I'm no final authority, at least not without doing some serious research, but I'd bet you a boatload of bullion this piece is not in the literature. The question is, dear girl, what are you going to do about it?"

Gillian's question. Buying a moment to collect her thoughts, she said, "This snippet from the next movement's really intriguing too."

After looking at the orphaned measures again, Mandelbaum nodded and said, "To my mind it's clearly the beginning of a rondo, and as such might well be the opening measures of a finale. But there's just not quite enough of it here to make any definitive pronouncements. Still, that doesn't answer my question."

Her eyes darted around her apartment. They rested fleetingly on the portrait on the wall she had made of her mother, an abstract in gouache done when she was much younger and fancied the idea she might become a painter rather than stick with this grand obsession about music. "I'm going to try to find the other movements. I'm going to do what that poor woman, both those women who lost their husbands, their whole existence in Prague, what they hoped somebody would do one day. Otylie Bartošová broke it up to save it."

"And you think it's your job to unbreak it to save it again."

"Isn't that what you'd do if you were in my shoes?"

"I'm not, though. May I?" he asked, carefully lifting the manuscript from the piano stand and turning its pages slowly, silently.

"Look," Meta said quietly. "We can go round and round the mulberry bush chasing attributions, but finding the other movements will not only help with that, it'll right a wrong."

"Admirably idealistic, my dear."

"It's come into my life for a reason and I think I have to honor that."

Mandelbaum couldn't help smiling, though he didn't glance away from the score. "I never knew you to be religious."

"It's not about religion. It's about devotion and responsibility."

"Well," he said, now turning to look her in the eye. "That's the very definition of religion, isn't it?"

She knew him far too well to take his proffered bait. Instead, without blinking or avoiding his kindly stare, she asked, "Will you help me?"

"What does your lawyer friend think about all this?"

Frowning, Meta said, "That's changing the subject. Will you help me or not?"

He held the first leaf up to the light, candling its watermark, then drew a notebook from his trouser pocket, whereupon he proceeded to sketch the watermark with his fountain pen. "The historian in me knows how small the chances are that, one, the other movements survived, and that, two, you—or anyone else, for that matter—will be able to find them. Slim to nil, I'd say."

Now Meta paced to the window and gazed down at the street filled with cars, trucks, jaywalking pedestrians. "When I was on the train headed out to meet this woman, I had the exact same thought in the exact same words. My chances of finding something of this magnitude in Irena's little house on Kalmia Avenue were slim to nil. By the same token, what are the chances anyone could sit down and write something as beautiful as that"—turning back and pointing at the manuscript—"and for it not to be published and heard by thousands, hundreds of thousands of people over the centuries?"

"It's not unprecedented."

"That's right. But it's definitely unprecedented in my life."

Mandelbaum saw that his protégée was at the edge of her patience. He might have felt guilty but for the fact that he believed it was his job to insinuate a bit of dull reason into her stardusted view of the matter. What was more—and this was a truth that stirred old thoughts he might rather not deal with—he had a good insight into just how valuable this manuscript might be.

"One last time," she said. "Will you help me or not?"

"In any way, shape, or form I can," he answered, walking over to her, suddenly dead earnest. With his long fingers he reached out and took Meta's hands, which were cold but clasped his in return with a surge of gratitude and trust. "Promise me you'll put it somewhere secure. No more moldy mothballs for this artifact, please."

"I was going to ask my mother to hold it for me, actually. Her apartment windows don't leak. And besides, women protected it all these years. Why change that?"

"I appreciate the impulse," Mandelbaum countered. "But at least let her keep it in a bank vault."

"For the time being," she said.

"Fair enough. With your permission, can I have a try at this too?" he asked, nodding his head toward her piano.

Meta let go of his hands. "As you noticed, my piano hasn't been tuned in a while," she warned.

"That's all right, neither have I."

She rolled her eyes.

Mandelbaum sat and arranged the manuscript before him. Straightened his back after adjusting the bench. Raising his hands to the keyboard, he began to play.

META NEVER SAW IRENA SVOBODOVÁ DORFMAN AGAIN. The woman had died alone in her bed a few nights after their meeting. Meta and Gillian did return to Irena's neighborhood, to attend her funeral at Flushing Cemetery. Standing with others, strangers all, amid the vast, amaranthine rows of graves in that metropolis of headstones and bones beneath trampled grass, they paid their last respects. One of the mourners was a handsome woman whose hair was styled in the same old-fashioned beehive Irena had worn.

After the brief service, they joined the handful of mourners for a midafternoon lunch in Irena's honor at a Bohemian restaurant in Astoria, Queens. Feeling out of place with the others, Czech immigrants and an Austrian gentleman who had been a friend of Irena's late husband, they ate what was ordered for the table to share. *Klobása*, roast pork loin with heavy dumplings, a fried breaded cheese called *smažený sýr*, and what had apparently been

Irena's favorite dish on the menu, *pečená kachna*, a crispy Long Island duck served with red cabbage and potato pancakes. They drank Czech beer and did their best to converse with these people who had known Irena. When Meta floated a couple of questions about the manuscript the deceased woman had placed in her care just days before, she was met with blank stares. None had ever met Otylie, but all had heard Irena speak of her best friend from the old days. Openly sentimental, they hoped the two women were now having their own lunch in heaven.

Most of their reminiscences were about Irena's little quirks and habits. The way she had sewn all her own dresses and coats because she could never find exactly what she liked in stores here. How her second husband had been a good man, a little given to drink, but she never complained. Meta was left with the impression that the woman she met just that once was precisely the one these people had known for years. Forthright, clearheaded, honest. If Meta harbored any doubts about Irena's story or how much the manuscript had meant to her, they were erased by the time lunch wrapped up and the bill was paid.

Before they rose from the table, Meta made a point of exchanging names and phone numbers with the woman whose hairdo matched Irena's and who proved to be her hairdresser of many years. Not that she would necessarily be of any help. Nor that Meta would ever dial the number. Just having it, though, made her feel as if her only tie to the sonata movement's past wasn't extinguished from her life.

The group stood chatting outside the restaurant, delaying their final leave-taking if only to postpone what would mean a last farewell to their friend. While Gillian shook hands with the Austrian gentleman, Meta, her mind adrift, listened to the half-English, half-Czech conversation around her until one detail caught her ear: a street near where Irena had lived in Prague. It was mentioned in passing, and Meta hadn't quite heard it. Fumbling in her pockets for a pen, Meta asked the name of the street again.

"Nerudova," one of them blurted in her direction and returned to the conversation.

Not wanting to draw attention to herself and not finding anything to write with, she decided to look into it later, making a mental note that the street name was oddly similar to that of the famous Chilean poet. One might speak of Prague and Kafka in the same breath. Or Werfel, Rilke, Klíma. Even the pre–Velvet Revolution rock group Plastic People of the Universe. These were Prague-souled artists all. But who in the world would associate Prague with Pablo Neruda?

Next morning, after lessons with a couple of her piano students, Meta bought herself a detailed map of the Czech capital at a shop near the Morgan Library and pored over it at the table of a local coffee shop. She could have looked it up online or gone down the list of street names in the index in search of a match, but chose instead to start by touring the city in two dimensions, taking a kind of sight walk hither and thither—a habit she'd developed on the concert competition circuit, when she rarely got out to actually see the cities where she performed. Not the easiest way to track down a name in the melted honeycomb that constituted Prague's tiny, twisty streets. Given how comfortable she was reading complex concertos and experimental piano works, some of whose late-modernist scores looked less like music notation than medical schemata for the nervous system of an alien species, she wasn't deterred. Her eyes watered and her vision blurred, but the real problem was that she heard in the back of her mind a small, skeptical voice saying, Can't you see? You're already wasting your time. Just look at the freaking index.

She shook her head as if to silence this inner speaker whom she fairly or unfairly identified with her absent father. Kenneth

Taverner, crashist, rationalist, abandonist extraordinaire. The doubter who even now in his audacious correspondence with her dropped hints, gilded by what he surely thought were appropriate hues of paternal concern, that she might want to consider looking for a real career, one with both feet planted in this world, as he had put it in his birthday note. But that was him through and through. Thinking that his daughter, whose life had always been her hands, ought to find her way into the world of feet. And planted feet at that. The same man who had never taken responsibility for the accident that deprived her of the perfect, unfettered use of one of her hands, the man who always blamed the other driver, though the particulars were murkier than he cared to admit or the police investigation managed to sort out.

Then she saw it. Nerudova. Hardly her Chilean laureate, she learned from the travel guide that she bought at the Strand on her way home. The street was named for the nineteenth-century Bohemian storyteller Jan Neruda, who'd lived there. And just as Bob Dylan named himself after the Welsh poet Dylan Thomas, Pablo Neruda—originally the unwieldy Neftalí Ricardo Reyes Basoalto—took the Czech writer's name as his own early in life and kept it. The son of a poor South American railroad employee honoring the son of a poor Prague tobacconist and grocer.

This would serve as her starting place. Irena had said that the only performance she'd ever heard of the sonata was in this same neighborhood, Prague's Left Bank, where she'd lived some sixty years ago. The chance of locating anyone who might have knowledge of such an event was more ephemeral than a grace note, but Meta had to begin somewhere.

During the few weeks that followed her morning revelation to Jonathan and her visit from Mandelbaum, she grew increasingly edgy. It was as if there were two Metas nervously circling each other. The new, strange Meta went surreptitiously to the Cooper Station post office to renew her passport without a concrete travel date in mind. The normal, familiar Meta made sure that when Jonathan's case was thrown out of court, she organized a private victory party for the younger attorneys in the firm at a local bar managed by a friend. Between giving piano lessons, she spent two days in her small kitchen preparing platters of hors d'oeuvres and elaborate finger foods for the celebration. After Jonathan left for work, the new Meta set about meticulously copying the sonata manuscript at her desk like some secular sofer writing out the Torah. And though she also had a friend make high-resolution scans of each page, which she then printed out on art paper that approximated the weight and color of the original, and even went to the unnecessary length of typing the composition into a Sibelius computer program, she knew that by writing it out in her own hand she would forge a more intimate connection with the heart and mind of its maker. Just as painters often honed their art by copying the masters, many composers copied out works of their mentors as a means of getting closer to the music, note by note, measure by measure. So why not she?

Evenings were about practicing piano to keep her fingers limber, making dinner, doing dishes. Days found her haunting libraries, reading histories about how the Second World War unfolded in Czechoslovakia, devouring books and monographs on sonata theory, poring over and playing unrecorded scores, immersing herself in recordings of every late-eighteenth-century piano sonata she could find, hunting for echoes, commonalities, sister notes and passages. At night, propped up in bed while Jonathan slept next to her or after he had left for the night, the insomniac Meta, who was strung out somewhere between her contented and restless selves, read and reread accounts of the Nazi occupation of

Prague, projecting herself into Irena's life, and Otylie's. They were just about her age when the sky fell in on them. How did they manage from day to day? What furious nightmares must have tormented them as they lay in their beds, knowing that when the sun rose, or even before the night was over, the Gestapo might come knocking? Would Jonathan, a liberal Jew, have been able to sleep in the dark, dangerous world Irena had survived and Otylie and her husband, Jakub, struggled against? Maybe so. He was pretty strong willed. Had Meta herself been bequeathed a handwritten sonata from a fond, eccentric father, would she have had the guts and the wisdom to split it into three orphaned movements in hopes of protecting it from the enemy?

She didn't know the answer, but she doubted that her strength ran to those depths. No one she'd ever met, she realized, wide awake at three thirty in the morning, possessed the courage that Irena and her clutch of friends and family had shown in wartime Prague. Was it possible that their defiant commitment to art in the face of violence, their heroic grasp of what it meant to give everything to preserve a tiny fragment of culture, was all but gone from the world?

By the hazy hot days of mid-August, Meta felt she was cracking up. She played the movement compulsively a dozen times and more every morning, and again in the afternoon. It was the first thing she thought about when she woke up, the last thing nettling her mind before she fell asleep. Not only had she learned its intricacies by heart, she could perform the work in its entirety in her head. Sometimes she urgently wanted to stop hearing it over and over, but couldn't. She felt as if she were nearing the pathological, so fully had the music infected her.

This Meta, the one whose life had become so obsessed with the score that she worried she was nearing a breakdown, finally decided to tell her best friend what had crystallized into an inevitability.

They met in the hospital cafeteria at Mount Sinai during Gillian's lunch break.

"So. Talk to me," she said after they sat down across from each other in the bright room, tuna niçoise salads on the table between them still in their unopened plastic clamshells.

"Gillie, I'm going over the edge," said Meta, flat as she could manage given the stirrings in her gut. "I've done just about everything I can do here. Unless you can convince me otherwise, I'm calling school and all my private students and telling them I need to take a leave of absence."

"What in the world do you mean?"

"I mean I'm going to Prague."

"Prague? Wow, Meta. Can you really afford to do that?"

"I've got some money saved up. Not a ton, but if it came down to it, I could always sell my piano."

"Never. You'd sooner die," Gillian insisted. "I have to wonder if going to Prague might not cause more problems than it solves. You've just started your dissertation. School begins in a few weeks. You're going to chuck it all? Plus, I thought you said you took on more students."

"I know, I did. Maybe I'm having some kind of early midlife crisis," said Meta, elbows on the table, face in her palms.

"And here I thought you were happy."

"I was," she said, eyes reddening as she reached out to hold one of Gillian's hands. "But I don't know what else to do. If I don't at least try to track down the other movements I know I'll always regret it. I'll be disappointed in myself for not living up to what I promised Irena. More than that. I'll be disappointed if I don't answer the call. I can't help it, Gillie, but crazy as it sounds I feel like I've been called."

"It doesn't sound totally crazy. But maybe you don't need to turn everything upside down. Can't you build it into your dissertation or whatever? Make it meld with the work you're already doing?"

Meta shook her head. "That's the problem. The work I've been doing these past years doesn't hold a candle to this. It makes my dissertation seem so mundane, even trivial. Can you understand?"

"I'm trying," Gillian said with an encouraging smile.

"Look, Gillie." Meta half-smiled in return. "I'm not sure I've got the right words to explain myself any better. The more I think about it, the less I understand. It's like"—she let go of her friend's hand and glanced at the fluorescent ceiling, then down, resigned—"like the harder you try to hold a fistful of sand, the faster the sand runs between your fingers. I don't think I'll be able to figure out what's happening to me unless I stop thinking about it so much and take a few steps, see what there is to see."

"You should eat," said Gillian, knowing that she was going to back Meta whether or not she believed her friend was acting on a hasty impulse. "I think you've lost weight."

They opened the plastic containers and started on their salads.

"People say Prague's the most beautiful city in the world," Gillian went on in the hopes of lifting the mood. "Maybe Jonathan can get some time off and go with you."

Here Meta hesitated for a moment before looking Jonathan's sister straight in the eye. "I need to do this by myself, Gillie. It's not a vacation."

"He means well. Eat, Meta."

"He means more than well, but there's a good reason it took me a while to tell him." She breathed in deep, her shoulders rising, then dropping as she exhaled and took an absentminded bite of salad. "I knew from the beginning he didn't understand music, and that's okay. Why should he? He's certainly more accommodating than my father ever was, running off to California because he got sick of every waking hour revolving around music."

"Music's your motherland, and Jonathan supports that," Gillie said, not wanting Meta to dwell on bitter memories of Kenneth Taverner. "He knows how important your studies are to you."

"Musicology's been a great fallback since I lost my concert career. Teaching's super fulfilling and I love doing the volunteer recitals you line up. But when Irena heard me gimp my way through Haydn's E-flat Major and decided to pass this manuscript on to me, it was like a chance at, I don't know, *rebirth*. My purpose was taken away in the accident. I've been industrious but meaningless. This gives me another shot at what I'd been working for all my life. This is my chance for meaning."

Gillian saw that the fingers of her friend's right hand were seizing up, as if they were grasping a crab apple made of air. "How long will you be gone?" she asked.

"I have no idea. However long it takes to find the other manuscripts or confirm they were destroyed."

"Well, you know I'm behind whatever you do." The two took the stairs back up to street level and said goodbye in the lobby. "I'm sorry, but part of me can't help wishing I'd skipped your birthday present this year."

Meta looked down, shaking her head. "Truth is, I'll never be able to thank you enough. It's the best, most difficult present anybody has ever given me."

Meta's year with Jonathan had been marked by such an even-keel calm that they sometimes joked about having become a settled old couple before they'd fully experienced being an adventurous young one. In spite of this, she could see that he had grown more and more troubled in the days since her announcement about Prague. She had taken the step of buying an airline ticket, nonrefundable, as a way of making her decision final. After all, she reasoned, Jonathan was the most skilled debater she had ever met, and her gallivanting off to the Czech Republic, solo, wasn't a move he blithely embraced. How could she blame him? She, too, was nervous about the decisions she was making. No, she was petrified. But she didn't want to give him the chance of orating her out of her resolve.

She needn't have worried. They both knew that if he managed to talk her into staying, it would be a Pyrrhic victory, no victory at all. One evening, over a glass of wine while they were preparing dinner together in his kitchen, he told her he admired her chutzpah and, despite his concerns, applauded her commitment.

"This is your chance to make your mark," he said, though she protested that he was putting a heavier spin on the project than it was likely to merit. They'd rarely been apart since they met, and it took them both some serious acting efforts to remain smiling and upbeat. She knew, glancing over at him while he chopped vegetables, that Jonathan's mood was darker than he let on. He had more than once offered to join her, but she had evaded the subject whenever it came up.

"You'd be bored anyway," she said, when that night he again raised the possibility. "I'm not going as a tourist, you know."

"There might be ways I could help. Some people think I'm a pretty solid researcher."

She set down her glass of wine, gave him a kiss on the lips, and said, "Don't worry, I don't think I'll be gone all that long. There aren't that many dots to connect, at least not from what I can tell. Mandelbaum's made a few introductions for me with people at Charles University in Prague, and a couple of others in Brno and Vienna. They're intrigued, but none of them has said anything overly promising or given me any real leads."

"Sounds like a lot of dots to me."

"Look, either I'll catch an unexpected break or else it'll be clear early on that it's impossible. I know it doesn't sound like it, but I'm being as realistic as I can."

Nothing further passed between them until they sat down to eat.

"I'm going to miss you," he told her, quietly, raising his glass.

"I'm going to miss you too."

Lying beside him in bed that night, sleepless again and restless without her books, she wondered what more they could have said. He was being honest with her, was all, and she with him. But missing each other wasn't going to change her mind. She felt as if her very life, her purpose, hung in the balance. Was this hubris? Kids, she thought, weren't capable of the cataclysmic downfalls of overambitious kings and warrior generals found in Greek epics. But if they clung to fantastic dreams while they aged into adulthood, weren't they setting themselves up for nasty falls?

Meta refused to give in to hubris. She needed to do this right. The time had come for her to validate everyone who had ever believed in her. Her mother, Gillian, Mandelbaum, her teachers and colleagues, her students. Jonathan, too, whether or not he fully backed what she was doing. She felt a deep, bristling need to come through for Irena Svobodová Dorfman, whom she'd known for all of an hour. And to honor Otylie Bartošová, whom she had never met and hoped but didn't expect ever to meet.

As she watched from the airplane window while the twinkling island of Manhattan disappeared below her in the gathering russet evening, she realized that all of the wishes she had made that birthday night not so long ago, after wandering through her apartment like a perfect fool, blowing out candles on sills, shelves, tables, stands, had risen into the realm of possibility. True, they had been the same wish. Charge my life with meaning. *Charge my life with meaning.* She had asked this in thirty different ways as she stood before each of the candles, improvising a theme with variations. Now it was up to her to make that wish come to pass.

· 3 ·

BOTH HIS FATHER AND MOTHER had played roles in naming the boy. And both had used the opportunity to weave their love of music into his name. Meta shifted in her cramped seat and turned the page of the book she had brought along for the flight. The boy's mother insisted that he should be christened Reinhard—*one wise in counsel*—after the hero in her husband's favorite opera. And his father called him Tristan, in honor of the master of Bayreuth, Richard Wagner. Both parents were disappointed, in their different ways, over their own ultimate failure to rise as high into the upper echelons of cultured society as they believed they deserved, and hoped their eldest son would one day ascend to a grander tier of accomplishment and fame.

Raised in Halle an der Saale—even his birthplace had a melodious ring to it, Meta thought—young Reini, as he was known, grew up in a household whose rooms were filled with every kind of music. His father, a gifted singer, aspiring composer, and generally inept social climber, served as the founding director of the first conservatory in the provincial town of Halle. His mother, the daughter of a musical dynasty in Dresden, had been trained as a pianist. The golden age of Wagner was just coming off its dizziest heights, but this was still a time when a musical education was considered an integral part of a proper upbringing, and their school was modestly successful.

With his mother, the boy went every Sunday to Mass, where his head swam with beautiful chorales that inspired in him a love for singing voices. By the age of five he had learned the art of music notation and was gaining mastery over his fingers by practicing thorny Czerny études on the piano. Beethoven and Bruckner played in his dreamy mind. So did his father's orchestral works and operas, with their simple, inspiring titles, like *Peace* and *The Eternal Light*. His violin lessons went well, and though he was withdrawn, a quiet child, he showed every sign of having a fine future. His mother taught him discipline and religion. His father instilled in him the desire to get ahead, to be creative and thrive. From the limited vistas of Halle, the First World War was not yet on the horizon, so the boy grew up in a world of relative calm.

As his parents became more involved with running their school, he and his older sister and younger brother were raised by their Silesian nurse. Left to his own devices, Reini began to change. He became, by daily shades, more and more stubborn, increasingly introverted. Try though his mother and nursemaid might to get him to run errands or play games with his siblings, he averted his eyes and turned his gaze inward. From the sanctuary of his growing isolation, whether sitting in the classroom or with his family at the dinner table, the boy showed a deepening disdain and iciness toward those around him. He spent a lot of time behind the closed door of his bedroom, sometimes practicing the violin, sometimes sitting in silence. When his mother saw fit to discipline him with a good Christian spanking, whipping him a dozen, two dozen times with the rod, he refused to cry. He would simply stare ahead until she finally gave up.

No one could say he wasn't a bright youngster. At the Reform-Realgymnasium he studied math, physics, history, and languages, and did well in all these subjects. His first love was chemistry. For a while he became convinced this was to be his life's work. But at the same time he continued to consolidate his role as angry loner, outsider, brooder. A slim rangy youth with a Nordic shock of blond hair, he took to walking down sidewalks, his chest stuck out like a spring robin's, forcing anyone coming in the opposite direction to step aside and make way. One day, just for show, he scaled the gymnasium building and leered at everyone below from its tallest peak. He lashed back in a fury when classmates started to tease him about his high falsetto voice and bony face, nicknaming him *die Hebbe*, the goat.

Was it after his adolescent voice finally dropped into a maturer register, when the same crowd began taunting him with the gleeful, contemptuous cries of *Isi, Isi—Jew, Jew*—based on a specious rumor about his father's heritage, that Reinhard Tristan Heydrich's fate jelled? His brother, Heinz, stopped the hecklers by threatening them with a knife, but had something in Reini snapped?

Maybe, but probably not that simple, it seemed to Meta, somewhere over the Atlantic, frowning at the biography on her lap. After the 1918–1919 German Revolution swept Kaiser Wilhelm II out of power and the narrow but comfortable universe of Halle an der Saale was destroyed, Reini would nurture a hundred other reasons to do what he did, to become who he became. Nor would anyone dare contradict those reasons when, in the early forties during the war, he had achieved a pinnacle of overwhelming power as the Nazis' Reichsprotektor of Prague. This boy, who even in adulthood liked to sit alone in his room and practice the violin to escape the world he had played such a prominent role in pushing to the brink of apocalypse, would become an iron-fisted favorite of Hitler. "Butcher of Prague" became his new nickname, one he liked better than *die Hebbe*. Better to slaughter the goat than be the slaughtered goat.

Yet in the end it all proved to be one fatal grand opera. Even in the final hours of his life, after his car had been bombed, he spoke to his colleague Heinrich Himmler—whose first name, he surely had noticed, sounded so much like his own last—about the nature of fate and death in musical terms. Evoking his father's fourth opera, his magnum opus, *Amen*, he quoted the lines

> *The world is just a barrel organ*
> *Played by God himself.*
> *We all must dance to the tune*
> *That happens to be on the roll*

which moved every one of the high-ranking Nazi officers and doctors who stood in shock around his deathbed. Himmler would later say that the martyred Reinhard Tristan Heydrich was one of the finest SS men he had ever had the honor of working with, never knowing how much Heydrich had despised him, just as he despised most people he met.

Having dropped her bags at the inexpensive pension where she was staying, Meta tucked her map, with Nerudova Street circled, into her pocket and made her first foray into the mid-morning streets of the same Prague that once had been governed by this man whose life, like hers, was rooted in music. As she strolled toward the town center to get her bearings, she couldn't help wondering whether Irena's husband had died as the result of Herr Heydrich's signature on a piece of paper. He had signed the death warrants of so many of Irena's countrymen with the same calm stroke of the pen one might use to sign a pub tab for stout and sausages. If Reini had only followed in his composer father's footsteps, would Meta be here now?

She reached the heart of the city, treading cobbled corridors not half as wide as the narrowest street in Greenwich Village, and emerged wonderstruck into Old Town Square. What fortitude the stucco and stones, the urban flesh and bones of this ancient place, had shown over the centuries. How many depredations it had survived, Meta thought, as she gazed in awe at the elegant spires of the Church of Our Lady before Týn, Heydrich's villainy being but one. And yet, look. Of all the major European cities that had suffered through the Second World War, which constituted the latest Armageddon—because there's always another Armageddon waiting in the wings—Prague had emerged as one of the most unscathed. True, the city had undergone its postwar restorations, but it was as if a protective spell had been cast upon it generations ago. A spell stipulating that its citizens were fated to suffer from era to era, but what they and their ancestors built up with their hands would remain as testimony.

A sudden chiming interrupted these thoughts as she found herself amid a gathering crowd beneath the medieval astronomical clock on the near corner of the square. Its hourly procession of carved and painted saints appeared from behind small doors, and she gaped as a skeleton, nodding "Yes," pulled a cord to ring a little bell beside a musician with a mandolin, who shook his head from side to side as if to say "No" to death.

Farther along, at the center of Staroměstské náměstí, a ragged quartet of old street musicians, who would have been right at home in Tompkins Square Park, had attracted a small audience near the green-patinated monument of the reformist Jan Hus. She listened to them play and sing "Bye, Bye, Blackbird." Rain clouds had collected low over Prague, forming a silver dome into which the city's tallest spires disappeared. Sun, dim through mist, made the grand assembly of buildings eerily glow, as if illuminated from within the stones and baroque pastel stucco facades. Meta was mesmerized by the singer who fronted the group with a cardboard megaphone in one hand and his trumpet delicately dangling from a finger of the other. Not a half-bad impression of Louis Armstrong, who was buried a stone's throw, or at least a trumpet blast, from where Irena now lay, in the same Queens cemetery as Dizzy Gillespie.

Dizzy and Satchmo, she thought. Twin Gabriels to announce Irena's arrival into the heaven she never quite believed in. This present Satchmo scatted with all the soul a freckled busker might ever hope to summon and, to Meta's ear, the homage was spot-on. His gravelly voice hit the nuanced notes of *Pack up all my care and woe* as if he had written it himself. When Meta tore herself away from this unexpected echo of home in order to head back across the Vltava to Irena's old neighborhood, the clouds shredded and fled, allowing the sun to shine into the square even as rain began lightly to fall.

Karlova Street was a gauntlet of souvenir shops. She passed windows filled with mass-market crystal, tray after tray of gold and garnet jewelry. Beneath a bronze plaque commemorating the astronomer Johannes Kepler were shop fronts cluttered with Don Giovanni puppets, pseudo-military Russian badges, rabbit-fur hats, postcards. The last made her think of Jonathan, as she dropped into one of these cramped shops to buy an umbrella. Would he consider a postcard from Prague somehow insulting? And what would she write? *Wish you were here?* He'd accompanied her to Kennedy Airport, seen her off. Had even helped her pack for the trip. But during their last days before her flight, it was painfully clear that he was straining to put on his best, most confident courtroom face. Subtle, sly digs had never before been in character for him, but he seemed unable to resist them now.

"You won't forget the little people when your discovery makes you famous, now will you?" was the ridiculous zinger that irked, or rather hurt, the most. Not knowing how to respond, she hugged him, remembering what it was like to feel somebody was about to abandon you. Her father still received his daughter's defensive barbs whenever they spoke. But this was different, she thought, as Jonathan apologized, "I so didn't mean that. I'm sorry."

The day she left, only yesterday, already seemed impossibly distant. Jonathan had taken the afternoon off from work to spend time with her before her flight. He'd booked a reservation for lunch at an outlandishly upscale restaurant. For dessert, he had ordered ahead as a surprise a platter of cannoli, profiteroles, and napoleons in honor of their first date. She thanked him, leaned across the table, and kissed him as conflicted tears welled in her eyes.

Jonathan's birthday ring glinted in the slanting sun as she stepped back into the street glazed by the short cloudburst and made her way to the Charles Bridge. Feeling guilty but at the same time certain the gesture was something she needed to do, she removed the ring and put it in her buttoned breast pocket.

She had read about the famous bridge, but none of the descriptions or photographs did it justice. According to tradition, the Czech word for Prague, Praha, derives from *práh*, or *threshold*. Meta, earnest fool or not, believed Prague was her threshold now too. As she passed through the archway of the Old Town bridge tower, she looked at the glistening soot-blackened statues of saints and other holy figures, then gazed at the green-brown water where wild swans paddled lazily upstream. Shimmering on the hill above this, Pražský hrad, Prague Castle, put her in mind of Sleeping Beauty's castle in Fantasyland but was so far beyond any Disney confection that she felt embarrassed by the comparison.

A scent of roses hung in the air together with that of stale sweat. She walked past vendors selling handmade jewelry and sketching caricatures of tourists. Past an organ grinder with a round crimson face, wearing lederhosen and collecting coins from passersby in a felt tricorne cap set out on the drying stones. Meta heard birdsong, the cries of children, hippies strumming untuned guitars on the far shore of the river, and church bells chiming the midday hour—an improvised symphony of the city's sounds. In the time it took her to cross to the other side, she heard people exchanging words in half a dozen languages. And how perfect was it that where the world's largest statue of Stalin once stood, now a seventy-five-foot metronome kept time for the whole orchestral city from atop the highest hill of Letná Park? If all the world was a stage, here was its bandstand.

She climbed up and down Nerudova Street, memorizing it as she might a score she was to perform. Then she began exploring nearby side streets and blind alleys. Not the grays and brick reds of New York, buildings here were pea green, mustard yellow, salmon pink, ocher, citron, pale blue. Although houses were numbered just like those back home, here they had two numbers—street and quarter. Many were also known by older signs fashioned of painted plaster, gilded wood, carved stone, or forged metal—the pictorial representations of something meaningful to those who first lived or worked within their walls. Twelve Nerudova/210 Malá Strana bore the sign of the Three Little Fiddles because it had once housed a famous school for violin makers. Elsewhere along her path were other emblems—a red eagle, a green lobster, a golden horseshoe. Near the top of the cobblestone street she located the House at the Two Suns, where Jan Neruda himself had lived. Here she lingered, marveling at how little must have changed since the writer had gone in and out through this door. She couldn't help wondering if Pablo Neruda had ever come and stood on this very spot to pay homage to his adopted namesake. Yes, she decided. He must have.

As she continued her ramble, Meta noticed that many of the businesses along the crowded main thoroughfares, but also in the echoing capillary side streets so narrow that only a single car could pass at a time, were beer halls, tiny pubs. She indulged in a Pilsner Urquell, then a second. Beer in the States didn't taste like this and, besides, wasn't she on her great adventure? Her meeting with the first of Mandelbaum's contacts was scheduled for tomorrow. Today was hers alone. Other than exploring the quarter where Irena and Otylie had walked more than half a century ago, and seeing what remained of the world they'd known, breathing their air, she had no plan. This was a full pause in the stream of her life. How wonderfully strange it felt, she thought, to be tethered to nothing but an idea. And a chimerical idea at that.

When she left the dark, smoky tavern to reemerge into the twisting and sometimes precipitous streets, she felt flush with freedom. The breeze was warming and fresh. The savory smell of a bakery drew her inside to buy a cheese sandwich, *hermelín* with tomato, on a roll still warm from the oven. As she ate, she wandered through alleys, filled with resolve about her purpose here. How impossible it seemed, as she walked the path along the top of Petřín Hill overlooking Prague, that such a magical, benign, and beautiful city should ever have experienced the repeated griefs of war, occupation, and oppression.

That evening, footsore in her tight, tidy room, having eaten dinner at a Vietnamese restaurant in Old Town after making her way all afternoon across bridges and through squares, Meta played the sonata movement slowly in her head. The excitement of the day had faded now, replaced by weariness and a germ of fear that unsettled her. What she feared hadn't gathered itself into any comprehensible image or idea. She wasn't afraid of failure. She wasn't frightened of being alone in this foreign place. What she felt was that simplest of fears. Not knowing what lay ahead on the other side of night.

PROFESSOR KOHOUT TAUGHT IN THE DEPARTMENT of music at Charles University. Meta showed up for her appointment half an hour early, having miscalculated the length of time it would take to walk from Malá Strana to his office overlooking the river. Just as Mandelbaum had promised he would be, Karel Kohout was a brusque, forbidding man. When Meta knocked on the open door of his office, he was sitting in a walnut swivel chair with his broad back turned, surrounded by a clutter of books and scores rising toward the high ceiling. His walls were hung with framed portraits of composers, university degrees, and playbills inscribed to him by various singers and musicians. Intent upon a monograph that he held close to his face, Kohout made no acknowledgment of her presence.

She knocked again. Again nothing. A long wooden bench stood beneath a bank of filmy windows across the hall, so she took a seat and waited until the exact time of her appointment. When it was ten thirty on her watch, she rose and quietly knocked once more.

"He's like what his name means," Mandelbaum had warned. "A rooster. My take on him is that he's very aware of the metaphysical ramifications of this. So watch yourself and don't get trapped in his henhouse."

"Lech?"

"No, I mean he's more like a seducer of ideas. A little headstrong, he has a way of ruling his roost. Let him weigh in with an attribution, if he can, and then thank him and go."

"Who is this guy anyway?" she asked, wondering why Mandelbaum would send her to someone he didn't fully trust.

"Besides being a player in more ways than one? Mozart man, mostly. The main thing is he's an expert on the minor composers of the period. Your largely forgotten Ignaz Pleyels and Joseph Gelineks of the world."

"This isn't minor music, though. At least not to my ear."

"Mine either. But he may surprise us by linking it to some lesser composer who might earn himself an upgrade in the canon. Besides, Karel's been in Prague forever, might know somebody who can tell you about its past. I wouldn't bring him into the dialogue if I didn't think there was more upside potential than down."

Now Kohout swung around in his chair. "Come, please," he said, motioning her in with a gesture so slow it made him seem as if he were underwater. His soft lips, heavy eyes, and plump pink cheeks did not lend themselves to the rooster image Meta had formed in her imagination. And if his comb was once rooster red it had long since faded. In his charcoal suit, rumpled white shirt, and polka-dot bow tie, Kohout appeared distracted, maybe a little annoyed at being interrupted.

She handed him the letter of recommendation Mandelbaum had given her, which he scrutinized unnecessarily, as she knew he'd already agreed to this meeting and had expressed interest, at least to Mandelbaum, in the manuscript.

"Your first visit to Czech Republic?" He smiled, sort of.

"Yes, I was scheduled to perform here many years ago but I had an accident and it prevented me from coming."

"Dr. Mandelbaum said something to this effect. I'm sorry."

"Well, it was half a lifetime ago."

Kohout cleared his throat, then continued in his accented but accurate English. "Let me see what you have brought."

"May I—I'd like to play it for you?"

"There is no piano here," he said, eyebrows rising toward the white thatch of coxcomb hair on his wide head, as if to verify that a piano was not even to be found there.

"Are there practice rooms in the building we could use?"

"I don't know what to suggest," glancing at his wristwatch, his curious smile now gone tight. "If you want my thoughts on the score Dr. Mandelbaum called me about, I must necessarily see it before you or anyone else plays it, *slečna*, Miss—"

"Taverner."

He was right, of course. Meta unzipped her pack and removed a manila envelope. She passed it to him, leaning over his crowded desk. Because the professor hadn't invited her to sit, she stood, shifting from foot to foot. He withdrew the pages, held the first one inches before his restless eyes, then lowered it, saying, "I don't understand. This is not an eighteenth-century manuscript. It was written two weeks ago, not two centuries."

"No, I apologize," Meta said. She had left in the envelope, along with the professional digital reproduction, her personal handwritten copy, which she'd brought along as a kind of security blanket. "My mistake. That's a transcript, my transcript of the original."

"Why would you waste time making a transcript in this day and age?"

Meta began to explain how the process of copying it brought her closer to the work. Then, reaching over and removing the transcript to reveal the scan beneath, she continued, "I'm sorry, I forgot that was in there. This is what I wanted to show you."

Eyebrows almost imperceptibly raised, Kohout studied the scanned pages in flat silence, offering her no critique one way or the other. She watched his eyes traveling back and forth, and waited. After an uncomfortably long minute, Meta decided to speak.

"What are your initial thoughts?"

Kohout ignored her for another wearisome half minute before saying, suddenly more animated, even courteous, "What are my thoughts. Well, my thoughts are that I cannot say I recognize the hand. If it's a copyist who wrote this out, his hand leaves much to be desired. I don't identify an obvious composer."

Meta opened her mouth to speak, wanting to offer again to perform it for him, but Kohout continued.

"'Either way, the chances are, as I'm sure you must be aware, it's most likely a nineteenth-century pasticcio, the work of some earnest amateur imitating some earlier masters. How should one put it, joining very different styles?" he pondered, knitting his fingers together.

"Grafting, splicing?"

"Yes, it seems too schizophrenic otherwise. That's why I think pasticcio. Withal, quite an intriguing oddity. Where did you say you bought it again?"

"I didn't buy it. It was given to me."

"Ah, that's right. Dr. Mandelbaum explained. May I keep it for a while?" he asked, his head cocked to one side, that skewed smile on his lips again. "I haven't time now, but I need to look through it carefully, even play it, when I'm not so distracted by a busy schedule. Only then might I be able to advise you."

His own oddly pastiched reaction to both his visitor and her manuscript, now haughty, now ingratiating, at once dismissive and involved, threw Meta off. She wasn't altogether sure she wanted his advice. With a cough, she said, "Of course. That copy is for you."

"Thank you." He placed the printout on a stack of paper on his desk, then picked up the monograph he'd been reading when Meta arrived. Seeing that their meeting had come to an end, she thanked Kohout, and found her way out of the building. She walked beside the Vltava, watching the swans bob calmly, indifferently, in the wake of a passing riverboat, and wondered if there was any way she could have made a clumsier first sortie into the small world of Prague musicologists.

That afternoon, nursing a residual awkwardness from her encounter with Kohout, she went to her second appointment. Not with another musicologist—her next such meetings came later in the week—but with one of Mandelbaum's former students, someone he thought might be a good person for Meta to know while she was there.

"He went to Prague on a concert tour at the beginning of what I thought was going to be a great career, fell in love, had a kid or two, never came back," Mandelbaum had moaned, with grudging admiration. "Daft as hell, if you ask me. But a real musician, not some damn piano player. Knows that musical tonalities are produced with the ear, not the fingers. Knows that music couldn't care less about fingers, that thinking your fingers produce music is pure lunacy."

Meta knew that idea backward and forward. Artur Schnabel, one of the towering pianists of the twentieth century. Modified in tone but not spirit from Schnabel's interview remarks in Chicago the same year Germany surrendered to the Allies. She also knew this was about as high a compliment as Paul Mandelbaum was capable of making. Schnabel's performances of the thirty-two Beethoven sonatas were possibly the only thing her mentor was capable of carrying on about ad nauseam. You were never going to enter his pantheon of star pupils unless you gave yourself over, heart and soul, to Schnabel's interpretation of Beethoven's *Klaviersonaten* and the virtuoso's idea that the greatest music was that which is "better than it can be performed."

Samuel Kettle was anything but a self-satisfied highbrow, which came as a great relief to Meta. Wearing an old lima bean–green sweater, baggy blue trousers, and nondescript lace-up shoes, he resembled one of those latter-day hippies she'd passed at the far end of the Charles Bridge, singing folk songs out of key and making up their own lyrics as they went along. His black hair was unruly and the puffy circles under his sharp blue eyes suggested to Meta that here was someone who had been burning his candle at both ends. His face was refined, as pale as vellum, and his thin shoulders were gently rounded. To her mind, he looked so Eastern European that it came as a surprise when he said hello in a northeastern seaboard accent thick enough to issue from the captain of a fishing boat. The only thing that gave him away as a musician, at least physically, was the graceful, delicate strength of his hand when they shook.

"Welcome," he said with a warm, eager smile as they sat opposite each other at a pub called Konvikt, across from the building where the Czech stooges of the Soviets had maintained their police headquarters in the Iron Curtain days, and a police compound had existed ever since. "Mandelbaum sang your praises to the point of—"

"Don't tell me," Meta groaned. "Ninth Symphony, *Ode to Joy.*"

At which Sam Kettle, without drawing breath, burst out with the famous first lines of Beethoven's finale in a strong tenor voice punctuated by rapping the table on the downbeats, "*Freude, schöner Götterfunken, Tochter aus Elysium*—how'd you guess?"

Meta looked at the ceiling and laughed. "It's an old joke between us. He put you up to this, didn't he."

"Sure did. He basically said you were a true daughter of Elysium and that I had to do anything I could to help you and, well, Mandelbaum's wish is my command."

"I appreciate it."

"But I haven't done anything. Save your appreciation until I've done something. For instance, have you eaten lunch yet?" he asked, his face a lively, endearing riddle of tics—quick hard blinks and random nose scrunches.

How different Kettle was from Kohout. He offered her a cigarette and she shook her head. She'd never smoked in her life but was, it seemed, glancing around, the only such virgin in this cloudy room. As Sam walked her through the menu, she realized that though she was no vegetarian, nothing could have prepared her for the meat-eating republic she had just entered. Pork necks, venison rumps, lamb knees, veal shins, beef-tail broth, blood sausages—the abattoir was fully represented. She told Sam she'd have whatever he thought was good. He ordered for them both in fluent Czech. Frothy pints soon appeared at the long table where others were also seated, engaged in conversations of their own, and the two Americans settled into an afternoon of such amicable discourse that a casual observer might have thought they were the oldest of friends.

From Mandelbaum they moved easily into their next commonality—abandoned dreams of a concert career. "After what happened to my hand I wasn't going to reach the far shore no matter how hard I swam, so I decided it was better not to drown" was how Meta explained herself to him, without further elaboration.

Sam was deeply sorry to hear it. For his part, he had continued to perform in France, Italy, the Netherlands whenever asked through his agency back in New York, with whom he maintained a cordial if ever-dwindling relationship. He had fallen in love not only with the Czech girl he met backstage on the last of his legitimate tours half a dozen years ago but with Prague itself. When not on the road, he began accepting piano students, and, over time, private and conservatory teaching had become his mainstay.

"But my story's just the same old expat tale. Boy leaves home. Boy falls in love. Boy rejects old life, makes new home away from home. Curtain falls. Scattered applause. Well, actually, you can scratch that applause part. Silence and sanity ensue. End of story.

Deal is, with the dreaded monkey of ambition off my back I'm happier than I've been since I was, like, five. Before I ever banged on my first piano key or tried stretching my thumb and pinkie wide enough to make an octave. I think you know exactly what I'm talking about."

"I do and don't," Meta admitted. When she was a girl her aspirations as a pianist were boundless and Carnegie Hall had been her promised land. But in the aftermath of the accident, and after all the operations and therapies, she'd found herself placing third or fourth in competitions, never first as she used to. The bows, bouquets of roses, curtain calls—now they added up to a moot point. She might wince at the rigors of the road, the shortcomings of the recording studio, the facile image-crafting, the dwindling sales of classical music recordings, but they weren't her problems anymore.

She had known all this for years. Yet how much more real it felt to review her path from this fresh vantage, away from home, sitting here with this man she didn't know from Adam and yet understood very well.

"But, look," Kettle was saying. "Your project sounds way more interesting than my own little capitulation to domesticity, at least from what our friend Mandelbaum was willing to say about it. So tell me what we're up to here."

Over the course of half an hour, sketching in the historical parts of the story that had taken place in Prague, Meta laid out what she knew about the unidentified manuscript. Sam listened closely, waiting until she'd finished before he began to speculate aloud.

"Did Mandelbaum think there's any chance that good old gold-standard Köchel made a mistake, for instance, if we want to say it's Mozart just for the sake of argument? Even the most anally retentive miss something now and then, why not K?"—Ludwig Ritter von Köchel being the nineteenth-century musicologist who exhaustively cataloged Mozart's works, hence the K system. "Maybe he left something out of the stew."

Meta liked Sam. *Koch*, cook. Punning away even as he pressed ahead toward a theory about what she might be dealing with. "He didn't say one way or the other."

"That means he believes it's possible."

"I hadn't thought of it, but you're right."

"'*He who knows does not say, he who says does not know.*' Perfect Mandelbaum Zen in action."

"Well," she said. "Köchel's possible failings aside, I think you'll find it's probably a little too weird for Mozart."

"The plot thickens. So when do I get to see it?"

"You can hear it as soon as you can get us to a piano."

"Where's the manuscript?"

"Back at the pension. But also right here," tapping her forehead.

"Let's get the Taverner out of the tavern then, and head home. I hope you don't mind playing before an audience of two noisy children who've made it their life's mission to sound like a concert hall's worth of coughers, sneezers, and snorters."

They split the bill and caught a tram to a nearby residential district, Vinohrady, where the Kettles lived in a modest apartment up several flights of worn marble stairs. Though clearly this had been an elegant building a hundred years ago, the plaster was cracking, the banister railing was wobbly, and more than one of the overhead lightbulbs needed to be changed. Most of the building's original art nouveau details had been removed by the Communists, Sam explained. The wrought-iron door and once spectacular Juliet balconies had been carted away for scrap metal. "My guess is that if they'd stayed in power for another decade or two they would have turned the whole town into a big, drab citadel of cement. Evil as they were—and don't misunderstand me, I know the Commies were choirboys by comparison—the Nazis at least had a modicum of appreciation for the art they plundered during their days here."

"It must be amazing to watch the Czechs reclaiming their country."

"Better than amazing. It's a daily miracle."

Kettle's wife, Sylvie, was so kind toward this stranger from America that Meta understood at once why he'd been persuaded to renounce his former frenetic life in favor of a settled one with her. And his boy and girl, David and Lucie, were anything but the little rowdies he'd jokingly mentioned. Open eyed and open mouthed, they sat cross-legged on the floor of a music studio lined with sagging shelves of books, albums, CD jewel cases, and unwieldy piles of sheet music. Along with their parents, they listened while Meta played the movement not once but, at Sam's urging, several times. He hovered behind her as she performed, his eyes riveted on her fingers traversing the keyboard.

"Brava, bravissima," he cried after the final resolving notes, followed by the rondo opening, dissolved into silence for the third time. The children, following their father's lead, applauded. "Bloody excellent, the setup in A-flat major, then off the cliff into the doloroso of C minor. It's like now you're young, in love, you're floating along in some beautiful alpine meadow on a perfect spring day—there's birdcall in there, Messiaen has nothing on this guy—and then, with no warning, you're plunged straight into hell. The meadow flowers wilt, the birds become bats, and the sky's the color of tar. It's eccentric, all right, but well within the classical parameters of Preromanticism. Can you imagine what this must sound like if the outer movements, assuming you find them, are as good as the one you've got?"

"How could they not be?"

"You know as well as I do that one masterpiece movement doesn't guarantee a brilliant symphony. Despite myself, I really love only one short movement in Bartók's *Concerto for Orchestra*. The rest I could live without."

"True," Meta conceded. "Paul McCartney wrote some monumental, immortal stuff. I could listen to 'Hey Jude' all day long. But he also wrote 'Silly Love Songs.' Not so hot."

"Except for Bach and Shakespeare, who I doubt were actually human, everybody's uneven. But what comes next? It's totally unfair!"

"I want to know what comes before too. That's the main reason I'm here."

"I can see why Mandelbaum had his knickers in such a twist. What's weird, though, is that there's something here I swear I've heard before."

Her heart rose. "Really?"

"No, never mind," he said, with a backhanded flick of the wrist, as if shooing away an annoying insect. "I'm just full of it. Wouldn't be the only time."

"Don't dismiss your idea so quickly," Meta pressed. "What's familiar?"

"Just bells in my belfry, ding dong ding."

"Are you absolutely sure?"

"I'm trying to think," he answered, seeing how intent his guest was. He got up from the piano and walked over to the balcony overlooking the murmuring street. It had grown dark out, and evening sounds from open windows of apartments across the way wafted in. Laughter, television racket, chitchat. But hushed, echoing like a memory of neighbors more than neighbors themselves home from their workdays. "Seriously, Meta. I know it sounds contradictory, but I've heard it and I haven't heard it. I mean, I can't place it in the repertoire but this thing is familiar somehow."

"Maybe it seems familiar simply because it's such an exceptionally beautiful piece," Meta tried, rising from the piano bench. She winked at David and Lucie, who were now quietly singsonging, "Ding dong ding."

"I don't follow," Kettle said.

"Sometimes when I hear music that's moving, upsettingly moving, if you know what I mean, I have the weird feeling of familiarity with it. Like it was a part of me already, hidden in my mind, and all it needed was to be awakened from the outside."

Distracted, he didn't answer.

"He knows," his wife intervened, looking at Meta with a conspiratorial nod, stroking her son's hair. "Sam knows about what you say. He has this feeling himself sometime."

"Well, it's just a thought," Meta added.

"I'm sorry," Sam said, shaking his head as if coming out of a daze. "Sure, I've had that experience too. I think most musicians have. It's just, this is going to pester me until I figure it out, is all. Would you like to join us for dinner?"

"Yes," Kettle's wife insisted. "Nothing much special. Over lefts."

"Leftovers," he corrected, with a fond smile.

"I probably should be getting back to my pension."

"What, so you can sit alone in your room? We won't hear of it. I've got a bottle of decent French champagne around here somewhere and this is a special occasion. It's not every day another Mandelbaum nut drops on my head," he said, breaking into laughter.

Meta looked back and forth from Sam to Sylvie, wondering what was so funny.

"Is not that good joke," Sylvie explained with a shrug. "*Mandel* mean in Czech a nut, almond nut, and *Baum* in German mean tree."

"Seriously, though," Sam chortled, "do stay. We'll drink a toast to the unknown soldier who wrote this piece of dark paradise, bless his troubled soul wherever it roams."

"Or hers," Sylvie added.

"Or hers," Meta and Sam agreed.

Her dinner in Vinohrady with the Kettles carried on until the small hours of the dawning morning. Lucie fell asleep with her head on Meta's lap long after midnight while the adults conversed about every musician under the moon from Copland to Coltrane, Saint-Saëns to Sting, Brahms to Beck. When Sam escorted Meta on a black-coffee tram ride to her pension through streets so empty it seemed as if they were the only people alive, she once again felt dizzy with the promise that this place was her destiny. By the time she washed in the shared bathroom at the end of the hall, stowed her clothes in the serpentine-front chest of drawers in her spare but clean little room, and finally crawled into bed, the Prague sky was already brightening with streaks of pink and apricot outside the second-floor window. For all the disappointment she'd felt after her clumsy meeting with Kohout, Sam Kettle and his family reminded her of who she was and why she was here.

DESPITE THIS AUSPICIOUS EVENING, the days following her arrival in Prague were a rich brocade of some highs and more lows. Steps and missteps. Crescendi, diminuendi. As she conferred with others among Mandelbaum's professional acquaintance, following up on contacts some of them in turn provided, she seesawed between hope and despair. More than once she scolded herself for not knowing what she was doing. Though she tried to hide it during her phone calls with Jonathan, the temptation was strong to cut her losses and return to New York in time to salvage much of her semester and reconnect with her students before they all found other teachers.

"Gillie and I had dinner last night," he said. "We toasted to your success there."

"Thanks," said Meta, heart sinking. "Miss you guys."

"You know you don't have to. You could be back here tomorrow."

"I'm sorry, but that's not possible yet, Jonathan." She wasn't surprised when he went silent on her, essentially ending the conversation.

Three fruitless days in Vienna and a sweltering bus ride down to Brno, on what proved to be straw-grasping exercises with music historians who were happy to examine the manuscript but were sorry not to be of much help, drained her pocketbook, not to mention her faith. A pregnant archivist at the Lobkowicz Palace in Nelahozeves was, along with Sam, the kindest among the experts she met. But even she could offer Meta only collegial encouragement and a chance to examine the original performance manuscript of *Le nozze di Figaro* from the vast Lobkowicz collection, which was being unpacked after years under Communist lock and key. Because the Mozart score dated from roughly the same period as the Prague Sonata, Meta was able to verify again what she already knew—that the paper, ink, and other elements were characteristic of the late 1700s. Disappointed not to have gotten more from the meeting—after all, the Lobkowicz princes were among the most important aristocratic patrons of Mozart, Haydn, and Beethoven—she consoled herself with the thought that there were worse ways of passing a morning than turning the weighty leaves of the *Figaro* folio with fingers sheathed by white cotton gloves she'd been given to wear. And how surreal was it to look out the archivist's office window in the palace perched on a promontory and see, down by the Nelahozeves village square, the house where Dvořák, son of the town butcher, was born?

It was all heady, yes, all very fascinating, but Meta caught the riverside train back to Prague feeling more lost than ever. Her initial enthusiasm began to seem the illusion of a dilettante. Rather than seeing light at the end of the tunnel, Meta saw an unending tunnel and no light at all. What was more, she still had to face the most renowned of Mandelbaum's musicological experts. Nor was he an easy man to pin down, whether or not her mentor had, in his own words, "softened his beaches with irresistible passion and inarguable wisdom." Mandelbaum was being half serious and half self-deprecatory, but his friend in Prague had proved to be more elusive than a fast-moving cloud. Two appointments had already been canceled, and a third, his sweet but harried assistant told Meta, had unavoidably been pushed back to the beginning of the following week owing to unforeseen circumstances.

This was Petr Wittmann. His widely read and translated biographies of such mainstays as Bach, Chopin, and Wagner were credited with generating popular interest in classical composers among the young, and were admired for their stylish, vivid portrayals even if some carping critics noted their reliance on the well-trod scholarship of others. Still, he was a phenomenon. There wasn't a field within the precincts of music he hadn't touched upon, if only tangentially, from bel canto to serial composition. He had even published a book, which Meta had read and enjoyed, about classical influences in the music of the Beatles. Meta had put off seeing him until she'd had time to confer with others, prepare herself to bring perhaps more to the table than the problem of the manuscript itself. That Mandelbaum had only ever spoken of this man in the warmest terms made her feel even more ill at ease.

"In Prague, Petr's the top of the heap, or he certainly was when I used to go there a lot. He'll be either your Canaan or your Elba," he told her over their promised New York lunch of steak, creamed spinach, and the rest, which took place after they spent hours combing through the score on Meta's piano one careful page at a time. Mandelbaum even missed his train and had to take a later one home. "Of course, I'm hoping he'll be the former. Who knows, but he might independently confirm my suspicion—and it's a wild one, I'll be the first to admit—about what you may have here."

"And what, old owl, would that suspicion be?"

"Let me rephrase. I won't be the first to admit. It's best kept to myself."

"That's not fair and you know it," Meta persisted.

"Haven't I always made it my life's cause to look after you?" he asked, slyly looking over a dessert menu his wife would have confiscated without comment had she been at the restaurant. He ordered a chocolate soufflé and filled the pause by adding, "Well, have I not?"

"Annalise wouldn't want you eating that, would she?"

"Answer my question."

"I think I just did. Why don't you answer mine?"

Mandelbaum may have canceled his soufflé order, settling for a double espresso instead, but did so with an air of friendly aggrievement. Still, he wouldn't tell her anything further about this theory of his, finally dismissing it as they left the restaurant as "madness." He telephoned her the next day, uncharacteristically apologetic. "I don't mean to be coy, especially in light of the importance of what the music speaks and what those who carried it had to go through to allow me the honor of hearing it. But you need to know, I'm no final arbiter here. My hopes for this may wind up being only that—hopes. Please don't let me jinx you with my own flights of fancy. Go meet these people I'm sending you to. Get their input. Branch out from there. Find the rest of the sonata if you can and don't ask me what I think anymore. Tell me, instead, what you learn."

"Thanks, Paul," she said. One of her rare moments of calling him by his first name. He was always *professor* or *old owl* or just plain *Mandelbaum*. With that one word, his given name, they both knew she had sealed an understanding.

Meta had followed his advice. All Mandelbaum's people came to the table with strong personalities and left behind differing opinions. Some were intrigued. Others saw nothing more to pursue than publication of the discovery in an academic journal where it might become, for a time, a seminar curiosity to dissect. One optimistically suggested that it might find its way into recitals as a newly unearthed rarity. Hadn't Schubert's first two sonatas survived as fragments? The first, in E major, was abandoned by the composer in 1815 after he finished only three of four movements. And the C major from the same year survives without a finale, which moody Schubert might have drafted and lost, or drafted and tossed. Even his third, the so-called "Grand Sonata," was a gathering of foundling movements from the broken families of other works. Yet that hadn't deterred a world-class virtuoso like Wilhelm Kempff from recording them.

Be content with what has already come to hand—that seemed to be the consensus. Which Meta, increasingly against her better judgment, still could not quite accept.

"Please to pardon," said one of the more engaging scholars she met, after allowing Meta to play it on her piano. A reed-thin lady named Gretja Toplová; she was the only woman other than the Lobkowicz archivist among the collective. "But what is to make you think there is some other movement to find?"

"Well, you can see the beginnings of a new movement on this last page."

"Could be this is just abandoned fragment. Maybe to use up the paper, not to waste. It was common practice, you know."

"I do, but that seems doubtful to me. Besides, as I said, the woman who gave me the manuscript in the first place told me the whole story behind the dispersal, specifically, of three sonata movements."

"And you believe her based on why?"

Gretja's English might not have been the most polished Meta had heard among the bilingual Czechs she'd met thus far, but her question wasn't without merit.

Folding her hands on her lap, Meta said, "I believed her because she had no reason to lie to me and every reason to tell the truth."

If the woman were looking Folly itself in the eye she couldn't have wagged her finger with any less charming affection. "First rule in life is never to ask why some people they say something. The second rule is not to believe them unless what they say can be proved. Me, I am, yes, a scholar of music. But any stories you tell me about this Irena Svobodová and Hitler and Heydrich and all the other, I can only trust so far and so you should."

Meta asked her if she recognized the work or could identify a composer.

"I have never heard this. To me sounds a little Haydn, but too what, wrong for him. Too, how to say it, peculiar."

"C. P. E. Bach was someone I thought might be a possibility."

"It is wild enough. The *Affekt* is there. I was thinking, when Doctor Mandelbaum called me, before I hear it, that Mozart has that second son, the one born fourteen weeks before his father dies—"

"Wolfgang Amadeus the Younger. Sure, I know what you're referring to." Sensing the dialogue was veering off course but willing, at this point, to listen to any idea, no matter how far-fetched, Meta said, "You're thinking of that unpublished rondo in G, but wasn't that for flute and piano?"

"You are almost right. No, I am thinking how Geiringer, or is it Walter Hummel, says that the rondo comes from a lost sonata in E."

This breached the boundaries of far-fetched, Meta thought, hoping her impatience and disappointment didn't show. Mozart's second son, burdened all his life with his father's weighty name—unlike Bach's son, who thrived—was an often miserable, peripatetic soul who had written four published sonatas between 1808 and 1820. They were late-Classic works by one whose talent sparked through now and then. It wasn't as though he hadn't studied with Antonio Salieri himself, a considerable teacher and force in his day despite his role nearly two hundred years later as a jealous fiend in *Amadeus*. But in this score, musical decisions were too dynamic, changes in mood too rash, and certain sonorities and emotions just didn't point to a lost Mozart *fils*.

"But this idea was wrong," Professor Toplová said, as if reading Meta's mind. "Bach is a much better possibility. Late Emanuel Bach."

"Well, thank you for your thoughts on it. Even wrong theories are helpful in that I can rule them out, narrow the field."

Gretja nodded in agreement. "It is most beautiful," she said when bidding farewell to Meta, whom she had invited to her apartment, unlike most of the others, who'd preferred the impersonality of offices or cafés. "I don't know what this is but it is good. Thank you for letting me know of it. And keep me on touch."

Meta gave her an embrace, then faltered back into the streets feeling she was leaving behind a woman who, for all her rules, would have believed Irena as Meta herself did.

Some of her best days were spent with Sylvie Kettlová—Meta had grown used to the feminine ending *ová* added to Czech surnames, but it still sounded strange on the American name Sylvie had taken from Sam. Sylvie had rapidly become Gillian's stand-in. With her help, Meta had located Irena's old address in the municipal records. Armed with this information, they met in Malá Strana and walked to the house where Irena had lived. Entering through a pair of large, undecorated wooden carriage doors, they crossed a courtyard and climbed a flight of outdoor stairs to a landing on the second floor, their footfalls echoing in the silence. These must have been the very steps down which Irena's husband was dragged to his death. Meta grimaced, glancing at Kettle's wife with an air of anticipation shaded by the unspoken question, Do we really think we're going to find anything here after so many years?

"Thanks for coming with me," she told Sylvie, then pressed the round doorbell knob.

A wiry, priestly gentleman of about sixty, with neatly combed yellowish-white hair and dancing blue eyes, answered the door. Sylvie, speaking in rapid Czech, apologized for disturbing him and explained Meta's purpose in Prague. To their surprise, he asked both women inside.

His English was no better than Meta's Czech, which was to say that the two couldn't communicate much beyond handshakes and wondering smiles. Sylvie acted as translator while they sat in his cluttered parlor. Lots of furniture, most of it very old, or at least very tired. In one corner stood a wickerwork dress form with an array of bowlers stacked on top of its metal neck. Paintings hung on the walls. They had been made by the man himself, as he proudly indicated by pointing at one and then at his chest after seeing Meta admire the canvases. Quiet geometrics in oil. Not bad, not great, Meta thought, but sensitive, striving. The room had a bachelor feel to it. One could see he had lived alone for a long time.

Sylvie asked him if he knew anything about the former residents there, the Svoboda family. Through those first few moments, Sylvie and the man spoke together. Meta nodded with an anxious smile whenever he looked at her.

"What's he saying?" she spoke up, not wanting to interrupt but impatient. Meta, following the music of their language as closely as she could, had heard both of them invoke Otylie's name along with Irena's. Her hopes were rising by the minute.

"He say that he never meet Irena. But he get a few letters from her long time ago."

"Does he still have them?"

"*Máte ještě ty dopisy?*"

Turning toward Meta, the man shook his head apologetically. "Not."

"What were they about?" Meta asked, forgetting for a moment that he couldn't understand her.

Sylvie translated the question, then explained that what he recalled was mostly about Irena's search for Otylie and Jakub. The man had no knowledge of Otylie, unfortunately, but had certainly heard of Jakub Bartoš, who had distinguished himself as one of the courageous resisters during the Nazi years in Czechoslovakia. Jakub was buried, the man believed, in the Vyšehrad Cemetery alongside other notable Czechs.

Before they left, Sylvie gave him her telephone number in case he happened to recall anything further. Meta did remember to glance at the floor in Irena's old apartment and saw that whatever boards had once hidden the manuscript had been long since replaced with newer parquet in a herringbone pattern. She shook her head. How thoroughly the evidence of a life, its harrowing struggles, its blood spilled, can be erased by as simple an act as replacing an old floor.

Without discussing their next move beyond exchanging the few words "We go, no?" and "Please, let's do," Meta and Sylvie walked down past Saint Nicholas Church to catch a tram in Lesser Town Square that would take them back across the river, where they could make a connection to Vyšehrad.

A breezy, cloudless day. Men fished the wind-riffled Vltava in the shade of willow trees. Magpies winged along beside the tram as if they were in a race. Meta marveled at how the city was transformed along this upriver stretch. Gone were the baroque and Gothic masterpieces of Prague's center, replaced by spray-painted graffiti and humble workers' housing as the tram neared a high bluff that had for centuries been the seat of power for Bohemian kings.

After getting off at Výtoň, they walked in silence up the undulant cobblestone roads through the Leopold Gate, where they startled a flock of pigeons. Apple trees were spangled with ripening fruit. The rhododendrons' leaves looked like burnished green leather. They climbed the hill, stopping to pet a brindled cat that looked well fed for a stray.

"Meta," Sylvie said, her tone downshifting out of the blue. "I must tell you one thing. I am sorry but I am now thinking this. Jakub probably is not here. We maybe not find."

"Why not?"

"The partisans, the resisters? They did not buried many. They killed by the Gestapo and the bodies destroyed, how you say, they mutilate. Or throw them in hole so nobody find. Many these fighters gone. And if they not gone, Communists will not let them to Vyšehrad."

"What about what the man told us, though?"

"He hope we find, but he is maybe confused. We look, though."

They strolled past Saint Martin's Rotunda with its petrified cannonball stuck in the wall—yet another war caught in the teeth of time—in order to view the river from the battlement overlook. Acacia trees, huge horse chestnuts, dwarf weeping cherries. Thickets of wild red roses cascaded beside the stone path. Far away, a dog yapped.

Despite Sylvie's warning about Jakub, Meta felt a deep serenity for the first moment since arriving in Prague. The stern Kohout of days ago receded; the illustrious Wittmann seemed but a distant wrinkle on her horizon. She experienced such an urge to take Sylvie by the arm and walk along like sisters, but shyness stopped her. The two entered the cemetery through an iron gate over which arched a sign that read "Pax vobis." Meta had managed all her life to avoid being in graveyards and now here she was in a second one in a matter of weeks. These cities of the departed weren't as depressing as she had always imagined. Instead, they inspired tranquillity. She wished Gillian were here to share this.

They found the resting places of other heroes of Meta's. Her three favorite Czech composers—Dvořák, Smetana, Suk. But while the graveyard was filled with Jans, Josefs, and Jaroslavs, the women discovered only one Jakub. A Jakub Kohout, of all things. Arranged on his tomb, which was far less grand than those of others buried here, was a curious crucifix fashioned of little stones and chestnuts. Other graves wore the same impromptu garlands of respect. Although this was neither her Jakub nor her Kohout— quite opposite poles of her experience—nor was the man whose remains lay in this tomb other than a Christian, unlike Jakub Bartoš, she sensed this was as close as she'd ever get to Otylie's courageous husband. She knelt on one knee and rearranged the nuts and stones into a musical note.

Rather than returning to her pension that night, Meta slept on the sofa in Sam and Sylvie's apartment. What started out as just another day that might have ended in disappointment had led her instead to a new vision of Jakub. Irena had told her what she knew of his final months but, ironically, he hadn't come to life as such until Meta visited Vyšehrad. It didn't matter that the old gentleman had made a mistake, didn't matter that Jakub wasn't entombed there. Otylie's husband may not have had any further physical presence in this world. No bones and dust beneath a marker. The rest of the sonata his wife risked everything to save, along with the culture it represented, was out there somewhere, though. Meta had to find it not just for herself, for Irena and Otylie, but for him too. The day had brought her face-to-face with the idea that she wasn't here shadowing an illusion.

What was more, Meta had been adopted by the Kettles. *"Meta Kettle, Keta Mettle,"* the children giggled over a dinner of herb-rubbed roast chicken and cucumber salad that night. Afterward, Sam played Debussy and some simple piano meditations by Federico Mompou, the—to Kettle's mind—scandalously underappreciated Catalan composer. He even knocked out a convincing imitation of Bill Evans doing "My Funny Valentine," having heard it earlier in the evening on a CD. What an ear, Meta thought.

All this was healing medicine to Meta, who lay down under a blanket in one of Sylvie's cotton nightgowns, still wearing her socks and clutching a chestnut nicked from Jakub Kohout's tomb. Sam and Sylvie didn't have much money, Meta now fully understood as she dozed. And their commitment to her was a real gift. Before she fell asleep, she promised herself two things. One, she would do something for the Kettles that they would never do for themselves. She didn't know what it would be, but a wonderful extravagance was appropriate, no matter that her own resources were beginning to run low. Two, after having met possibly the only man alive who could confirm Irena once lived here, she would not give up until every last possibility had been exhausted.

Many of her hopes would vanish when, a few days later, Petr Wittmann showed up at the Slavia, a crowded art deco café across from the National Theater, where Meta had been waiting for over an hour to finally meet him. Her nerves were already as tense as taut wires when she arrived, but after three espressos and countless glances at a wall clock, they quivered, much as they had before competition concerts in her youth.

After sitting casually in a chair at her table, Wittmann ordered himself a coffee and lit a cigarette, saying in passing, "Sorry I'm a bit late." He spoke in an impeccable Oxford accent and looked older than in his dust-jacket photograph. High forehead, aquiline nose, impatient full lips. He wore his salt-and-pepper hair long with sideburns that gave him an unexpectedly dashing, raffish air. Round wire-rim glasses framed his dark gray eyes.

"It's an honor to meet you," Meta said, not knowing whether to reach across and shake his hand. She decided it was better not to.

"I'm also sorry to say that something unexpected has come up at the university, so I'm afraid we won't have much time."

"Paul Mandelbaum told me to give you his very best regards."

"Yes, we spoke on the phone, as you know" was Wittmann's oblique response, and to the waitress who just then delivered his coffee, he said, "*Zaplatím.*"

Was it possible, Meta wondered, that he had just asked for the check?

"So now," after a sip from his cup.

"Thank you for making time to see me. I know your schedule's tight."

"That I won't deny. I'm back from sabbatical with my new book in dire need of its introduction and a final redraft before it goes off to the publisher."

"What—"

"Mahler, but I could have used more time off."

"I look forward to reading it."

"Mahler's not why we're here, though. We're here to discuss your lost Mozart sonata, or was it Beethoven?"

"I know, I mean I see obviously how busy you are. But if you could spare just half an hour, fifteen minutes—just to listen to it once. I'd so value your expertise."

Here Petr Wittmann snapped cigarette ash into the tray, leaned back in his chair. "Paul is someone I've known since our student days. Met him at an international conference in Paris. We've been in touch ever since. He is a man of considerable knowledge and not a little imagination. Sometimes quite a lot of imagination. I haven't had the pleasure of making your acquaintance until today, but I would think that you must be a good musicologist if only because you studied with my friend and because he says you are good. I don't want to waste your time, his, or, for that matter, mine. Having looked into it a little, I've come to the conclusion that it's just that. A waste of time."

She was floored by how coolly he delivered this judge-jury-and-executioner sentence. He even underscored his out-and-out dismissal of her project with a brief, apologetic smile. It was everything she could do to keep from jumping up and running out of the place.

"But you haven't seen it," she said, doing her best to maintain composure.

"Actually, that's not quite true. I have had the opportunity of seeing what you left with my colleague, Karel Kohout. As forgeries go, my sense is that it's quite a distinguished fabrication. In fact, as forgeries go, I'd be willing to state for the record that this is one of the more sophisticated works I've had the occasion to see in years. But if you think it's worth investing a lot of valuable time in the thing, as Mandelbaum tells me you intend to do, I can only urge you, with all due respect, to put your energies to better use."

"Maybe the scan isn't clear enough for you to work with. To me, there's no question about the legitimacy of the original."

"Look, don't get me wrong," Wittmann retorted, raising both hands in the air as if Meta were pointing a pistol at him. "While it's true the original might make it easier to date the thing, and while it may well be old, that's not what I'm talking about."

"I must be missing something here," she protested.

"Maybe so. I am talking pure music. Whoever concocted this nifty mélange really knew his stuff. An impressive amalgamation of phrases and technical conceits borrowed from Mozart and Clementi. Some traditional transitions and modulations sounding fresh. Too much Beethoven, not enough Beethoven. It's really quite a mess, for all its corrupt instances of beauty and clear moments of inspiration."

"But there's nothing messy about it."

"You still misunderstand. As music, to our contemporary ears, it's a marvelous construct. Were it authentic it would be revolutionary. I mean that as a forgery it's a brilliant, messy stew. Riddled with anachronisms, impossible musical moves for the era it purports to come from. Miss Tavener, I'm sorry, but so-called lost masterpieces out of the workshops of ingenious forgers have a long and storied history, and I believe yours is likely another chapter. It's just not the book I can help you write right now. I hardly have the time to write my own."

Meta opened her mouth, closed it. She didn't bother to correct his mispronunciation of her name.

"I'm truly sorry," he went on. "Don't think these things never happen to the best of us. I put in a lot of work years ago on what I'd become convinced were some unknown Bach fugues. As it happened, they were probably the work of someone in his circle. Friends with Anna Magdalena, I speculated at the time, though I later repudiated that. I remember wanting them so badly to be by Bach, there at the beginning of my own career, that I forced them on the poor man, who wouldn't have been very grateful."

"I'm not making any such claims, you realize." Meta was struggling to regain some semblance of equanimity. "I'm coming at this from another angle than you were when you were working on your Bach. This manuscript has a story behind it, a place in history, and it's only part of my work to try to identify the composer."

"Identification strikes me as critical to understanding its value, if it has any value, cultural or otherwise. Am I wrong?" As he asked this question he pulled some coins from his trouser pocket and paid both of their tabs.

"Doesn't value have multiple criteria? Why shouldn't its beauty give it value?"

"I said corrupt beauty. That's not the same as genuine beauty."

"You've given this enough time and thought to be confident beyond a reasonable doubt about what you're saying?" she asked, hearing echoes of Jonathan in her question.

"I'm making a subjective call based on objective frames of reasoning. I think you have something interesting here, but an oddity. Why do you think that woman who had it all those years never let anybody publish it?"

So he had listened to Mandelbaum, and with closer care than she'd thought.

"You're going to say it's because she knew it had a dirty past."

He nodded. Any earlier coolness toward her was gone now. He seemed to feel sorry for her, even sympathetic. "Wouldn't surprise me. If you want to pursue a potentially interesting line of thought, trace the provenance back to its original owner. I would wager you will discover that the forger and the family who owned it all those decades had some relationship. You might find a fascinating narrative there. Still and all, I can't imagine your talents wouldn't be better used on other projects."

"Well," Meta said, numb as stone.

"I wish you nothing but the best. Mandelbaum speaks glowingly of your other work, you know. I'm sorry to be in such a rush and I apologize again for being late. If you're ever back in Prague, don't hesitate to call me. It would be a pleasure to see you again under less pressured circumstances."

"Thanks for giving the score a look," she said. As she finally shook his hand—hers was damp, his dry—she realized that Kohout's judgment about the work was, by default, the same as Wittmann's.

He said "Good luck," and left.

Dazed, Meta wandered back across the river to her pension. Her sight was blurred, her head ached. Hubris, she thought. Hubris again. What philosopher said that hubris is the flip side of faith? She lay on the bed for a time, eyes tracing a long crack in the ceiling, like a crease in a plaster palm. Imagining it as her lifeline, she tried to divine where on its serrated curve she had arrived today, and what twists and turns her future had in store.

"Ridiculous," she said aloud, finally, then sat up and walked to the window, her mind skipping like a dull needle across a scratched vinyl record. Give up, go home. Give up, go home. Give up, go home. How had she never noticed that the word *Elba* was hidden in the middle of her mentor's name, she thought, remembering Mandelbaum's words about Petr Wittmann. Well, he had turned out in fact to be her Elba, not her Canaan, hadn't he? "Ridiculous," she said again, feeling rotten for thinking of Mandelbaum this way. It wasn't his fault things weren't going well. I'm no better a musicologist than I am a damn pianist. Second-rate, third. All those years wasted, and she sat down to dial Jonathan's number on her newly and grudgingly purchased cell phone.

"Suffice it to say I tanked" was her response to his hesitant, "How's it going?" She raised her voice as she spoke, a preposterous habit from as far back as she could remember while making overseas calls. As if the ocean between her and whomever she called required Meta to shout in order to be heard. It had the effect of making her sound hysterical. Not so inappropriate at the moment.

"You needed to follow an interesting lead, and that's what you did," Jonathan reasoned. "This isn't the end of the world or your career. Don't beat yourself up over it. Nothing's really changed."

She was speechless. Everything had changed, had it not?

He was still talking, consoling her, offering to meet her at the airport, to restock her fridge, when she heard him say "—did discuss the manuscript with a colleague—"

"What do you mean?"

"Well, even if you did discover the other parts and manage to figure out who wrote it, it's highly unclear as to what ownership rights—"

"Jonathan, rights and ownership are the lowest of my priorities. Especially now."

"I'm just trying to help."

It didn't take a lifetime of training for Meta's ear to register the neediness in his tone. That, and a hint of acerbity. Way out of character for him, she knew, sensing it was best left untouched. She thanked him, assured him that she missed him too, and hung up feeling more dispirited than before, not to mention more distant from him, fairly or not, than she'd ever felt. She paced back and forth, wishing she could call Gillian, but couldn't bear to tell her the news yet. Not from embarrassment but because she knew Gillie was going to blame herself, and Meta couldn't take the compounded heartache of that conversation just then. Instead, she dialed her mother.

"Good news?" Kate Taverner asked, her voice resonant with excitement.

"Nothing of the kind."

Meta described her conversation with Petr Wittmann, not dulling the razor edge of his criticisms or softening the raw force of his dismissals or hiding the fact that he had offered her encourage-ment as well—encouragement to do something more useful with her fledgling career. The sole detail she withheld was that the man had been over an hour late and made only the most perfunc-tory apology. That would have sent her mother into a fuming tizzy.

"And that's the last word on the subject?"

"He wasn't the only one who had serious doubts."

"I think you might want to take a deep breath and have some serious doubts about their serious doubts," Kate scoffed, launch-ing into her dual role as protector and champion. She had devoted herself to her child prodigy after her own marriage had gone south and even in the aftermath of the accident, and she wasn't about to stop now. "My advice, if you want it, is to get away from the music mafia, follow your own nose. Are you at least enjoying yourself a little? Is Prague glorious?"

Meta did take a breath. It was true, she was enjoying herself, in a way, and if what she'd learned so far was how little she knew, it was more than made up for by her friendship with Sam and Sylvie. "Prague's everything it's cracked up to be and more," she responded, trying to sound upbeat. "I promise I'll tell you when I'm home. No need to run up more minutes on this cell."

"I'm proud of you. You're doing everything right. Just a bumpy road is all."

"I failed," she said.

"Well, then unfail."

From the precincts of an anxious dream which seemed so vivid, so real, but began to vanish the moment she opened her eyes in the darkness of the room, Meta fumbled for her cell phone vibrating on the bedside table.

"Hello?" she asked, groggy, dislocated, switching on the lamp and looking at the clock. Two in the morning. Abruptly awake now, she panicked, thinking that something had happened to her mother, or maybe Jonathan, Gillian. People never call in the middle of the night with good news.

"Meta? Really sorry to bother you at such an ungodly hour."

"Sam? What's wrong?"

"Nothing, no, nothing's wrong. I couldn't wait until morning to tell you," he said. He sounded—not drunk, but exuberant. "I should've waited."

"Tell me what?"

"Remember when I thought I recognized your music that first night you came over?"

"I do, of course."

"Well, I think I may know where I heard it. Not all of it, just those introductory measures to the outer movement that get cut off on the last page. You said Irena used to live in Malá Strana?"

"Yes. I went up there with Sylvie a few days ago."

"She was saying. That's what got my memory going."

Meta could hear Sam take a long drag off his cigarette. If ever she had been tempted to smoke, now was that time.

"At first, all I could think was I somehow knew that movement you were playing, emotional roller coaster that it is, eccentric as it is. Now I'm sure that was wishful thinking, me trying too hard to help you piece together your puzzle."

Feeling a little lost, Meta waited for him to continue. A quiet breeze drifted through her open window.

"Maybe when the entire sonata is rediscovered—"

"You mean *if*," she interjected.

"—my sense, or hallucination, that I'd heard that movement before will be proved by its musical relationship with the rondo movement. Unlikely but possible."

"Sam, why are you calling?" Maybe he was drunk, after all.

"I'm sorry, Meta. Because if it's about anything, it's all about the rondo. The rondo. That's what I think I've heard before. It has such a simple but strikingly original theme. I don't know what sort of procedure you follow as a teacher, but with many of my students whose parents can afford a good piano, I go to their places to give lessons."

"Sure, I do that. Especially if they're young," still wondering where Sam was headed with these tangential thoughts.

"Better they work on their own instrument, and plus, they don't need to get home safely since they're already home. Anyway, I have one pupil, Andrea, she lives in a house on a blind alley up in Malá Strana, a block off Nerudova—"

Nerudova. She took a sip of water from the glass on the table.

"Hear me out. You know when you've read a line in a book that really stayed with you, one you meant to underline but didn't have a pencil handy, so you just kept reading? And when you wanted to find it later you could picture perfectly where it was on the page, even knew it was a left page or right, but not which page it was?"

"I've done it many times."

"Well, it's like that except the book is Malá Strana and the page is somewhere in the vicinity of Andrea's. When Sylvie mentioned you'd been exploring together, it triggered a memory, and I thought, I could swear I've heard that line, that rondo theme, in Malá Strana. Same key, though it's truncated in your score and— and it fell into place tonight, when I was prepping for a lesson in that neighborhood. Mulling it over, I'm pretty sure I've heard those notes myself walking to or from her lesson. Or maybe even at her house. Her parents have a boarder upstairs who Andrea adores. Sometimes when I get there he's noodling around on the piano with her. Maybe it's something he's played. I don't know. Now that I'm saying this out loud, it sounds pretty nuts."

"No more nuts that I am. When's your next lesson with Andrea?"

"Day after tomorrow."

Eyes closed, Meta asked, "Is it all right if I come along?"

"I'll do you one better. After breakfast, I'll call her mother and see if we could drop by and speak with him in the morning. I'd love to find out myself if he remembers it and knows what it is. Long shot, but worth a try."

"This whole trip is a long shot, so of course it's worth a try. Thanks, Sam," she said, and they hung up. She turned off the lamp and lay back on her bed. Not since the night she'd returned from Kalmia Avenue with Irena's gift of the Prague Sonata score had she felt so wildly wide awake. She tossed from left to right, sat up, again lay down. She heard a couple whose amorous voices and uneven footfalls echoed on the cobblestones outside suggested they'd had quite a night out on the town. Unthinking, a little lonely, she rose and went to the window in the dark to watch them sway their way down the narrow lane. She didn't recognize the song they were more or less singing, but she knew that Sam, as aurally hot-wired into the universe as anyone she'd ever met, probably would. She felt happy for the couple and grateful beyond expression to her new friend as she climbed into bed again, suddenly exhausted, but never did get back to sleep.

*   *   *

JAKUB BARTOŠ'S ROAD TO A GRAVE, whether marked or not, was longer and thornier than he would ever have wanted his wife, Otylie, to know. His declaration of refusal to comply with the whole idea of a Nazi Protectorate, his writing the single word *Odmítám* on a placard and posting it in his shop window that raging fifteenth of March, 1939, had been the beginning of a new life for him. Or no, he thought, not really a beginning. The end of a life he had worked so hard to build.

Now as he waited in the shadow of a leafing tree along a street in the Prague suburb of Holešovice, trying to look inconspicuous though his mouth was dry from fear, fondling the gun in his pocket, he knew his life as a resister was likely at its end. Today was assassination day. Sometimes, as one of his fellow conspirators said the prior evening when they gathered in secret to finalize details of the plan, you must kill to cure. He was right, of course, but Jakub couldn't help thinking about the moral consequences of what they planned to do. Murder was murder, Otylie would argue. He could almost hear her voice rustling with the breeze and birds in the green canopy above his head, urging him to abandon his post. But the target in their crosshairs was an assassin himself, he contended, looking up into the splinters of light that came through the greenery. One of the worst ever to have drawn a breath of sweet spring air freshened by the Vltava. Heydrich needed to stop breathing Prague air. Berlin air. Any air.

Often during his underground exile Jakub questioned whether he had made a rash, crazy mistake. He loved Otylie more than any person alive. Treasured her more than he did his own life. During low moments, he reassured himself that he had at least managed to spirit her out of occupied Czechoslovakia to the safer shores of England. Yet, by joining the resistance, he'd lost everything that once had given him joy. His wife, his home, his friends, his work. All was gone except for the hot anger he felt toward the false proprietors of his homeland, and a wrenching disgust he couldn't suppress when watching some of his countrymen capitulate to, or even collaborate in, what he saw as mass cultural suicide.

His wife was speaking to him again through the susurrous leaves. Chiding him, saying that he had always been a kind man. Gentle-spirited. Why do you insist on doing this?

She wasn't wrong to press him. Hadn't he lived for over three decades never once imagining he was capable of helping put a fellow human being to death? And though this was the strange, dark path down which his life was taking him, he wondered if his decision to walk it would carry the weight of any moral authority when judged by God. His ancestors' faith promised that when he died, his soul was to be placed on one divine scale of justice and a feather on the other. Would his determination to fight back, to kill, tip the afterlife scales against him? He had no simple answer for the question he heard Otylie, his conscience, asking. It came down to an ineffable belief, forged on the very first day of occupation, that the gentlest man must stand up for what he loves, for those he loves. This was why he stood here, waiting with others farther up the road who were the vanguard he was to aid if his help was needed. Today was the crucible moment he had both longed for and dreaded, the day the Butcher of Prague would himself be butchered.

When it was announced the year before that the first Reichsprotektor, Konstantin von Neurath, had to step down for reasons of health—in truth, Hitler ousted him for being far too lenient with the Czechs—and the infamous Reinhard Heydrich was named his successor, Jakub understood the implications. The Czech resistance was about to come under merciless attack. Defiant acts of sabotage, such as cutting phone lines to hamper enemy communications or blowing up a German fuel depot or munitions works, were no longer of much use. The godfather of the Final Solution, the Führer's choice to take over the Third Reich one day, Heydrich was also the head of the Reichssicherheitshauptamt, whose authority carried every last syllable of the weight of that very long title. He was not being sent down from Berlin to tolerate a ragtag clique of Bohemian resistance fighters, to put up with any resistance from any quarter, underground or above.

Not that the Butcher hadn't initially courted the Czech work-ing classes with what Jakub recognized as skillful savvy. Heydrich knew the mongrels were starving. Many were exhausted by fear and hopelessness. Wages were low. Clothing and shoes were as scarce as fresh vegetables. Productivity and morale were in the ditch. How could they be expected to build tanks and trucks and armaments for the German military if they weren't fed, paid, clothed? If Heydrich was to turn these riffraff Czechs against the underground opposition, wasn't it best to show them what Ger-man generosity was like? For two and a half long years, in Hey-drich's view, the Reich had mismanaged the Czech situation. A fed dog doesn't bite.

When Heydrich assumed control of the Protectorate, on a pleasant late September day in 1941, his first move was to gain the confidence of the people. Rather than going directly after the Jakubs in the resistance, he made it his first priority to root out black marketers who were profiting from the misery of others by choking off food supplies and illicitly raising tariffs. Posters went up all over the country. Announcements were made on radio and in the papers. Rewards were offered to citizens who named greedy racketeers suspected of illegal slaughtering and price gouging.

His program was a grand success. For a few months, more pig-stickers, cattle slayers, animal skinners, cutters, boners, and meat vendors were hanged than intellectuals and political agitators. This wasn't such a bad thing, as far as more than a few hungry people could tell. Heydrich was careful to project a show of fairness, ar-resting some expendable Germans in the mix along with Czechs and Jews, and even some in the upper classes. Jakub was floored by how many in the hamlet of Nehvizdy, where he'd been holed up for three months, bought into the Reichsprotektor's clever deceits.

False hope settled like so much fairy dust over the Czech moth-erland. The initial panic over Heydrich's entry into Czechoslovakia, and the widespread terror that he would surely bring the country under control through an orgy of blood, now seemed the exaggerated propaganda of agitators. To many Czechs, all was well and would continue to be well, thanks to Heydrich's initiatives. Canteens were established in factories across the country to feed malnourished workers. Unemployment insurance was instituted. Clothing was distributed to threadbare families. The Protectorate-run press hailed these initiatives as triumphs over the resistance, whose members were denounced as spoilers and troublemakers. Morale soon began to take wing among the lower classes. Thousands registered themselves as German citizens, changing their surnames to Schmidt, Klein, Meyer, and christening their children Frieda, Dieter, Hans, even Adolf.

Emboldened, Heydrich soon enough began to orchestrate his real work. Prime Minister Alois Eliáš, suspected of secret collaboration with the exile government in England, was summarily executed. Czech cultural organizations were suddenly, systematically, shut down. Deportation of Jews and other unwanteds to concentration camps in Poland and elsewhere gained momentum and soon became such an everyday occurrence that some bystanders no longer bothered to avert their eyes. Intellectuals were back on the firing line, and Heydrich now clearly planned to keep all universities, those breeding grounds of dissent, closed for good. The police force was officially annexed by the Gestapo.

In the Butcher's view, the country was coming around nicely. In his self-ascribed role as patron of the arts, Heydrich began to dream of resurrecting Prague as the crown jewel of German musical cities. This place so beloved of Mozart would one day be the home of the greatest opera house in all the Reich. Heydrich fervently supported the city's up-and-coming German Philharmonic Orchestra and attended concerts in the elegantly refurbished Rudolfinum, a hall that in the nineteenth century had seen performances by such towering German composers as Anton Bruckner, but was later converted by the Czechoslovak government into a dismal Chamber of Deputies. To think that a beery rabble of Bohemian bureaucrats had ordered the demolition of the very pipe organ Bruckner himself once played, in order to install doors connecting one legislative chamber to another. The whole idea made Heydrich furious. It was further proof that these people were incapable of civilized behavior and thus needed one of two things to set them straight. Aryanization or extermination.

Jakub was one of the last of the underground Jews to remain uncaptured. He was no thespian, as he well knew, but became marvelously inventive when it came to creating variations of his identity. He became a shape-shifter. Grew a beard, dyed it, shaved it off, let it grow back only to dye it again. He blended in, managed to look old or young depending on what the moment dictated. For a time Jakub disguised himself as a woman, hunched with a cowl over her head, quasi-infirm, complete with cane and convincing limp. Once a man who loved nothing better than putting his head down on the same pillow every night, he turned into someone who didn't trust the same beds, the same hiding places. Attics, closets, outbuildings. He learned to stay on the move. Somewhat to his surprise, he became an intrepid insurgent, working daily to disrupt Nazi operations in small ways. He helped to hide others, helped to keep the network of fellow anti-Nazis organized and active. He nearly got caught once cutting the brake lines on a troop carrier in the middle of the night. Turns at engagement and sabotage such as these gave him meaning.

His rare correspondence with Otylie took place through intermediaries whose lives were forever in danger. He apologized in every missive for exiling the two of them from each other. Wrote that he loved her and wished he were with her. Never knowing whether his letters would arrive in her hands, he told her the truth. Told her if he could relive his life, he would run with arms open across that meadow and wrap himself around her.

My courage was cowardice, he confessed in the last letter he ever wrote to his wife. She, he declared, was the brave one. The real believer.

Heydrich was living large by this time. A bright blond sun shone radiantly on his every initiative. Productivity was up. Morale, up. The resistance, suppressed. A majority of Czechs, he believed, now saw things the same way he did. He had single-handedly turned the country into the most prolific arms producer the Reich had at its disposal. Rumors began to circulate that he was about to be redeployed to France and Belgium, to work the same miracle in those countries now that the Czechs were pacified. The government in exile knew that he had to be stopped lest he turn Paris and Brussels into the next Pragues, just as the man himself was convinced he'd set Prague on its way to becoming the new Nuremberg.

The Reichsprotektor resided with his family on a pastoral estate at Panenské Břežany, twenty kilometers outside the city. On his way to and from work, he defiantly displayed his confidence by having his driver ferry him through the streets and suburbs of Prague in his polished open-air Mercedes. He loved feeling the cool wind flooding over his long, proud face. It was the feeling of mastery, of unchecked control. Sometimes he ordered his chauffeur to let him take the wheel so that he might drive himself. Pure heaven.

Now, Jakub, after two years of youthful military service before engineering school and much time in the underground, had the will but still not the elite English commando training of Jozef Gabčík and Jan Kubiš, who had been assigned the task of assassinating Heydrich. Jakub's impromptu shadow role as he saw it was to help provide whatever backup they required. Five long months would

pass between their parachuting under cover of night from an RAF
Halifax just after Christmas, and the twenty-seventh of May 1942,
the sun-bedazzled day Heydrich was scheduled to fly up to Berlin
to accept his promotion from the grateful Führer.

Working out of his safe house just east of Prague, Jakub wasn't
mobilized to play any role in Operation Anthropoid, as it was code-
named. But he found himself involved after a local miller and a
gamekeeper discovered Gabčík and Kubiš, injured and disoriented, having been dropped in the dead of night many miles away
from their planned point of entry. Fortunately for the resistance,
the two Czechs were ill-disposed toward the Nazis and helped the
paratroopers get in contact with Jakub and others whom the Gestapo had not yet run to ground. The infiltrators needed to be fed,
sheltered, covertly moved into position. Jakub helped as best he
could, trading boots with one of them, who had sprained his ankle
during the jump, and giving the other his only pair of warm gloves.

The assassination, like the parachute drop, was not fated to
go off quite as planned. After surveillance of Heydrich's routes
and routines that winter and into the spring, it was decided that
a hairpin curve on a hill in Holešovice gave them their best shot.
Heydrich's car had to be braked and downshifted to make the
turn. He would be, for a brief promising moment, very vulnerable.

On the day of the attack, however, it seemed to Jakub from
his vantage point a bit farther down the street as if the man were
above and beyond death itself. As if Death had too dear an accomplice in Reinhard Tristan Heydrich to want to see him destroyed.
When the Mercedes Cabriolet B convertible made the sharp right
turn from Kobylisy Street onto Kirchmayer, Jakub saw Gabčík
emerge from where he'd been hiding, take aim, and try to fire
his Sten submachine gun. Nothing happened. Had he neglected
to release the safety? Was the gun jammed? To Jakub's horror,

an undaunted Heydrich stood in the passenger seat as the car ground to a halt. The Nazi quickly unholstered his own pistol and fired at his assailant, who dropped his gun and fled. It was then that Kubiš stepped forward and threw his high-powered grenade, a Mills antitank bomb, at the Mercedes. An explosion rent the air.

Though no one had instructed him to do so, to be there as a witness to this moment in history, Jakub held his ground. He had no training as an assassin. Everything he knew about acts of insurgency he'd learned on the fly from others in the underground far more skilled than he. Whether from instinct or shock, he stayed put, the gun the gamekeeper had given him still concealed under his jacket, and waited to see if Kubiš needed help. He saw Heydrich collapse on the street, still trying to shoot his attackers.

Silence descended over the neighborhood. Out of the corner of his eye, Jakub saw a man in uniform rush past, a blurry figure that abruptly stopped, turned, and glared at him where he stood loitering suspiciously under his tree. Jakub was about to pull out his pistol and fire, but the dreamlike quiet was broken by a baby's crying somewhere behind an open window. The man, having memorized Jakub's face, turned again and hastened to help the fallen leader. Glancing around, Jakub saw that both assailants had gotten away, one on foot, the other on his bicycle. As discreetly as he could, he walked from the scene himself while others helped Heydrich into the back of a baker's truck, where he lay on the floor in obvious agony, though he neither cried out in pain nor showed the least sign of fear.

Later, when he learned Heydrich hadn't died that morning—it would happen a little over a week later, of blood poisoning from the limousine fender and seat shrapnel, dirty horsehair stuffing, and bits of cushion springs—Jakub wondered if he should have finished off the wounded man himself. During the last hours of his own life he couldn't help questioning if he would have been able to pull the trigger. Otylie, whispering to him in the capricious spring breezes, assured him he had done what he was meant to do.

The SS and Gestapo cordoned off Prague. The attempt on the Reichsprotektor's life gave the Nazis free rein in the capital and countryside to round up and execute anyone they pleased. Jakub had no chance of slipping past them back into the rural woodlands. If his father-in-law, a soldier he never met, had been right that all wars begin and end with music, Jakub could only hope that this violent, ecstatic, percussive gesture not only opened the finale of Heydrich's dark interlude in Prague but served as prelude to the golden requiem for the Reich. He was certain he wouldn't live to know the outcome.

As he made his way toward Malá Strana, his last act of resistance was to head for the Svobodas' house before being captured, or to find Tomáš, to give one of them the sonata movement. He had no idea whether his old friends were still to be found there. Or if they were alive. The manuscript his wife entrusted to him had for these years been his only possession. He no longer owned any of the clothes he was wearing when he left Josefov. Even his wedding ring had at one dire turn meant the difference between buying off an informant or being turned in. His onetime go-between, Marek, had disappeared nearly a year ago. It was like that with people in the underground. One day they were there. The next they were gone. He didn't dare ask around about his young colleague, for fear of betraying himself. But the sonata had never left Jakub's person.

Sometimes, alone at night, he would try to read the score by candlelight. To recapture in memory that single performance by Tomáš. He remembered how lovely his wife looked that evening, in her dark blue silk dress that set off her favorite pearl necklace. She'd worn her hair down for the occasion, and Jakub remembered with fantastic precision how it swept, wavelike, across her bare shoulders. He couldn't recall what the music sounded like, except in the most nebulous of ways. But he bravely improvised in his various secret caves and haylofts, following the scales that ran up and down the staves, making up passages as he did. The manuscript he sometimes tenderly placed to his face, as he believed its paper still bore the scent of his wife. It smelled of gardenias, he thought, and somehow of the sea.

Now he walked along with it hidden under his shirt, held tightly against the curve of his gaunt, drumming chest. One day this war would be over, and his Otylie would return to look for him. She would not find him. But if she found this, she would know that he never stopped loving her, that he never gave up. It was their only chance at reunion.

II

What seems so far from you is most your own.
—Rainer Maria Rilke, *Sonnets to Orpheus*

· 1 ·

WHEN THE WALL CAME tumbling down on the ninth of November 1989, Gerrit Mills reveled along with the teeming floodlit multitudes in Berlin. A sea of ecstatic women and men and children sang and chanted and waved banners and hugged and kissed each other, rejoicing in their newfound freedom. Witnessing this mass jubilation, Gerrit had never felt so exhilarated, despite the fact that this was neither his country nor his liberation.

He wasn't even supposed to be here. Germany was a side trip, hastily added and wholly unauthorized, on his way from Paris to Prague. His editor at the newspaper in New York, where he worked as a stringer for the foreign desk, had been keeping a close eye on the wall weeks before it finally fell. Gorbachev's perestroika was gaining such unstoppable momentum that reunification no longer seemed impossible. But Margery Raines didn't ask Gerrit to go to Berlin, and for all the elation he felt experiencing firsthand that pivotal moment, Berlin wasn't his story to cover. Instead, he needed to return to Czechoslovakia, where he was convinced an even more depreciated people were about to shake themselves free after Communist-strangled decades. Though his home base was still nominally Paris, he had filed stories from Prague as recently as September, and had kept in close touch with his contacts there as the situation developed.

"Poland got out from under the Soviets in June," he had earlier reminded Margery, calling her from his studio apartment in Montmartre, jotting notes almost as quickly as he spoke, aware that he had to make a strong case for himself to score the assignment. "And now there are workers straight out of the Gdańsk shipyards sitting side by side with Red party bureaucrats in Parliament. This playwright Havel and his rock-and-roll pals are next in line to topple a regime."

"You've done good work there, it's true," said Margery, thinking out loud.

"Plus, don't forget I have dual citizenship and friends in the middle of the unrest. They might be able to help me drill deeper into the student dissident underground than your more senior journalists."

"All right, so when can you leave?" she asked her youngest reporter in the field.

Gerrit was thrilled. The byline wouldn't necessarily be his, but some of the inside research would, and maybe he would get a "with reporting by" credit. Either way, he didn't want to let Margery down. She had been his advocate from early on, when he came to the newsroom as a fledgling intern straight out of Columbia's journalism school. While he understood why she dispatched her most seasoned staff reporters to above-the-fold historic scenarios like the Berlin Wall, he also knew it was thanks to a soft spot in her mentoring heart that she'd sent him to help cover the opening of the Hungarian-Austrian border earlier that spring, a watershed event in the sundering of the Iron Curtain. No one, not even the astute Margery Raines, had guessed that fifty thousand East Germans, many pretending to go on holiday in Hungary, would cross the open borders into Austria when the checkpoints were relaxed and frontier fences ripped down. But they did, old and young, all seeking a new life in the West. When Gerrit heard that East Germans were scaling the walls of the West German embassy in the Prague neighborhood of Malá Strana after abandoning their tin-can-cardboard Trabant cars on the streets, keys left in the ignition for anyone who cared to drive them home, Margery sent him there straightaway. He found several thousand refugees crammed into a makeshift camp in the gardens behind what used to be the Lobkowicz Palace while diplomats negotiated their safe passage to West Germany; then he talked his way into the Associated Press office to wire the story to New York. Heady days. The oppressed and disenchanted were rising up across the globe. In Sofia, in Timişoara, in Bucharest, in Tiananmen Square. A political tsunami was cresting and for a brief flicker of time there was no stopping it.

He thanked Margery before they got off, and said, "Consider me already there."

Still, he couldn't resist the temptation to make his way back to Czechoslovakia via West Berlin. Despite his devotion to Margery, Gerrit occasionally stretched the rules when he felt it was for a good cause. He wasn't in it for the money, since there wasn't much to be had anyway, or the transient glory of seeing his name in print. No, he liked working in the field because he wanted to see raw history for himself, breathe it unperfumed, hear it live and unfiltered. When he was a boy, history had seemed to him not a series of events left behind but an organic, swirling storm worth chasing. And this time his small sin of traveling roundabout in hopes of catching up to it paid off. Celebrating with exultant Berliners that epic day, taking a hard swing himself at the symbol of tyranny with one of the sledgehammers being passed around, Gerrit knew that luck and curiosity had converged in his favor. On the train down to Prague, he wrote in one of his ever-present notebooks a detailed reminiscence of what he had seen, heard, and in his small symbolic way participated in. This act was an integral part of Gerrit's life, as ordinary and essential as breathing.

He stayed, as always, with friends on Kampa Island, in the heart of Prague. The Pelc family, who'd known his parents and grandparents, had a spare bed that was always his for the asking when he was in town. He'd wired ahead to let them know that he'd probably be there for a while, unlike his whirlwind in-and-out in September, and when he arrived, his hosts set out a spread of baked ham, *knedliký* in paprika sauce, and boiled potatoes.

Since they hadn't had time to talk earlier that fall, they sat down to catch up on family news. How were things going at his father's shop? His mother, still enjoying her public school teaching? And how was Gerrit's life in Paris? Didn't he feel a little betwixt and between living neither in America nor his native Czechoslovakia? He looked thin. Was that French girlfriend of his feeding him enough? What he needed was a good Czech girl. One who could cook a Bohemian pork roast with all the fixings, make him some nice fried cheese.

So the conversation with three generations of Pelcs always went, a comfortable stroll down a familiar path. Nothing much had changed since Gerrit was last here. At least not on the surface.

But the streets were about to fire to life. Gerrit had felt it the instant he got off the train. Aging Anton and Lenka, along with their son Pavel and his wife, Věra, seemed to sense it as well. The elderly couple's politically active grandson, Jiří, who studied painting at Charles University, certainly did. Every last soul in Prague, to differing degrees, knew something was in the air. It was as manifest yet shrouded as the layers of autumn mist flowing inexorably along the river embankment.

For good reason. The next day would mark the fiftieth anniversary of the death of Jan Opletal. A soft-spoken, middle-class medical student shot dead by Hitler's police during an anti-German rally in 1939, Opletal was one of the Czechs' most revered martyrs. No activist who struggled against the Nazis, nor any who later rose up against the oppressive Communist regimes, failed to embrace Jan as an inspirational comrade in arms.

After dinner, Gerrit invited Jiří out for a beer. They both knew where to go. U Fleků was the pub where Opletal's wake was held half a century ago, a place popular with students then and in a way hallowed to them now. The hangout overflowed with young people, many wearing buttons and badges with pro-democracy slogans, everyone in high spirits, scoffing at Czechoslovakia's buffoonish party leader Miloš Jakeš and his hard-line stooges.

So, you think I look too thin, Georgie? he asked his friend in Czech, raising a glass. Gerrit's unruly black hair, subjected to a barber's scissors only once a season, was threaded with a few strands of premature silver at the temples. His taut face and green eyes, flecked with gold and framed by fine wrinkles, made him seem older than his twenty-five years.

Don't listen to my mother. She loves you like a son, that's all. Anyway, you've always been lean as a pole. *Na zdraví.*

Gerrit thanked him, said he was lucky to be part of the Pelc family. After taking a swallow of beer, he set his mug on the table and looked around at all the students, trying to read their faces. Most were about Jiří's age—nineteen, twenty—and there were faculty types in the crush as well. The room was thick with cigarette smoke and edgy camaraderie.

You want to know what's going to happen, don't you.

Without a change of expression, he glanced at Jiří and then went back to surveying the crowd. Everyone here wants to know what's going to happen as much as I do. Why, do you know?

Can I ask you a question, Gerrit?

Jiří's face was not unlike the photograph Gerrit had seen of Jan Opletal himself. Bright crescent eyes that turned down at the corners, ruler-straight nose with flared nostrils, confident full lips over a strong cleft chin, and cheekbones as prominent as a pair of apricots—a sturdy youthful face that projected nothing but the most promising future.

Of course, fire away.

Are you here as a Czech or an American?

I'm here as a journalist.

A man without a country, in other words.

I never thought of it like that, but I suppose so, in a way.

You know we're friends, right?

I should hope. Our families go back forever and then some.

So don't get me wrong. I'm not telling you what to do.

That may be, but you've never been shy about speaking your mind.

Jiří chuckled, took a deep drag off his cigarette, exhaled. I hope you can be in your Czech skin while you're here. It's important that the world knows what's actually going on, that the uprising is real.

That's my intention, Jiří. What are you getting at?

What I'm saying is that if push comes to shove I hope you'll help us protest, as a fellow Czech, as my friend, instead of standing there, just watching and writing.

Be dispassionate and passionate at the same time? Be both observer and actor?

Jiří shrugged and said, Guess that's one way to put it.

Gerrit took a swallow, stared at the foam on his beer after he set it down. He hadn't been in Prague a full day and here he was already plunged deeper into the story he'd been dispatched to cover than he might have wanted. Jiří, no fool, was asking that he commit the cardinal sin in journalism. Take sides, bias his report. Or worse, become one of the players in the story itself. While Gerrit couldn't honestly claim that he didn't feel a strong affinity for the endless stream of East German families fleeing across the Hungarian border into Austria earlier that autumn, he hadn't helped carry the fugitives' luggage any more than he had written a slanted account of what he'd witnessed.

Jiří, if the world needs to know, don't I need to write it down? You can do both. I know you, Mills.

Jiří rarely called Gerrit by his last name. It was disconcerting, but brought into tight focus what was at stake.

Where's this idealism coming from, Pelc? You're my reliable cynic, the guy who insists that the Czechs have always been burned by history. That dashed hopes are spliced into the DNA of your national psyche.

Your psyche? It's ours. That's what I'm saying, man. Be with us on this. You were just in Berlin, you know about the huge demonstrations in Leipzig, right? Everybody here in Prague does too. If Poland, Hungary, and now East Germany did it without reprisals from the Soviets, why not Czechoslovakia?

Jiří's points, forcefully posed, were much the same as those Gerrit himself had impressed upon Margery. They both knew that the great promise of the post–First World War governments of Tomáš Masaryk and, later, Edvard Beneš had ended with the invasion and iron-fisted rule of Hitler. And that the end of the Second World War merely set the stage for Stalin to take over. A glimmer of hope arose in the spring of 1968, when the head of the Czechoslovak Communist Party, Alexander Dubček, tried to lift some of Moscow's more oppressive restrictions. But, as sure as water evaporates, the hopes of Prague Spring vanished, and by autumn Dubček was arrested and tanks clattered into Czechoslovakia to crush its people once again.

Let's not forget, said Gerrit, my folks fled this country when I was very young and you weren't even floating in your mommy's womb yet. I hate Jakeš and the rest of these Communist assholes as much as anybody, and I resent this long occupation too. But I'm here to report on what I see. There's international interest in what's going on, don't think otherwise. If you want people outside Czechoslovakia to know what's happening—

I want people to change things. So do all my friends. Since others won't do it for us, we have to do it for ourselves.

You and I have no quarrel, Georgie. But we've talked about professional practices and you know I've signed a contract with my paper about conflicts of interest, so don't push too hard. I'll do my best to be who I am.

I know you will, said Jiří with a broad smile, touching the base of his glass to Gerrit's on the table. Friends?

Always.

Gerrit spent the rest of that evening and the week that followed taking notes on what Jiří Pelc had learned at plenary meetings, shadowing him as he attended gatherings about planned demonstrations and strikes that were to come. When he wasn't with Jiří, Gerrit interviewed student leaders. He snapped pictures with his worse-for-wear Nikon. His pockets rattled with film canisters and microcassettes as his notebook filled. He converted his data into articles, then transferred the work to his contact in Prague or phoned it in to the rewrite desk in New York, repeating the spellings of difficult names and double-checking details over transnational phone static.

Walking the restless streets, Gerrit thought about his conversations with Jiří. He understood his friend wasn't wrong. The
boundaries between observer and participant had already slipped
in Berlin—although he hadn't been there as a freelancer—and
the frailer-than-iron curtain that kept these impulses separated
was difficult, once opened, to close again. It was going to be hard
not to go native.

Organizers had anticipated a crowd of as many as three or four
thousand to gather in front of the Institute of Pathology, the spot
where Jan Opletal's funeral procession had begun fifty years ago.
Fifteen thousand came.

Speakers recalled Hitler's bloody crackdown in November
1939, when he'd closed down Prague's universities and had the
Gestapo round up nine leaders of the student union, executing
them without trial in the SS barracks at Prague-Ruzyně. They
condemned his henchmen, who broke down doors of residence
halls throughout Prague, murdering students who resisted and ar-
resting twelve hundred others, promptly shipping them to a concentration camp in Oranienburg. To the cheers of the crowd, they
called for the resignation of the current government, which was
nearly as repressive in its slow-boil way as the National Socialists
before it.

Jiří and the rest of the chanting throng carried flags, flowers,
and candles and sang the national anthem. Pressed in among
them, camera dangling from its strap around his neck, Gerrit
marched up to the Slavín, the cemetery on a bluff overlooking the
river where the demonstration was supposed to end. He pulled
his recorder from his pocket and started talking into it, trying to
describe every last detail of what transpired. Somebody handed
him a candle and, in the middle of recording a statement from a
woman about the "living altar" that the streaming mass of protesters had now become, he took it without thinking. Among the many

impressions flooding his mind as evening fell was that history, to these people, had nothing to do with textbooks. Jan Opletal might as well have died that morning, so present and passionate were these children of his struggle. Then Gerrit remembered who he was—a Czech American, yes, but a reporter—and snuffed the candle, stuck it in his pocket.

What happened next happened quickly and without permission from the authorities. The growing crowd didn't want to disperse. Gerrit heard calls from every side to continue the march back to Wenceslas Square. It was then, as everyone reversed course and headed down the hill, that he realized he had lost track of Jiří and his friends. Alone in the crush, he continued to record what he saw.

At first the mood was lighter, more exuberant than before, although rumors abounded that riot police had cordoned off Gottwald Bridge and were blocking other routes to the center of town. As the demonstrators made their way along the Vltava, tram and bus drivers blew their horns while their passengers disembarked to join the human river that now spilled into every side street. Local residents along the embankment leaned out of their windows to cheer them on, waving the tricolor, hanging impromptu homemade banners with fresh-painted demands for reform. More and more onlookers were drawn into the miles-long flow of protesters, whose ranks had by now swelled to over fifty thousand. Turning at the National Theater and proceeding toward Wenceslas Square, those at the front of the march shouted that they were unarmed and wanted no violence. *To the square and then home*, they cried in near unison.

Gerrit knew that his press card probably wouldn't save him from spending a night in jail if he remained in the midst of the throng, but he managed to wend his way toward the choke point, where protesters and cops stood in a face-off. His heart beat hard as he took photo after photo of boys and girls younger than Jiří sitting in the middle of the street together with men and women old enough to remember the Nazi days of Jan Opletal himself, holding carnations and singing "We Shall Overcome." Thousands of others jangled their keys overhead to protest their jailers. All of this reminded Gerrit of the old Czech saying *Co Čech, to muzikant.* Short and sharp on the tongue, easy to remember, it translated simply, One Czech, one musician. Was there ever stronger proof of its truth than here with so many hands held high in the air chiming dissent?

Suddenly overwhelmed, he threw his head back and listened with eyes closed. The elation he had felt at the Berlin Wall returned to him in full spirit here in Prague. House keys, car keys, skeleton keys, keys to offices and stores and schools and brothels and bakeries and churches. Keys to safeboxes and keys that no longer fitted in any lock, all ringing like bells of freedom, accompanied by voices caroling the national anthem in a tangle of musical keys, off-key, and there in the middle of it all the melee began.

Fifteen hundred policemen in full riot gear managed to segregate and surround more than five thousand people trapped at the front of the demonstration. The thick curtain of cops soon parted, offering a single route of escape down an arcade lined with yet more police, truncheons raised, standing at the ready. They beat everyone who fled, screaming, tripping, stumbling, single file down this narrow corridor. In the sickening crush heads were bloodied, eyes blackened, teeth broken, the fallen were kicked by the enemy and trampled by innocent friends. Gerrit's jacket was torn off his back, his camera yanked away, and when he resisted, twisting and falling to the ground as he grabbed his notebook and recorder and shoved them under his belt, a billy club repeatedly struck him from behind. His notes safe, he abandoned his jacket and camera, and surged forward with the others, finally emerging into Mikulandská Street, his face a Rorschach of blood, gasping for breath. Hundreds were injured, the youngest thirteen, the oldest born before Czechoslovakia became a nation. Staggering back to Kampa Island, he saw people cudgeled as they tried to enter metro stations or board trams and buses headed toward home.

Before withdrawing to file his report, Gerrit filled the Pelcs in on what had happened, insofar as he was able to understand why and how such a peaceful protest had devolved into bloody chaos. Jiří was nowhere to be found. His family almost hoped he was in jail rather than lying injured or unconscious in a hospital somewhere. Phone lines were mysteriously jammed, so they would have to wait to find out.

As the kitchen sink ran pink with blood and soap, and Věra Pelc dressed his wounds, Gerrit realized he needed to find an answer to Jiří's query back in U Fleků. What was his role here? Exactly who was he supposed to be after this? Behind the closed door of the room he shared with Jiří, he sat awake writing in his bloodstained notebook every last detail he recalled about the demonstration, confronting the dilemmas that were raised for him that violent and pivotal night.

META GREETED SAM at the western end of the Charles Bridge. From there they walked toward the foot of Nerudova Street. The day was drenched with crisp light, and the smooth-faced cobbles winked as if they were wet. A dwarfish man in a brown double-knit jacket and clown-like baggy gray pants stood in the shade of Saint Mikulaš Cathedral feeding a flock of cooing, pirouetting pigeons from a sack of bread.

"He's something of a fixture here," Sam said, nodding in his direction. "Nobody knows where he lives, but it's said that after dark the pigeons fly him up to the castle towers where he nests with them. In the morning, they carry him back and set him down by the local baker, where he buys two loaves, one for them and the other for himself. It's good luck to put a little change in his cap."

Meta said, "Well, I could use some luck," walking over to where the man stood before the baroque facade and depositing some coins in his upturned porkpie on the steps. When she rejoined Sam, she added, "That's one of the things I love best about Prague. Everything and everyone seems to bring a fable to life."

"Home of the Golem and crazy Rudolf's equally crazy alchemists, not to mention Kafka's bug."

"Some days I feel a little like Gregor Samsa myself."

Sam laughed, but his expression was serious as he turned to her and said, "Meta, I may be totally wrong about this. You know how sometimes ideas that come in the middle of the night look different in the morning? I just hope I'm not wasting everybody's time."

"No worries, Sam. I'm grateful for the lead however it pans out."

They strode up the hill on the narrow stone sidewalk, which forced them to step into the street at times when oncoming pedestrians didn't give way.

Sensing they must be nearing their turn, Meta asked, "So tell me again who this guy is? What's his story?"

"He boards with the Hodeks, Andrea's family. She's crazy about him, has a big crush. Dual citizenship, Czech American. He wrote one of the best books I've read about the Velvet Revolution, and was one of the founding staff members of the *Prague Post*, which originally was a small paper for American expats but now it's read all across Europe and overseas. His name's Gerrit, easy enough to remember since he lives in the garret apartment in her family's building."

A steep flight of stone steps down off Nerudova and a hard right turn at the bottom put them on Jánská Street. The house they sought was near the end of this blind alley. Sam pressed the Hodeks' buzzer and they were welcomed inside, then led up another flight of stairs and into the living room, where Meta was introduced to his piano student and her mother. Andrea, the thirteen-year-old daughter of Gerrit's landlords, was a button-bright precocious girl with a ready smile. Meta liked her at once.

"I go up to his floor, see if he home," she said in English for Meta's benefit. "He tell you he don't know about this music, though."

"We'll see, Andrea. Music's sticky, like honey or tree sap. You never know when it will get into your head and stay there."

"Tree sap?"

"You know, like the clear blood that comes out of a tree when you cut it."

"I see. Tree sap," said Andrea, giving Meta a quick nod as she turned to go upstairs.

Smiling back, Meta admired Sam's impulse to help people find their way to things. Whether toward an understanding of music or English or, in her case, a shot in the semidark at a lost sonata movement, Sam seemed always ready to engage.

Reflected sunlight washed through the street-side windows, giving the room a deep golden glow. Andrea's mother having excused herself, the two Americans were standing at the window nearest the piano, looking out over the rooftops toward the lush green foliage on Petřín Hill, when Andrea reentered the room with Gerrit.

Shaking Sam's hand with a firm, friendly grip, Gerrit said, "I know we've met in passing, but it's good to finally meet you for real. Andrea here thinks the world of you."

"Unless I make her practice her scales too much when she'd rather be listening to Madonna. Then the world she thinks of me isn't such a wonderful place."

"*Lháři*," Andrea shouted, with a genial frown. Liar!

Sam turned toward the woman hovering at his side. "This is Meta Taverner, another fellow traveler in the land of music."

Until that moment, Gerrit hadn't looked directly at her. As they shook hands he finally saw the face of this young woman whose chestnut hair was coppered by the sunlight. Her burl-brown irises took on a golden hue in the changing light. She smiled, or half-smiled, as she said hello. It was clear at once to Gerrit that she was nervous, tucking her hair behind her ear, which in turn made him feel a bit nervous. When he let go of her hand, his eye held hers for an extra moment.

"By fellow musical traveler, you mean you two," he said, breaking the brief spell.

"You play too, don't you?" Kettle asked, finding his opening quickly as they sat, Meta and Sam on a divan between the windows and Gerrit in a green baize wing chair opposite.

Andrea, perched on the chair arm next to Gerrit, with the confident familiarity of a daughter, said, "Sure" at the same time Gerrit said, "No."

Kettle saw no reason not to press ahead and, after a good-natured laugh, continued. "Andrea wins the point on that one. I'm pretty sure I've heard you playing once or twice."

"I took piano lessons when I was a kid. But I fiddle now, is all. That is, if one can actually fiddle on a piano."

"Your technique is unpolished, I'll admit, but I really like what I think I've heard you fiddling."

"Well," Gerrit said with a slight shrug, wanting to direct their focus elsewhere. The last thing in the world he thought Andrea's piano teacher would come to Jánská Street to discuss was his less than stellar pianism. He barely had technique to polish, for heaven's sake. "You live in Prague too?" he asked Meta, turning to look at her again.

"New York," she said. "This is my first time in Prague."

"So, what brings you here?"

"Music," Kettle answered for her.

"You're performing somewhere?"

"Actually, I'm looking for two lost manuscript movements of a piece of music that was broken up during the Second World War, somewhere in this neighborhood. That's why Sam and I are here."

Trying to keep up, Andrea asked Gerrit for a translation into Czech as Meta detailed what she knew about the sonata. Gerrit listened intently to the wartime story she related, then turned to his young friend, who was leaning lightly, a bit possessively, against him, and filled her in. The more Meta spoke about the Prague Sonata, the more Gerrit felt perplexed by the visit. It was left to Sam Kettle to make the connection for him.

"This may sound like a pushy question coming from somebody you don't know, but do you have any classical compositions committed to memory? Something you 'fiddle' from time to time?"

Puzzlement settled on Gerrit's face. "Classical compositions committed to memory?"

"I'm sorry," Sam went on. "I don't mean to sound mysterious. It's just that I know I've heard a passage from the score that Meta here has discovered, the beginning of what could be a rondo that follows at the end of her manuscript, but I don't know what it is myself. I thought I might have heard it here. That's why I ask."

"I know a few old standards," Gerrit said, "but none in their entirety. When I play, it's more guess-as-I-go improvisation than any traditional readings of your Brahmses and Bachs."

"In the eighteenth century, improvisation was considered the true mark of a virtuoso," Meta said.

"Only problem is, I'm not a virtuoso and it's the twenty-first century."

Meta bent forward, clasping her hands out before her knees, on which she rested her wrists. She had such an earnest look of supplication in her eyes that Gerrit felt sorry for her. Her attitude was almost of prayer, given how her long fingers knotted themselves so tightly together. He half expected Meta Taverner to ask him to sit, then and there, and perform, as best he could, every single work he knew.

"Look," he proposed, "maybe if you play me the piece, I might recognize something."

"Of course, happily," said Meta.

"Andrea, all right with your mom, you think?" Sam asked.

"Sure," delighted to hear someone else play her piano.

"Shall I play the whole movement or just the rondo?" Meta asked no one in particular.

"Play it all," Gerrit said.

She adjusted the stool height and sat. Without saying a word, she closed her eyes and for the hundredth time let herself be lifted away into the introductory phrases that by now were second nature to her. Andrea and Sam were mesmerized by the music. Hearing it again made Kettle realize once more why he had become an activist, if that was the right word for his role, in Meta's quest.

As for Gerrit, he couldn't help staring at her hands. He tried his best to listen to the music, but his attention was divided. He had not seen anything in a long time so compelling, so stirring, as those hands. The blood vessels that fanned into deltas across the backs of them, threading between her knuckles, were a healthy blue beneath her skin. Her hands were as beautiful as the music they created with every press and release of the keys. And yet, wasn't there something off about the right one? What was the story behind the white wormlike scars that crisscrossed those blue veins? Her fingers seemed more curled too, and reminded him of the spidery tendrils of some graceful orchid. Whenever both hands hovered above the keyboard, the left was motionless while the muscles in her right were clearly cramped and palsied a bit, as if it were much older than its mirror-image twin.

When he forced his eyes away from her hands, he couldn't help but furtively trace her outline. Her profile was, to Gerrit, as classic as some maiden's in a painting by Vermeer. Her eyes were shut, though it wasn't as if she had closed them, as some musicians do, for dramatic effect. She just clearly could hear things better that way. In his untutored view, her whole approach to the keyboard was restrained, calm, masterful. Her back and shoulders were straight but not stiff. She was exceptional not because of any extravagant glamour but because of simplicity and depth of spirit.

He was startled when the performance ended and the room dropped into fast silence, but also because her eyes were wide open and staring directly into his with the question she wanted him to answer, if he could, here, now. He fumbled through an apology and asked the first question that came into his mind. "Who did you say wrote this?"

"I didn't say, because I don't know yet. Finding the other movements would make that part of the process a lot easier."

"Especially," Sam added, "if the composer's name is on the first page."

"Makes sense" was all Gerrit could think to say. "I'm sorry, but would it be possible for you to play to it once more? Especially that rondo bit?"

Instead of offering him the impatient frown he felt he deserved, Meta said, "No problem."

He too shut his eyes this time, and when she reached the rondo fragment at the end, he realized the melody was indeed familiar—he had heard these notes before. But what was it? He tried his hardest to search through the melodies he knew, or kind of knew, and had dabbled with, on hotel uprights or friends' spinets in France, Germany, England, wherever his job had carried him. Even now, during quiet patches of an evening when the Hodeks were out, he would sit at their piano and improvise, reimagining in skeletal play-by-ear notes, approximations of what he had once studied, had maybe heard. He loved to run simple scales for the pleasure of feeling his fingers produce something more than the hollow clacking sound of his banged-up Olympia portable and computer keyboard.

"Anything?" Sam asked, once she finished.

"Not sure. I don't want to raise false hopes, but I do think I've heard this before. Especially that last bit."

"The rondo opening?" Meta pressed.

He nodded, searching his memory for where he possibly could have encountered it.

"Well, that's promising," said Sam. "Now I don't feel so alone. What about you, Andrea?"

The girl shrugged.

"Can you give me a little time to think about this?" Gerrit asked, glancing first at Sam, then at Meta. "Who knows, maybe I'll remember where I picked it up if in fact I did."

"Of course," Meta said. "I'm so grateful." She took a pen from her leather knapsack and wrote down her mobile number on the back of Professor Kohout's business card, since she didn't have a piece of paper. It gave her a bit of satisfaction crossing out his name and university address on the front. "This is how you can find me, at least until my money runs dry and I'm forced to head home."

They rose at the same time. Gerrit hesitated before shaking her hand again, oddly unwilling to part company with Meta yet.

Could he really have recognized what she played? Or was it wishful thinking born of the impulse to help this young woman find what she was looking for? Trudging back upstairs he felt compelled to make a few notes about the encounter before returning to his article on marionettes. He'd been a journalist too long not to recognize the scent of a good story. Even if it proved to be a minor composition, it had political and human implications that went beyond music. He would bide his time, but wanted to see her again, knew that something had just happened to him, for better or worse, beyond merely a lead, beyond meeting a stranger who played for him a beautiful piece of anonymous music.

BLACK FRIDAY WAS FOLLOWED, as Gerrit and Jiří and everyone else who attended the Jan Opletal demonstration quickly saw, by a barrage of sketchy information. Of misinformation, disinformation, and no information at all. Shaken by both the number of demonstrators who had descended on Wenceslas Square and the nationalist zeal they'd displayed, the besieged authorities in Prague Castle cranked their pettifoggery machines into high gear.

How can they lie like that? Jiří fumed as he read the Communist Party newspaper, *Rudé právo*, with disgust. But for the fact that his fist was wrapped in a gauze bandage, he might have pounded it on the table. Like Gerrit, though neither knew it at the time, he'd been one of the unfortunate several thousand corralled by riot cops and forced to run their gauntlet. Jiří had tripped, been trampled, then wandered home in a daze hours after Gerrit got there. His badly sprained hand looked like a fresh-skinned baby rabbit in a butcher-shop window.

Gerrit, you work for a newspaper. How can they lie like that and get away with it?

All media make mistakes, but I don't work for any *Rudé právo*, Georgie. You know as well as I do, their job isn't reporting, it's about keeping the proletariat calm and ignorant. Sedated as a patient on an operating table.

Rudé právo—Red Right, Jiří sneered. It ought to be called *Žadné právo—Nothing Right*.

Jiří only grew more frustrated when official state news reports downplayed the massive protest as the work of antisocial dissidents and drunken hooligans. Both the head counts of those who participated and the tally of heads busted by the police were skewed. The minister of health assured the country that fewer than a dozen troublemakers had been sent to the hospital. Yet at the same time, as Gerrit discovered that Saturday morning when he managed to get a call out to his girlfriend in Paris, Agence France-Presse was reporting, wrongly, that four students had been killed in violent clashes with police, and that the students had provoked the bloodbath. Clear government plant, he thought.

What did your paper say happened? Jiří pressed Gerrit, as they walked toward the city center to attend a matinee at one of the many theaters where the first strikes were to begin. They had no real interest in the play that was billed, but wanted to be there to see if the performers, as promised, would abruptly switch roles onstage from actors to dissidents.

I don't know yet, but when I reached my contacts here in Prague and New York, I reported the story as I saw it. What really happened will get out, don't worry.

Gerrit didn't tell Jiří how close he had come to losing his notebook in the fracas. Phone numbers and addresses he wouldn't want the secret police to know, including Jiří's, were scribbled in the back of that book. Not good. The anxious Czech leadership was, as Margery had phrased it when Gerrit finally reached her, "pissed as hell at Western newspeople right now. Just don't get yourself in trouble."

"I won't," he'd answered, knowing that to stay close to the center of the upheaval he had to put himself right back in harm's way. Still, he made sure to switch to a fresh, blank notebook in which no sensitive information would be written, not even his own name.

As they entered the theater hall, his worries receded when he and Jiří witnessed what took place. The actors didn't perform a single line of dialogue for the packed Saturday-afternoon house. Instead, they read aloud the students' edicts against the government and announced that actors, directors, playwrights, producers, set designers, musicians, ticket takers, and everyone else involved in theater around the country were going on strike. The audience rose in a standing ovation and began to sing the national anthem.

That evening Gerrit and Jiří joined others at the statue of Saint Wenceslas in an impromptu display of perseverance. Dozens became hundreds became thousands. Candles were lit. Banners unfurled like vesper flowers. The chanting began. *Who if not us, when if not now?* A group of protesters formed a human cross and, mobilized by what Gerrit noted as a "common intuition, many bodies inhabiting a single idea," they made their way down the long public square, intending to march to the very gates of Prague Castle, the seat of Communist power. Twenty thousand streamed behind them.

This is it, Gerrit jotted in the fresh notepad. *The revolution. Roll over, Stalin, and tell Karl Marx the news. More strikes to come, more protests. But the weight of inevitability is behind these people and they feel it. So do I.*

A mile-long phalanx of policemen with Plexiglas shields and billy clubs at the ready blocked bridges and surrounded the castle, thwarting the marchers. It hardly mattered. Their voices were heard at the top of the hill. A call for calm on Sunday night by a high-ranking member of the Central Committee was met with derision. By Monday, students and their professors had shut down every university in Prague and many more across the country. Artists and nontheater musicians joined the actors' strike. Cinema screens went black and moviegoers used the auditoriums for political discussion instead. Metro station walls were papered with typewritten announcements and handmade posters that went up faster than police operatives could tear them down, and Gerrit, using a camera he'd borrowed from Anton Pelc, photographed them to wire to New York.

The mood was charged with excitement inside the classrooms and lecture halls where students organized, even though many felt sure that tanks would come clanking across the cobbles any day, just as they had in times past. Václav Havel and other core dissidents met in the basement of the Magic Lantern theater and within a few fast days emerged as a unified opposition group, Civic Forum, with specific demands. The hard-line Communists were to resign. Prisoners of conscience were to be released from Czech lockups. Officials behind the violence wrought upon innocent protesters on Black Friday were to be brought to justice.

Elegant in his old-school suit and tie, Alexander Dubček joined the messy-haired Havel on a balcony in Wenceslas Square and addressed ever-larger crowds as the revolution hurtled forward. Everyday citizens—bakers, housewives, truck drivers, janitors, secretaries, mechanics, stonemasons, factory workers—now outnumbered the students. Volunteerism rose. Crime fell by two-thirds. An almost idyllic spirit of community was seen in Prague and beyond. *Be kind to one another* was one of the altruistic chants Gerrit often heard, and rather than sounding naive, the words shimmered like diamonds, hard and brilliant.

By November 25, certainty had set in. Three quarters of a million strong, peaceful but adamant protesters sang and cheered in Letná Park, within earshot of the government offices on Hradčany. That there was no retaliation, no bloodshed, was one more sign to many in the crowd that collapse was imminent.

Gerrit continued relaying reports to his contact in Prague and met his deadlines, sending dispatches to New York, interviewing prominent protest leaders, and detailing what he observed. But more and more he found himself singing and cheering and jangling keys over his head along with the others. Jiří and a circle of his friends had become Gerrit's constant companions. Even he could tell that his reporting had drifted toward a pro-revolutionary posture. When he wrote of the Communist regime, terms such as "willfully blind" and "intransigent" peppered his language. The wry sense of humor shown by demonstrators—a facet of the Velvet Revolution that was coming to be seen as one of its hallmarks— now cropped up in Gerrit's descriptions of events. When he transmitted to New York that *Rudé právo* was turning from red to white, he became the target of protest himself.

Margery's first words on the phone were "What the hell's going on over there?"

He hesitated. "You've been getting my filings, right?"

"Oh, I've been getting them." Her voice combined worry and anger. "'Economic destabilization, understandably frightening to many in the labor force, may be, according to various forward-thinking members of the Student Strike Coordinating Committee, a necessary endgame to bring down the implacable Old Guard'?"

"I wrote that? 'Forward-thinking'? 'Implacable'?" he feinted, silently scolding himself for putting them both in this awkward position.

"Well, I sure didn't. Nor will I run it. Nor am I inclined to edit it into anything even slightly approaching impartial journalism. I'm surprised by you, Gerrit."

He hardly knew what to say.

"I guess I may have gotten a little partisan recently," he admitted.

"You think?"

"I'm sorry," he said, wincing. "I didn't realize how much all this would affect me. I'll make sure it doesn't happen again."

"Do. Because if it does, I'll have no choice but to send you back to Paris. Put you on a story that doesn't get your blood boiling," she warned him. "Now get back out there. Give me the straight goods. No more gonzo cowboy stuff."

Despite his disappointment, Gerrit recognized that Margery had done him a real favor. As a freelancer, he wasn't even owed two weeks' notice or severance pay. She could've wired him train fare home and written him off. But he knew she believed in him, had from the beginning, and didn't want to lose her young reporter because of some overzealous statements. He knew her criticism was right. Knew that the very notion of journalist as propagandist was against everything he stood for, especially after seeing it up close and personal here during the rusty old Iron Curtain days.

The catch was this. Gerrit had come to understand that he was in Prague now as much for himself, his past and possible future, as for his fledgling career. A mini-revolution had been building within him from that first night. There was no more turning it back than the larger revolution he was in Czechoslovakia to cover. He knew that the resignation of the general secretary, Miloš Jakeš, and the implosion of the Czech Communist presidium were at hand, and he didn't want to read about any of it in Paris, or see the images streaming out of Prague on his girlfriend's portable black-and-white set. He wanted, needed, to be right here.

Life spun itself out with spidery quickness after the Velvet Revolution went down. Gerrit kept his roiling thoughts to himself, at least in the written accounts he turned in. The Communists were gone, replaced by a cadre of dazzling nonprofessionals who took back their country from outsiders for the first time in over half a century. If some of Gerrit's dispatches were tinged with giddiness, Margery understood it to be a function of the prevailing mood in the newly minted republic.

Gerrit returned to Paris that winter just long enough to invite his girlfriend, Adrienne, to move to Prague with him. Since she no more wanted to leave than he wanted to stay, they agreed to remain friends. When Gerrit kissed her goodbye at Gare du Nord, he looked into her eyes and knew he faced many a night ahead when he'd regret this move. Two valises in hand, he found himself back in Malá Strana not a full month into the new year, greeted by gray snow, gray skies, and silvery glowing optimism in every face on the street.

His primary order of business was to find a place to live. The Pelcs offered to put him up for as long as he liked. He needed his own apartment, though. Having lined up some gigs writing for additional news outlets as well as doing some translating, he could afford it. Anton Pelc had friends with space to let, rooms formerly inhabited by relatives who'd emigrated to Canada the minute the borders were opened. Accompanied by Anton and Jiří, Gerrit strolled from Kampa Island up the narrow lanes until they reached the even narrower lane of Jánská, where he was introduced to the Hodek family. The rooms offered were in dire need of plaster and paint. The plumbing had a medieval cast to it and the kitchen was rudimentary. But the apartment was airy, with vistas out the windows. Seeing winter sunlight glancing off the cubist array of red rooftops and whitened terraces of Petřín Hill in the distance, Gerrit immediately felt at home. Monthly terms were easily settled, an informal agreement was signed, and he moved in the next day.

The first letter he sent from his new address was to his parents. He wondered what they'd think of his decision to live in Prague. To say they had a long-standing ambivalence about the mother-land was an understatement. Was it possible, though, they might be curious about this experiment that was about to shed the be-draggled name of Czechoslovakia and become a democracy? More likely, they would think he had lost his mind.

A FEW NIGHTS AFTER THE MEETING on Jánská, Meta found herself walking across the Charles Bridge with no destination in mind. Mandelbaum's contact list was exhausted, without much progress to show for it. And for all of Sam Kettle's good intentions, her hopes were pretty much shattered. She hated to admit it, but naysaying Wittmann might have given her the best advice. Give up, pack up, leave.

She looked at the lights dancing on the black river from mid-span. The Vltava was running high. Its shallow falls just upstream roared, their wide cascade barely visible in the gloom. A brightly lit sightseeing boat with a few night-owl tourists aboard chugged under the great stone bridge. As Meta wandered toward the Old Town tower with its pinnacled wedge spire glistening in ambient light, she reflected on how many souls as perplexed as she had passed through its Gothic stone archway over the centuries.

Small comfort. A wretched smirk played on her lips. She couldn't remember being so down on herself. Her mood was as dimly churning as the river. Then there was the matter of Jonathan.

When she first arrived in Prague, she spoke to him daily. Within a couple of weeks, their calls had tapered off to Wednesdays and Sundays, with the agreed-upon excuse that they were costing too much. A new timbre colored his voice. Darker, rounder. More pavane than sarabande, she thought, lurked behind his fading encouragements. Without a doubt, Jonathan had modulated into a minor key, and gone, or at least diminished, were his earlier encouragements to return to New York and salvage her studies and teaching.

"What stones are left for you to turn?" he'd asked when she called to let him know that the visit with Gerrit proved inconclusive.

Jonathan had just come back from her apartment to water the plants. Simple as the task was, she could hear that it irked him. She hesitated before admitting that she and Sylvie planned to start asking around the three places—Wenceslas Square, Malá Strana, and Josefov—where Meta knew the manuscript had been when it was intact.

"You're telling me that you intend to go door-to-door and talk with strangers, in a foreign language, I might add, about something that went astray sixty years ago?"

It did sound ludicrous when laid out in such blunt terms. "It's all I've got left to work with. Every one of the musicologists came up empty-handed. Besides, Sylvie and I did this before when we went looking for Jakub's grave in Vyšehrad."

"Yes, but you didn't find it."

"I found it wasn't there. That's its own kind of important verification, isn't it?"

Jonathan sighed. His exasperation was so thinly disguised that Meta was sure even he must have heard it.

"Sylvie and I are going back to the municipal archives," she went on. "We'll look for exact addresses for Jakub and Otylie's apartment, his shop, whatever else we can find. If I come up with nothing, I'll be on the next flight out of here."

"I've heard that before," he said, and immediately apologized.

She forgave him the wisecrack, tried to quell the defensiveness rising in her. If this was to be her last-ditch effort, she wasn't going to let Jonathan's skepticism dampen her determination. "Sam Kettle is being nice enough to let me take on a few students he doesn't have time for in his schedule. Only ones who know a little English."

"That's kind," Jonathan said, recovering his equilibrium.

"He and his wife have offered to let me move in with them, save some money. I'm going to crash in a sleeping bag in his piano studio. Well, actually, under the piano. I'm moving over to Vinohrady tomorrow."

With this, Jonathan's misgivings seemed to subside. He even ventured, "Far be it from me to be upset with anybody who's so committed to an idea," and added that he'd known investigators in the past who were often reduced to just such primitive methodology as ringing doorbells, canvassing neighborhoods.

"I know the pressure's really on once I move in with them. They're being generous, but I can only sleep on Sam's floor for so long before going mad. Last thing the Kettles need is a madwoman living under their piano."

Mad, or outlandishly hopeful, as she might be, her saner self had begun to believe that Sam was wrong. The only other option was that Gerrit, or someone somewhere, had improvised a line or two, stumbled upon a brief phrase that by sheer chance resembled the passage at the end of Irena's manuscript. Twelve brave little notes constitute the Western chromatic scale. Though it might seem the possibilities for their permutations were all but endless, there were still chances of overlap or glancing echoes. Whether on purpose or by accident, the rising arpeggiated figure that opens Beethoven's first piano sonata is identical to the opening of the finale in Mozart's G Minor Symphony, just one whole step down in the key of F minor, both in second inversion. And how many blues songs were based on the same three-chord sequence? Quotes, echoes, accidental replications are part and parcel of music.

Much as Gerrit—what was his last name?—seemed to want to help, he too had failed to connect what she played in Andrea's house with any music he knew. While she was on the phone with Jonathan, she'd ignored an incoming call, which proved to be from Gerrit with nothing to report other than apologies. "Just wanted you to know I'm still sifting through my memory here," he said in his voice mail. "Call if you need anything."

Call if she needed anything. What she needed, Meta mused as she wandered toward Old Town, was a miracle. She found herself thinking about Gerrit, the air of self-reliance that surrounded him, the warmth, even intimacy, he conveyed. His familial kindness toward Andrea was endearing, and Meta hadn't been blind to his gaze when they were introduced. It was not a come-on, more a frank assessment, and it hadn't left her feeling small.

But small or not, her feelings were now beside the point. Meta was in fact running lower on funds than she was able to admit to Jonathan. Gillie, bless her, had offered to send enough money to get her through another month. "A loan to be paid back either someday or never, whichever comes last," as she put it. But Meta couldn't in good conscience agree to the offer. It wasn't as if Gillian had vast resources to draw upon. Besides, only the week before, Paul Mandelbaum had posted her a money order for what she considered an extravagant three hundred dollars.

Finally got around to your big bad B-day present, he said in an accompanying typewritten letter, since e-mail and money transfers were technologies he refused to embrace, not unlike Meta, who only reluctantly participated in the digital world. *Ten dollars a year for you, though you deserve far more. Take yourself out. Get the best seats in the house at the Prague State Opera or the National Theater for you and Ma and Pa Kettle. Make it Mozart. Then dinner, something gourmet, no damn goulash on my dime. Bonne anniversaire!*

She wanted to tell him she couldn't accept this much money, but knew he'd be offended if she refused the gift. She didn't let him know that after paying off her pension bill and setting aside the rest for food and sundries, she barely had enough to go see a movie, let alone a production of *Die Zauberflöte*.

Meta had long desired to take a seat at one of the outdoor restaurants that fronted the Týn's towers and idly watch passersby in the Old Town Square. Were Mandelbaum here, he'd scold her if she denied herself such an innocent indulgence. She sat under one of the large umbrellas warmed by big propane heaters and ordered a drink, facing the resplendently ancient square as she people-watched and listened to the distant strains of live jazz emanating from a cellar club somewhere. This was to be her last night at the pension, where she'd never enjoyed one good night's sleep. Tomorrow the endgame would begin. In his message to her, Gerrit had said, "Keep up what you're doing here. It's important." And it was true. This was important, what she was trying to do, worth those sleepless nights.

The after-theater and postconcert lingerers gradually trickled away, along with the tourists. Only a handful of customers still loitered under the canopies as restaurants extinguished their spirit stoves and nightlife retreated indoors to dance clubs and blues bars. Breaking in on her reverie, a waiter asked if she wanted anything more.

"*Děkuji, ne*," she said, signing a check in the air with an invisible pen in case he couldn't understand her foreigner's Czech.

As she finished the last of her wine, she heard the voices of two men entering the square from fashionable Celetná Street. Their footfalls echoed across the cobblestones. Meta stood and edged past the array of empty tables and chairs. While she was setting off toward the narrow lanes that would take her to the pension, one of those voices caught her attention. She hadn't spent more than twenty minutes with the man. Half an hour, tops. But Petr Wittmann's baritone had a depth of confidence that made it unmistakable. He and his companion were laughing, speaking rapidly back and forth.

Meta followed them, weighing whether or not to interrupt, say hello to Wittmann, let him know she was still here working on her project. He would at least have to acknowledge that she was no quitter. More than once she'd wondered if he would have engaged her more about the manuscript if he hadn't been in such a hurry the day they met. The two men passed the Jan Hus monument as she came up behind them and blurted, "Professor Wittmann?"

Wittmann turned, said, "Yes?"

Even caught unawares, he had recognized an American accent and responded in her language.

"*Dobrý večer*," she said, as amiably and with as careful an accent as she could manage.

Her heart sank as she looked into his eyes. What did she think she was doing? How she wished she had stayed within her wine-warmed cocoon.

"Good evening to you too, Miss Tavener. A pleasure to see you again." He bowed a little, shook her outstretched hand. The self-assurance Wittmann exuded was breathtaking. His white silk scarf against his white turtleneck and black jacket suggested the kind of elegant poise she'd seen only in famous conductors and composers. Hadn't Stravinsky affected a scarf like that?

The other man turned around to see who had broken in on his pleasant dialogue with Wittmann. Under the faint stars that hovered over the broad plain of stones in Staroměstské náměstí, Kohout acknowledged her with a nod.

"What brings you out so late?" Wittmann asked.

"It was a beautiful evening. I decided to take a stroll."

"How is the research coming along?"

"Well enough."

Kohout shifted his weight from one leg to the other.

"That must mean you've had some success then."

"You know how it goes," she hedged, hoping he wouldn't ask further.

"I don't, actually. But I'm glad to hear that you're making progress. Please let me know if you have anything new to show me. I'd be interested in looking at it."

This was a very different tune from the one Petr Wittmann had whistled during their earlier truncated encounter. While he awaited her response he pursed his lips as if he were about to whistle in fact, then startled her by warmly smiling.

Seeing Kohout's impatient expression, she thanked Wittmann for the offer and, drawing her jacket lapels with both hands around her neck, bade them good night. As she moved to leave, however, Wittmann stopped her, saying, "My colleague and I were just parting company. Perhaps you and I might have a quick word, Miss Tavener?"

That was unexpected. She turned toward Kohout in time to see the surprise on his face slide into the awkward smile she remembered from their meeting.

"A pleasure to see you again," Kohout told her, then raised his eyebrows at Wittmann, saying, "We will talk again tomorrow," before striding across the square.

Facing him directly in the uneven light and shadows, Meta waited.

"I find," said Wittmann, "that some of my obligations at school have cleared up, my Mahler is done, and I have a bit of unexpected time at my disposal."

Again Meta just looked at him, unsure how to respond.

"So, I wanted you to know that while I still have serious reservations about the manuscript you and Paul Mandelbaum brought to my attention, I believe there are aspects about it that merit further consideration."

"I'm glad you think so," she said, wary but open. "I'd be pleased to meet with you again, maybe play it for you this time—"

"No need. I've already played it myself from your copy. Not the performance I'm sure you would give. Be that as it may, I wonder if we ought to address it in the context of historical musical fraud. As I said before, it's both too good to be true and too unpolished to be false. Working together we might approach it as optimistic skeptics."

Meta bit her lip. "I appreciate it, but that's not the research I want to be doing right now. Optimism and skepticism have their places. What's important to me is finding the other movements. If I can do that, I'll eliminate all these subjective issues."

"Well," said Wittmann, undiscouraged, "if you change your mind, give me a call. And if, by the way, you have the original with you, I would like to see it."

He pulled out his wallet, withdrew a business card, and handed it to Meta. She thanked him, shook his proffered hand, and said good night a second time.

Under the dirty peach light of a rising moon she hurriedly found her way to the Charles Bridge, running the gauntlet of its statuary on either side. Her hard-won calm had been scuttled by this encounter. She had no idea what to make of Wittmann's sudden collegiality. Rather than feeling heartened, she felt confused, mistrustful.

Maybe she was tired, maybe a little tiddly, but instead of walking straight to her pension, Meta found herself climbing Nerudova toward Gerrit's house. Not that she could explain what compelled her to do so. She had met the man only once. She knew little unto nothing about his life. But she sensed he might understand, somehow, why she was unsettled by what she'd just experienced. She made her way to Jánská and soon enough stood before the Hodeks' building, looking up at what she believed were his windows. If she was right, Gerrit was home, since the lights were on. For a few minutes she stood there, swaying a little while weighing what to do, then left without ringing his bell.

WITH SYLVIE AT HER SIDE, Meta began to trawl for information in the Josefov quarter of the city. After days of false leads and bad information, they had finally identified, through copies of pre– Reich Protectorate documents found in the state archives, the address of Jakub Bartoš's antiquities shop on Veleslavínova. Meta, bucking weariness and self-doubt, began there less because the location held the greatest possibility for a breakthrough than because the street was short. Just a block between the much busier thoroughfare of Křižovnická, fifty paces away, where cars rushed and clanging trams ran; and Valentinská, which terminated at the Klementinum, where Meta had only a few days earlier attended a free concert of Beethoven's Fifth in the Mirror Chapel, performed by a string quintet and, of all things, a saxophone.

Since Irena said Jakub's shop had been pillaged by the Gestapo soon after the Nazi takeover, the chances were good they wouldn't encounter one soul who knew a thing about the Prague Sonata. At least this way, Meta figured, she'd be able to rule out one of the three locales where she knew it had been. She had joked with Sam over breakfast, when he raised an eyebrow at their plan, that it was "failure as a form of accomplishment"—a quip Jonathan would not have found funny.

Now a modest books and prints shop—an *antikvariát* and *galerie*—occupied Jakub's former premises. Its proprietor, a peaked man in a nubbly argyle sweater, had heard that the space once housed an antique store of sorts, but knew nothing about its former owner. When he excused himself to talk with a customer who'd entered the shop and asked about a volume on one of the high shelves, Sylvie gave Meta a shrug. Clearly, this was a dead end. Meta used the brief moment to marvel that the sonata movements had actually been together, as a single work, in this room. Two of her lifetimes ago. Whatever exhilaration the idea aroused in her was quickly undermined when she conjured images of Jakub's terror within these walls. And imagined, as best she could, what the SS troopers breaking down the door must have looked and sounded like as they began to ransack his *antikva*.

"You all right?" Sylvie asked her.

"Sorry," she said. "Just thinking."

After the bookseller rang up his sale, he returned to the two women, apologizing for the interruption. Business was business, Sylvie assured him.

"Ask if he has any customers old enough to remember Jakub's shop back in the days before Communism," Meta told Sylvie.

Following some back-and-forth with the owner that lasted for a few minutes but felt, to Meta, more like an hour, Sylvie reported, "He does know people who family lives here then. He gives me the address."

"Really? Wonderful," Meta said and turned toward the bookseller, clasping her hands and gratefully nodding her head. "Would you mind letting him have your telephone number in case he thinks of anything else?"

Sylvie wrote her number on a piece of paper the man gave her, then thanked him.

The first address was across the street, three doors down on the same block. *Langová* was typewritten on the buzzer label for the second-floor apartment. On either side of the stucco building's rough-carved double doors were alcoves whose entryway statues had long since been stolen. An empty beer bottle stood forlorn in one of them.

Her voice distorted by the antiquated intercom, a woman asked who they were, what they wanted. Sylvie apologized for disturbing her and explained.

"*Jděte pryč,*" was the woman's lightning response. Go away.

Meta and Sylvie looked at each other. Her brusque dismissal felt like a blind-side slap after the warmth they had encountered across the street.

"*Mohly bysme s vámi na chvilku mluvit?*" Sylvie gently persisted. Please, can't we speak with you for just a moment?

"*Nechte mě na pokoji.*" Leave me alone, the woman answered before launching into a rush of garbled words. She sounded to Meta not so much guarded or standoffish as hostile.

"She say we leave our name and phone on paper. Put in her letter box."

"Well, at least that's not a definitive no," said Meta, taken aback by the woman's vehemence. "Were you able to tell her everything?"

"As much as she lets me."

Sylvie wrote their names along with the Kettles' address and telephone number on a sheet of paper torn out of Meta's notebook.

"Write at the bottom that there's no reason for her to be afraid of us."

"She not call."

"You're probably right, but you never know."

Meta opened the creaky door to the rusted mailbox marked *Langová, J.* and dropped the folded slip into the receptacle.

"Onward?" she asked Sylvie, who agreed, "We go," and read the next address on the shopkeeper's piece of paper. Žatecká, another tiny street, one block over. Walking back down Veleslavínova, about to turn right toward the library to head to their next stop, Meta gave in to an urge to glance over her shoulder. A frail woman with hair as white as any flag of surrender was leaning out the second-story window of the building they had just left, staring at them. For a moment, Meta wondered if she had changed her mind and was willing to speak. The woman, however, seeing Meta hesitate on the sidewalk, ducked swiftly inside.

Žatecká Street proved to be a kinder call despite the enormous bat-winged devil figure over the door of the sooty pre–World War I building. The Novák family listened to Sylvie's story and invited her and Meta inside. Three generations of Nováks gathered in their front room. A girl and boy in their late teens showed every sign of being thoroughly westernized. Both wore bell-bottom jeans, and the girl, whose hair was raven black with red highlights, sported a Metallica T-shirt. Their mother, a handsome, work-worn woman in her early forties, greeted Meta in halting English. It was her father, who had lived there his whole life, to whom Meta directed her attention. He spoke no English, but his grandchildren were eager to bridge the language gap on his behalf.

"Could you ask him if he remembers a man named Jakub Bartoš who had a little shop around the corner on Veleslavínova? This would have been in the mid- to late 1930s."

Both asked their grandfather at the same time. The girl, who was a year or two older than her sibling, told Meta, "He say he was only a boy, but his father used to go there. He played chess with the man who had this shop."

"With Jakub?"

"S Jakubem?"

The grandfather gazed first at Meta and then, taking a wistful drag off a cigarette, out the window as he spoke.

"I don't think he can remember the name. But he say his father liked this man very much, and his wife too."

"Otylie?" Meta asked, catching the old man's cloudy blue eyes. A smile of recognition broke on his face. "Otylie."

Meta half-jumped out of her chair. "Otylie? Otylie Bartošová?"

He nodded, looking past Meta as if seeing the woman there with them in the room. "Otylie Bartošová."

"Oh my God," Meta cried out. "Sylvie, ask him what he remembers about her."

As it happened, Antonín Novák remembered quite a lot about Otylie Bartošová. Rapt, with the excitement of a beggar who has stumbled upon a bag of gold, Meta listened through a potpourri of memories that his two grandchildren and Sylvie by turn told her in translation.

Otylie loved sweets—just like Irena, Meta thought. She always had hard candies wrapped in shiny paper in the pocket of her skirt. She adored children too, was a benign pied piper, Antonín laughed quietly, but instead of playing a pipe she doled out treats to the children of the neighborhood when she came by the shop to bring lunch for her husband. Antonín was older than most of the kids, and often he would give the younger children the candies she handed to him after she'd left. He just liked to be near her. She was, he said, kind and sad. She had no children of her own. So all the youngsters in this part of Josefov kept a sharp lookout for Mrs. Bartošová when the sun was moving into the early afternoon.

"What else?" Meta asked, touched by what she was hearing. As close as she felt to Irena, her direct benefactor, and to Jakub, whose traces she'd been following, this was the first time she had been able to sketch a picture of Otylie in her own mind.

She always wore nice clothing and saw to it that her husband's shirts and suits were stylish and made of good fabrics. The old man could remember, now that he was thinking about it, a suit of—what was her husband's name again? Jakub, of course—herringbone wool, glorious dark gray it was, with beautiful bone, or perhaps antler, buttons. Antonín always hoped he would one day grow up and wear such a regal suit.

As much as Meta wanted Sylvie to interrupt his streaming oral history and ask about the Prague Sonata, she realized it was better to let him wander the streets of his childhood, building a portrait that might in itself somehow lead her where she needed to go.

Otylie worked in the *antikva* with Jakub. She oversaw everything having to do with money, as far as Antonín could tell, he who knew little about such things then. She spent many hours in the back room doing their bookkeeping, recording inventory, paying bills. How did he know this? Well, because he was often invited to accompany her to the bank where she made deposits and withdrawals. And why did he recall such a boring little outing as that? Because afterward they always strolled together down toward the river, where she bought him a lime ice or a *trubička*, a sweet cream pastry.

Jakub loved music. Otylie always claimed she never cared for it but Antonín didn't believe that. Her father had been a conservatory teacher, and had taught her. She tuned the instruments in the shop. Violins, lutes, mandolins, harpsichords. Anything with strings. She was rumored to have had a beautiful singing voice, although he only ever heard her hum.

"What did her speaking voice sound like?" Meta asked Sylvie, who translated.

It was low, he said, and, looking at the captivated Meta after his words had been translated for her, he dropped his own voice. A low voice like this. Her husband often tried to get her to sing for the children who hung around the shop, but she never would. It was said that one of the reasons she didn't attend church services or go to synagogue with her husband was that she couldn't stand listening to the hymns and other religious music.

This was Meta's moment. Had he ever heard her speak of a music manuscript that she inherited from her father? A sonata for piano?

When Antonín lifted his hand to scratch his head she saw on his forearm the telltale blue numbers. She said nothing. What was there to say? He looked down at the worn Afghan rug on the floor, then back up. Meta could tell he didn't want to fail her, and sensed that he didn't want to lead her astray either.

"Nepamatuju se. Nejsem si jistý, vopravdu ne," he answered.

Sylvie told Meta, "Means, he not remember but not sure."

"Why isn't he sure?"

They exchanged a few slow words. That his grandchildren had fallen silent meant to Meta that either she had run up against another wall or her quest was about to break loose.

"Ne, promiňte. Vopravdu si nevzpomínám," he said, looking meekly back and forth at the two women as he stubbed out his cigarette.

No, sorry, he really couldn't recall. He knew nothing about any manuscript. He apologized that he was a tired old man with a faulty mind. He appreciated what these young ladies were trying to find. He was young once too. He lost a fountain pen when he was in his early teens. One that his grandfather had given him at his bar mitzvah. He'd made the mistake of lending it to a school friend who proceeded to misplace it. Even after all he had been through in his long life, that fountain pen haunted him. He could still see its black and chocolate-colored lacquer barrel, its nickel hardware. Now it was out there somewhere in the world, being used, he hoped, by somebody. Maybe a writer of beautiful poems.

Both Meta and Sylvie took Antonín's story of the fountain pen as a signal that the time had come to leave. Sylvie asked if they could visit again if Mr. Novák remembered other details about the Bartošes. The smallest recollection might be significant, you never knew.

Telephone numbers were exchanged and hands shaken. Her letdown aside, Meta thought it astonishing that strangers from such different pasts could meld so freely through the catalyst of loss and memory. She even dared to lean down and give the still-seated old gentleman a kiss on the cheek, so close did she feel, through him, to Otylie and Jakub, then left Žatecká Street in a state of quiet euphoria.

For days after their encounter with the Nováks, Meta and Sylvie traipsed around Wenceslas Square discovering exactly nothing. The apartment building where Otylie and Jakub once lived had been converted into a commercial property on the ground floor and pricey residences above. No one they asked had ever heard of the Bartošes.

Doing her best to remain undeterred, the euphoria she'd felt so recently starting to wane, Meta was now prepared to canvass the upper reaches of Nerudova and adjacent streets and alleys in Irena's old neighborhood. The Kettles' daughter had come down with a cold, forcing Sylvie to beg off as Meta's Sancho Panza, as Sam jokingly called his wife—since who was Meta if not Doña Quixote?—until the girl recovered. Sam was meantime drowning in students, despite his American boarder's help with the overflow during evenings, and unable to step in.

After meeting with Gerrit and getting his voice mail, Meta had found herself musing about him at the oddest times. When brushing her teeth. As a pupil ran melodic minor scales on Sam's piano. She had to question whether these stirrings, or whatever they were, these private and inadvertent one-sided encounters with Gerrit, weren't somehow a specious response to her downward spiral with Jonathan. Maybe yes, maybe no. Either way, she knew she had to focus on what was before her. So she called him, but insisted to herself that this was purely business, nothing more. He'd offered, after all, and she did need something.

"If it's not too much of an imposition—" she started, hoping to sound neither sheepish nor presumptuous.

"Not at all," he said, his voice encouraging. "What's up?"

After explaining, she added, "I was just thinking that it's your corridor of Malá Strana, and you already know the area. And your Czech's as impeccable as your English."

"Not always impeccable, but more than serviceable."

They agreed to meet at an outdoor café up near the castle. Unthinking, she put on her best dress, but just as she was about to leave decided she looked absurd, so quickly changed into jeans and a white blouse. One last glance in the mirror before heading out brought her down to earth, if bringing her down to earth was what the moment required. Her pale drawn face and the bluish rings beneath her eyes betrayed just how exhausted she was from her up-and-down search. She splashed some cold water on her face, toweled dry, and left.

The day itself was radiant. Prague stretched below the aerie café, its many spires and steeples bristling out of a choppy angular sea of red-tile roofs. Above was a dense blue sky accented by wispy clouds, where a dirigible floated along like an anachronism whose pilot, with a handlebar mustache and monocle, had lost his way from another century. Kittiwakes circled over the Vltava while sparrows flitted in ivy that draped the wall beneath the palaces. The white-noise hum of the city could just be heard as Meta and Gerrit shook hands and sat at a wooden table.

"I appreciate your taking the trouble to help me," she said after they ordered coffee. "I've got to warn you the chances are good you'll have wasted your time."

He shook his head. "I don't believe anything is finally a waste of time. Wasn't it Thelonious Monk who said there ain't no wrong keys on the piano? It's sort of like that. Besides, I was overwhelmed by what you played the other day."

"It's magnificent, isn't it?"

Gerrit thanked the waiter for the coffee. "This may sound a little layman-naive to a musicologist but the music seemed really biographical to me, like somebody's story being told in those notes."

"I know what you mean," she agreed, stirring sugar into her cup and noticing the dirigible's reflection flexing on the black liquid mirror. "It's hard to imagine the composer wasn't thinking of himself or someone he loved. I'm so obsessed with it that sometimes I wonder if it wasn't written for me."

"As obsessions go, you could have worse ones," Gerrit said. "No question that the rondo bit, short as it may be, is a total *Ohrwurm*."

"Rondos as earworms," Meta echoed. "Hadn't thought of it that way, but it's true that rondos can get caught on the cortical loop. The thing has so completely taken me over that it's like some glorious illness I don't mind suffering even though it causes pain." She glanced up to see a complicated look of admiration and concern on his face and, suddenly self-conscious, continued, "So, Sam says you're a journalist. I hope I'm not taking you away from your work."

"Unless I'm on a breaking news assignment, I more or less set my own hours."

Meta nodded. "What sort of things do you write about?"

"Right now I'm doing something on Czech puppet theater, which you may know is pretty renowned. Puppets kind of freak me out, actually, but my editor back in the States arranged a generous fee for me to write about it for the Travel section. Honestly,

I write about everything under the sun. I've even written about things over the sun, if you count a piece I did for the *Prague Post* on the Meade mirror telescope they recently installed in the Štefánik Observatory not far from here." He chuckled, shaking his head, went on. "When I got started I was doing field research for a big New York paper, covering the region for them in the late 1980s. It's a story for another day, but during the Velvet Revolution I found my objectivity was harder to maintain than I expected."

"What happened?"

"Well." He raised his right hand, cupped as if it were holding an invisible ball, "I took objectivity"—then he raised his left in the same way—"and subjectivity and joined them like this," bringing his hands together to form a single sphere. "And out of that came a book about how I personally experienced the revolution."

"Sounds hard to do."

"I won't say it wasn't. But in the end it was well worth the struggle," he said. "Plus, I seem to have maintained my credibility—at least, I still get assignments."

They chatted as they drank their coffee. Meta asked Gerrit about his background, his translating; she talked about growing up in New York, studying piano. When he asked about her family, she shrugged, massaging her right hand with her left. "I grew up with my mother. As for my father, he's long gone, flew the coop. He disowned us, so we disowned him."

"Doesn't sound great," Gerrit said, and then, "Is your hand all right?"

Instinctively, she moved it onto her lap under the table. "It's nothing."

"I hope you won't despise me for being so up-front, but I've been wondering what happened. Looks like an injury."

Journalist or not, no one had ever been so undisguisedly direct about this. Other than her mother, nobody—not Mandelbaum,

not Jonathan, not even Gillie, who knew the whole sorry story—
was able to avoid looking at her hand with pity. But Gerrit's eyes,
his whole face, held no pity or judgment.

"You say you're not a real pianist, and I believe you."

"Wise move," he said, which made her feel a little more at ease.

"Well, this is why I'm not one either," placing the hand between
them on the table.

"Absurd statement, but go on."

"It's kind of a long story."

"Tell me everything," he urged her, ordering another round of
coffees.

"Well, I was a mistake. My parents were crazy in love back in
the sixties. He was premed. She was an art student. She got pregnant, and instead of listening to him and aborting me—he never
wanted to be a father—she went ahead with the pregnancy."

"Not very Age of Aquarius of her. So they got married?"

"Yeah, for a while. They broke up when I was in my early teens.
He got a job offer in California. Moved to Los Angeles, met a
younger woman, and remarried. Rode off into the sunset in his
predictable red Mustang—"

"You're not kidding, are you? About the red Mustang."

She shook her head and they both laughed for a moment.

"How'd you get started with music?"

"I had this toy piano when I was a little kid, one that sounded
like tin ducks being shot in a penny arcade. It was my favorite possession. I named it Molly."

"Molly the Piano?"

"'Fraid so. I loved my Molly, started picking melodies out on her
when I was just a toddler. Thing is, I accidentally tripped over
her while I was running around one day, more or less smashed
her to smithereens, which my mother tells me was a disaster—
apparently, I cried my eyes out. Our next-door neighbor came

to the rescue. She had a real piano, and I started taking lessons from her before my feet could reach the pedals. By age four or so, I moved on to professional teachers. Then High School of Music and Art, Juilliard, the whole thing. Bored yet?"

"I'll stop you when I am, how's that?"

Meta gave him a genial shrug. "When I was twenty-one, I was out in L.A. to play in a competition with other emerging pianists from around the world. My father may have run away from my constant practicing when I was younger, but he saw this as the golden chance to show me off to his new friends and my step-mother. I played Rachmaninoff, not my favorite composer, but a crowd-pleaser and technically heavy-duty stuff. After I placed first, Dad threw a party that went on forever. I was staying with the other musicians at a hotel—God knows I didn't want to stay at his place—so at three in the morning, he finally drove me back downtown from Pacific Palisades. Ocean fog had rolled in. I remember the streets being so eerie, like everything was behind a billowy gauze curtain. I was half asleep myself, but knew he was speeding like a maniac—"

Gerrit saw where her story was going, and stopped her. He reached out, taking her right hand in both of his. "I'm sorry I brought it up, Meta."

"No, that's all right," she said, remembering, as if she'd ever truly forgotten, why she so seldom spoke about the accident. "That's my sad little tale, such as it is."

"Little, no. Sad, yes. I appreciate your telling me," said Gerrit, his voice quiet. "One thing it does is make what you're doing here clearer to me than before. So let's move forward. What's your plan for this walkabout of ours?"

Meta excused herself, went to the washroom, splashed water on her face for the second time that morning. She looked at herself hard in the mirror, past the pasty skin and shadows beneath her eyes, more inward toward her deeper self. What's happening to you? she whispered, not as an admonishment but as a question. She had no answer, not just then, so straightened herself and headed back outside. Returning to the table, she explained to Gerrit what she had in mind.

"I know it sounds preposterous, knocking on doors, asking around, but I've run out of any other way I can think to proceed aside from giving up."

"Not preposterous," he assured her, considering how he himself would approach such an investigation, even as he felt a little guilty for having hastily jotted a few lines in his notebook about Meta while she was away. Old habit. Plus, the more he heard, the more he realized there was a compelling story here, about both the lost manuscript and Meta herself. Not that he would write it, since helping her out of friendship, or whatever this was, while compiling notes behind her back, would constitute a rotten conflict of interest, would it not? Interrupting his discomfiting thoughts, he told her as he got up from his chair, "Sometimes shoe leather is the best tool in the arsenal. Czechs, as I think you may have seen, are really open for the most part. Good people. They're the main reason I'm not inclined to leave."

"Sylvie Kettlová's been wonderful to me. And your Andrea seems like a darling."

"If I ever had a daughter, she'd be the one I'd want," he said.

Meta stood and turned to look out over sprawling Prague below. The dirigible had disappeared behind and beyond the castle. "So, Gerrit—what's your last name?"

"Mills."

"Well, Gerrit Mills," she continued. "Are you going to tell me more of your story sometime? It's not fair that you listened to my dreary tale of broken families and broken bones and I don't get anything in return. You owe me."

"I promise, but first let's hit the road," he said, putting money on the table to pay their bill. "By the way, what's that?"

While they'd conversed Meta had absently torn her paper napkin into a mess of small shreds. They lay like white fluttering petals around her empty cup. She reached down, closed her hand around the little pile, and put it in her pocket.

"Confetti," she improvised, turning to leave.

"For when you find the needle in the haystack?"

"For when I find the needle in the haystack."

The streets were full of midday crowds as the two descended into Malá Strana to begin their search. So many of the pedestrians seemed to be in a buoyant mood that Meta too felt unwarranted hopefulness rise within her. What was the line? Nothing hoped for?

Gerrit led Meta downhill toward Nerudova. "I've done my share of wandering this neighborhood. For example, I know there are exactly forty-nine steps from Nerudova down Jánský vršek to Jánská. Also, I'm no barfly, but I do happen to know every last pub in the area, including the ones tourists don't, where some of the elder statesmen of the quarter hang out. What I propose is to give you a guided tour past houses where I've heard musicians playing, because Sam probably heard his notes from an open window, not from me. Or I got a few of them and passed them to him, like some melodious virus."

"Okay," she agreed.

"One last thing you may already have noticed. Prague's not a city. It's just a bunch of small villages set side by side, like a honeycomb. And this neighborhood in Malá Strana's one village inside another village. Point is, walking around in the summer when windows are open everywhere, you get to know a lot about the lives of people inside without ever setting foot in their homes. You want to knock on doors, we'll knock. And when you're tired of that, we can haunt a few places like U Kocoura—At the Cat—and Baráčnická rychta, a pub that's more off the beaten track. Ask around if anybody knew this pianist from the early days. What did you say his name was?"

"Tomáš."

"No surname?"

"I'm afraid not."

"The haystack just got bigger and the needle just got smaller." He turned right off Nerudova toward the very steps he'd just mentioned, thinking to head down toward the German Embassy, which was situated in the old Lobkowicz Palace, and venture out from there. "It's an impressive old pile," he told her. "Complete with stone statues of the Valkyries on the roof. Well, macho Athenian maidens, anyway."

"How many palaces and castles did that family have, for the love of God? I visited another one a while ago in Nelahozeves. The manuscripts they own from the same period I think this sonata comes from are astonishing. They're still sorting out what's left in their archives after all those years of Nazis and Communists confiscating everything imaginable."

"Blatantly and brazenly stealing, you mean," Gerrit said. "What I have to offer is a little less edifying than your Lobkowicz treasures," pointing down the cobblestone street at the foot of the steps. "Our first musicians in the neighborhood. One's an aspiring electric guitarist who lives there on the left, bless his tattooed heart. The other's a singer with a voice that sounds like industrial noise, farther down across the way. I've often thought I should introduce them. They could start a band."

"They could call it the Forty-Nine Steps."

Gerrit enjoyed this small talk with Meta. Not to mention the inherent pleasure of walking beside a woman who had the capacity to move him with such simple gestures as a quip, some torn pieces of paper, the story of a smashed toy piano.

This was dangerous terrain, he knew. Soon enough, when her quest ended, whether in triumph or failure, she would leave Prague, and he'd miss her. Not that his life was lonely or bad. He hadn't dated anybody seriously since his breakup with Adrienne. Casual nights now and then with casual friends, nothing serious. "Friends with benefits," as his friend Jiří, always current with English jargon, referred to it. But Gerrit hadn't sensed any real absence in his life that needed filling, and he loved his work, its variety, its engagement. So he had to ask himself what gave him the temerity to anticipate missing Meta Taverner. Preposterous, he thought. Still, he had to admit there was nothing he could've done to prevent these feelings—real as a pebble in his shoe; real as a wind that might make a kite soar—from the instant he saw her standing, nervous and serious, in young Andrea Hodek's gold-tinged piano room.

· 2 ·

NINETEEN THIRTY-NINE was the year the World's Fair opened in New York and Italian physicist Enrico Fermi confirmed the successful splitting of the atom. It was the year Rudolph was introduced as Santa Claus's ninth reindeer, not by a children's-book writer but by the Montgomery Ward dry-goods company. The same year *Gone with the Wind* and *The Wizard of Oz* were Hollywood's biggest hits. The year Batman comics hit the racks and the great Irish poet William Butler Yeats died. In the United States, average life expectancy was not quite sixty. A gallon of gas cost a dime and a postage stamp three cents. The first televised heavyweight boxing match—Max Baer versus Lou Nova—was broadcast that year. The very year Germany invaded Poland after signing a nonaggression pact with Soviet Russia, and Franco sacked Madrid, ending the Spanish Civil War. The Yankees won the World Series that year, while Italy invaded Albania, and Hungary broke off diplomatic relations with the Soviet Union. The song "Jeepers

Creepers" climbed to the top of the pop charts that year, the year Albert Einstein wrote to inform President Roosevelt that nuclear chain reactions could possibly be used in bombs. It was the year England and France declared war against Germany and the *Physical Review* published the first paper about the discovery of black holes. It was the year Prague was kidnapped and a mass cultural tyrannization began. The year in which the Stockholm committee decided that no one in the world deserved to be awarded a Nobel Peace Prize.

It was also the year in which Jakub Bartoš lost contact with his wife. The year he arranged for her to leave besieged Prague for England. The year she passed into his hands the third movement of that star-crossed sonata. It was the year Jakub, like so many of his friends, should have been arrested and executed.

Somehow, over the course of the three excruciating years that followed, he managed to slip past the Nazi dragnets. Though he was grateful to have carried on his work in the underground, he thought often, alone at night in some hiding place, trying and failing to sleep, about how unfair this was. How brutal. Fair or not, brutal or not, he knew his luck had run out the morning in May 1942 when Heydrich was attacked.

Otylie always called her husband *Kocourek*. Little tomcat. Sometimes, after they made love, she liked to stroke his soft reddish beard and he would make her laugh by purring. Now his ninth life was about to be spent. No reason to hope otherwise. As he half-stumbled beneath flowering chestnut trees, ducking into niches in walls, into the sheltering shade of doorways, he thought of his wife. He wished he could feel her palm on his cheek once more. Wished he could lie with her in bed and hear her say, "*Můj kocourku*," and they could kiss.

Instead, he heard sirens screaming all across the city. He heard sporadic gunfire. His side ached and he was breathing hard. How badly he wanted to sit and rest. But he didn't sit and rest. He pictured his wife and pressed onward.

Jakub would have been happy if, by some magic, he could have known what Otylie was doing that day, her one day off during the week. She had been assigned to work as a staff secretary for Beneš's chancellery in the Putney area of London. To fill her empty evenings she decided to do some volunteer work at a hospital. Soon enough her English was quite good, a fact she attributed to her musical upbringing. She acted as a nurse's assistant and sometimes a translator for the wounded—those who had made it out of not just Moravia, Bohemia, and Sudetenland, but other Eastern European theaters. Fugitive fighters, underground agents, escapees, informers, fellow exiles committed to the cause of thwarting the Reich who had managed to make the difficult passage from the widening front to England. News of Jakub himself rarely reached her, although she was persistent in asking. When it did, she rightly questioned the veracity of what she was told. She wrote him letters almost daily and kept them in a discarded medical supply box with the intention of sitting him down to read them together, like an open diary, one day when the war was over.

Colleagues of hers who worked for the government in exile respected Otylie and felt sorry for her. She had arrived in their company shaken, if not shattered. She made friends easily enough but allowed no one to get particularly close to her. Since coming to England, she'd lost her appetite. The couple of dresses she brought with her hung on her body like mismeasured drapery. Any rosiness that once spread across her cheeks had blanched away under the damp Thames fog that rolled across the river from Bishops Park and directly, it seemed, into her foreigner's lungs. Nor did she ever go out with the others for an evening's entertainment in downtown London. Glenn Miller, Tommy Dorsey, none of the swinging big band music stirred a bit of joy in her heart.

Her closest friend was another displaced woman, an American nurse whose fiancé was stationed in France. She'd volunteered to transfer to London because she felt closer to him here than sitting around back home in Texas.

Even as Jakub made his dangerous flight through the streets toward Irena's house, and Tomáš's, Otylie and Jane Decker were enjoying their Wednesday afternoon walk to a nearby movie house. Though the Blitz forced leaders in the exile government to relocate to three rural villages in the Aylesbury Vale district of Buckinghamshire, Otylie and others remained behind in London to assist with daily operations. Matinees constituted her one weekly escapist treat. Today a new picture starring Cary Grant was showing. Jane claimed to have seen every movie he had ever made, from *This Is the Night* forward.

"His bad ones are better than anybody else's good ones, if you ask me."

Otylie didn't mind. She liked most any movie. She even enjoyed the newsreels and cartoons that came before the feature. The news often offered grainy footage from the front, with pro-Allied voice-overs that stirred pride and patriotism in her despite her hatred for the war. And the cartoons made her chuckle, silly though they were with their Daffy Ducks and Bugs Bunnys, who always found themselves in dire straits but never, ever died. She sometimes wished the world were animated. In a cartoon universe, you might get thwacked on the head with a frying pan but your head always sprang back. You might be blasted to smithereens with a shotgun but once the smoke cleared, there you were, blackened from head to toe, still standing, arms crossed and tapping your foot.

After paying the cashier and handing their passes to the ticket taker, a gentleman old enough to have served in the Crimean War, the two women entered into the smoky womb of the theater.

"So, Tilly. If me and Jim have a son first, you know what we're going to call him?" Jane asked, while they walked, half blinded by the sudden blackness, down the aisle.

"Cary?"

"No, that's too obvious. Grant, of course."

"What if it's a girl?"

"Why, then she'll be Carrie with two *r*'s and an *ie*. You see, I got it all figured out."

They laughed and settled into their seats near the front row, where Otylie gave her friend a handful of gumdrops she'd smuggled inside in a worn paper bag.

Otylie had never written as much in any of her many unsent letters, but she was convinced that if Jakub ever came to serious harm she would know it at once. She'd gotten the idea in her head sometime early on during her exile from Prague, and by now it had formed itself into a fixed article of faith.

The movie was good. Romance, psychological thriller. Jane whispered that she'd seen Cary play a dandy, a playboy, but never a potential murderer before. It was a revelation, yet another facet of his genius. But Otylie's thoughts were not centered on the screen. They wandered from its fake Sussex black-and-white sets back to the realities of Prague. She would never finally ascertain the exact time or circumstances of Jakub's arrest and would learn only scraps and minims of what happened to him once he was taken into custody. As she sat, however, watching Joan Fontaine vacillate between trust and terror on the screen, she felt a murmuring, a dark whispering, in the reaches of her intuition.

When she read about the courageous attempt on the Butcher's life in the papers the following day she was gripped by panic. In her room, on her knees, in tears, she prayed that Jakub hadn't been apprehended by the Gestapo. His life wasn't a newsreel, pumped up with impossible hope and narrated in heroic tones of valiant sacrifice and victory. It wasn't a cartoon whose violence ended in instant rebirth. She kept writing him letters. More furiously than ever. As if writing them would somehow keep him alive. She told him she had a friend here in England named Jane who spoke with the funniest accent. How he needed to see a Cary Grant movie sometime. How lovely the gardens were here. The magnificence of the English roses and leafy commons. The boys rowing beneath the Thames Embankment, war be damned. The sweet brown wrens flitting in the hawthorn bushes. She kept telling him how proud she was to be his wife. But her headstrong conviction, the stubborn belief she once held that he would someday sit beside her on Petřín Hill and read her letters one by one, had evaporated.

For his part, Jakub managed to get close to Irena's courtyard flat, but the streets were crawling with Waffen-SS and collaborating Czech gendarmerie. He had no stomach for testing his fake identity card on them, especially since he knew he reeked of fear and guilt. They would probably have searched him anyway, and the manuscript would have been confiscated even if he'd managed to talk his way out of trouble.

He had one last hope. If he was able to skirt the forested hillside that backed the Lobkowicz Palace and cut across the cloistered gardens behind the Franciscan hospital, he might make it to Tomáš's place on Šporkova Street. He'd have to do some trespassing. He would have to scale walls and hope nobody saw him. But he was out of options.

The final leg of his trek was more difficult than he'd anticipated, though not because of soldiers or police. As he neared the last wall in the Vlašský špitál complex, hopelessly tall and barren of trees with overhanging limbs that would set him down on the far side, a dog started barking at him. Brown as liver, with yellow fangs bared, it was tethered to an iron post. The animal strained against its leash, heaving hard at Jakub, who stood thirty feet away from both it and the wall. Without a second thought, Jakub made a dash for the stone bulwark, grabbing at the ivy that covered part of it, and abruptly found himself tumbling over, all akimbo, onto a cobbled walk on the safe side of the garden. The dog continued to bark, invisible to him now. Its owner, who had apparently come outside to see what all the racket was about, shouted a string of epithets that could have been directed at either the dog or Jakub. He got up and looked in both directions before hurrying down Šporkova to his destination.

As he knocked on Tomáš's door, trying to slow his breathing, he had to wonder whether his old friend lived here anymore. Wondered if he were even still living. For all Jakub knew, some boy in a Hitler Youth uniform was about to answer. Or a finger-pointer who might view him as good fodder for trading with the Gestapo.

He looked at the fob watch he'd bartered for some cigarettes in a safe house back at the hamlet of Nehvizdy. How was it possible it had taken so long to get here? Several hours had passed since the bomb detonated, tearing into the shiny metal of Heydrich's Mercedes convertible. How had he not heard the noontime church bells tolling?

Unbeknownst to Jakub, as he waited for Tomáš to answer the door, Hitler was already on the telephone with Karl Hermann Frank, whom he designated temporarily in charge of Prague, authorizing a cash reward of ten million crowns for the assassins' capture. Hitler was apoplectic. Ten thousand people, he demanded, must die at once. It scarcely mattered who, just so long as they were Czech. Himmler refined Hitler's demands by ordering that the chief concern should be the immediate detention and mass murder of any of the intelligentsia suspected of favoring the opposition. The capital, the entire country, had to be cut off from the rest of the civilized world until these perpetrators were found. One of the largest manhunts in European history was about to begin just as Jakub's friend, the pianist who once had performed Otylie's sonata so brilliantly, opened the door, gripped him by his forearm, and without a word pulled him inside.

"*To snad není pravda,*" Tomáš said, embracing him. This can't be true.

They walked down a hallway and at the rear of the apartment sat at Tomáš's kitchen table, each man stunned to be in the other's company. Tomáš had shuttered his windows after he'd heard about the assassination attempt on the radio, so the room felt safe, cave-like. Not that the Gestapo would be inclined to bother him, but he couldn't bear the inevitable cacophony of mobile loudspeakers and the drone of planes circling the city. Jakub saw how the years of occupation had aged Tomáš and it made him wonder how he himself must look to his friend. Not only older, but leaner, wearier. All but broken.

Tomáš described the many times he'd heard that Jakub had finally been caught, tortured, deported to a death camp, executed. He had never expected to see him again but here he was, like a miraculous flesh-and-blood apparition. What could he do to help? he asked. Did Jakub need money? Did he need food, something to drink?

I know it's impossible, but I would love a taste of our old favorite from back in the days when life made sense.

Slivovice? Ah yes, this is possible, said Tomáš, who briefly left and returned with a bottle of the traditional hard plum liquor. Jakub raised his eyebrows at Tomáš's having such a luxury on hand, when rations were so tight. As Tomáš poured him a glass, he asked if Jakub had heard about Heydrich, suspecting the answer was yes and that it had some connection to his sudden appearance in Malá Strana.

"*Nejen slyšel,*" Jakub answered. "*To jsem viděl na vlastní oči.*" I didn't just hear. I saw it with my own eyes.

Both wonder and terror crossed Tomáš's face in the light of the milk-glass ceiling lamp. He knew that Jakub's presence in the kitchen of his house constituted treason against the Protectorate. If his friend had anything to do with what had happened in Holešovice that morning, Jakub was a walking corpse in search of a grave. He also knew that Jakub, no fool, understood that Tomáš had done what was necessary to survive. He would never have been so well off had he not taught lessons to some of the best and most promising children of Nazi officers and Protectorate bureaucrats. He had even performed from time to time for German audiences and spoken highly of Heydrich's many efforts to enhance Prague's musical culture. Indeed, Tomáš was scheduled to perform the very next evening in a program that was part of the Reichsprotektor's pet project, the spring music festival. And, of course, all through the dark years, it hadn't hurt his chances of ingratiating himself with the occupiers that his last name was German. Tomáš Lang. He and his sister had both used the heritage suggested by their surname to avoid trouble.

But Jakub, suppressing a flash of rage at what the liquor clearly meant, did not press him. Instead, he thanked Tomáš for the drink. Thanked him for taking him in off the streets for a moment to catch his breath, and at considerable personal risk, though he needed to leave now. Something in Jakub's eyes told Tomáš that, despite any misgivings the fugitive might have, he believed that Tomáš wouldn't turn him in, that the pianist was still worthy of trust. Jakub then made a gesture that would stay with Tomáš Lang for the rest of his long life. He unbuttoned his shirt, carefully pulled out a sheaf of paper he'd concealed there, and without uttering one word or taking his eyes off Tomáš's, passed the manuscript across the table.

"*Kde je zbytek?*" the pianist asked, after looking through the pages. Where's the rest?

Jakub explained quickly and finished by saying, "*Ujmeš se toho?*" Will you take care of it now?

In this moment, Tomáš felt that every mistake, every poor judgment he had ever made in his life could at least be partially erased. Confronted by the wisdom he saw in his friend's face—for this is how he viewed Jakub, not as a broken man but whole—Tomáš was ready to do more than safeguard the sonata manuscript. He wanted to right his wrongs by helping Jakub, protecting him, using his connections to spirit him out of the country. It might take a while given the uproar that clutched Prague at the moment. But he felt sure it could be accomplished. Gushing, he expressed his willingness to harbor Jakub, help him to safety.

"*Pozdě,*" Jakub said as he rose from the chair and offered to shake Tomáš's hand. Too late. He asked only if he might wash his face and comb his hair. Afterward, the pianist accompanied him to the door, where they shook hands again.

Jakub's last words were consoling. Thank you, he said, for your offer to shelter me, but you can't protect what I've asked you to protect if I'm here. If it should ever be possible to get this back to Otylie, I would consider it the greatest favor anybody ever did for me. I know where to go now.

Good luck to you.

Good luck to us all.

Jakub had learned from Marek, the last time he saw the boy alive, about a safe house on Malostranské náměstí where a friend of a friend could help him if he ever got into a mortal jam. Since few of Jakub's activities had been centered in Prague proper, he had nearly forgotten. Remembering tidbits like this, however, had saved his life in the past. It was a long shot, but worth a try.

The best way to avoid being noticed, he decided, was to walk right down the street in plain view with his hands in his pockets. No one special, just a person on his way home as directed by martial law. He climbed Šporkova and the stairs that led up to Nerudova, and strode down toward Saint Nicholas Church, as nonchalant as if he were going to hear an organ concert there or attend a christening. Not looking behind to see whether he was being followed, he stopped at a nondescript house just before the church square and knocked on the door. A voice asked who he was and what he wanted. For the second time that day, Jakub made a leap of faith. Looking furtively left and right, seeing nobody nearby on the street, he stated his name and needs. Without a single further question, he was immediately taken in by a partisan—there were many hidden around Prague—who risked everything for the cause.

At dusk the city was all but immobile. The railways into and out of town had been shut down. Buses and trams and all other means of public transport had been suspended. A curfew was announced on Prague radio and by loudspeaker trucks that rumbled over the stones in every quarter. Jakub sat cross-legged with several others in darkness, not daring to speak above a whisper, listening to the sounds that filtered in through an open second-story window. Two other men and a widow with a little boy sat listening to a city that hovered in limbo before the onslaught.

Soon enough it came. Not long before midnight Prague broke into the music of war that Otylie's father had spoken of on his last night with her. The grinding engines of the Nazi motor corps that echoed in the streets. The marching feet of three battalions of Wehrmacht that spread across the cowering city. The shouted orders, the reverberations of doors being knocked on, then knocked down, the shattering of glass, the pleas and cries of people dragged out into the streets for questioning. Every member of the SS, the SA, the secret police, right down to the lowest-ranking cops, fanned out from Nusle to Dejvice, from Libeň to Košíře, in search of the would-be killers. The siege lasted longer than any of the resistance fighters holed up in that room might ever have expected.

But for them, at least, it did come to an end. The woman, hungry and tired of sitting around waiting to be caught, left with her boy and one of the men, hoping to reach the forested outskirts of Prague as they had done in times past. Their host, an elderly lady named Jana, was urged by the two remaining men to walk away from the house and stay with friends elsewhere. In all these years she had never been suspected by the Gestapo. It was not the time for her to risk being interrogated with anti-Nazis hiding in her upstairs study. She agreed, reluctantly, knowing that if they were caught it wouldn't be long before she was too. She brought them the rest of the foodstuffs from her kitchen cupboards. Told them to take anything from her house they needed—clothes, blankets, medicines. Shook their hands in farewell and departed. Before noon the next day, Jakub and his companion were discovered and detained. While their individual interrogations took the inevitable turn from being questioned under threat of torture to being questioned while undergoing torture, they did manage to keep their stories about Jana straight. No, they didn't know her. Yes, they'd broken into her house. No, they had no idea where she was. They could only hope the ruse would work.

As for the assassins Jozef Gabčík and Jan Kubiš, Otylie initially heard through the exile government grapevine, and then read in the London papers, that they managed to evade the Germans well into the month of June, hiding first with families in safe houses in Žižkov and elsewhere in Prague, then later in the dank, lightless crypt of the Church of Saints Cyril and Methodius. Betrayed by a fellow resister named Karel Čurda, who, in Gestapo custody, spilled the Judas information needed to lead the enemy to the church, they were soon besieged by some seven hundred German soldiers. Every effort to smoke them out of their subterranean refuge, to flood the crypt with the help of the fire department, to kill them with grenade blasts and gunfire failed. Ultimately the Butcher's assassins took their own lives as a best-case means of avoiding capture and execution. Years later, Otylie learned that the informer Karel Čurda's guilt-inspired attempt at suicide was unsuccessful. He was convicted of high treason by a tribunal after the war and hanged. About her Jakub there was no news, private or public, to be had.

· 3 ·

CLIMBING DOWN Jánský vršek's forty-nine steps, Meta silently counted to see if Gerrit's numbers were accurate. She wasn't surprised that they were. At the bottom of the stairway, Jánský vršek continued straight ahead, but Gerrit turned right where two other narrow streets forked. Meta recognized the short street on the right. Jánská, where he lived with the Hodek family. To the left was Šporkova, down which she'd never wandered. They passed by an ocher house, with its gated front garden, at the crossroads.

"There are a couple ways to get to the embassy. This one's my favorite because of a friend you'll meet in a minute, I hope."

They walked along, their footfalls echoing in the corridor. The street took a hard left at a small triangular open area. Here Gerrit knelt down, squinting under several parked cars of locals, and whistled a two-note call—an E followed by a C at a regular interval done quickly a few times in one breath.

Soon enough a shaggy, ancient, pearl-eyed cat came striding out from under an old Renault. Gerrit stood, pulled a small plastic bag from his jacket pocket, and handed it to Meta. "If you want to really know this neighborhood, this is where your lesson begins. Meet Socrates, our mayor."

Meta grinned, took the bag, shook out a few of the treats onto her palm, and, stretching out her hand, whistled the same notes Gerrit had.

Socrates made his way toward her in slow slinking strides. He was clearly listening and smelling, but not seeing a thing. First he walked up to Gerrit, rubbed against his calf, and then warily approached the crouching Meta. The cat took his time but once he found his way to Meta's palm he ate the dry nuggets, sat down, and promptly, elegantly began to clean his matted fur.

Gerrit said, "Looks like Socrates has given you his blessing. I imagine his great-grandfather's great-grandfather cruised this street back when your manuscript was still in one piece. A shame he can't talk."

"He probably can. Just that we don't understand him," handing Gerrit back the bag of treats.

They continued down Šporkova in silence. Near the bottom of the lane, Gerrit stopped and pointed to the left. "There's a piano, a bit out of tune, in this house, on the parlor floor, I think. This one's memorable because I feel sorry for the pianist. Decent player who deserves a better instrument. I don't know how he can hear what he's doing through all the *rámus*."

"*Rámus?*"

"Noise, din. Your vocabulary word for the day. The piano makes its own racket I'm sure he or she doesn't intend. Do we knock?"

Meta did, but no one answered. She made a mental note of the place and they moved on. From the square in front of the German embassy they proceeded first down Vlašská, nipping into courtyards where Gerrit believed he had heard a flutist, a soprano, somebody attempting reggae on a reedy Farfisa organ. If he'd ever heard the plink of an African thumb harp or the drone of a didgeridoo, Meta was certain, he would have gone ahead and pressed the door buzzer. His sole criterion was music. When she asked if it wouldn't be more efficient to focus on keyboards, his response was, "Probably. But again, don't forget this is a village and we want villagers to talk to each other."

Whenever a door was opened, Gerrit apologized for the intrusion, explained what Meta was looking for and, after the occupants shook their heads, he handed them his card, just in case. Meta found his deliberate, carefully spoken Czech easier to make out than that of most natives, whose words barreled past her limits of comprehension like lightning-quick glissandi. More often than either of them had hoped, people directed them across the way or a couple of streets over, to where a musician lived—thus expanding their circuit and, Gerrit hoped, their chances at success.

Has anyone heard of Otylie Bartošová, Jakub Bartoš? Meta gently coached Gerrit.

Sorry, no, was the response, over and again.

Irena Svobodová, survivor of Terezín?

This grandmother or that grandfather might have known her. There was more than one Svobodová who lived around here for a time. But one died last year, of emphysema, and the other in Dachau.

I know a Tomáš who plays piano, but I'm afraid he's only seventeen. Apologies and good luck with your search.

Having spoken with more than a dozen other neighborhood residents without luck, and seeing that the light was fading, they said farewell, albeit reluctantly, and agreed to get together and continue their search the next afternoon.

Seven fruitless hours of touring the quarter the following day seemed less tedious than it might have—but each encouraged the other to continue, in part because the objective was so important, but also because their conversation was so warmly engaging. By the time they started up Břetislavova, the sun had set and it was getting to be dinnertime, too late in the day to disturb strangers. Not ready to part company, they agreed to have a pub supper at U Kocoura. After a couple of pints of *řezané*—a measured mix of dark and light beers—conversation meandered through music, inevitably, then work, family, daily life. The things new acquaintances talk about. When Meta mentioned she'd celebrated a landmark birthday in this millennial year, talk turned to New Year's Eve. Gerrit described watching fireworks from the palace ramparts with his friend Jiří Pelc and his family. Meta said she'd gone with her boyfriend to Times Square early in the morning to see Jumbotron broadcasts of the celebrations from tiny islands perched on the cusp of the International Date Line.

"It was eerie," she said, blushing at her reluctance to make any further mention of Jonathan. "Imagine standing there just before dawn, bathed in Times Square neon and watching people in the South Pacific on islands like Kiribati and Fiji up on the screens who were, technically speaking, a whole century ahead of you. A whole millennium."

"You must have felt pretty medieval," he said.

"Still do," she replied with a straight face. "Who but somebody way behind the times would go chasing after an eighteenth-century sonata manuscript when what the twenty-first century really wants is hip-hop, rave, and electro?"

Gerrit was tempted to ask about this boyfriend, but didn't. Instead, they talked politics, art, books. They compared places where they had been. She had performed in Vienna when she was young, an unmemorable recital but a chance to see some breathtaking

art, which prompted Gerrit to rhapsodize about Brueghel's paintings in that city's Kunsthistorisches Museum.

"His finest series is of the seasons," he said, hardly containing
his enthusiasm. "He did six panels and three of them are there.
Another's in New York at the Met."

"I know that one. It's made up of harvest scenes?"

"That's right. Rumor has it your famous Lobkowiczes own one,
also about the harvest, that was confiscated by the Nazis and then
reconfiscated by the Stalinists when it was their turn to occupy
this country."

"That makes five. Where's the sixth?"

He lifted his glass, finished off the last of his *řezané*, set it down.
"It's lost. I imagine a whole multitude of Metas have searched for
it over the centuries, but nobody's ever found it. Chances are, I'll
get to see the Czech-owned panel one day. But that last painting
in the cycle will always elude me."

"Unless you go find it."

He smiled. "Let's find your lost sonata movements first.
Brueghel can wait. By the way, I apologize," as they got up to leave.
"There's no such thing as a multitude of Metas."

Neither had been oblivious to the flirtation in all this. Gerrit
walked her to her tram stop and waited close beside her. Even in
the wake of a long afternoon and evening together, neither felt like
parting company. Their animated conversation was now thrown
into restless silence which Gerrit broke, asking, "So should we get
together again, keep going?"

"If you have the time, I'd love nothing better."

"We can meet at the same café as the first day."

"You know, I wouldn't mind going right back up there now."

"Well," he said, taking her hand, "shall we?"

Without thinking, she leaned toward him and, tentative, even
timid, pressed her lips against his cheek, then his open mouth,

before settling into an embrace that felt strangely natural. After a long minute, they caught their breath, Meta's heart beating hard, and held each other at arm's length, not knowing whether to apologize or simply kiss more.

"I—" Gerrit began, but Meta tenderly placed the fingertips of her injured hand on his lips. "Please, let's not say anything," while thinking, This is a perfect moment and not one to be ruined by language.

Too soon her tram pulled into the stop. After a final kiss good night, Meta reluctantly climbed aboard and found a seat from which she waved at him on the curb. In the tenebrous light he waved back, then watched the streetcar recede between the facades of shops and houses before disappearing around a curve.

As the tram crossed the river Meta stared at the glossy shimmer of city lights on the unsteady face of the water. What had just happened? The whole encounter should have felt like a dream, she thought. But there was nothing dreamlike about any of it. Gerrit was the most wakeful and awakening man she had ever met.

Loyalty was one of her cornerstones, probably the result of what she'd suffered at the hands of a disloyal father. Awakening or not, wonderful or not, this development presented problems. Feeling guilty, she got off the tram, pulled out her phone, and gave Jonathan an unscheduled call. Maybe she should reconnect with her real life, distant as it had become.

When she didn't find him home, a surge of distrust ran through her. How hypocritical. She didn't leave a voice mail—he might catch something in her voice or the wording of her message—so she tried him on his BlackBerry. Again, no answer. What had she been thinking all these weeks, now going on two months? That Jonathan would just sit by the phone? Tend to her persnickety orchids and scrawny ficus tree while she roamed around overseas, knocking on strangers' doors like an imbecile? She walked the rest of the way back to the Kettles', chagrined with both Jonathan and herself.

Sam Kettle, up after the others had gone to bed, was a little surprised but also accommodating toward his friend when she asked if he had something in the house to drink. "Anything so long as it's nice and stiff, please."

"Sure," he said. "What are we celebrating?"

"What makes you think we're not mourning?"

"Fair enough," as he poured a couple of strong whiskeys. "So what or whom are we toasting then?"

"Brueghel."

Sam took a drink, squinched his face, asked, "Brueghel the Elder or Brueghel the Younger?"

"Brueghel the Lost."

"Well, then. Here's cheers to Brueghel the Lost," he said as he raised his glass, having no idea what she was talking about.

Over their nightcaps, Meta, not quite meeting Sam's eyes, described to him what she and Gerrit had done that afternoon. Sam tactfully refrained from pointing out how many hours ago the afternoon had ended. He had, in his own way, grown to adore his houseguest, and hadn't had the courage in the past weeks to rain on her parade. Hadn't even mentioned to his own wife behind closed doors, their heads on pillows in the quiet of an otherwise sleeping household, how much Meta had begun to worry him. She wasn't sleeping well, he knew, as he could hear her rustling on the other side of the thin wall of his bedroom. She rarely sat at the piano to play for her own joy, and she'd ceased playing the sonata movement altogether. Maybe it just meant that she had grafted the piece so fully into her cortex that there was no need to bring her fingers to the dance. But could she be getting tired of it? In some ways, rotten as Sam felt to think such a thing, he hoped so. This latest business of touring the streets beneath Nerudova frankly struck him as hysterical. He'd never developed a strong sense about her boyfriend. Kind of surmised he might not like the guy if they ever met. Still, he found himself uncomfortably in league with the lawyer about the folly of her carrying on like this much longer. She had a life to lead, to reclaim, and an article to further research and publish on the movement that had already come into her fortunate hands.

Pouring her the last of the whiskey, he ventured, "So, my friend. I have a question for you."

"Shoot."

"Don't hate me for this, promise?"

"Promise," she said, returning his gaze. She had never seen Sam quite this serious.

"You know you're welcome to live under my piano for the rest of your life. Barring your getting married and starting to raise a family under there. But don't you think it would be wise to set yourself a deadline? Christmas, say. Easter. Cinco de Mayo, whatever you like. You know, just as a reality-check kind of thing."

"I hear you," she told him with a frown, setting her drink on the kitchen table. "I've been wondering myself whether I'm losing my grip on reality."

"Don't misunderstand me, all right? I'm not pushing. Just a thought."

She stared at the empty glass in her hands. How could she drink so much and still be this sober, she wondered, dismayed. "I hear you and you're right. Let me think on it."

"Go easy." He placed a fraternal hand on her forearm. "Maybe the wind feels good in your sails. I just want you to do what's best for the good ship Meta. No sinking now."

Nodding off that night, Meta felt her thoughts drift in directions that branched like the fork in the road leading up Jánská and down Šporkova.

Jánská took her to Gerrit. Resisting the easy, arbitrary met-
aphor, she dismissed the voice inside that warned her that he,
like Malá Strana, might be a capricious dead end. Gerrit was no
more a dead end than the sonata itself. She was still convinced the
manuscript could be somewhere in Irena's old stomping grounds,
and thanks to him she believed she still had a chance of locating
it. When she set off for Prague, she'd assumed fellow profession-
als would pave the way. Not this writer who lived alone in an attic
apartment and claimed a precocious young girl and a moth-eaten
alley cat as friends. As for the rising affinity, the affection, she felt
for him, Meta tried to write it off as simple forgivable loneliness.

The other path, the Šporkova fork, as she conceived it, contradicted the first. Call it the shoe-leather fork, the walking-in-
circles-of-desperation fork. Gerrit's image of Irena's onetime
neighborhood, now his, as a nest of villages, made a pretty picture, but knocking on doors hadn't produced a result yet, had it?
Jonathan once told her that when a crime's committed—a murder,
the abduction of a child—with every fleeting hour the evidence
evaporates, the trail disappears, the case goes cold. Pounding on
the door of every musician in Prague was not going to change the
inescapable fact that seven hundred or so months, half a million
vanished hours, meant there was no trail left to trek.

The bifurcated road was, she realized, like the second sonata
movement itself. One path full of hope; the other, despair. The
optimistic seeker, the forlorn loser.

What was she missing here? What was she overlooking? Was it
nearing time to admit defeat? Kind people had tried, were still trying, to help her. Others hadn't the time, will, or interest—which
was fair enough.

Then it struck her, as she lay in her sleeping bag under Kettle's
piano. That Langová woman across the street from Jakub Bartoš's
former antiquities shop on Veleslavínova. Why had she responded

to Sylvie's narration about the manuscript with such bald anger or fear? And that look on her face when she leaned out the window. What possibly lay behind that tableau of paranoia?

Dead tired as she was, Meta crawled out of the bag and quietly slipped into the hall. She retrieved the Prague phone book from the drawer of the telephone table and brought it back into Sam's studio. Sitting on the piano bench, she turned on the gooseneck lamp used to illuminate music scores on the piano's rack. She flipped through the pages to listings for *Langová*. Not surprisingly, there were a number. Running her eye down the column, she located the name *Johana* on Veleslavínova.

"Just who are you, Johana?" she asked in a whisper.

Glancing farther up and down the list of names she paused when she saw an address on Šporkova. Lang/Hašková. Her breath quickened. She'd walked right past the house earlier that day, may have knocked on the door. Probably meant nothing. She calmed herself, leaving the phone book splayed open to the page on the piano and turning off the light. But it might be worthwhile to see if the Lang in this Lang/Hašková listing knew anything about a white-haired namesake in Josefov and why she might have acted as if she'd seen a ghost.

LIKE A WRIT OF CONDEMNATION, the manuscript of the third movement of Otylie's sonata lay on Tomáš's kitchen table for several days and nights before its new trustee could bring himself to carry it over to the piano. He had placed on the manuscript, as a paperweight, a polished ivory egg, a keepsake from a trip to Berlin before the hostilities began. And there the movement had rested until he could gather the courage to address the fact of its presence in his life, and all its presence meant. Jakub's last word still echoed in his memory. *Pozdě.* Too late.

After his old friend had dropped by for that feverish quarter hour, Tomáš couldn't bear to touch the thing, stained with sweat where Jakub had held it against his chest under his shirt. Tomáš was drawn to it and terrified of it by turns. More than once he found himself wishing he'd never met Jakub Bartoš and his wife, never encountered these anonymous handwritten pages. Life would now be far simpler if he hadn't. He remembered so well that evening when he played all three movements for a select group of friends. Even now he could hear the opening notes in his memory. Every one of them sounded the word *sympathizer.* Or, worse, *collaborator.*

It had occurred to Tomáš that he could surrender the manuscript, tweak enough details about how it had come into his possession to exonerate himself from any hint of guilt by association. If the authorities believed his story, there was a chance that in return he might expect even more preferential treatment than he already enjoyed as a result of keeping secret tabs for the SS on Czech students' parents who managed to earn enough money to afford such luxuries as piano lessons.

He could burn it, bury the ashes in his tiny garden, erase all memory that Jakub came here. That is what his sister would have insisted he do if she'd had any inkling that he had turned up at Tomáš's door. Fortunately, Johana—who even before the war broke out had scorned his friendship with the Jewish Bartoš—wasn't likely to be dropping by for a visit. Like others in Prague, her movements were restricted until Heydrich's would-be assassins were run to ground.

Or else he could claim it was something he had always owned—who could contradict him?—and dump it into the thriving black market in antiquities. Maybe Johana's lover, who himself was a member of the secret police, would be willing to help him in exchange for a cut. But no, he concluded. Altogether too dangerous. The officer who had taken Johana as his mistress, who lived with her in a large apartment that had been confiscated from a family in Josefov, always seemed to have his eye on Tomáš. And more to the point, despite his wavering, fearful heart, Tomáš understood that he had to seize this second chance Jakub had placed before him. He had to take care of the manuscript as if it were a foundling displaced by the harlotry of war. He owed it to his friend, to himself, and to the music.

While his thoughts seesawed about what to do, he knew he dared not ask around about poor Bartoš. Any display of curiosity about an enemy of the Protectorate would raise suspicion. And to raise suspicion meant you risked putting not just yourself but all those you knew before a firing squad in the ever-bustling execution grounds in Praha-Kobylisy. The Gestapo saw insurrectionists in every shadow. Though he had friends in middling-high places, he knew that in the current state of emergency such friends wouldn't think twice about turning on him.

As the clampdown in Prague continued, Tomáš went outside only to buy his rations and *Der Neue Tag*, the Reich-run newspaper, which he pored over at home, looking in vain for Jakub's name on the long lists of the condemned. Restaurants, cinemas, shops, pubs were closed. Heydrich lay unconscious, stricken by septic shock, in the Bulovka Hospital, even as his beloved fellow Nazis were making great progress on other fronts. Rommel was marching across North Africa like a fiery sandstorm. A quarter of a million Soviet troops had surrendered to the Germans in Kharkov. Murmansk bowed to the Luftwaffe. It seemed that the war was going nicely everywhere except, because of this outrage visited upon the Reichsprotektor, for Prague.

When it was announced that Heydrich had finally died, four days into June, Tomáš's vigil, his turmoil, came to a head. The martyr's body lay elaborately in state in the main courtyard of the castle, having been conveyed there on a gun carriage by the most elite German troops throughout the Czech lands. No civilians were allowed to be present during this solemn processional. It was as if a god were being borne across the city of his divine creation to a resting place in Hradčany, the seat of ancient Bohemian kings, of astrologers and metaphysicians of old. Once the catafalque was arranged with appropriately grandiose stagecraft, huge lit torches flanking the flower-bedecked bier and a large Iron Cross serving as a backdrop—made not of iron but of wood, yet impressive enough to awe the rabble—the gates of the castle were thrown open so tens of thousands of mourning Czechs could file past, paying final respects whether they privately hated the Nazis or not.

Tomáš knew he had to attend. He put on his best suit and mechanically tied his black cravat. These were the darkest days of the occupation, days in which every window framed a prying eye as neighbors spied on neighbors. If anybody had happened to see Tomáš's visitor acting out of the ordinary, it would have been only a matter of time before the SS came knocking. *Aren't I just a musician?* he thought. *What do I know about politics and the workings of power?* Then he bitterly smirked. *Such hollow words.*

Before making the short walk up the steps to Nerudova and toward the castle, where he would stand in line for hours so he could pass by Heydrich's coffin, he finally worked up the courage to touch the manuscript. Whatever dampness had remained from Jakub's sweat was now dry. It took all of Tomáš's nerve to carry it over to the piano by the shuttered window in his first-floor parlor. He took a deep breath and played the opening measures.

Strange, that. The music at the top of the first page began midstream. Had Jakub lost one of the earlier leaves? What a shame, but wasn't everything that had happened these past years shameful? Weren't everyone's beginnings cut off from their ends?

Blinking away a pathetic tear, he turned the page and continued. It was as if another life, his earlier life, were being opened to him again through the music. He had lost so much. Lost any claim to moral purpose. Not that he'd been a terribly useful informer, so far as he knew. Maybe an arrest or two, none that triggered deportation. Not like Johana, who seemed to take a grim, patriotic satisfaction from turning people in. He had always suspected she was behind the arrest of the Bartošes' friend Irena Svobodová and the execution of Irena's husband for having sheltered Otylie—a gentile loyal to her Jewish husband. And that was only the people closest to home. Still, each innuendo he had imparted was like a great chunk chiseled away from his diminished sense of self-worth. A paltry rat bent on saving his own pelt, he couldn't even feel sorry for himself.

But here, now, the music Tomáš played proposed that nothing in this world was ever completely lost. Or if something had been lost, it could be recovered so long as one was alive and willing to dedicate oneself to setting the matter right. He played the movement, a rondo, several times, realizing that it was missing but a few introductory measures that could be reconstructed from repetitions of the theme. After closing the lid of the piano, he hid the manuscript and set out to join the multitudes in their cowed mourning of Herr Heydrich's death.

He dreaded what he was about to do, raise his right arm in the Hitler salute as he passed the fallen Reichsprotektor. No one would be the wiser that his bloodshot eyes had nothing to do with the loss of the Butcher of Prague, the infamous Hangman as many secretly called him. None would know he wept for Jakub Bartoš, not Reinhard Heydrich. Cloaked in music, he climbed the hill to face his sometime master and his marrow-deep shame.

Rather than walking back to Jánská after saying goodbye to Meta, Gerrit set out toward Kampa. His mind was traveling in circles like the waterwheel of the Grand Prior's Mill on Čertovka, the Devil's Stream, on the island's west side. The man he most needed to talk to right now was his old friend Jiří Pelc—Jiří possessed deep common sense and was never afraid to tell Gerrit what he thought.

As luck had it, his friend was home. When Jiří graduated from Charles University after the revolution, he found a job working evenings as a waiter in Old Town, and this was his night off. The wages and tips, though by no means lavish, were enough to pay for canvases, brushes, and tubes of colorful oils, as well as his portion of the cheap rental of an unheated industrial studio a half-hour tram ride upriver, where he painted during the day. Knowing that under the Communists he would have been vigorously dissuaded from squandering time and materials on the large abstract images he was driven to paint, Jiří didn't take his newfound freedom lightly. That he continued to live with his parents was, as Gerrit knew, nothing unusual. Many of their unmarried friends either lived at home or piled into small shared flats.

What's happening, man? Jiří asked, opening the door to find his friend standing there.

Free for a couple, Georgie?

Always, he answered, taking his frayed black leather jacket from the coat tree and stepping outside into the evening.

I'm surprised to find you in, Gerrit said as they crossed the park in the purple light back toward Malá Strana. I figured you'd be getting ready for your open studio out in your warehouse.

My atelier, you mean? I was there earlier but paint's like laundry. It's got to dry before you can do anything with it.

They walked over to a favorite local dive and ordered beers as Jiří lit a cigarette. Shaking his match and dropping it into an ashtray, he said, So what's up? You seem a little off.

Gerrit finger-kicked a coaster back and forth a couple of times before telling his friend about the unusual visit Meta had paid to the Hodeks' house, the backstory that brought her to him, and the afternoons he had just spent walking the neighborhood with her in search of a lost manuscript. It was obvious to Jiří that his friend was smitten not just with Meta's story but with the woman herself. It was so obvious, in fact, that it need not be broached, Jiří thought, until and unless Gerrit wanted to discuss it. But when Gerrit mentioned, as a throwaway detail in passing, that she'd shown the sonata passage to, among others, Petr Wittmann, Jiří started in his chair.

Wittmann? he sneered.

Right, Petr Wittmann, Gerrit said, startled by the sudden vehemence in Jiří's voice. I knew the name when she mentioned it. Classical-music scholar. He pops up in the cultural news from time to time. What, is there some problem with that?

Jiří wrapped both hands around his pint glass as if it were a neck in need of strangling and said, And how do you think he managed to build such a pretty reputation for himself, unless he had Party connections? He was a two-faced bastard during the revolution. I actually heard him speak at an underground meeting in favor of Havel. When I called him on it afterward, he asked me my name.

What happened?

Nothing except I suddenly found myself on disciplinary probation.

I remember that. You're sure Wittmann was behind it? He wasn't even in the art department.

I know, but the fucker had pull. Even kept his position at the university after the Marxist brothers were thrown out of power. The man's a master apparatchik. Your friend better watch out who she's running around with.

Meta was told he's a master musicologist too.

May well be, probably is. But in the old regime days he wouldn't walk your crippled grandmother across the street unless there was a payoff waiting for him on the far corner. I hope your Meta counted the rings on her fingers after shaking his hand.

Meta doesn't wear rings, Gerrit said, then took a long quaff from his beer. Jiří raised his eyebrows but said nothing.

With slow deliberateness, Gerrit set his glass down and said, Speaking of the bad old days, you remember when I showed up in Prague to cover the revolution and you told me to report what I saw but also to jump headfirst into the protest?

Same advice I would give you today if you asked, said Jiří.

As a matter of fact, I don't remember asking your advice back then.

Jiří laughed, knocking some cigarette ash into the tray.

This time I do want to ask you something.

About this woman?

About her, yes.

If you want to know whether I think you should marry her, I'll have to meet her first.

Ignoring him, Gerrit said, When I heard her story—Meta's, and the women who saved it, the sonata, I mean, its incredible history, its potential significance—my first impulse was to grab my pad and start taking notes.

You mean you didn't?

Well, no, I did. But I felt guilty, like I was stealing from her.

Jiří shook his head. You gave up thinking that way about your work years ago.

What can I say? This is different.

Looking away, Gerrit's friend scanned the crowded pub as he continued. Well, I'm not a New York editor, obviously, but 1989 was a revolution. The stakes were too high for you to watch from the sidelines. At the end of the day, you managed to cover the revolution, be part of it in your way, and write a book about it too.

This isn't the same, and you know it.

So this time you either break what could be one of the most interesting stories you've uncovered—music, human interest, history, all that—and lose a chance at love, or you chuck the rules of journalism, not to mention a potentially big byline, and offer yourself up as this girl's romantic research assistant. Either way, your life gets in the way of your life and you lose. Am I right? leveling his eyes at his friend.

Gerrit knew it would be unfair to be angry with Jiří. He'd asked for what he was hearing, had he not? After all, wasn't Jiří one of the two dedicatees of his book, along with Margery? The highly passionate and strictly dispassionate set in type, side by side, on the dedication page? He managed to say, You know it's not that simple a dichotomy.

Or, okay, third possibility. You tell this Meta what you have in mind.

That's the problem, said Gerrit. If I tell her I want to write about her and her project, she's going to think I'm just interested in her for selfish reasons. She wouldn't be wrong to accuse me of being an opportunist. And I can't just spy on her, write about it without saying anything. It'd be more than a betrayal, it'd be a breach of professional ethics.

Jiří toyed with his cigarette before replying. I don't mean to make light of this. I know how strongly you believe in your professionalism. But I also know that you're capable of hiding behind your notebook.

Gerrit ordered another round and changed the subject. Together they strayed away from their dialogue about Meta, manuscripts, journalism, art, love, objectivity, and all the rest. Only when they were saying their good nights did Jiří bring up the issue again.

So what're you going to do about Meta?

Try to help her find that manuscript. And try to do my job.

In other words, you have no idea?

In other words.

Back at Jánská, he let himself into the house as quietly as he could. It was late. He was tired. Jiří's marathoner endurance with pilsners, bocks, and porters would always exceed Gerrit's, but he was relieved to have sifted through concerns with his old friend. The inchoate feelings he had for Meta guaranteed nothing in return. He needed to listen, in that old phrase, to head and heart alike.

As Gerrit climbed the stairs he made a promise to himself that he'd seek out Petr Wittmann for an interview. He would have to invent a nimble reason for their meeting, so as not to disturb whatever relationship the professor had, or scarcely had, with Meta. If he decided not to write about lost music manuscripts, at least he might write about lost musical souls.

The next day, he called New York. Margery listened to Gerrit describe Meta's story, and those of Otylie, Jakub, Irena, and the others, but her first question caught him off guard. "That's all very interesting, but who composed it?"

The Czechs have a phrase for when something is hidden in plain sight—*Pod svícnem je největší tma*. It's darkest under the candlestick. Gerrit had been so enthralled that this rudimentary detail had gotten sidelined in the narrative shuffle.

The rest of the conversation went more or less the same way. Had he asked Meta who she thought the composer was? Not yet. What had he confirmed about its purported history? Not much.

Had any outside experts verified its legitimacy? No, but that count at least he'd anticipated, though his interest in interviewing Wittmann was more personal than Margery needed to know.

"I haven't yet tapped into those aspects of the story," he said. "Right now I'm just feeling you out on the lead. What's seemed most important to me so far is the cultural legacy that inspired the original owner during the war and Meta's quest to reassemble this thing that was partitioned, not unlike Germany itself, though for different reasons, of course. The manuscript was broken up to save it from the Germans. The Germans were separated to save the rest of us from them."

"Let's stay with attribution instead of manufacturing metaphors," said Margery, which made him grin as he jotted down the words *Partitioned, like Germany itself.* "Gerrit, you're onto something intriguing. As it stands, it's not news by any stretch. Move the thing along a little more, and then we can pitch it to Arts, see what Arthur or maybe Clive thinks about all this."

After hanging up, Gerrit looked through the telephone directory for Petr Wittmann and found both his office and residential numbers. Deciding it was best to contact him at the office, Gerrit wrote the number in his notebook and went out to get some air while he thought through how exactly he was going to frame his questions. This was how he had always preferred to work, walking a story through as far as he could before actually interviewing a contact—assuming Wittmann would agree to it.

Atypical of how he worked, his subject matter was not clearly delineated. He was sort of pursuing Wittmann for Meta, sort of pursuing him for Jiří, and sort of doing it for himself, and none of it aboveboard. But he continued to propose to himself possible articles that Wittmann might find worth sitting down with him to discuss. Something just generally about Czech cultural heritage? No. Progress being made by the present government in supporting

the musical arts in the decade after the downfall of Communism? That angle might draw him out, but it could also make him suspicious and defensive if Jiří's all but KGB portrayal of Wittmann was even partly accurate. What about asking him about the music they used in these ubiquitous puppet theaters for which Prague had a growing reputation around the world? That piece was due in a couple of days and at least had the possibility of looking entirely legitimate since Wittmann would probably see it published soon enough.

Gerrit phoned the music department, asked the secretary if Dr. Wittmann was in his office. She put him through and, first surprise, the professor picked up. After introducing himself and making apologies for such short notice, Gerrit asked if Wittmann might be willing to make himself available for a brief interview for the *Prague Post*. Second surprise, Petr Wittmann agreed. Owing to a canceled appointment, he happened to be free to meet at eleven.

Great. I'll see you then, and Gerrit hung up before Wittmann had a chance to change his mind.

Meta's thoughts were anywhere but on the lovely Chopin mazurka she was teaching that morning. The A Minor, op. 17, no. 4. Her student was as earnest as death. He knew all the notes, had memorized them like multiplication tables. One day he would grow up to be a damned good industrial engineer. Or maybe a devoted math teacher. But whatever ineffable quirks of neural, auditory, haptic coordination were fundamental to gifted pianism, this boy didn't have them in quite the right balance. Still, Meta's role was not to dampen his enthusiasm but to ignite it.

You must play it from here, she said in her rough Czech, placing her palms on her chest.

Students like this usually inspired her to try her hardest to encourage them to reach beyond their natural skills. Today she felt impatient. What was she doing instructing a twelve-year-old boy whose parents were hoping to round out his education, rather than pounding the streets with Gerrit?

"*Ne, takhle ne,*" she said, breaking into her thoughts to correct his fingering.

"Like this?" he asked, trying again.

"*Ano.* Like that."

The door to the studio had meantime been noiselessly opened. Sylvie did not want to interrupt. Sam had once advised her to break in on a lesson only if the building was on fire. And if she thought there was time for him to finish and still get their family and the student out safely, the rule was not to disturb.

"Sylvie?" Meta asked.

"You have a phone call."

Meta told the boy to practice that troublesome passage until she returned.

"Who is it?" she said, walking toward the entrance hall where the phone sat on a small table next to a chair. This foyer, which had doors at either end, was the most private room in the apartment, despite the fact that one of the doors led to the common corridor outside.

"Antonín Novák. He remember more something. Say important to talk to you."

Behind her, Meta could hear her student busily working. "Can you translate?"

Meta hovered beside her, catching phrases here and there. But when Sylvie thanked Antonín and hung up, Meta understood the look on her face with ease.

Late morning, not yet noon. Meta and Sylvie brought the Kettle children along to Josefov after Meta finished her lesson. They

had no time to find a sitter, and Sam was going to be out all Friday into the evening with teaching appointments. On their way from the tram, they stopped long enough for Meta to buy a small basket of wrapped hard candies, as Otylie might have done, and an inexpensive but pretty fountain pen in a nice dark blue box as presents for the old gentleman. Antonín's granddaughter greeted the four of them at the door. Her hair had already changed, now entirely bright red, and her fingernails were painted with silver glitter. Today she wore an orange jumpsuit, one strap stylishly undone, over a striped T-shirt. The Kettle kids were dazzled and both eagerly accepted her offer of sodas.

"He is waiting for you in there." The granddaughter pointed, leading the children away toward the kitchen.

On seeing the two enter the room, Antonín greeted them with a kind of impatient urgency that would have been alarming but for the spirited shimmer of his faded blue eyes and the childlike look that larked across his face. He thanked them for coming so soon—At my age you can forget things even before they happen to you, he muttered in Czech—while setting the candy basket on the table to share and carefully sliding the pen into a pocket of his double-breasted sweater.

There is a woman, he began, after they sat across from him. A woman he'd been trying to remember after Meta and Sylvie had left last time. This woman knew Otylie and Jakub. Her name was Langová, Miss Johana Langová.

Meta and Sylvie exchanged a glance.

After their first meeting, he found himself reminiscing about his youth, he continued. He'd been thinking about the music manuscript they were looking for, and had suddenly recalled with the absolute clarity of an old man who has become a stranger to sleep that Miss Langová had a brother who back in those days was friends with Jakub Bartoš. This brother used to come by the *antikva* now and then to play chess with Jakub while he, Antonín, and other young chess fanciers watched. He was a good chess player, the brother. And he played piano like a dream. Whenever Jakub got in a new instrument, a harpsichord or pianola, anything with keys, Miss Langová's brother dropped in to play it and argue with Jakub over its aesthetic merit. Sometimes his sister came with him.

The neighborhood kids all called her "Zlá Johana"—Nasty Johana. He remembered she was of German extraction. Maybe from Sudetenland, he couldn't be sure. Part of the reason he might have forgotten about her when Sylvie and Meta first came by was because he didn't care for the woman. She wasn't mean to him, but she struck him as cold, brittle, distant. She was nothing like Otylie, who was memorable for her kindnesses.

Sylvie translated, though by dint of sheer focus Meta was comprehending some of what he said. She nodded, as a way of urging him to go on.

Well, Miss Langová. During the worst years of the Nazi occupation, so many people in this district were forcibly taken away to camps, only the fortunate few to return—here he held up the tattooed wrist Meta had noted before. She didn't suffer such problems. People did what they had to do in those days, Antonín said, shaking his downturned head. The world was not in its right mind. This does not make such things forgivable.

Sylvie asked, unprompted by Meta, What was the brother's name?

That was the crazy part. He knew his memory was faulty and fading, but he couldn't understand why recovering this man's name, the name of someone he liked before the war, stumped him, while recalling the nickname of the sister, whom he loathed, was easy. He supposed it was simply because the brother was gone while she was still his neighbor, an unpleasant apparition in the local bakery from time to time.

His face, shrouded in the blue smoke of his cigarette, was keen, thoughtful. Earned wisdom was present, Meta thought, in its rivering wrinkles.

Here was the main point. After the Germans surrendered and Antonín came back home to Josefov with his mother, having lost his father in Auschwitz, he had walked through his old neighborhood in shock. Forced by the exigencies of war to grow up in a far bigger hurry than most, he wasn't naive about what had caused so much destruction, displacement, and misery. But even though he'd been told by grown-ups that Prague was in much better shape than cities in firebombed Germany and faraway atombombed Japan, he was speechless when he walked past his old school, his friends' homes, past places where he used to like to go before everyone's life was shattered.

When he went to see if Otylie and Jakub might be at their *antikva*, he found it abandoned. The whole street was a mess but for a couple of apartment buildings that were still partially occupied. He volunteered to help with the restoration of his city, though he was far too young to heft a sack of sand or do more than tote a cobble at a time. But he got to know people and heard the scuttlebutt. One name from his past that he did recognize was Miss Langová, who it turned out was now living across the street from where Jakub's shop had been. Thinking that maybe she knew what had happened to the Bartošes, he went by her apartment and knocked on the door. She wasn't there, but a man answered. It was the same man who used to play chess and piano at Jakub's *antikva*. Antonín couldn't have been more excited when he saw the man's face in the dim light of the shabby hallway.

"*Pamatujete si na mě?*" he asked. Do you remember me?

No, the man answered, suspicious. He was unshaven and his eyes were black holes. Antonín remembered peering past him into the flat and being surprised at how nicely it was appointed. Fancy wallpaper, upholstered furniture, landscape paintings in gold frames.

"Jakub Bartoš a jeho žena," he added. Jakub Bartoš and his wife. I used to visit them across the street.

The man shut the door in his face. Puzzled by this odd response to his innocent question, he started asking around. Miss Langová's brother, people said. A collaborator who may have worked both sides of the fence. They say the Nazis burned his place in Malá Strana in the days of the uprising, when the Germans were destroying everything they could as they exited Prague, and he fled to Josefov. They say that he was afraid of the Nazis but now he was even more afraid of the Soviets. When Antonín told his story about the brief, unfriendly encounter, people weren't surprised. The war had driven him insane. Anyone who bothered to think about him believed he was just another example of what war does to people. And just imagine, someone added. He used to be such a promising pianist. But he was reduced to a poor withdrawn drinker who, deep in his cups, would sometimes bray about how he owned an original Mozart manuscript that the Nazis never confiscated.

"Mozart," Meta interrupted. A shiver shot through her.

Shaking his head disdainfully, Antonín blurted, Mozart one night, heaven knows who the next. Nobody took his ravings seriously. I felt sorry for him myself.

Meta asked if Antonín had ever seen this manuscript.

Of course not. Nobody saw it. Why? It didn't exist. But one thing is for sure. When the Communists took over all the art and artifacts the Germans had confiscated, this crazy man shut up about his imaginary manuscript.

"Sylvie, please, I'm sorry to interrupt," Meta said, her hands gripping each other. "Could you please ask him if he knows what became of this pianist brother?"

He was afraid he didn't know. He'd grown up and become interested in things that mattered more. Anyway, his mind was a holey sock. How he wished it was something that could simply be darned or, better yet, replaced with a fresh one made of silk.

They laughed politely at his joke.

Girls, he said. All this was generations ago. Times then were so bleak they seemed barely worth remembering other than to shrug at the craziness of mankind. Jakub and Otylie, this Miss Langová and her brother, me myself, every single person in this world of Prague and far beyond—what were we all but pawns in a game of impossible brutality and lunacy? I hope this remembrance will help, flawed as it is. Flawed as I am. It is all I have.

"A ted' si dáme bonbóny," he said, reaching his opened hands toward both of them and gesturing toward the basket of sweets. Now let's share some candy.

A voice from inside acknowledged Gerrit's knock on the pebbled glass of the door, and he entered Petr Wittmann's office. The two men greeted each other with an amicable handshake and the warm smiles of cautious strangers, and Wittmann offered his visitor a seat.

May I? Gerrit held up his portable tape recorder.

Of course. Now what's this piece you're working on? Wittmann asked, as he leaned back in his leather office chair. You mentioned puppet theater.

Puppet theater, Gerrit affirmed, clicking on the battery-powered recorder and hoping his ruse wasn't transparent. Its Czech roots and heritage and its now internationally recognized genius. As I've been researching and writing the piece, I find myself wondering why, with all the theatrical possibilities that puppetry has at its disposal, our puppet theater companies keep going to opera for repertoire.

Instead of what?

Of course there's a tradition of folkloric material that's drawn upon, but I'm thinking, why not Kafka? Shakespeare? Maybe Beckett?

Wittmann unexpectedly warmed to the train of thought.

Beckett's not good for marionettes because he already writes for human marionettes. He thinks we are all puppets to begin with, so his theater needs the plasticity of actual actors in order to highlight their essential puppetness, their being hoisted on strings they don't even know exist.

A damned sharp answer, thought Gerrit, especially for being off-the-cuff and not really directly situated in Wittmann's field. Maybe Jiří had him figured wrong. Who was to say that with an agile mind one couldn't negotiate the bureaucratic byways of small-minded tyrants and minor despots without having to sell one's soul?

Still doesn't answer my question, Gerrit said. Why all the nineteenth-century and earlier operas as formula?

The obvious answer? Because their audiences are now mostly foreigners, Japanese and Brits, Italians, Greeks, Americans and the rest, a real international stew, and they want to feel that they're spending an evening out doing something that's fun and cultural at the same time. Most of these puppet shows are meant to attract tourists, and most tourists would rather see *Don Giovanni* lip-synched by wooden actors and done as slapstick than go to the Estates Theater and see it performed by actual opera singers with years of training.

And you think it's just that simple?

I know it's just that simple.

I wasn't living in Prague during the Communist years, Gerrit ventured. What did the Party make of puppet theater back then?

Wittmann sat forward at his desk and folded his hands together, instinctively wary. The Communists were every bit as cynical about this aspect of our—you are, I gather, Czech?—

Born here, raised in the States.

Wittmann oddly smiled.

—of our culture as you seem to be.

Cynical? Gerrit said, admiring Wittmann's rhetorical skills again. A blatant attempt to put the interviewer on the defensive as a means of getting the upper hand.

Seamlessly, Wittmann switched into English, "Look, let me offer you this, since I don't fully understand the purpose of this interview. My bottom line on contemporary puppet theater relying on the musty, dusty classics of operatic compositions to get people to pay a few crowns to fill their playhouses? Where's the harm? Besides, who knows whether some who attend these events on a whim come away thinking Rossini or Berlioz or whoever is not musty and dusty but quite wonderful. Maybe it moves some recordings, or actually gets them to buy tickets to the Estates to see and hear the real deal."

Sensing there was no way to maneuver Wittmann back to a discussion about his days under Communism without looking manipulative, Gerrit said, "Good point. You're an educator, so it makes sense you'd locate the silver lining here, in terms of pedagogy, or proselytism."

"Proselytism? What do you mean by that?"

"Nothing, really," Gerrit said, noting that the word had struck its intended nerve. "Certainly didn't mean to upset you."

"I'm not upset. Just busy. And unless you have other questions that deal with music and musicology, I don't think I'm going to be of much use, I'm afraid."

"I did have one other question, strictly about music. I've been thinking about doing a piece about restitution of artworks confiscated by the Communists, or maybe as far back as the days when the Reich seized power—specifically music manuscripts, which don't get the media coverage that paintings and sculptures seem to attract. You're as knowledgeable as anyone about the policies that the Party had in place, I'd imagine, about what music was authorized for broadcast and dissemination, and about how some of the great Czech music collections of famous patrons, Jewish and otherwise, were handled by the regime."

"It would make an interesting article," Wittmann breezed back, showing no sign of disquietude. "But, alas, on this subject I'm going to be of even less help to you than on your puppet-opera piece."

"No insights based on your own experiences with the Communists?"

"Like so many, I was a putative member of the Party. It was strictly understood by the authorities that my membership was for show. I've been fortunate to enjoy a reputation that extends beyond Czech borders, and early in my career it was made clear that in exchange for my not denouncing the government at home or when abroad, I would be free to pursue my work. What's pertinent is that this work never extended to any serious involvement with government affairs. Pertinent, and the truth. So, you see, I have no information for you."

Gerrit hadn't come intending to broach Meta's manuscript as such, but hoped that Wittmann might mention it himself. Since that now appeared unlikely, he tried one last, more direct approach.

"I'd imagine that more and more manuscripts and musical artifacts that might have been hidden from the authorities over the years are now beginning to come to light in the first decade after the Velvet Revolution, no?"

Wittmann offered Gerrit a broad, friendly smile. "Perhaps so, Mr. Mills. Do you have a particular work in mind?"

"Nothing in particular, no," Gerrit lied, having no ready alternative.

"I would be most interested in hearing of any such musical artifacts you may discover. Now is there anything else I can help you with? I need to keep an eye on the clock."

Gerrit rose at the cue, thanked Wittmann for his time, and shook his hand.

"Let me have a copy of whatever you write, would you?" Wittmann said, as he walked with Gerrit to the door. "Czech puppet theater is, for better or worse, one of our most popular attractions, after our marvelous architecture and potent beer, maybe in that order, with beer at the top of the list."

"I will," said Gerrit, feigning a chuckle. "And again, thanks for your time."

Gerrit had done hundreds of interviews since he signed on with his New York paper, branched out to do foundational work at the *Prague Post*, then freelanced for other European newspapers and magazines—that Rolling Stones concert in Prague, the first time liberated Czechs could hear "Satisfaction" live from a stage, sung by Mick himself? Gerrit covered that, scoring a few pithy backstage remarks from the band—but this was his weakest performance. As a professional he should have had no problem directly asking questions about Meta Taverner's sonata manuscript that might have unearthed fresh insights. Instead, he went dog-paddling and basically drowned.

Well, he thought as he walked home, at least he could add that nice aperçu about Beckett, give Wittmann his attribution, and turn in the article. Further, he could tell Margery that he'd consulted with an expert, though Meta's manuscript hadn't been the focus.

Then he had an idea. Pulling out his cell phone, he called an older colleague at the *Prague Post* and asked if he wouldn't mind running a quick LexisNexis search on Petr Wittmann. The results gave Gerrit pause. Book publications, public appearances, numerous articles on music—these came as no surprise. But he hadn't known that Petr Wittmann's name was once floated for a top position in the ministry of culture. Under cloudy circumstances, the professor had withdrawn from consideration. When Gerrit's journalist friend commented, "I remember this guy. You have a lead on him or something?" he answered, "Not really. Talked with him for background on a story and was just curious."

Whether or not he would tell Meta about his encounter with Wittmann and what he'd learned from his colleague was another matter. What had he finally gleaned? First, that the professor wasn't someone to dismiss; second, that Wittmann's not-so-subtle dodginess was, if nothing else, perplexing. Gerrit could see no clear reason why Wittmann would bother to be elusive or unforthcoming with him or Meta, neither of whom posed any threat.

Much as she wanted to rush straight from the Nováks' home, past the Klementinum, and around the corner to buzz Johana Langová's apartment and find out who and where her half-mad brother was, Meta knew the Kettle children had already been thrown off their regular routine by coming with her and Sylvie to Josefov. They'd had a fine time with Antonín's charming postpunk granddaughter, but now they were tired and cranky. A visit would have to wait for another day. She and Sylvie talked all the way back to Vinohrady. If even a fraction of what the old gentleman recalled was accurate, the sonata manuscript had traversed quite a landscape of human highs and lows during the past century.

After they got the kids home, she returned to the telephone book, wrote down the exact address of the Lang who lived on Šporkova Street, and walked out again into fading afternoon light. It was impossible to attempt any contact with Johana right now, since Meta knew she would need a translator, that anything said would have to be conducted in careful Czech. But she was too jazzed by Antonín's revelations to settle down into a domestic evening with the Kettles. No harm in wandering over to see if the listing was right.

The evening air was soft. Meta got off the metro early to weave her way through the Little Quarter, strolling along tiny quiet side streets, alleys that opened into small squares between noisy Karmelitská and the river. Her thoughts, as both her pace and breathing slowed, floated away from Antonín Novák's recollections and instead she found herself thinking of Jonathan and Gerrit. Flightiness, fickleness, and flirtation—three troublemaking F's—had never been part of her character. She was, as Gillian mock-scolded her more than once, sinfully unsinful.

"All that virtue without being a Bible-hugging child of the catechism," her friend chided her before Jonathan entered her life. "You need to do a little less concertizing sometimes, and a little more clubbing."

Gilliespeak. She was a fine one to talk. Had probably never been to a Meatpacking District club in her life and had the same steady boyfriend since forever.

Silly thought, maybe, but if the middle movement of the sonata declared in no uncertain terms that happiness can plummet with immediacy into grief, could its opposite equally apply? Might it be true that she and Jonathan had reached the end of their partnership and she and Gerrit, whom she barely knew, had together opened a new theme?

Meta always found the idea of love at first sight a bit suspect. Her father had once told her that this was how he'd experienced the blind date in Chelsea with his future first wife, her mother, but it hadn't endured in the end. The concept was sentimental at best, bankrupt at worst. It would be so easy to fall in with Gerrit, who had hardly hidden his interest in her. Much as she was drawn to him—his wise eyes that reacted so openly to nuance, his endearingly unruly hair, his intellectual sensibility, not to mention the urgency of their kiss—she sensed it was better to keep her guard up for the time being, as best she could.

Here she was again, back in Gerrit's and Irena's neighborhood. Its streets had become so familiar that she turned, almost by rote, up past the German embassy, and entered Šporkova, climbing its gentle and narrow rise, enveloped by its flanking houses.

Then she heard it. A piano. Echoing down the tight corridor of stucco and stone. Not her sonata, probably not her composer. But a piece she knew well. Haydn's Sonata in E-flat Major. A passage from the beautiful first movement. Roughly played, to be sure. The pianist was either quite young or quite old, hard to tell. But one of her favorite of all late-eighteenth-century works for piano filled the lonely alley as Venus rose and the first faint stars began to blink above.

Other sounds accompanied the Haydn. The percussive sounds of dishes being washed. The ever-present televised voices. A siren, far off.

She could not identify with certainty that the piano, whose notes seemed to emanate from a garden behind one of these buildings shuttered against the coming night, was Lang's. But she did confirm that a Lang, along with a Hašková, lived right here on Šporkova. It was all she could do not to knock on the door, but it was getting late and anyway the moment was too perfect to shatter. She would come back the next day. For now, she stood in the gloaming and listened until the pianist, whoever he or she was, stopped playing.

She walked past Socrates's corner toward the foot of the forty-nine steps that led to Nerudova and hovered uncertainly in front of an ornately sgrafittoed building at the foot of Jánská. Gerrit's flat was just a few paces away. She could so easily ring his doorbell, lead him by the hand to the spot where she'd heard the Haydn, stand there with him, and hope the pianist would play some more.

Instead, as before, she climbed the stairs and headed back down Nerudova, toward the river and Vinohrady beyond. She gazed up at the Milky Way, unusually bright against the ambient light as it stretched like some nocturnal silver rainbow overhead. It wasn't as if noon tomorrow, when they'd agreed by phone earlier to meet again, was all that far away. Despite her doubts about love at first sight, Meta did surmise that from the moment she and Gerrit met they'd been improvising a duet on either side of the river. A duet that wanted to evolve into a fugue. One whose harmonic and rhythmic structures moved toward the same resolution.

· 4 ·

OTYLIE SIGHED IN GRIM RESIGNATION when she heard through a fellow Czech exile about the new Prague Music Festival. The Reichsprotektor, it was said, considered it one of his proudest cultural achievements. Rumor had it he'd approached its planning with all the high-minded tenderness of a doting father raising his favorite child. The German Philharmonic Orchestra was specially scheduled to perform that first year. Other ensembles and virtuoso soloists were being imported from all over Deutschland to play alongside the best musicians in the Protectorate. Simultaneous performances were to be held up at the palace, over in the Valdštejn Garden, and down at the handsomely renovated Rudolfinum. In a display of evenhanded altruism toward the occupied Czechs, Heydrich instructed organizers to open the festivities with works by Mozart and Dvořák. This way, both German and Czech musical legacies—the Praguers claimed Mozart as in part their own—would weave through the gentle spring air in the Reich's subverted jewel by the Vltava. Or rather, the Moldau.

As a particular treat, the German Music Society invited the Bohnhardt Quartet all the way from Heydrich's hometown of Halle to perform a romantic chamber work composed by the Reichsprotektor's late father. The piece enjoyed a warm reception in the banquet hall of the Valdštejn Palace the very evening before assassins attacked their son's limousine. In all likelihood, Heydrich *fils* never read the review of this special performance, as he lay mortally wounded when it was published in *Der Neue Tag* a few days later, on May 29. His festival went on, at least for a while. Bach and Beethoven and Bruckner—celestial music filled the city as the secular sirens bawled and jackboots beat the paving stones.

Hearing this intelligence, Otylie couldn't help but remember the last night she saw her father alive. All his carrying-on about war and music, music and war. Yes, her poor father had been drunk and half out of his wits with fear. But she recognized that there was more truth in his reckless doctrine than she had believed.

Reports out of Prague were sketchy at best, and Otylie assumed that much of what she read or heard was wrong. When, however, she learned of the announcement on Czech radio that anyone involved in the attack would be shot along with his entire family, she knew in her bones this was accurate information. As the news finally came in early June that Heydrich had succumbed to his wounds, Otylie shared none of the general elation felt by the English and expatriated Czechs around her at the Czechoslovak Institute on Grosvenor Place. Beneš and his government in exile proclaimed that the people were rebelling against their oppressors and that the Reich's power had been delivered a true deathblow, but Otylie could only imagine what grisly reprisals the Nazis would mount now. She wondered if the music-loving Reinhard, evil as he was, hadn't been less destructive alive than dead. Many years would pass before she learned that the man she worked for, Edvard Beneš himself, had factored Nazi retaliation into his assassination plans. His strategic hope was that Heydrich's demise would spur the SS to such a reign of terror that the Czech people would rise up as one, winning the admiration of the Allied world as they fought back.

Wheels within wheels. Those turning them, those caught in their cogs.

Otylie's feelings of helplessness only increased as the war ground on. Nor did they end when Beneš reentered Czechoslovakia to assume control of the government, triumphant after the Germans' retreat in the spring of 1945. Hitler was dead, Heydrich's successor, Karl Frank, was sentenced to death, the Protectorate itself was dead, and by every indication Jakub was dead. Stalin—whose Red Army marched into Prague as liberators after Eisenhower made the fateful decision to halt Patton's advance in Sudetenland—was Prague's new ally. About him Otylie had strong misgivings, despite Beneš's embrace of the Soviets, in part because Jakub had never trusted Communists. On the other hand, what did her opinions matter? Everything she'd once known had now collapsed.

Left behind, she was forced to go forward. But where? Jane, her best friend in London, was reunited with her American fiancé after D-Day and the couple moved back to Texas, where they got married. Otylie herself returned to Prague, where she found nothing and no one waiting for her. Retribution against Germans was the order of the day. Czech militias rounded up German soldiers and civilians alike, painting swastikas on their backs and belongings, deporting thousands, interning some, and murdering others. A simmering chaos defined the mood of the city. She asked around about Jakub, but just as she had expected, he had vanished. As for Irena, Otylie assumed, despite what she'd heard, that her friend must have perished in a concentration camp, for her flat was full of strangers' possessions and empty of life save for a family of mice that had nested comfortably under the floor where some of the boards had been pulled up.

No, much as she'd always loved Prague, now she couldn't bear to walk the streets of Josefov or Malá Strana, much less Nové Město, where she and her husband had lived. A specter stood sentry on every corner, and she was little more than a specter herself. The great square named after good King Wenceslas, where she'd had such a charmed life with Jakub, repelled her. It was generous of the Beneš officials she'd worked with to offer her a job in the new government, but she was bereft of any ambition beyond distancing herself from her war-marred city, and so reluctantly returned to England.

Postwar London didn't hold more than stale memories for her either. Its fogs tasted of rotten fruit. Its Thames smelled of feces. Its pubs might have been as inviting as those in the old country but Otylie was never much for alehouses and drunken blather. She became a hermit, a woman in her middle thirties at a dead end beyond which she could see nothing of worth. Besides bitterness and hopelessness, all she'd learned during the war years was English. And if she couldn't bear to live in her motherland—the only place on earth where her native tongue was spoken—or here in England, then she would have to follow this new language to some other country where she at least stood a chance of being understood. Not that she felt she had much left to say now that Jakub had slipped into the ether.

During a long walk one drizzly afternoon in Hyde Park she formed a plan. For half a year, she worked in a shop in Hampstead that sold musical instruments and sheet music. She still didn't care to be around music, but it was one thing she knew well, and if she was forced to capitulate a little in order to afford to move on with her life, so be it. What was more, despite her antipathy, she had to admit that practicing the piano did lift her spirits. Once she'd saved enough for a third-class cabin on a passenger ship to America, she set out for the New World. Aside from her wardrobe and wedding ring, she carried little with her beyond what she'd originally brought to Prague as a young orphan. The photograph of her parents, one of Jakub, and the sonata movement.

Otylie asked around in New York about old friends of hers, even brought up Jakub's name whenever she happened to encounter someone from Czechoslovakia in her various wanderings. But Manhattan was a leviathan of a city. Long avenues, right angles, straight lines—the opposite of medieval, patchwork Prague. A teeming clamor of humanity on sidewalks, in streetcars and autos, on trains running overhead and underground, and every one of them in a rush, flying along in the shadows of impossibly tall skyscrapers. She was rootless, friendless, utterly divested of any shared personal history in this place, yet she had to admit she was drawn to some ineffable peculiarity she saw in many of these faces. An unburdened optimism, almost embarrassing for all its green rawness. Even after a war that had brought them so much loss, these fresh-faced Americans, immigrants all in such a young country, seemed unfazed by the weight of the past. In Prague you lived in the same houses, walked the same squares, shopped at the same farmers' markets where others had for centuries. You moved through—indeed, became—another concentric ring in the trunk of an ancient tree. Here in Manhattan, life was invented day by day, idea by idea, girder by girder. These people seemed innocent of the concept of yesterday. It struck her as equally a strength and a weakness, enviable either way.

She wondered what Jakub would have made of this bustle and rumpus. Sometimes she asked him, softly but aloud, what he thought of it all. Talking to him was a comfort, but not wanting to turn into some muttering half-wit, she weaned herself off this habit. She reminded herself that she was stuck with her bad memories, her good health, and maybe as much as half a century to live. Better to pull it together rather than be sucked into the black pit that had taken up residence where her heart used to be.

Her first job was as a cleaning woman for Czech immigrant families who had lived in the city for decades before she arrived. This charwoman work was a grind and more isolating than she might have imagined, despite the fact that her employers often could speak in the old tongue and talk about the homeland in a way that afforded her some sense of having a foothold in the world. When she was offered the chance to work as a housekeeper who doubled as a daytime nanny, she took the job and counted herself lucky to have a child to look after, though the young boy spoke no Czech and was in and out of trouble at school. Otylie didn't have it in her to scold Douglas when he broke things—a vase, a china plate, objects that exploded into sharp-edged shards—and even when he was caught rummaging in her purse, she didn't tattle on him to his parents as she probably should have done. When he hit her arm one afternoon so hard that a plum-shaped bruise blossomed overnight, forcing her to wear long-sleeved blouses during the hottest days of August, she knew he was beyond her. She gave notice, never betraying the boy, but never wanting to see him again.

Her fortunes turned. Answering a newspaper ad, she got herself a job as a live-in nanny for a well-to-do couple who had distant relatives in Moravia. East Eighty-Sixth Street was a new world cocooned inside the New World. She had her own maid's room, small but cozy, and a life regimented by the daily needs of the two Sanders children. During her interview when she was asked where the rest of her family was, she said she had lost everyone in the war.

"That's terrible, tragic," Adele Sanders said. "Your children too?"

Assuming her employment depended upon having raised children, she blurted, "Yes," and immediately regretted it. After all, what did she know about mothering? Douglas had been proof enough of her incompetence.

"How many did you have?"

"Like you," she said, unblinking.

"Twins?"

"No, but two," improvising away. "A boy and girl."

"What were their names?"

Without hesitation, Otylie said, "Jakub. And Irena."

"Grace and Billy are too young to really understand what the war was all about, so maybe it will be best if we—"

"Not to worry," Otylie said. "I do not have pictures of them. So they needn't know."

"If you wouldn't mind terribly. They'll learn about such things soon enough."

"I prefer it that way."

"When can you begin?" Adele Sanders said, standing and offering her outstretched hand to Otylie, who took it with a modest, embarrassed smile. "And by the way, you should feel free to talk to me about your poor children anytime in private. Sometimes it helps to share with another mother. Who understands such things better than we?"

Otylie gazed down at the labyrinth-patterned Oriental carpet that filled the Sanderses' living room and said, "Perhaps is best we not talk of it either."

"Whatever makes you most comfortable."

It was surprising to the Sanderses, adults and children both, how quickly the displaced Czech settled into their household routines, becoming something of an extended family member within weeks. Because she was reticent about her past, they couldn't know that she had been twice torn by war from the comforts of a settled existence. Whether or not she intended to be an inveterate survivor, Otylie was just that. As for the Sanders kids, they took to Otylie and she to them.

Some things in her life hadn't changed. The silver print of her parents and a framed photograph of Jakub hung on the wall over her bed. The sonata manuscript lay in the bottom drawer of her dresser, hidden under folded sweaters. But just as she had done when her father was killed in the Great War and she was sent to live with an aunt, long dead now, in Vyšehrad, Otylie gathered her memory wraiths into a secluded corner of her consciousness. Besides keeping her sane despite her grief, it freed her to remain as open as possible to whatever life she found herself in next.

Central Park became her new Petřín Hill. She walked Grace and Billy there every afternoon after school, except when rain or snow kept them indoors. In the park's generous embrace she sat with other women, many of them continentals, fellow refugees from a shattered Europe, and watched the children race in circles playing games of tag, or sitting on the grass chattering with dolls, or floating model schooners in the boat basin. Sometimes Otylie would get swept up in the nostalgic memories the women shared about prewar days in France, or Austria, or Hungary, or even Germany. More often than not, she minded the twins and gazed at the buildings that rose at the edges of the park and kept to herself. Like Petřín, which overlooked its bustling city from the quieter vantage of nature, Central Park was an urban refuge where her thoughts could settle. It was here she wrote letters to Jane and made entries in the pocket diary she kept, fantasizing that Jakub was standing behind her, reading her words over her shoulder.

This diary was her only concession to the old language. Now that she'd left Czechoslovakia behind, including those immigrant families she'd worked for, she was determined to speak, think, write, even dream only in her adopted English. On Tuesdays, Thursdays, and Sundays she attended night class to improve her grammar and pronunciation. She would always in her heart be Czech, but she wanted to recapture, in some small way, the simple comfort of not feeling like an outsider, an alien. For the same reason, she determined to become an American citizen as soon as she was eligible.

Grace, seven, became Otylie's favorite charge. In Grace, she caught unmistakable glimpses of her own childhood self. A lively if moody girl with a full-moon face, she had honey-colored hair cut short like a boy's, eyes the color of nutmeg, and a delightful singing voice. Otylie, ever the musician's daughter despite herself, caught the girl humming one morning while dressing for school.

"What tune is that, Grace?" she asked, standing in her bedroom doorway.

Startled, the girl turned. "I don't know. I just made it up."

"It's pretty. Here, let me help you with that," walking into the room and sitting on the edge of the bed to button Grace's dress. Without pausing to think about the consequences of her words, Otylie asked, "Have you ever thought about taking music lessons?"

"What for?"

"So you can learn to play the piano and sing like the angel Maria Callas someday."

"Aren't angels dead people in heaven?"

"No, she's a famous opera singer. The greatest in all the world. Here, we better hurry up. It's time to go."

"You really think I can be as good as, what's her name again?" Grace was tying her shoes and grabbing her book bag for the walk with Billy to school.

"Maria Callas. You'll never know unless you try."

This tossed-off conversation marked the beginning of a new, unexpected phase in Otylie's life. She perfectly remembered her pledge never again to listen to men who talked war, and never to sing or play music. Refusing to speak of war presented no problem, especially now that the defining wars of her lifetime had ended. But she'd already bent her other vow when she worked at the music store in London, and planting in Grace Sanders the idea of studying music broke it altogether.

"*Byla jsem tehdy mladá, co jsem mohla o životě tušit?*" she asked herself, breaking yet another pledge by slipping into Czech. I was young then; what did I know about life?

The Sanders family lived in a "classic seven" apartment, and in the long living room, opposite a wood-burning fireplace, was an ebony Baldwin upright. The piano was more a handsome piece of furniture than a musical instrument. Its bench was neatly stacked with oversize art books, its music stand held a display of old botanical prints, and its top was forested with a dozen framed family photos. A visitor might spend an hour in the room without noticing it hidden beneath all the bric-a-brac. Enthusiastic at the idea of her daughter's sudden desire to try her hand at music lessons, and not a little surprised that Otylie was an able, if rusty, pianist, Adele helped her daughter and nanny clear the piano.

"Play something," Grace begged.

"It's been quite a while," Otylie apologized, then sat and began to play one of her favorite works from when she was young, the prelude to Bach's Partita no. 1 in B-flat Major. She spun it out gently, slowly. Her trills, especially those in the left hand, were uneven. Notes were missed here and there. The passing of the prelude's celebrated theme from treble clef to bass and back was nowhere as smooth as she'd once been able to perform it. But for someone who had been mostly estranged from this instrument she'd known so well as a child, Otylie was surprised by her memory of Bach's peerless phrases.

Adele and Grace applauded when she finished.

"Beautiful, beautiful," the mother said, placing a hand on Otylie's shoulder. "Would you like to learn to play like Otylie, Grace?" It was settled then and there.

Scales, she wrote in Czech in her diary. *Jakub, I had forgotten what soulful things scales are! The perfection of flowers here in this park, the flowers that know just how many petals and leaves are needed to grow every spring to find their way into the sunlight, that's what scales are. The musical logic of plants, the vegetable logic of music! This girl is learning them so quickly, eager as a kitten confronted by a bowl of cream. I feel both joy about this and shame that in my stubbornness I refused to open this part of me to you. Like a wife denying her husband a meal or the pleasures of the bed. Please forgive me if you can. My amends are in teaching this girl to play, as best I am able.*

Billy ran his scales under Otylie's patient eye too. But where he managed merely to do well, Grace excelled. She worked for a few months with a vocal coach who came to the apartment, but it soon enough became apparent that the girl's talent was in her fingers. Grace possessed a lilting soprano ready for a church chorus maybe, but no challenge to Maria Callas. She shrugged it off and redoubled her efforts at the piano.

Otylie was diligent with her responsibilities in the Sanders household. She shopped for most of the food, took clothing to the dry cleaner, escorted the kids to and from school, prepared meals. But her favorite effort went into making sure Grace did her exercises, practiced her assignments. The girl particularly liked Franz Schubert, so Otylie took the bus with her to Patelson's, the best sheet-music store in town, and bought all the Schubert it had in stock. Most of this Grace couldn't begin to play. But she adored sitting with Otylie and reading through the scores while they listened to recordings on the phonograph of Arthur and Artur— Rubinstein and Schnabel.

After a year working with Otylie, Grace reached a point in her development beyond which she couldn't progress without moving on to a professional teacher. This was, at any rate, Otylie's opinion. Grace vehemently disagreed.

"We're doing fine together," the girl protested. "You haven't taught me everything you know, have you?"

"No, I haven't," Otylie said. "But I worry my old habits are hampering yours. My father, who taught me all what I know, worked at a music academy for a living. He kept up with new technics— techniques, I mean."

"So, there. That's good, right?"

"It was good in the early years of the century. But now? It is like you are studying in nineteen-teens instead of the fifties. I don't want to hold you back."

Adele and Otylie by her side, Grace auditioned with a professional instructor and was accepted to continue her studies. It gave Otylie no small joy in being complimented by Grace's new teacher for the splendid job she had done bringing the girl along this far. At the same time, it was bittersweet to listen to Grace grow away from her. *Rather like standing on a pier and watching a boat you've helped to build with your own hands take its maiden voyage, seeing it disappear over the horizon on its voyage elsewhere. This was something my father sometimes found painful, Jakub, losing a student to his next musical port of call, but I was too young to understand how he felt*, she penned in her diary one night.

Time feathered by, months blurring into years. Otylie was no longer the gaunt, haunted-eyed woman of wartime London. With the extra income Mr. Sanders had given her for the music lessons, she'd purchased modest but fashionable clothes on the Lower East Side, and cut a stylish figure whenever she ran errands for Adele. She sometimes joined the twins at the cinema, but now that Grace and Billy had outgrown the need for a chaperone, Otylie found herself left to her own devices more than in times past. She still went to night classes, although her English had become polished, and aside from her whisper-light Slavic accent, she often passed for a second-generation citizen of her adopted country. Her life seemed to her rich enough, full enough. Acquaintances from her Central Park days stayed in touch, and occasionally they would get together for lunch or tea. During one such rendezvous, however, the contentment she'd taken for granted came into question.

"You are too beautiful to go on living like a widow lady," a friend told her over a glass of port. They'd met in a French bistro just off Madison Avenue on a Saturday evening Otylie had off. "You oughta come with me to dance tonight. Downtown, where there are many nice men to meet."

"I don't think so," Otylie said. "I've never been much of a dancer."

"Well, what do you do to entertain yourself, wallflower?"

"I like the movies."

"Movies? That's no place to meet a man."

"I never said I wanted to meet a man."

"Every woman wants to meet a man."

"Well, I already did that. He's gone now."

The woman, a well-meaning former nanny who now had a job in midtown working in a secretarial pool, was about five years younger than her Czech friend. She felt, not without reason, that Otylie Bartošová was slowly but surely headed toward early old age and a life of unqualified loneliness. "Yes, but you're here."

No arguing that point. Otylie shrugged one shoulder.

"Tell me," the woman continued, "did this man of yours love you very much?"

"Of course he did."

"Did he love you so much he'd want you to sit around and be lonesome the rest of your life?"

Otylie took a sip of her port and set it back down on the scratched zinc bar. All this talk of Jakub made her uncomfortable. She'd grown used to speaking with him in her own way, having him to herself. It felt wrong to discuss him like this. She answered, "He never wanted anything for me but my happiness and safety."

"Your happiness he wanted? Well, then, let me ask you. Are you happy?"

The woman was just a little tipsy, but spoke not accusingly or aggressively. Otylie knew she meant no harm.

"Yes. Happy enough. Anyway, 'happy' is one of those words in English that seem to me not to make a lot of sense, if you really must know."

"Honey, I don't mean to pry. Just I was thinking you might enjoy getting out and meeting other people. Let your hair down a little."

"I appreciate your concern."

"You're not coming then?"

"I need to get back pretty soon," Otylie fibbed with an apologetic smile.

That night in her room she sat down to write a long entry in her journal, but wrote to Jane instead. Maybe, she thought, the time had come for her to move on from New York. Grace and Billy were getting older. Soon they would be sent to boarding school or an academy. Grace continued her piano lessons, but now that she was blossoming into adolescence, she had begun to listen to music besides Franz Schubert. Frank Sinatra, more like it. And Otylie's pork schnitzel, once her favorite dish, wasn't quite as dreamy as a cheeseburger and chocolate malted down at the soda shoppe on Lexington. The girl still loved her nanny like a second mother, but she'd begun to fledge, was starting to take wing.

All natural, all for the good. Yet everything Otylie read about life in the old country was discouraging, convincing her that

Prague wasn't a place to return to, although the uncertainty she felt about venturing farther west was strong as well. All the bucking broncos and saloon brawls, the stagecoach robbers and vast wide-open untamed space that Otylie had seen in innumerable Saturday-afternoon cowboy-and-Indian movies gave her pause. None of that hullabaloo on the screen was real beyond the darkened cinema, was it? Either way, unspurred and saddleless as she was, she told Jakub after turning out her bedside lamp, whispering into her warm pillow, it was time to move on, and the only contact she had was across the Hudson into yet another world.

· 5 ·

NOON BELLS HAD JUST FINISHED their pealing when Meta and Gerrit, back at the café below the castle, sat at the same table as before, after saying hello with a kiss and hug somewhat more tentative than their parting at the tram stop had been. Though they had traded places, neither seemed to notice.

"I'm really happy to see you again," he told her, reaching out to hold her hands.

"Me, too, you," putting hers in his.

"We're good?"

"Completely." So it wasn't an aberration, that embrace the other night. Well, this trip was into uncharted territory, she thought. She'd just have to continue trusting herself, see where things led. "Listen, though. I may have something," she went on.

"Tell me," he said, marveling that Meta looked more fatigued and yet more radiant than she had a couple of days earlier. An unfettered excitement was there in her quick-moving eyes.

"All right, but it's less a matter of telling you than taking you somewhere."

"Don't you want a coffee?"

"I've already had too much coffee this morning, if you want to know the truth."

Gerrit left a tip for the waiter who approached to take their order. "*Prominte,*" he apologized, then, following Meta's lead down the stone declivity of Ke Hradu, he asked, "So where are we headed?"

They walked close enough that their swinging arms touched in an amicable jostle. Each was aware of how easily they fell into the comfortable rhythms of attraction.

"Socrates first. Then you'll see."

As they descended the castle heights, Meta reflected aloud on how her trip to Prague had in recent days come to resemble less a scholarly search for a cultural artifact than a personal journey to uncover a family history. "This whole venture," she said, as they turned left and made the trek down bustling Nerudova, "is starting to feel like one of those trips immigrants' great-grandchildren take to track down their roots in the old country. I don't think there's a drop of Eastern European blood in my veins, but this seems more and more like a hunt to locate ancestors. Does that sound ridiculous?"

"Not at all," he replied.

"It's strange how close I feel to Otylie's husband, Jakub. I met his wife's best friend. I've met a man who remembers watching him play chess. I've stood in the place where his shop once thrived. From what I've heard, he was braver than any man I've ever known. When Irena first told me the story and gave me those pages, I thought it would be Otylie's footsteps I'd be tracking. But it's all been Jakub."

"Where did Otylie wind up after the war?"

"I wish I knew. Irena looked but couldn't find her. I know she worked for the Czech exile government in England. I figure I can always pursue that angle if I don't turn up anything in Prague. There must be records of refugees who fled there and helped with the anti-Protectorate movement."

"Any chance she'd still be alive?" he asked, wondering whom he might know in London who might be able to help.

"Well, a chance, yes. She'd be around ninety, from what Irena told me."

"Same age as Socrates," said Gerrit, crouching down to see if the old cat was loitering under one of the parked cars at the elbow of Šporkova. "Not here today."

"I hope that isn't bad luck."

Standing again, Gerrit shook his head. "Socrates would probably say there's no such thing as luck. So where are we going?"

"We're pretty much already there," and gave him a description of her second visit with Antonín Novák, his recollection of a Johana who seemed to be the J. Langová on Veleslavínova Street, and her discovery of another Lang in Malá Strana. She recounted her stroll on this very lane the night before, and the unpolished, ethereal piano music she'd heard.

"You were here and you didn't stop by?"

She apologized, blushing. "You don't need a sonata zombie knocking on your door in the midnight hour. Besides, I was a little shy about bothering you."

"For future reference? Don't be."

"I won't." She explained that after a mostly sleepless night, she'd come straight back to Šporkova. Thinking there was nothing to lose, she knocked on the door, and—

"—and, no way."

Meta nodded, giving in to a suppressed smile. "Remember me telling you about a performance of the complete sonata that a friend of Jakub's gave before the war?"

"Of course."

"I've not only found his daughter—she's the one I drank all that coffee with this morning—but when I told her I had to run out, I promised I'd come right back with someone who speaks Czech. And don't look now, but we may be able to meet the man himself."

They walked the remaining short distance and stood before the Lang/Hašková house. Gerrit turned to Meta and said, "Same door we tried the other day, right?"

"Sure is."

"Well, maybe Socrates will have to offer a revised version of his philosophy of luck. Something more optimistic, like luck is the progeny of persistence."

She tapped the lion's-head brass knocker and they waited for an interminable minute. Meta nervously glanced up and down the rows of tidy sunny houses with colorful painted facades, their window boxes spilling over with early October's late flowers, their trellises laden with turning vines. Had the woman experienced a change of heart after Meta excused herself to run and fetch her friend?

Finally a voice inside called out, *"Moment, moment."* When the door opened, Marta said, "Hello again, Meta," and then, "You must be my neighbor Gerrit," in heavily accented English. She had broad cheekbones, limpid gray eyes, dark blond hair plaited on either side of her head. Regal in her way, she wore a billowy linen blouse with sleeves rolled up, and jeans. "Please, both, come in."

The foyer was dark, with a black-and-white-checkered marble floor and stuccoed walls hung with old prints of mountain scenes. Shepherds, flocks, hilltop châteaus. Bygone eras. They followed her through the house toward the back.

"You know, I was thinking after you left. Your name is close to mine. Marta, Meta. It is so beautiful a day, not cold, so we will go talk in the garden."

As they passed a shutter-darkened library in which a closed piano stood, and through the kitchen hung with old copper pans and dried herbs, the woman asked, "You will take some more coffee? A brandy?"

Distracted by nervousness, Meta didn't respond at first. Instead, Gerrit spoke. "You said you already had enough coffee?"

"Three brandies then," and with that Marta gestured toward a table outside where she left Meta and Gerrit alone in a walled arbor. A pair of heavy gloves and pruning shears lay neatly stacked on the face of a granite sundial. Along the nearby wall was a tangle of wisteria suckers that had just been cut. Meta told Gerrit, "That must be why she was slow to get to the door. She was back here doing end-of-season gardening."

Balancing a tray laden with glasses, a decanter, and a small bowl of almonds, Marta returned. After pouring, she handed her guests their glasses, which they raised in a toast.

"Na zdraví," Meta said. "Thank you so much for meeting with me again. Did you have a chance to discuss what I mentioned earlier with your father?"

"I did," she said. "And what I can tell you is this. I think you are looking for what my father has. Would you mind if we continue in Czech?" then asked Gerrit if he would translate. Meta had told her earlier that she'd picked up just enough Czech to snatch bits and pieces of conversation, as a cat might jump at a proffered string and once in a while grab it away, but Marta spoke too quickly for her to glean much. Both were grateful to have Gerrit as intermediary. His translation leapfrogged a phrase or so behind when the woman paused.

"'You surprised me this morning,' she says. 'I have known about this manuscript for years, but we never did anything since we had no clear idea what to do. Many times my father considered giving it away to a museum, but my aunt thinks it should be sold, that's it's worth money—'"

Museums, Meta thought. If she failed to find Otylie herself, visiting more museums and other institutional repositories would be next on her agenda. Back in New York she had, however, gone through the databases of numerous music collections and come up with nothing. Not that there had been much to work with.

"'We had it privately examined by a friend or two who knew a bit about these things. Nobody could identify what we had exactly, so we just kept it. Those Russians were even more idiotic than the Nazis'—I like this woman, by the way," Gerrit quickly added as an aside, then continued translating even as he realized Marta understood what he'd just said. "'They thought they grabbed every last piece of culture but they didn't.'"

Meta struggled to quell her mounting hopes as she replied, slowly and articulately, "So, again, it would be late eighteenth century, a movement of an unpublished sonata that would run roughly ten pages, give or take, about this big"—she gestured—"written out in sepia ink." She glanced from Marta to Gerrit and asked him, "Do you need to translate that?"

"You all right?" was his response.

"I'm—I'm fine," she stuttered.

Marta paused before nodding at Gerrit to begin translating again. "'I don't know what century it is,' she says. 'I don't know much about music history. It is old, this I know. And it was given to my father during wartime, the occupation, by a man who came to this house running from the Gestapo.'"

"Was his name Jakub Bartoš?" Meta asked.

Uncrossing her legs, Marta sat straight in her chair. "Yes, that was his name. He was in the underground."

"My God, I can't believe what I'm hearing," said Meta, leaning forward. "May I ask where the manuscript is?"

Marta continued, through Gerrit, saying, "'Here is the strangest thing. All these years have gone by and my father kept it safe, hoping Jakub's widow would return to lay claim. Now, just this week, two people have shown up asking for it.'"

Meta said, "You mean Gerrit and me."

"'No, another. A professor from the university. He had first asked my aunt Johana if she had this piece of music.'"

The joy, the excitement that had illuminated Meta's face disintegrated into a look of bald shock. She swallowed hard. "Is his name Kohout?"

"'I don't think so. I have his card in my study,'" Marta said, noting the change in the girl's demeanor. She and Gerrit glanced at each other.

"Wittmann? Petr Wittmann?"

"That's right. Is he a colleague of yours?"

"No. Yes, no. He's a musicologist here in Prague. I asked him for help with this and he told me I was wasting his time—did your aunt give him the manuscript?"

As Gerrit continued to translate, he noticed his heart was beating harder. He could only imagine what Meta was feeling. "'She doesn't have it. My father does. This Wittmann explained he found her because he'd heard rumors about my father and some music. Father lived with her in Josefov after the war, and the professor thought he was still there. So my aunt sent him to me.'"

"Would you mind saying whether Professor Wittmann made any mention of me and my role in all this?" Meta asked, doing her best to conceal her shock from Marta.

Gerrit's voice rode along just behind Marta's. "'He did say an American brought a fragment of the manuscript to his attention. He told me he had a copy of it in his office and asked if he could take my father's part with him for examination at the university. He seemed impressed by its apparent authenticity—'"

"Impressed? Apparent authenticity?" Meta coughed, incredulous, looking at Gerrit, who found himself wondering just how much Wittmann had sidestepped him during their little interview.

He was distracted enough that Marta had to repeat her response for him to translate. "Wittmann wanted to come back, she's saying, with another expert to see it."

"Kohout. I should've known."

Gerrit, looking askance at Meta, saw that her rising anger about Wittmann and Kohout threatened to capsize all the goodwill that Tomáš Lang's daughter had for her. An early lesson he'd learned when covering a story, interviewing people be they hostile or helpful, was to avoid showing emotion. Not knowing the myriad ins and outs of what was happening here, he decided to toss caution to the wind and make Meta's case for her.

"*Paní Hašková*," he said, knowing that once again he was about to lie, or at least fudge, just as he had in Wittmann's office, and continued in Czech. I have met Petr Wittmann. Yesterday, in fact—

Gerrit paused, looking quickly at Meta, and was relieved to see that she appeared not to have understood his admission.

—and I can confirm that he's a well-regarded music scholar. I've heard less than flattering accounts of his biography, I might add, but that's often the fate of someone who has a high profile. What I want to say is that this young woman here from New York— gesturing toward Meta, who was leaning across the table toward him, straining to understand—made a discovery that was possibly quite important, and has sacrificed a lot to pursue her research.

This is clear, I admire it.

Well, my suspicion is this professor may be trying to interfere with what she's doing. Far be it from me to tell you what to do, but at a minimum I think in fairness you should let her have the same access to the pages as he did.

"Meta, I have a question for you," Marta said in English, shifting focus as she shifted in her chair. "Were you in Josefov the other day? Did you and a friend try to visit a lady on Veleslavínova?"

"We just wanted to talk with her, see if she remembered anything about Jakub and Otylie Bartoš," Meta answered, recalling the hostile woman.

"My aunt Johana. She told me about you. Don't hate her for sending you away," and she continued in Czech, after nodding to Gerrit. "'Like so many during the war, she had to make hard, life-and-death choices. She has regrets about some of those choices, but she did look out for my father during his worst days. So when Professor Wittmann came asking for the manuscript, speaking of patriotic duty, and you came soon after, as if led there by Otylie Bartošová's ghost, it was too much for her to handle.'"

"I'm sorry," Meta said gently, wondering just how giving Wittmann the manuscript would constitute an act of patriotism. "My friend and I had no intention of frightening her. And we had no way of knowing about any of these other factors."

Marta offered a consoling smile. "My aunt is old. She's tired. The sad truth is, she does not like people anymore. Thinks they are more bad than good."

"She may be right," Gerrit said. "But I hope you understand that Meta's intentions are obviously of the latter kind."

Realizing what was at stake and that she needed to argue her own case, Meta leaned forward toward Marta. "I don't think this is about patriotism or good or evil. It's about music, and all I ask is that you allow me to see the manuscript. I'd be pleased to play for you what I'm fairly sure is the second movement of this sonata. It'll be clear immediately if the two are by the same composer, part of the same composition." And over the next quarter hour, Meta told Marta, through Gerrit, everything she had learned and what she hadn't. The names Otylie Bartošová and Jakub Bartoš, Irena Svobodová and brave young Marek who worked at Jakub's *antikva* were like an intimate weft throughout the larger warp of the manuscript's place in musical and political history.

Irena's final wish was that I seek out the missing movements and reunite them as a way of honoring her lost friend Otylie, Gerrit translated into Czech.

"*Milá Otylie. Otylie je tady?*" Dear Otylie, came a voice from the shadowed doorway that gave onto the garden. Is Otylie here?

"*Ne, táto,*" Marta replied, rising to take her father's arm to help him outside into the bower. "*Tohle je Meta. Přijela z Ameriky, aby našla Jakubův rukopis.*" No, Papa. This is Meta. She's come from America to find Jakub's manuscript.

Impossibly frail and so stooped he resembled a hunchback, Tomáš rested his cane against a stone bench in order to shake her hand. His sudden appearance, the living and breathing Tomáš, left Meta speechless. Gerrit, seeing this, jumped in and introduced himself with a respectful bow, explaining that he was Meta's friend and lived in the neighborhood.

"*Je tady s Wittmannem?*" Tomáš asked, squinting at Gerrit with irises glazed as white by cataracts as Socrates's. Is she here with Wittmann?

His daughter steadied him as he lowered himself into the nearest wrought-iron chair, then explained what brought Meta to Šporkova. Tomáš listened intently as familiar names from the distant past drifted by him like the first notes he had ever learned. Yes, he had sat with Wittmann not that many days ago. He had been impressed by the scholar's erudition. Yet as ancient as Tomáš now considered himself to be, he was, when lucid, endowed with enough street smarts that he wondered, after the spirited professor left, whether he'd been taken in by some apparatchik. He'd seen a cavalcade of Wittmanns in his time. They were ever smooth and often smart. They spoke with grace and ease. But here now was a woman who, on first impression, seemed not to be cut from that fancy brocaded cloth. Her hands fairly crawled all over themselves like nervous little animals.

"Jak se daři Ireně, po takové době?" he asked her. How is Irena doing after all this time?

Gerrit continued to translate for Meta, answering Tomáš by saying that before Irena died she recollected the faraway evening recital of the sonata here in Malá Strana. Years later, she still marveled at how Tomáš performed the work with great artistry. She never forgot that night, she'd said.

I'm sorry she's gone. Fate of the old. But yes, it was a night none of us would ever forget, Tomáš mused. I'm the only one left alive in all likelihood who remembers it.

Seizing the moment, Meta asked Tomáš if he'd mind telling her more about his recital and also what happened after Otylie's manuscript was delivered into his care. Fill her in about his years as its custodian. This was not the kind of question that Wittmann had bothered with. Even if it had been, Tomáš might well have concluded the man was a spy come to gather more evidence against him, dredge up a life's worth of the guilt that had already broken him in flesh and spirit. But this open-faced woman appeared genuinely interested in breathing life into the story of the manuscript, and that swayed him.

Tomáš turned to Marta, asking if she might sketch a portrait for the young American. If it's all the same, he admonished his daughter, forgetting that one of his guests spoke fluent Czech, tell her in a way that she'll not think ill of me. Gerrit sat as mute as the paving stones beneath his feet until Marta asked him if he would continue as interpreter.

"'You see,'" Marta began through Gerrit, "'the Nazis were always, how to put it, good to my father during the years of the Protectorate. By good I mean they allowed him to go about his business as a musician undisturbed. In truth, this made my father's life both easier and harder. The threat of being deported to one of the camps didn't hang over his head like a black cloud, but those that the Gestapo did harass mistrusted him. With the Nazis, though, the time for being in their good graces was always going to be limited. When they heard rumors that a suspicious man had visited him on the day the insurgents went after Heydrich, they began calling him in to Petschek to ask questions. They never arrested him. But they kept a close eye on him after that. He had fallen from favor, that much was clear.'"

Meta noticed Tomáš shift in his seat, discomfort creeping across his wrinkled face.

"'When the uprising started near the end of the war, some of the last of the Germans killed Czechs before fleeing or being killed in the streets themselves. My father hid with Aunt Johana, who had managed to stay above the fray, until the Russians marched in to liberate us'"—she traced quote marks in the air. "'When he returned home he found the house had been burned to the ground. This place he loved was a black shell.'"

Here she paused to collect herself.

"I'm sorry," Meta said. "What did he do?"

Marta replied in English. "His piano was his saddest loss. It was all burned, but the brass pedals and part of the—what do you call this?—music board with the Bösendorfer?"

"The soundboard, yes," Meta said, and explained to Gerrit, "A Bösendorfer's like the Stratocaster of pianos."

"The label on the soundboard didn't burn completely. So he saved that."

Tomáš recognized the word Bösendorfer and glanced over at Meta, who'd been eyeing him as his daughter spoke. From the crestfallen look on his face, it was clear that hearing his life recounted was painful, and the mention of his Bösendorfer particularly so.

"'The second floor of the house had collapsed onto the first and the roof had caved in,'" Marta went on as Gerrit followed in English. "'He'd been very wise to anticipate problems, and had given the sonata pages to Johana, who hid them behind her bureau where the wallpaper had come loose. After the fire, he stayed on with her. There was nowhere else to go. He wanted to fix the house he'd inherited, but the Communists confiscated the property, and anyway, why did this lowly pianist with a German surname deserve better than his Czech comrades? He could get some training at a vocational school, do something useful with his life. Learn how to repair a tractor or glaze a window. Music that wasn't made to energize the masses was as much a capitalist abstraction as going to church and praying to a god who didn't exist.'"

"What about the manuscript?"

"'It stayed where it was behind that bureau. Since my aunt Johana didn't have a piano, he never played during those days. He kept his head down and learned how to be a fair stonemason. To make a long story short, he married a neighbor of my aunt and she moved in with them. That's how it was in those postwar days, generations of families crammed into apartments like maggots in rotten logs, just getting by. I came along. My mother died when I was only a baby, so I was raised by my father and aunt—'," and here, for a moment, Marta switched into English—"I don't think he likes for you to know this, but he lost his will after my mother died. He was much more in the pubs. He had nothing but me and that manuscript, and he liked to talk about it, what is the word, bragging? But nobody cared. Later, I married a man who has a little money, not rich, but enough. Like my father here, he was a man who can do anything with his hands."

"Was?" Meta asked.

Marta nodded, looked away, abstracted, then back once more in focus, glancing at Gerrit, who continued. "'After the Communists were ousted, we applied for restitution of this property. Once our paperwork came through and it was retitled to my family, my husband and I built the place up from scratch. And like too many things that happen in life, just when he'd finished the house and was really looking forward to living in it, he had a heart attack, and died. That was when I asked Father to come live with me here so I could take care of him and not be alone. We got a piano so he could play again. It had been a long time but his fingers still remembered.'"

Meta and Gerrit glanced at each other. Seeing how hard this was for Marta and her frail father, Meta offered, "Would it be better if we came back another day? I'm so sorry about your husband."

"No, no," the woman said, noticing that Tomáš was staring at Meta.

"Marta, may I ask, does your father still play the piano?"

"He will sit and play some evenings, you know, with open windows for fresh air. I love it when he does. His fingers pain and he is not so agile, but these are the only times I know for sure he is happy."

"Does he sometimes play the sonata movement?"

"Now and again. He has to improvise the opening since it was missing from Jakub's pages."

Meta bit her lip, hopes rising. "It'd be very possible for him to reconstitute it, since the nature of a rondo is that its theme repeats." Turning to Gerrit, she said, "That's what you must have played, you and Andrea that day, if Sam really heard you. Or else he heard it himself, Tomáš playing some version of the rondo melody. It's catchy, easy to recall."

"Well, his piano is part of the Malá Strana soundscape. I've lived nearby for a decade, so it's feasible I'd have picked up echoes of what I heard walking by. Or that Sam, who really has an ear, would have."

Broadly smiling, Meta shook her head. "Not just feasible. I'm convinced it's what happened." Turning to Marta, she said, "Thank God your father likes playing with the windows open."

They sat in silence for a moment. Then, knowing he had far less to lose if the question was met with resistance, Gerrit put into words what each of them knew must come next. "Do you think it would be possible for Meta to see the manuscript?"

"For me, I think, yes, she must. But it's my father's decision." She asked, *"Můžu jim to ukázat, táto?"* Can I show them, Father?

Meta would never forget the look on Tomáš Lang's face as he nodded. Some mirror, some reflection of his troubled life, but also of the simpler times before the war, illuminated his eyes. When Marta brought the manuscript out and handed it to her, Meta, fingers nimble as a surgeon's, unwrapped the tissue paper that protected it and knew at once just by its physical presence—the paper, the staving, the hand—that this was it. She read the first page, her hands now lightly trembling.

Yes, yes, yes! Here was the mid-phrase continuation of the rondo theme that launched into empty silence at the bottom of the last leaf of Irena's manuscript. Pure eighteenth century, simpler by far than the dramatic narrativity of the earlier movement, Mozartean but with some curious chromaticism in the episodes that followed the exposition, not to mention notated dynamics that were more extreme than anything she'd seen in Mozart. While she turned the pages, delicately and carefully—this part of the manuscript was in far worse condition than Irena's—it was all she could do to restrain her joy.

Gerrit broke into the music soaring in Meta's head to ask, "Is it right? Does it fit with what Irena gave you?"

Blinking away tears, she nodded while looking over at Tomáš. "I feel like the most blessed person on earth right now."

Marta translated for Tomáš, who, sitting in the stippled light, lifted his outstretched arms toward Meta. Handing the manuscript to Gerrit, she went to the old man and gave him a long hug. Overwhelmed, Tomáš buried his face in his squarish, muscular fingers when Meta stepped away. The sun had begun to sink, and a rose-gold glow settled within the confines of the bower. He excused himself and left the garden, waving his daughter away. At the doorway, he slowly turned and thanked Meta and Gerrit for what they'd done.

Tomorrow afternoon, he said in Czech, if you are willing, I would like to hear you play Otylie's music. My fingers are too stiff to manage the faster passages in tempo. It would give me great pleasure to hear the sonata movements performed as they deserve to be.

Invite a few friends, Marta added. Four o'clock, say? We will celebrate.

Gerrit translated Meta's response, saying that nothing would make her happier but that she'd do a better job if she could take it home and practice overnight.

A suspicious, or maybe mischievous, twinkle shone in Tomáš's rheumy eyes. No, he said. The first time Otylie Bartošová let me play it, she allowed me little opportunity to practice. You're a very good pianist, I imagine. I saw your fingers as you read those first measures. It will be a wonder to hear both movements after so long. Tomorrow, then.

After checking with Gerrit to be sure that she'd understood Tomáš, Meta said, "*Tak zítra*," repeating his final words, honored and intimidated by his challenge. If that was how he wanted to do this, that was how it was going to be. Both her strong hand and her weak one would have to work harder than they had in some time.

After they left and—dumbstruck, enraptured—made their way up Šporkova, Gerrit stopped. "So now what?" he asked.

Grabbing his hands, she let out a shriek of joy. "Now what? Now we're going to share the best bottle of champagne they have in Prague is what. Or at least a decent bottle of Moravian wine. Even the mighty Professor Wittmann can't ruin this moment."

Neither Moravian nor any other wine had ever tasted better to Meta, celebrating with Gerrit in one of his favorite nearby pubs. When she reluctantly decided to head back to the tram, knowing she had to get some rest before performing the next day, Gerrit walked hand in hand with her to the stop, and kissed her again on opened lips as they stood, swaying a little, anonymous in the lamplight. They lingered as one tram passed—"I'll catch the next," whispered Meta—then another. Boarding the third tram, Meta waved goodbye and Gerrit walked home to Jánská. His mind was swirling with the wine they'd shared, but more potently with his new self-defining interests in life. Meta and Meta's quest.

Falling in love with her, which he could not deny he was doing, was one thing. He had never met anyone so fired by talent, devotion, unself-conscious elegance. And yet—this damned dilemma again of being drawn to her narrative, skewing her into a subject. Not since the heady days of "the Velvet" had he come across a human interest story so fundamentally compelling to him. He admired Meta for wanting to curate a lost fragment of the world's culture, with no clear gain in mind other than to set something right. But hiding his increasing little hoard of secrets—his not-quite pitch to Margery, his so-called interview with Wittmann, and now, this late evening back in his rooms, his compulsive note-taking about the extraordinary encounter with Tomáš Lang—was becoming more and more troubling.

Pathetic. Enviable and pathetic at the same time. Hadn't he lost Adrienne those years ago, when he left Paris to chase history? This was even closer to the bone. Meta couldn't be separated from the history she herself pursued, and he felt unequal to chasing both of them.

Like some gone-native ethnographer, Meta found herself stepping away from the scholar's role into the living world of the sonata itself. The recital, she realized, meant that she was herself becoming a part of the manuscript's history. When she knocked on Sam and Sylvie's bedroom door, giddy from her celebration with Gerrit and their good night kisses, the three of them danced like ecstatic children in the semidark, Sylvie in her nightgown, Sam in his boxer shorts, Meta with her coat still on. A drowsy note of complaint from David and Lucie's room brought them to their senses.

"Why in the world didn't he give you a chance to practice?" Sam whispered.

"I don't mind. Anyway, this sonata seems to live by its own rules. I hope it's okay if I make a couple of phone calls. I promise I'll be quiet."

"No problem, we'll talk in the morning. Huge congrats and sweet dreams."

When Meta telephoned Gillian and Jonathan behind the closed door of the piano studio, their reactions were wildly dissimilar.

Gillie screamed, dropped the phone. Meta laughed as she heard her friend enact the same celebratory dance, an ocean away, that she herself had just done with Sam and Sylvie. When Gillie got back on the line, she said, "I knew it, I knew you'd do it! Now listen, girlfriend. My birthday's coming up at Christmas, so I insist you play it for me as a present."

Meta wanted to point out that she hadn't really *done it* yet, and might never finally marshal together the whole sonata, but allowed herself to be happily, tidally swept away in the moment, promising Gillie that one way or another she would come through with this command performance.

Though glad for Meta, Jonathan was less exuberant. "I guess you'll be coming back pretty soon then?" he said, after offering congratulations. She changed the subject. If anything, the discovery would keep her in the field searching for the first movement, assuming Tomáš's manuscript was, as she believed, authentic, and Wittmann hadn't somehow beaten her to the other missing piece. There was, as well, the issue of Gerrit. Instead, she told Jonathan what Wittmann was up to along with the shadow man Kohout. This did get a rise out of him.

"You've got to call Mandelbaum and demand that he read his friend Wittmann the riot act. I'll make the call myself, if you want."

"Before I go accusing Mandelbaum of throwing me to the wolves, I ought to hear Wittmann's side of the story, don't you think? It's not impossible that I'm being paranoid because I don't like his friend Kohout." She caught her voice rising and, remembering the sleeping children in the bedroom behind her, lowered it again.

"How freaking naive can you get, Meta? You already know his side of the story. These guys are totally in cahoots. They're using your discovery to advance their own twilighting careers."

"Wittmann's career is hardly in twilight. He doesn't need to filch other people's scholarship in order to get ahead. He *is* ahead."

The silence that fell between them was, she thought, as deafening as the John Cage piece in which silence was the music. In

266 THE PRAGUE SONATA

which the music consisted of the coughs and sneezes and squirming noises the audience made in the concert hall while the pianist
sat onstage without playing one note.

When Jonathan finally spoke, his voice dropped into a register
of warm impatience. "Look, it's your life, your search. It's your
time and money and effort. But I think you're being foolish by
refusing to call Mandelbaum and at least ask him to discuss this
with Wittmann. By the way, how do you know Mandelbaum himself isn't involved here in some way?"

"You're delusional."

"And you're blind, tunnel-vision blind, as well as guileless, and
if you don't mind my saying so, you're acting like a horse's ass."

Meta had no idea how to respond.

"I apologize," Jonathan continued, a bit breathless. "I know I'm
overstating my case, but that's how I feel."

"Your case? You're not my attorney, Jonathan." She was struggling to keep her voice to a whisper. "I'm sorry but I think we ought
to get off the phone. I finally get a chance to hear—to play—some
of the music I've been searching for and I don't need all this per-
cussion crashing around in my head all night. I'll talk with Petr
Wittmann myself. I'm a bigger girl than you think."

"I never said that."

"Well, in fact you did. But let's drop it."

"The way you've dropped me?"

"That's not funny," she said, her ears warming.

"I'm not trying to get a laugh here. I'm telling you, you've come
unmoored, you're gone, I don't know what to do with you anymore."

"Do with me? You make me sound like I ought to be put away."

"Well, sometimes I wonder, Meta. You've given up everything
you had going here. And for what? If you want to know the absolute truth—"

"Absolutely."

"—I don't think you're up to this quest of yours. I've had a lot of time to come to this conclusion and I'd like to lay out my reasons for you."

"That won't be necessary. Goodbye, Jonathan."

Fitful in her sleeping bag and adjusting and readjusting her pillow, Meta admitted to herself that the schism between her and Jonathan seemed all but unbridgeable. Absence made the heart grow harder? And there was no denying that her growing attraction to Gerrit served to undermine any sense of groundedness left to her. She was out to sea, was she not? On the other hand, wasn't that the nature of exploration?

Still, Jonathan wasn't wrong about Wittmann. She was now certain that he and the Rooster had been consulting, if not colluding, from the beginning. It was clear as ice water. While it was true that their shady behavior actually underscored the importance of Otylie's sonata, Meta had known something was off since that night in Old Town Square. Wittmann, so polite, so solicitous, had been—well, too polite, too solicitous. Jonathan once told Meta that the only reason she wouldn't have made a good lawyer was that she lacked the "killer instinct."

"That's because I have no desire to kill," she quipped. They'd been walking toward Chelsea, mitten in glove, as late-afternoon snow twirled down around them, on their way to meet friends to see a movie. "I feel bad swatting a fly, as you know."

"My point exactly. You have every other necessary quality."

"Being?"

"Being, a phenomenal memory. Good verbal skills. You're insightful, empathetic. Dogged as can be. A sixth sense that lets you, when you're willing, see through the malarkey to the heart of matters. You're persuasive, attractive, and don't think that doesn't matter in a courtroom because it does, fair or not. Above all, you're not judgmental. But, but, but"—his breath was billowing several small frosty clouds. "Zero killer instinct."

"Well, if that's a shortcoming, it's one I don't mind having," she said, and drew him closer for warmth as they crossed the darkening blue avenue.

The swirling, teeming confusion Meta felt was reminiscent of the days when she used to amble down the hallway of practice rooms at Juilliard. Although the doors were closed they were not altogether soundproof. You could hear all the pianos behind them being played at the same time. Shostakovich, Ravel, Bartók, even somebody sneaking a little Scott Joplin ragtime into the mix. What a lovely, crazy cacophony, she thought. Music of the spheres!

Whereas that charming chaos brought a smile to Meta's face, this was just plain old turmoil. To rub out all the inharmonious voices, she turned her mind to rondos. Deliciously sane, sane-making rondos. Rondos in which the musical theme was stated, followed by a subordinate theme, then back to the main theme to reassure the listener—sometimes with a simple ornament or filigree—before a second subordinate theme emerges, all in an amity of braiding, a settled pattern.

Next morning, hasty arrangements were made by phone. Because it was a Sunday, nearly everyone invited was free to join them. Aside from a couple of the Langs' neighbors, elderly Šporkovans, Meta felt a kinship with all the invitees. Tomáš and Marta would of course be there. Sam had canceled his couple of Sunday lessons in order to go with Sylvie and the kids, and invited several favorite students, Meta's struggling Chopin pupil among them. Gerrit was to attend with Andrea and her parents. Even Gretja, the musicologist whom Meta had encountered when she first came to Prague and who'd asked to be kept "on touch" with progress, was invited. Only Jiří, who wasn't able to get anyone to cover his restaurant shift on such short notice, couldn't make it.

She still had one phone call to make, Gillian having agreed to call Meta's mother on her behalf. However upset she was about things Jonathan had said, Paul Mandelbaum needed to know what was happening.

"Are you sitting down?" she asked.

"At my age, I don't care for standing anymore. So, yes, consider me seated."

"At your age," she mocked. "Stop it. I have something important to tell you," and in a tumble of words, her excitement returning now that she was speaking with an ally, Meta explained that she'd found another of the movements and would be performing it for a small gathering that very afternoon. "Not only that, but in the home of the man who protected it from the Nazis and the Czech Communists over half a century."

Mandelbaum's end of the line was silent as he processed. Finally, to Meta's surprise, he said, "I'm going to book a flight out of Newark. I've been envious of you hanging out in Prague ever since you left, so it's a perfect excuse to come over. Be nice to see Sam too. Can you get me a hotel room? You have a moment for such mundanities?"

"For you, old owl? Just let me know when your flight's arriving and I'll meet you at the airport. I'll be so glad to see you, and there are other things we'll want to talk about when you're here."

"Such as?"

Meta hesitated. "Well, for one, I'm finding your friend Petr Wittmann increasingly, what, confusing. First he dismisses out of hand the manuscript I showed him. Then I find out he's doing everything he can to talk the owner into giving him the original of this third movement, saying it's of great importance. Help?"

It struck her as odd how long it took for Mandelbaum to respond. When he said, "Let me talk to him. Meantime, it's best you steer clear," Meta caught a tone she'd never heard before in her mentor's voice.

"All right. Maybe I'm misunderstanding something," she agreed, but it did make her wonder. "I have a request myself. Pretty big nuisance of a request."

"Shoot."

"If you really are coming, would you be willing to go into the city before you grab your flight? I can ask my mom to get the manuscript out of the safe-deposit for you to bring, and—"

"You sure you want to risk that?"

There was that unfamiliar tone again. "How else can we definitively compare all the physical continuities, unless we see the originals side by side?"

"You can do that when you get it back here, Meta."

"But he hasn't given me the manuscript, and there's no guarantee he will. He's just letting me play it. This may be our only chance to actually see them together. I know it means a couple extra hours and I promise I'll make it up to you somehow. I'll buy you chocolate soufflé every night you're here and won't tell Annalise, how's that?"

"Tempting, but you don't have enough money to buy me chocolate soufflé every night, and my waistline doesn't need it anyway. Look, what if my plane goes down? What if they try to confiscate it at customs? Anything might happen. It's safest where it is."

"Why would they possibly confiscate it? Besides, it's not like the manuscript has an appraised or intrinsic value, as such. Aside from you, and maybe Wittmann, no one believes it's of any serious worth except me. And I questioned myself at every turn. I can't force you to do this. But I'd appreciate it."

"Well, I think you're being hard-headed, but it's your call," Mandelbaum said. "Just so we're clear, I'm on record as strongly against it."

"Thanks, Paul. Besides, what better place to rejoin them than here in Prague where they were originally separated?"

"That's too saccharine an idea for me to respond to."

Ignoring him, she said, "I need to tell you something else you won't want to respond to. I think it's over with Jonathan. And I think I'm falling in love with someone else."

"Boy problems," Mandelbaum sighed. "All the more reason for me to get overseas as soon as possible. See if I can't save you from yourself."

When they hung up, Meta stared out the back kitchen window at rusting balcony railings and empty clotheslines, wondering whether she had made a mistake mentioning Gerrit to Mandelbaum, however much of a father figure he might be. What in the world possessed her? She hadn't even articulated to herself the idea of falling in love. Curiously, Beethoven came to mind. The poor bastard fell in and out of love every time he met the pretty sister, the buxom cousin, the handsome wife of a new friend. He rarely just fell either. He plunged, plummeted, crashed and burned in love. He was in love with love, much to his lifelong distress. Her own father, Kenneth, was a little like that too, she thought, and look where such impulsiveness had landed him.

Seeing the breakfast dishes stacked in the sink, she mechanically started washing them. As she ran the soapy scrub brush in circles around a dirty plate, she questioned her own impulsiveness. Had she been pulling a Kenneth Taverner since her birthday, stepping out of her settled life because she had fallen in love first with a manuscript and then with a man? Just as well that Sylvie wandered into the kitchen, unintentionally interrupting her thoughts. Enough,

Taverner, Meta scolded herself. Impulsive or not, her purpose right now was this sonata. It, and seeing where intangibles led her with Gerrit, and making sure she didn't break any of these dishes.

"Why you washing? I take care of them."

"That's all right, the warm water feels good on my hands."

Sylvie shrugged, grabbing the dish towel and drying the plates and cups Meta had placed in the rack by the sink. "Today is the day you looking forward to since I know you," she said. "Sam still think it crazy this Tomáš not give you the music to practice."

"I would have kept you up all night if he had."

"We do not care."

"It feels like something in a fairy tale, that whoever plays the music has to be tested to prove they're worthy. Anyway, he's allowing me to show up an hour early to run through it a couple of times, so I won't be doing the whole thing cold. I don't think he's ready to let it out of his sight yet. Can't say I blame him."

After finishing the dishes, Meta retired to the piano studio, where she put on the best clothes she'd brought with her. She was used to dressing in dark attire when she performed, a suggestion made by one of her coaches, as a way of pushing the focus away from the pianist and toward the music instead. She slipped on a burgundy silk blouse and a black silk skirt from her favorite East Village secondhand store. Sylvie lent her an antique floral scarf her grandmother had given her, also silk. Meta did her hair up in a loose bun before spending half an hour at the piano running through warm-ups. Since she was to sight-read a rondo, she rehearsed by playing a couple using Sam's sheet music—the last movements of Mozart's *Eine kleine Nachtmusik* and Beethoven's Sonata in C Minor, op. 13, the "Pathétique." She didn't practice Otylie's unattributed movement if only because she wanted to hear it fresh today, not as a lonely orphan but with a sibling score to interact with. Sam and Sylvie wished her luck, told her they'd see her later at Šporkova, and she left to catch the tram.

Gerrit had offered to meet her early and walk her to the Langs', but she had declined.

"I appreciate it," she told him on the cell from the streetcar. "But this is something I have to do by myself. We'll be together afterward, whether I tank or triumph, right?"

"You'll triumph. You already have."

Marta answered the door, then led Meta down the hall to an arched entryway that gave onto the parlor. The shutters were all flung aside today. Midafternoon sun streamed into the room. Marta had arranged a hodgepodge of chairs—upholstered, wooden ladderback, even a couple of the wrought-iron ones from the garden—into rows in the room, salon-style.

Tomáš was sitting at the far end of the parlor by the window. His white hair glowed in the light as he rose to shake Meta's hand, which was, despite her efforts to calm herself, mildly trembling. Both Tomáš and Marta saw her nervousness, but rather than view it as a shortcoming they understood it as another manifestation of how important this was to her.

"*Budu vám otáčet stránky*," he said, placing the score on the music stand and miming his words. I will turn for you.

Meta thanked him, adjusted the height of the bench, spidered some arpeggios up and down the keyboard to get a feel for the action. Sluggish but better than she'd anticipated. As promised, it was out of tune—the *rámus* Gerrit had mentioned when their search began—but not so much as to prevent her from being able to hear, deeply hear, what was written.

Tomáš sat on a stool next to her as she slowly read through the pages. Every so often her fingers would drop onto the ivories to sort out the phrasing of a passage, but for the most part Meta followed her settled routine of hearing a score first with her eyes before ever playing a note. *Air your errors in your head, not with your hands*, one of her earliest teachers had advised her, and it stuck. Over the years, Meta had gotten so adept at mute sight-reading that she could almost hear the movement as it might have sounded on Tomáš Lang's original Bösendorfer Imperial with its characteristic sweet singing tone, and was so moved by it that she could no longer see the score. She rested her hands on her lap for a moment, composed herself after wiping her eyes with Sylvie's scarf. Tomáš asked if she was all right, if she needed a handker-chief, and Marta translated. But Meta, who had wept for joy more in the last two days than she had for any reason, happy or sad, in the past two years, shook her head.

For all its occasional idiosyncrasies, flashes of genius, it was soon clear this was an archetypal third-movement rondo with its constant return of the opening line. And just what any listener would expect—though sonatas could be unruly little monsters that defied cut-and-dried theory—was a resolution at the end. The human ear begs for the reassurance of the tonic key. Dah *dah*. We're *home*.

Nor was it by a minor composer. For its overt niceties of con-vention, this music was too quietly quirky to have come from someone who wasn't a bit headstrong, who didn't view music from a different angle. C. P. E. came to mind again as did Beethoven, hard as that reasonably was to imagine. Haydn and Dussek still couldn't be ruled out.

Again, though, speculating about composers wasn't the imme-diate issue. She needed to get through the piece itself. Nodding at Tomáš with a blanched smile, she tucked a loose strand of hair behind her flushed ear, and began her first foray. She moved nimbly through the opening theme, Tomáš turning the pages at just the right moment, a measure and a half ahead of her fingers. As she played, a calm settled over her, the kind that harkened back to her youthful days when her mother baked bread and the apartment filled with its savory aroma. Sure, she dropped notes in some of the more vexing phrases. But by the time she neared the end, the original theme naturally recurring there like a welcoming echo, Meta experienced a childlike rapture. She played it again from the top at a livelier tempo. Tomáš indicated passages in the movement where she might adjust her fingering and dynamics.

After her third run-through, quiet settled over the room. Not since she first performed some of her favorite variations in Bach's Goldberg set, a girl not yet in her teens already reaching for mastery, had she felt this enthralled. Whereas true keyboard virtuosity would forever elude her, Meta sensed that her Prague Sonata might not.

This was the concluding movement she'd been searching for. Not only did historical accounts of its provenance line up, but both the manuscript and its music fit together like an old architectural blueprint that had been torn and could now be mended so the building—a sonorous temple, as far as Meta was concerned—might be seen for what it was meant to be. And to think another wing of this temple, with its facade and front gates, was out there waiting to be discovered.

Marta was speaking to her after Tomáš had offered a few emphatic words in Czech.

"I'm sorry," Meta said, recalling herself. "You're saying?"

"He wants to make sure you understand he doesn't mean to interfere. Just that he's had many years to think about this music and you've had minutes."

"I'm open to every idea he has," said Meta. "Ask him if he'd prefer to perform it himself and let me play the second movement? It'd be a duet that way. It would bridge the time he performed it for Otylie and Jakub and Irena with today, here, now."

Marta translated for Tomáš, who, with a grateful shrug, held his gently palsied hands before her. His daughter said, "He says he likes this idea, but his fingers are too old to do proper justice. He says he can draw, but you paint it."

"Mine are pretty ruined and rusty too, but I'm good to go ahead as planned," she told Marta, as the first guests were heard ringing the doorbell. She added that they might have to live with some flubbed notes, but the overall performance of the movement would be much more coherent thanks to Tomáš's suggestions.

"*Můžu vám říct víc, jestli chcete,*" he said, intuiting her words, the fingers of his right hand resting on the keyboard. I can tell you more one day, if you want.

"*Ano,*" Meta said, nodding at Marta's translation. "*Prosím vas.*" Yes, please.

Marta left the parlor to answer the door, leaving the two pianists alone together for the first time. They regarded each other with open stares, benign but intense. The moment was not unlike that when a handshake between strangers goes on a touch too long, or people walking down the street who have never met catch each other's gaze and allow it to linger until they pass. Meta didn't know Tomáš. Never really would. She hoped that keeping his promise to Jakub Bartoš would allow the sonata of his own life to resolve at least into a tonic minor. Then, unexpectedly, he removed the manuscript from the piano stand and presented it to Meta with a slight formal nod.

"*Není to moje, takže vám to nemůžu dát. Ale dává vám to Jakub, abyste to vrátila Otýlii,*" he whispered. This is not mine to give you. Jakub gives this to you so you can give it back to Otylie.

Buoyant, Meta needed no translation. Nor did Tomáš when she held the score in both hands and said, "Thank you. I will do my best."

Tomáš, unburdened from his wartime promise to Jakub, felt lighter as well. His buoyancy was limited, though. This earnest, gifted American girl was not going to be very happy with him, he feared, when she found out what he'd done. Nor was his sister, Johana, going to be anything less than livid once she learned he had given the original to Meta. Maybe this had been his great character flaw all along. Hedging his bets. Coming to a crossroads and trying against the odds to take both paths. He might have learned by now, might he not, that it was better to make the wrong choice and live with it long enough to correct the mistake than to embrace opposing sides.

Meta gently pressed the manuscript to her breast, then replaced it on the piano stand for her recital. Smiling one last time at Tomáš, she noticed his features weren't as calm as a moment ago. All of this must be overwhelming for him, she figured. Then, hearing voices in the corridor, she turned to face the entering guests.

What began as a brief recital evolved into a lively musicale. After Meta finished an encore playing the sonata movements a second time, she asked Sam to come to the piano and show them what a real pianist sounded like. Scoffing at the comparison, he sat and gave an account of Beethoven's "Les Adieux" that was so sure and solid it transformed Lang's limping piano into an exultant instrument. Andrea was coaxed to the front of the room next, where, after bowing extravagantly to the applause, she made Sam proud with a not-half-bad crack at the first waltz of Erik Satie's slow-dreamy *Trois Gymnopédies*. And for her own encore, a noisy version of "Louie Louie," as Gerrit and Meta cheered her on. Caught up in the spirit of the afternoon, Tomáš himself was finally cajoled into playing an excerpt from the middle movement of the very Haydn sonata he'd performed in the 1930s during his gathering with Otylie and the others in the ghost of this room.

"You should play too," Meta nudged Gerrit, as Tomáš hoisted himself up on his cane to more applause.

"No way. It's like asking a meadowlark to listen to a toad croak."

"I don't think toads croak."

"Sure they do."

"Toads don't make any sounds, do they?"

"Better yet. My point exactly."

Everybody had come with wine and beer. The Hodeks brought a basket of local cheeses, fresh bread, ripe figs; and the Langs' cupboards and refrigerator were opened wide. An impromptu party began. Another party Mandelbaum was going to miss, Meta rued, toasting Tomáš, who in turn raised a glass to Otylie and Jakub Bartoš. Sam and Andrea found the stereo and began to spin an eclectic mix of Bo Diddley, Aretha Franklin, the Ramones—all bootleg stuff that Marta's husband had obsessively collected in the Iron Curtain days. It was out with the old longhair music and in with the new longhair music. Sam asked Gretja if she'd like to dance. Andrea dragged Gerrit by the hand out onto the improvised dance floor that spilled from the parlor into the kitchen. Even Tomáš, who hated pop music, sat at the kitchen table and tapped his cane absently to the beat.

Meta watched this revelry feeling curiously maternal. If she never did another good thing in her life, she had come this far, made it to this day. She knew about the butterfly effect but had never really believed it before. Yet right now, just for a passing instant, wasn't she herself the butterfly who flapped her wings and created a weather system on the other side of the world? All these people were here because she had taken the subway out to Kalmia Avenue on a warm summer day to visit Irena Svobodová Dorfman, regift her some Polish chocolate, and listen to a life story from the precincts of hell. She had to admit to herself, if nobody else, that she'd never fully believed she'd locate a sister movement to go with Irena's. If she'd been reasonable, pragmatic, whatever the word was, she would not be here now. Well, she thought, sometimes the haystack needle is found.

"He wanting dance with you, Meta," Andrea said, snatching her out of her thoughts.

"You sure you don't mind sharing him with me?"

"He wanting you."

"Andrea," Gerrit warned. "Stop it already."

"Shall we dance, mister?" Meta said, ignoring his embarrassment and offering him her hands. Gerrit pretended to frown at Andrea, then smiled at Meta, who had transformed herself from an elegant classical musician in a black silk skirt and sensible black shoes to a barefooted terpsichorean tossing her hair from shoulder to shoulder with abandon. Sylvie, who hadn't known what had developed between them, saw it at once. She and Sam, as they swung slowly back and forth in an embrace to the Marvin Gaye ballad that came next, felt as if they suddenly had an older daughter, one who was impossibly close to their own ages. In Czech, Sam whispered, We'd better get a bigger piano, if you know what I mean.

A few hours fled by. Most of the guests, not a little tipsy, said goodbye, thanking Marta and Tomáš for the hospitality. Andrea pleaded to stay with Gerrit when her parents announced it was time to go. Her father told her that they had no need of a chaperone, even an indulgent chaperone like Andrea. She responded with a compliant pout.

Gerrit told her in English, "I'll catch up with you later."

Satisfied, the girl gave Meta a kiss on both cheeks, and the Hodeks gathered their things and left. While Marta busied herself with seeing guests to the door, Meta and Gerrit sat with Tomáš. Now that the nexus between the two manuscripts had been established, Meta saw no reason not to immediately begin her search for the first movement, the one Otylie had kept. With Gerrit acting as interpreter, she asked Tomáš if he had any idea what had happened to her after she split up the sonata and departed for England.

Taking a sip of beer and setting the glass on the table with such focused care that one might have thought it was fragile crystal holding some rare elixir, Tomáš pursed his lips and told Gerrit what he recalled about her time in London.

"He says what I think you already knew. Jakub helped her get work with the Beneš exile government, maybe as a secretary. He says he thinks the couple always believed that when the war was over they would reunite in a free Czechoslovakia and take up their lives where they'd left off—I'm sorry, *můžete to zopakovat?*" Could you repeat that?

Staring at his tabled hands, Tomáš filled in what Gerrit had missed, and then continued.

"'Such optimism, but that's how they were. Infectious idealism, not a cynical bone in their bodies.' As for Otylie, he says he knows she was in Prague after the war."

"How does he know? Did he see her?"

"He got a letter from her, he says."

"You're kidding. Ask him if he still has it."

Tomáš nodded and conversed with Gerrit for a minute.

"What's he saying?" Meta interrupted.

"If I'm getting this right, she wrote to him a couple of times and he wrote back, but he thinks she never got his replies because she never answered the questions he asked her, didn't respond to his offer to return the manuscript. Strangest of all, she never requested details about his last encounter with her husband. That seemed very much unlike her. So he assumes she never read what he wrote."

"Can we see her letters?" she asked, unable to contain her stirring impatience.

Before Gerrit had finished translating Meta's questions, Tomáš reached into his jacket breast pocket, pulled out several sheets of folded paper, and handed them to Meta.

Tell her, he said to Gerrit, that there were some others from London, but they're gone now. These are all that I have left.

Heart racing, she opened and flattened them with her palm, then looked at the front and back of each sheet of the two missives. Otylie's tidy signature was there in blue-black ink at the end of both, and each began *Milý Tomáši*. One bore the dateline *Praha, 1946,* and the other, *Prague, 1978.* She handed them to Gerrit and sat shifting in her seat as she waited for him to tell her what Otylie had written.

There wasn't much to translate. Written in a carefully rounded script on blue, billet-sized paper, the first letter was brief. How much useful information could be there, Meta wondered, trying to curb her hopes.

"*Dear Tomáš,*" Gerrit translated. "*Praise heaven this horrid war is over! I'm back in Prague looking for my Jakub. Do you have any news of him? And you? Where are you? I came to your house but it is in ruins like too much here. You can find me at the Inn of the Golden Hart. I long to hear from you. Your affectionate friend, Otylie Bartošová. P.S. I address this to your Šporkova house and hope one day it may reach you.*"

"Does that hotel still exist?" asked Meta.

Gerrit queried, and Tomáš assured him it closed long ago.

Undeterred, Meta said, "I think I already know the answer to this, but could you confirm that Tomáš never saw her?"

Gerrit asked the old man, who shook his head as he spoke.

"He didn't get the letter until several months after she wrote it, he says. He went immediately to the inn but she'd checked out."

"What about the other one?"

Written on cream stationery, the second letter ran to two sheets. Gerrit read it through, then translated for her.

"*Dear Tomáš, You have been on my mind these past years, and as fate would have it I met a boy today, a new piano student, whose name is Tom, and I thought to write. I wonder if you are still alive and, if so, whether you ever feel lonely for those days as I sometimes do. Oh, I have friends in this new world, that wonderful girl I met during the war years away from home who I've told you about, and now even a man, a very good man, although sometimes I wonder if I am living two lives, one as a ghost and the other waiting to become one. I write this knowing you may never see or read it. How I loved our lives back in the old days. We had no idea how fortunate we were. Did you ever hear anything of Jakub or Irena? Do you have any idea what became of the sonata manuscript? I can't forgive myself for ever having broken it up. Your friend forever, Otylie.*"

"Is there a return address on that second one?"

Gerrit turned the leaves front and back, said, "No, just Prague and the year."

"Could you ask him if he still has the envelope? Maybe she added it there."

The old man told Gerrit that his sister had probably thrown it out. He was able to salvage these letters, but Johana was never comfortable with his friendship with the Bartošes, and he had no idea what else she might have tossed. "'The Nazis may have been defeated,' he says, "'but prejudice is less easily overcome.'"

Meta clasped and unclasped her hands, suddenly aware that they ached from the strain of the performance, then laid them flat on her thighs. "Unless you can think of more questions, I don't know what else to say other than to thank Tomáš for sharing these with me. It's heartening to know that Otylie made it through the war and beyond."

"Let me ask him about this wonderful girl she mentions," Gerrit said, then translated Tomáš's response, that he only remembered they were together in London. Beyond this, his memory was a blank.

Tomáš continued speaking for another minute before Gerrit told Meta, "He says she sounded so sad in the later one that even if he'd known where to reach her, it would have been a hard letter to write. He knows the truth about what happened with Jakub, or he's pretty sure. It would have been terrible to be the bearer of the news, though at least he could've returned the manuscript."

"Tell him—," she started, looking not at Gerrit but at Tomáš. Gerrit hesitated before asking, "Tell him?"

"Tell him if Otylie's still alive, I swear I'll put it into her hands myself, just like he put it in mine."

When they left Šporkova Street that evening, the manuscript wrapped in the same brown envelope it had been stored in for years, Meta's first concern was to figure out the safest place to keep the treasured pages.

"Much as I trust the Kettles, their children tend to get into things, like all little kids do," Meta said, as they passed Socrates dozing on the cobbles. "And there's also an endless parade of students and their parents into and out of Sam's. Just too much risk."

Gerrit thought for a few quiet paces. "There's an old writing desk at my place, one of those antique secretaries with a lid that folds down. It's got a lock and key. Just a generic skeleton key, I admit, more symbolic than secure. But I think it'd be safe there until you find a better spot for it. It certainly has the virtue of anonymity."

"You're sure you don't mind?"

"Why would I mind? It'd be a privilege."

Meta hadn't yet been up to Gerrit's attic apartment. She was struck by its spartan yet lived-in, comfortable look.

"Would you like something to drink?"

"What are you having?"

"Boring as it sounds, I could use a cup of strong black tea."

"Me too," she said. As he left the room, she asked, "Okay if I look around?"

"Feel free," he answered, checking to make sure his notebook that contained observations about Meta's quest was still in his jacket pocket.

One wall was papered with color photographs he had snapped all over Europe on assignments. Judging from a number of the images, he had seen firsthand his share of history, some of it triumphant, some of it violent. Another wall was lined from floor to ceiling with shelves of secondhand books. History, poetry, biography, philosophy, novels in several languages—his interests were broad. Gerrit's desk by the window was stacked with manuscripts, microcassettes, recorder and earphones, newspaper clippings, and more books whose pages were tagged with slips of paper, no doubt references for projects in progress. A porcelain jar held a quiver of pencils next to a laptop that centered the workspace. The furniture in the front room was eclectic, from distressed baroque to unornamented nouveau. An imaginative apartment, she marveled, lived in by an unassuming, thinking inhabitant.

Until now, Meta had always found herself drawn to bright guys, who were, in a word, slobs. Jonathan's one-bedroom was the archetypal New York bachelor pad with laundry growing in every corner, a sink full of unwashed dishes, a bed that never got made until his once-a-week cleaning woman came by to set the place in temporary order. Not that he didn't always put himself together like the professional he was. His shirts were impeccably pressed, his suits handsomely cut. But looking at him from the outside, one would never guess at the not uncharming mayhem that was his apartment.

How unlike Jonathan was Gerrit, who presented to the world at large a persona far closer to the way he lived: precise without being fussy, smart without being overbearing. She felt at home here and was struck by his—for want of a better word—maturity.

"I love your place," she told him, turning to see that he'd returned from the kitchen to the main room through an open arched doorway. "So who are these people?" pointing to a framed collage of black-and-white photographs on the dormer wall beside the desk.

"Key players in the Velvet Revolution. That's Alexandr Vondra, and that's Jiří Křižan, Michael Žantovský there, and this is Havel speaking at a huge rally in his heyday."

"I didn't realize you were a photographer."

"I wouldn't characterize myself that way," he said, "but as a freelancer I have to be my own photographer sometimes. And anyway, I like to take pictures of people and things that interest me. I thought about bringing my camera to your sonata party this afternoon."

"Why didn't you?"

"Because it was your moment, and my taking pictures might have distracted you," he responded, only then realizing that if Meta and her sonata were to become a feature story, he'd blown an opportunity to record a milestone in her search. Jiří would likely have applauded this bit of negligence.

"Just as well. I was nervous enough as it was."

"Besides," said Gerrit, "you can't photograph music, which was the main point of the gathering."

Meta took a sip of tea, and commented, "You're more of a world traveler than you let on. Is this the fall of the Berlin Wall I'm seeing in this one?"

"I wasn't supposed to be there, but yes."

"You have any pictures of yourself when you were young? Shots of your parents, where you grew up?"

"I'm happy to show you, but I've got an idea. I have a sort of family portrait gallery where I'd like to take you. My best friend, Jiří Pelc, is a painter. He has an open studio coming up, and if you'd like to join me, I'll show you my walk-through family album on the way. Game?"

"Sounds intriguing. And I'd love to meet your friend."

"Done," he said. "Now I have a present for you."

He set down his cup, went into his bedroom, and returned holding a vintage leather dispatch case, dark-brown calf with roan edging and brass hardware tarnished to a mellow gold. "I bought this in France years ago. Saw it in an antique-shop window and thought it was the most beautiful thing I'd ever laid eyes on. I've never owned anything precious enough to put in it. Here, it's yours now. To protect the manuscript."

"I can't possibly."

Gerrit took the sonata manuscript from where it had been sitting on his worktable. He undid the straps on the leather brief, carefully laid the sonata inside, then stepped over to the antique writing desk he had mentioned. After sliding the brief under a shelf of pigeonholes, he lifted the mahogany lid into place, and locked it. Handing her the skeleton key, he said, "There you go. It was always meant for you. I've just been its custodian for a while."

The rest of her world and those in it were swept off into some other verity. One that seemed less solidly real or comprehensible than what was here in this room. Without another word she slipped herself into Gerrit's arms and kissed his warm face, his mouth. Silent, with no words or music to accompany her, she crossed the threshold from her old life into this new one about which she knew little, but fully understood she had to enter. It was almost as if she had taken her own hand and led herself into the refuge of another Meta. She could feel his heart beating against her own chest and wondered which of them was more amazed.

· 6 ·

MANDELBAUM WOULDN'T ARRIVE until the next day. Anxious as she was to see him, Meta welcomed the brief respite. Once he was in Prague, a kind of hard, home-based reality was going to enter the scene. Any self-deceptions Meta might have been relying on to get from hour to hour—about the sonata, about Wittmann, not to mention Gerrit and Jonathan—would burst like so many bubbles against the sharp needle of Mandelbaum's pragmatism. Even if, deep down, she welcomed the reality check he represented, these radiant hours were going to be hard to leave behind. Not that all was happiness. Not in the least. But all was directed toward happiness.

The morning after the recital, she showered at Gerrit's flat before returning to the Kettles' still wearing her performance outfit.

"Don't ask. You already know" was her hasty, mildly embarrassed greeting to the grinning Sam when she arrived in Vinohrady. Before he could respond, she changed the subject. "Will you be coming with me to fetch the maestro at the airport?"

Sam reacted to her obvious deflection with a widened grin. "I'd love to tag along, but I think you ought to go by yourself. Our boy's flying here because of you, not me. That said, I'm looking forward to our big reunion dinner in Old Town."

Meta removed Sylvie's scarf and carefully folded it, intending to wash it and return it to her later. Sylvie and the children were out somewhere, given how quiet the apartment was. "You know how he pretends to hate kids. Calls them puling pip-squeaks, filthy little rugrats, and like that—I'm sure you've heard him on this topic. But I think under all the crustiness, he actually loves them."

"He'll love these, I hope. They're the only ones I've got. Will you be able to book him a room in the hotel I suggested, or do you need help with that?"

"We got it all organized earlier this morning, thanks," said Meta, thinking, Listen to me, already using *we*.

"Where's the manuscript?" Sam asked, nodding at Meta's empty hands.

"Under lock and key at Gerrit's, temporarily. You don't have a safe-deposit box at the bank, do you?"

Sam's second grin was like his first. Nothing patronizing. Just the tender hint of a fraternal smile. "How long have we been living cheek by jowl—your smooth cheek, my stubbly jowl? What possible use would I have for a safe-deposit box? This here's all I got, girl. A family and a piano, none of which would fit in a bank drawer vault. The pages are safe on Jánská."

"I'm sure you're right."

Sam glanced at his watch. "Look, I have to leave for a lesson now but I had an idea and insist you agree. You should take a day off from all things sonata. When Mandelbaum gets here, I'm not sure which way the wind's going to blow, but I'm sure it'll blow," he said, rubbing the back of his neck, a tic that Meta interpreted as his way of expressing kindred exhaustion. "I'm going to sub your lessons while he's here, and won't take no for an answer. You have more important things to worry about."

Meta hugged him, and said, "Thanks from the heart, Sam. That's the best idea I've heard in ages. I have something I need to do with a clear head, and this will help."

Sam held her away, looking her fondly in the eyes. "Now go change your clothes."

"Yes, sir," she said, grateful for such a sane and decent friend.

It was true, she thought, when the rooms fell into a rich silence after Sam departed, there was something that needed doing. And now, not later. She had been abroad far longer than either she or Jonathan ever anticipated. The tectonics of their once content relationship had shifted in ways that, last summer, would hardly have been imaginable. Occasional friction in some of their earlier phone conversations had given way to calls that invariably ended up in ditches. Jonathan's voice, formerly softened by a solicitor's training, now often blazed with frustration, even anger.

He had every right, she supposed. Open-eyed, she'd left him behind while she went off chasing after chimeras. But now that she'd actually caught one? Impulsiveness had never been in her nature, Meta thought. Duplicity either. She'd never slept with another man behind a boyfriend's back. Even when the boyfriend— one of her pale, slender, undeniably gifted musician boyfriends back in her early twenties—thought *monogamy* was some obscure rule of harmony used in Gregorian chants, or that *fidelity* really only referred to sound quality on an old LP. When she and Jonathan began thinking of themselves as boyfriend and girlfriend, monogamy and fidelity were unstated, unquestioned pacts. But that had changed. Standing by the kitchen sink, she drank a glass of water before dialing Jonathan on her cell.

"What time is it anyway?" he asked, in lieu of any hello.

"Why are you whispering?" Meta asked in turn.

"Three in the morning, for crying out loud. Look, hang on a second."

She could hear muffled talking before Jonathan said, in his regular voice, "I'm glad you called actually. I was going to try to reach you today."

"Well, it's good that I—" she started to say.

"No, listen," he interrupted, a delicate resolve underscoring his words. "I do have something I need to tell you, Meta, and I've been racking my brain to find an easy way to say this, but there is no easy way, except—"

"We both know things have changed. I feel bad that—"

"Please, Meta. I need for you to know that I'm seeing someone else."

That did silence her.

"Someone else," she echoed, flat as ice. "Does Gillian know?"

"Nobody knows. It only just happened. You were going to be the first person I told."

His announcement was so blunt that Meta felt faint. Sure, she knew it wasn't fair to expect him to sit home while she dashed around Prague for two months now hoping to bag "phantom butterflies with a net full of holes"—one of Jonathan's nastier criticisms of her quest during yet another recent exchange. But for all the strife and her own guilt about Gerrit, she hadn't really believed it would come to this. Leaning hard against the countertop, she tried to think what to say next. Surprise, anger, relief, an absolutely unfair trace of jealousy, curiosity, a weight lifted—Meta experienced quick waves of contradictory emotions, some of them riptides, others calming a rough sea.

"So, well, I guess I'm happy for you," she managed, voice cracking, hearing the words issue from her and knowing how insincere they sounded.

But Jonathan felt compelled to continue. "Gillian told me you're looking into selling your piano. I wanted you to know I'd like to buy it and give it to you as a kind of peace offering, or whatever you'd want to call it."

"That's kind but I don't think so. Who is she?"

"No one you know."

"Somebody at the office," she conjectured aloud, not as a question or an accusation. It occurred to her that the other voice she'd heard must have been Jonathan's new lover in his bed at this very moment.

"Yes. Her name—"

"That's all right." Her face felt warm and cold at the same time. "As you say, I don't know her."

"Meta, I'm sorry. It all happened very unexpectedly. I've told her everything about you and she feels terrible about the situation, but she really respects what you're doing."

She had called to confess to him about Gerrit but hesitated. A rotten damned-if-she-did, damned-if-she-didn't dilemma. She needed to come clean, but had no desire to appear competitive. Was the best compromise to leave her confession until later? Jonathan was not like past boyfriends. He was a good man, just not *her* good man.

When she didn't speak, he continued, "I want to help you if there's any way I can. A loan, whatever you need."

"Oh, God, no. That's all right, Jonathan. I'll get along."

More silence poured over the line before Jonathan filled it with a last offer. "I can still take care of your mail and plants and the rest until you get back."

"Watering my ficus tree is not a priority. Honestly, don't worry about it. I can ask Gillie to pick up the slack."

"If she's too busy—"

"My mother can help out, or give them away. You need to move on, Jonathan, make a clean break. Maybe one thing you could do would be to take your clothes out of the closet, whatever other personal stuff, sometime before I come home."

"To be sure," he said.

"Oh, and the ring. I can either send it back to you, or when I get home we can make some arrangement."

"Keep it, please."

"No, I'm sure you paid a lot for it. That's not fair."

"Listen, do me a favor. Would you sell it, and keep the money?"

Meta wanted neither to sell the ring nor to keep any money from its sale, but hearing the awkward strain in his words, she knew it was best to drop the matter. "I'll give it some thought. Meantime, I'm sorry I haven't handled things better on my end. I mean that."

They hadn't finished saying goodbye for five minutes before Meta called him back to admit that she hadn't been a saint, hadn't been faithful, and gave him the faintest sketch about Gerrit Mills and herself. It was imperative to get this off her chest. Even though she knew it didn't matter anymore, she needed to apologize.

"So we're even, looks like" was his curiously toneless response, neither accepting nor rejecting her apology.

"It's not about being even," she said. "That's not how I see things. I just didn't want you to feel bad that you were the only one who strayed."

"I'll take it all under advisement."

That was him, she thought after they hung up the second and final time. That was the Jonathan she could never fully wrap her life around.

Gerrit was waiting for her in front of the Sternberg Palace, museum tickets in hand. When she saw him waving, trepidation about what she was doing receded, though she still felt the pressure of threatening tears. "Picture album, then Jiří's opening?"

"I'm all yours," she said.

"You okay?"

She nodded. "So this is your family portrait gallery?" She held his hand, stayed close to him as they entered the museum.

In the first years after he'd settled in Prague, Gerrit often found himself wandering the halls of the Sternberg Palace, a baroque pile that housed the National Gallery's collection of European art. So many favorites were here. El Greco, Rousseau, Kokoschka, not to mention Brueghel. Whenever he needed a break from an assignment, wanted to clear his head, he had haunted the Sternberg. What compelled him about the paintings was not so much style and period, but rather the people depicted in them. To Gerrit, the faces weren't of long-deceased painters' models. Instead, they were regular people one might encounter on any given day. Costumes and equipage might change, the scenery might be of other eras, but in a good painting the faces were always as contemporary as his friends and family. These were real people who lived in real times, ate, drank, loved, fought, prayed, hoped, and died.

"Would you like to meet my mother first?"

"It seems only polite."

He led her to a second-floor gallery. Frans Pieter de Grebber. *Portrait of a Young Lady*, 1630.

"Not everything here is exactly right. Grebber got a few details wrong. But this is basically her."

"She's lovely."

"The eyes are probably the closest. Hers are exactly this blue. The high, broad forehead is right on the money. And my mother has rosy cheeks just like this. She blushes on a dime."

"What's her name, your mother's?"

"Helena," he said, adding, "and my father is Alex, American-
ized from Aleš when they moved to the States, which is kind of
funny since he insisted we speak Czech at home until I was in
grade school. He's in another wing. You'll have to forgive him his
tights and rapier. Usually he wears a business suit."

"Shall we visit him?"

"I want to show you somebody else first. His name was Emil."

Gerrit had grown serious, an almost imperceptible shadow
passing across his face. She now sensed they were here for more
than a lark.

The galleries were all but empty, earlier crowds having left as
the sunlight in the tall windows dimmed. Meta and Gerrit walked
hand in hand past sarcophagi and still lifes, their footfalls resound-
ing on the polished wooden floorboards.

"Here he is."

Meta squinted at the placard. *Saint John the Evangelist on Pat-
mos*, circa 1520. Giovan Francesco Caroto. A moody oil of a young
man with luxuriant long brown wavy hair, seated on a rampart,
abstractedly watching a black bird peck at an open Bible.

"Early sixteenth century," she read. "Your friend Emil is even
older than your mother," turning to Gerrit to offer him a smile for
bringing her here, introducing her to the people in his life in such
an endearing and original way. But Gerrit's face had fallen. She
waited, looking from the dreamy idealistic saint to this pained
man who unconsciously squeezed her hand. "You want to tell me
about him?"

"This isn't Emil, obviously. But I think if he'd lived and grown
up, at one point in his life he might have looked a little like this.
He was my brother, ten years older than me. He died in the Prague
Spring."

"He was only, what, thirteen at the time? You said you were
three when your parents fled the Communist crackdown."

Gerrit led her away toward one of the triple-height windows along the corridor that looked out over a series of walled gardens and tile roofs beyond. Meta leaned against him as he described how his brother had joined some friends protesting the Soviet tanks and wound up getting shot in the stomach. At first it seemed he was going to pull through, but he apparently suffered a sudden hemorrhage in the hospital one night, couldn't be saved. Gerrit's parents buried him in a cemetery near the small cottage they rented each summer up in the mountains, and after the service they decided to continue over the border with their younger son rather than risk staying in a brutalized country. His grandparents followed soon after that, the whole family settling in and around New York.

"In all these years," he continued, "even after the revolution, my parents have refused to come back to visit me. I used to plead with them, tell them everything's different now, but I gave up a long time ago. I get their trauma and have to respect their adamance. Every so often I visit Emil on behalf of all of us, put flowers on his grave, clear the leaves."

"I'm so sorry, Gerrit." Her voice was as soft as the fading light. "Sorry for your parents too. Do you have any actual photos of him?"

"I'll show you sometime," placing his lips briefly against her temple. "But really, I prefer seeing Emil in that painting, thinking of him as somehow still around."

Together they toured other galleries, pausing now and then as Gerrit showed Meta oils in which his grandfather, grandmother, old girlfriends, college pals were depicted. Meta joined in herself, telling him that the young woman in a seventeenth-century portrait looked much like her friend Gillian.

"Just that Gillie is allergic to lace. Gives her a rash."

Although he might not have fully understood it before, Gerrit realized that Meta's presence here in Prague kindled a reawakening in him beyond the love he'd begun to feel for her. The fall of the Berlin Wall, the Velvet Revolution—not since those days a decade ago had he felt history as raw and unfettered as he did now, seeing Meta's frustration and joy, hearing Tomáš's story, holding in his own hands manuscript pages from centuries before. Finding himself again in the midst of living history gave him a jolt of purpose.

For her part, Meta realized as they left the Sternberg Palace that she'd never felt closer to anyone. She knew her breakup with Jonathan, which she'd tell Gerrit about later, was sad, a loss— music might better express what she felt than these paltry words— but in its way it was also a blessing. She knew, too, that war had never directly touched her life, while Irena, Otylie, Jakub, Tomáš, and Gerrit had all been shaped in one way or another by different wars, different political conflicts. Now their wars seemed to be reshaping her.

After a quiet tram ride up the river, they walked to Jiří's warehouse atelier. As they made their way down the long central corridor of the industrial building, which had been divided into individual studios, Meta was reminded of the small pulsating galleries back home in Soho and Chelsea. Some of Jiří's fellow artists were at work on sculptures and paintings, visible beyond open doors. Pop and jazz music emanated from these colorful interiors, as did the mingled odors of oils, acrylics, and welding. It was, Meta thought, the diametric opposite of the Sternberg, which was hushed with dignified calm and smelled of floor polish and the faintest perfume of female museumgoers.

Vivid and kinetic as the art was that she glimpsed in passing, nothing prepared her for the explosion of crimsons, cobalts, viridians, ebonies, and other hues in the spectrum that greeted them when they entered Jiří's studio and pushed through the noisy crowd. His canvases were enormous. Some were rectangular while others stretched into idiosyncratic shapes, octagons and trapezoids. It was immediately clear that Jiří was both serious and radical.

"Amazing," she said, raising her voice over the loud chatter and louder music as she looked around the room.

Amid the friendly jostle, Gerrit felt an arm drop over his shoulder and turned his head to see Jiří grinning ear to ear. A bottle of beer was dangling from his hand against Gerrit's chest, and a half-smoked cigarette hung between his fingers.

"You didn't say it was going to be a rock concert, Jiří."

"Not just any rock," Meta asserted, with a smile of her own directed toward them both. "Anthrax covering Joe Jackson's 'Got the Time.'"

Jiří looked at her admiringly. "You like thrash metal?"

"I was really into this album when I was twenty. *Persistence of Time*. It still kicks."

Freeing his arm and offering her an energetic handshake, Jiří said, "So you must be the famous Meta."

"Not famous, but happy to meet you. Gerrit tells me you're best friends."

"He worships me. I tolerate him," Jiří said, straight-faced, taking a swallow of beer. "You both need something to drink. Come."

As they threaded a path away from the sound system, Gerrit leaned toward Meta and asked, "Is there any music you don't like?"

"Some takes me to the mountaintop, some doesn't. But I couldn't live without it."

A makeshift bar had been set up in one corner of the room where it was a little quieter, if not much. "I hear that you guys went to the Sternberg to see all those old-fogy masterpieces and now you've come to see what real art looks like?"

"I showed her my family portraits," said Gerrit.

Jiří asked Meta, "Did you see the one where he's on horseback killing a dragon with a lance?"

"You never mentioned you'd slain a dragon."

"Well, I do have those bragging rights."

"Here," Jiří said, opening two sweating bottles of beer and handing one to each of them. "Don't you Americans have a phrase, *Honesty is the best policy*? I think it's very honest of Gerrit here to admit his age by showing you those antique paintings of himself and his relatives."

Feeling oddly uplifted, lightened, by this mention of honesty, Meta said, "And yet he doesn't look a day over a hundred."

Jiří drew on the cigarette and exhaled contemplatively. "Well, a hundred and fifty, anyway," giving his friend an appraising look, deadpan.

"How kind of you both. *Na zdraví*."

"*Na zdraví*," Meta echoed, and Jiří tapped his bottle against theirs, saying, "Cheers."

"So, listen, are you going to let us see your paintings or are we here to watch you blow smoke rings?" asked Gerrit.

Meta could hear that his mood had recovered, as had hers in tandem. "Yes, I'd really like to see your work."

Crushing the cigarette against his beer bottle, dropping it in, and leaving it on the bar, Jiří led them from canvas to canvas, pausing to greet others, introducing Meta to painter and musician friends, as well as to his parents, Věra and Pavel, who were leaving but stopped to give Gerrit a hug.

We're his Czech family, Věra told her proudly, and she understood without Gerrit's having to translate. After they left, Meta fondly teased, "You're a man of many families."

Anthrax gave way to Pantera, Pantera to Lamb of God.

"Beautiful," Meta said, raising her voice as they stood before a dynamic painting, the largest in Jiří's exhibit, one she felt might be described as twitchy, restless—impudent forms wanting to jump out of their frame.

Gerrit placed his free hand on his friend's back. "Really impressive work, man."

"Never enough," the painter said, taking a cigarette from a woman standing next to them and squinting at the image, a mix of bright multicolored cloudlike abstractions with suggestions of muted figures either in combat, Meta sensed, or having an orgy. Maybe both.

"What would it take to be enough?" she asked. "What's missing?"

"In art, is it ever possible to do enough? Being alive, man, it's about stretching as far as you can. As many good friends and ideas, as much music—" He gestured around the room, waving the cigarette like a baton. "—As much color."

Meta raised her bottle in another toast. "I envy you. Finding your passion and living it. Gerrit told me you didn't hold back during the revolution either."

"I don't hold back," Jiří replied, "and maybe you don't either. I've heard some very interesting stuff about this search of yours."

For a lightning-quick moment, Gerrit feared that his friend would forget what part of their conversation had been in confidence and what not.

But Jiří continued, "I was sorry to miss your recital on Sunday. Maybe one day I can hear this music?"

"I'll happily play it for you anytime," Meta said. "But right now we're here for you. What's the title of this piece?"

The open studio went on for another couple of hours. Eventually, the crowd having slowly filtered out, the space finally empty, the three decided to head back to Malá Strana for dinner and a nightcap at Baráčnická rychta, where the wooden booths were private and the lighting was low. The conversation, like Jiří's paintings, was full of energy, and it brought out a liveliness in Gerrit that was new to Meta. That these two were close friends spoke volumes about him.

When talk veered briefly to Petr Wittmann, Jiří didn't hide his deep dislike of the man and his "supernatural abilities" as a con artist.

"'Supernatural' isn't how I'd put it, Jiří," said Gerrit. "Brilliantly opportunistic. And smooth as single malt Scotch."

"I don't like scotch any more than I like Wittmann," Jiří groaned, downing yet another beer and changing the subject.

Though Meta made a mental note of Jiří's opinion, she stayed true to the promise she'd made to herself about taking a temporary respite from the sonata manuscript, Tomáš, Wittmann, Kohout, even Mandelbaum.

Hours later, back at Jánská, lying in Gerrit's arms as he slept, Meta marveled at how in balance she felt despite the way her mood seemed to swing from elation to gloom to hope to sadness and back again. He had surprised her on their way home from the pub, by asking, "Did you speak with Jonathan this morning?"

Was it good or a little dangerous that the person you had fallen in love with possessed a sixth sense about you? Did loving, really loving, and being in love mean losing the privacy of hidden worries and reveries? She told Gerrit what had happened.

"I find that hard to believe. I'm prejudiced, but I can't imagine anyone leaving you. Listen, Meta, would you rather be alone right now? You must be upset."

"Yes, I'm not going to lie. When we were good we were good. But more than anything, it relieves me, if you want to know the truth," she said. "I hope that doesn't worry you."

"Why on earth would it?"

"Isn't it a lot safer to fall in love with somebody who might not be available? You've been pretty content here in Prague on your own. Aren't you worried that with me suddenly free, the life you've set up for yourself's a little in jeopardy?"

She tried to smile, but her own worry made a mess of it. She opened her mouth to add something but he put his forefinger to her lips.

"I think there may have been as many as three questions there, but however many there were, the answer to them all is no."

A clock in the next room ticked like a distant dripping sink, a liquid metronome, and it gave her curious solace. She shut her eyes and settled closer to Gerrit. It seemed inconceivable that one woman could fall for two such dissimilar men. Looking back, she was able to explain why she'd been attracted to Jonathan. Stability, security, a bedrock dependability that had been the great yawning absence in her youth. He was all the things Kenneth Taverner hadn't managed to be. But here she lay beside Gerrit, listening to him inhale and exhale. As her own breathing slowed and sleep came over her, she thought, Was her life meant to be a column of ciphers that added up? Much music was, in its way, pure, measured math. Notes were audible numbers. Add some here, subtract some there. Multiply, divide. It was only when the inspired composer pushed computations and reckonings over the edge that those notes morphed into a song, a symphony, a sonata. Gerrit went far beyond the simple math of adding up. This man had become music for her. How else could she put it?

THE ROOSTER DIDN'T THINK it was a wise idea. But for Wittmann this whole business had metastasized into a personal cause. The copy Tomáš had provided him was not good enough, neither as an intellectual tool nor as an artifact of value. So when he announced to Karel Kohout that he intended to go back to Šporkova to get the original, it was clear to his partner—for they had by now formed a loose if unstated partnership in the matter—that he had best come along if only to make sure Petr didn't push things too far too fast.

"*Jenom ho vystrašíš*," Kohout warned. You're only going to frighten him.

You're wrong, my friend, Wittmann assured him when they spoke on the phone. You play the Good Samaritan while I play the prosecutorial public servant. If we persuade him to give us the original it would be best for all involved.

He's stubborn, Kohout argued. I don't see him changing his mind.

Yes, but he's also a fellow Czech musician. I have to make our needs clearer, that's all. Now that we've had a chance to look it over a little, certain questions arise. For instance, what if there are errors in the transcription? Things as small as wrong notes or dropped notes could change the meaning of a passage.

Even at his age he ought to see through that, Kohout retorted.

See through what? I mean what I'm saying. We must have the original in order to do the necessary work on this manuscript to draw accurate conclusions.

In other words, the fact that the original has worth beyond mere scholarship is beside the point?

To Tomáš Lang it ought to be beside the point, Wittmann said with a frown that Kohout could not see, but easily imagined. And if it isn't, I propose to help him come to the realization that the manuscript is, how shall I put it, *bigger* than he is. He must relinquish it, and in doing so he can be assured of a nice little footnote in history. Nicer than what he probably deserves.

A good angle, Wittmann thought. A decent ruse. It shrouded the fact that, as in any enterprise, musical discovery had its commercial side. Scholars who weren't aware of this were, as far as he was concerned, naïfs who deserved what they got. Or didn't get. And that included an apostate like Mandelbaum, who'd once benefited from such a philosophy but now forswore it—just as he must have thought Wittmann had done, or else why so self-righteously dangle such temptation as this manuscript in the first place? Maybe he did overstate his doubts about the thing—dismiss it, in fact—during his initial meeting with Meta, but his investigations in the weeks since had brought him closer to the idea that it wasn't a pastiche. Wasn't a fluke or forgery.

Wittmann had never openly spoken with Kohout about negotiating a possible sale of the manuscript either to an institution or, more likely because more quietly, to a private collector. Proper ownership of the document the young American had brought to their attention seemed tenuous, and if a sale, or a donation with tax implications, was to be made, proprietorship would have to be established first. At least, established adequately enough to withstand any questions that might arise. And if the girl would not relinquish it as valueless, she would have to be otherwise convinced to let it go.

But, again, they had not expressed these concerns in any detail to each other. Such thoughts had silently grown around them like accumulating shadows since Meta Taverner's arrival in Prague, all wrapped up in the musical significance of her find. Or, that is, not *find*. But what had fortuitously fallen into her neophyte hands.

No, as Wittmann saw it, to find something meant to search for it. Everything else was pure chance, an accident, blind luck. Tracking down Johana Langová and, through her, Tomáš Lang—the minor Nazi collaborator fink whom the Communist bosses hadn't considered of sufficient importance to detain as either a drunken nuisance or a failed proletarian—*that* was a find. And to persuade the daft old goat to show Wittmann the treasure he'd stashed for decades? Neither accidental nor lucky. Wittmann had already been in touch with trusted colleagues at Freies Deutsches

Hochstift in Frankfurt, the Universitätsbibliothek in Mainz, and even the Deutsche Staatsbibliothek in Berlin, with whom he shared various tantalizing measures and asked, in strictest confidence, provocative questions that centered on specific years in the penultimate decade of the 1700s.

Wittmann and Kohout met in front of the German embassy at half past seven that evening and strolled up Šporkova. Marta answered the door thinking that perhaps one of her guests had forgotten something at the recital. She recognized Wittmann from his earlier visit, but Kohout was a new face.

"Večírek skončil. Je mi líto, ale všichni už odešli," she told them, after Wittmann said hello, introduced Kohout, and asked if Tomáš was in. The party's over. I'm sorry but everybody's already left.

Her response was confusing, but Wittmann forged on.

We won't take up much of his time. We happened to be in the neighborhood. Met to discuss the manuscript, in fact, and I thought it would be nice for your father to meet my colleague here who is working with me on this project.

Leery but polite, Marta left them on the stone stoop while she went back inside to see if her father was open to more company after an already busy afternoon. She found him sitting in the parlor beside a window, half-contemplating the day, half-dozing toward the night. When he learned who the two men waiting outside to see him were, he agreed to speak with them. Both Professor Wittmann and Meta Taverner needed to be informed about the decisions he had made regarding his dispensation of the manuscripts, original and copied, so he figured he might as well get some of the unpleasant business of disclosure out of the way. Confession now to Wittmann, and maybe the next day to the American, and his obligations would be fulfilled.

Marta allowed the men inside, warning them that her father was tired. Whatever it was they wanted to discuss, if they could keep it short and to the point, that would be best. She left them alone in the dwindling light and withdrew from the room to the hallway, where, out of sight, she eavesdropped on their conversation.

After presenting Kohout, Wittmann said, I hear you're fatigued. Had a party this afternoon.

Yes, we did.

Good, good. I hope you had a pleasant time.

Very nice, Tomáš said, weighing whether or not simply to use this as his opening.

But Wittmann continued, I wanted you to meet my brilliant colleague because he agrees with me, after spending considerable time reviewing your copy of the third movement side by side with the second, that we really must insist, with all due respect, that you give us the opportunity of working with the original.

Otherwise, Kohout added in a more docile tone of voice, it's like you are sending us on a journey through unknown terrain with a map that's only approximate.

Tomáš knew there were no errors. He himself had meticulously transcribed it in the fifties against the possibility that the Communists might confiscate the original.

I assure you that my copy is exact, Tomáš said, looking back and forth at the two men.

That may well be true—, Wittmann began.

But also I think you should know that I have put the original into the hands of the young American scholar, who, it seems, listening to her account, has raised this issue out of obscurity after so many long years, and intends to restore it to its rightful owner.

Tomáš's two visitors sat stunned for a moment. Kohout, knowing his colleague's unruffled demeanor masked a silent diatribe, gathered his own expression back into an uneasy smile and said, That seems reasonable. And who would this rightful owner be?

Otylie Bartošová, Jakub Bartoš's wife. It's a long story. Miss Taverner will tell you.

Wittmann said smoothly, That's fine. We will be sure to consult with her. All we're asking is that you tell her you want it back once she's finished looking it over. This way you can provide us with the original, so we can proceed with our own independent analysis.

That won't be possible, Tomáš said. You will have to work out something directly with her. My role in this is over now. I'm an old man. I've done what I can do.

Wittmann folded his hands into a tidy bundle on his knees and leaned toward Tomáš, looking into his eyes. Let me get this straight. I want to be sure I understand. Did you give it to her, or lend it to her, or did she take it away of her own volition? Is there a chance she made an unfortunate assumption?

Well, Tomáš hesitated.

If she did, Kohout said, I'm sure it was done in all innocence. We're not here to cause her any trouble.

Of course not, Wittmann said, and proceeded delicately to make his case about the national interests that must not be overlooked, concluding, Music is the art form above all others that goes beyond borders, but its archival treasures are like archaeological discoveries and must not be looted by tomb raiders, be they innocent or not.

Tomáš's heart hammered. Of course he had given it to the girl. He had never asked for this responsibility, had always been ambivalent about it, no matter how hard he'd tried to rise to Jakub's bequest. Here were two qualified people who urgently wanted it. One promised to fulfill Jakub's dying wish. The other had located and charmed, or rather cajoled, his sister into believing that such a national treasure should be kept out of any but Czech hands, and should be given only to him—in consideration for an honorarium, the sum of which had yet to be disclosed—for safekeeping, study, and eventual transfer to the republic.

The republic! he'd loudly scoffed when his sister mentioned this last idea. As if any government had ever done anything other than wreck their lives.

No, Tomáš had chosen to seize this moment with both shaky hands. In a way, he believed, he was providing the manuscript two very different opportunities to find its way home. Be it Wittmann or Meta, he reasoned, one of them would carry his albatross the rest of the way. Rather than a betrayal, this was its best chance of survival. It was not unlike what Otylie herself had done. Surely she would have approved.

Now, though, he was stymied as to how to account for it. Only hours before he'd thought this whole business was nicely settled. He had to admit that Wittmann and Kohout, two distinguished fellow countrymen, sketched a fairly credible case for keeping it in Czech hands despite Tomáš's own disdain for what he saw as Johana's gullibility. But he didn't know what to tell them. Best, he thought, to feign confusion, buy himself time to think.

"*Myslím, že jsem jí to dal. Ale kdoví, komu to opravdu patří,*" he tried. I believe I gave it to her, but who owns it may be unclear.

You *believe* you gave it to her? Wittmann chided.

I need a moment to remember.

Let me help you, the professor continued, his voice lowered, as if to prevent its being recorded by hidden microphones. We know about you, your past. Let me tell you a bit about us. We too have had to work with occupiers in order to pursue our dreams. You and I both understand that a man has to look out for himself while making sure not to harm the homeland. It's a delicate dance. For hundreds of years, artists and scholars of every stripe have had to toady to patrons they sometimes hated in order to keep benefactors' money coming in. We stand near the bottom of the social order, despite whatever flattery the middle and ruling classes toss our way. You have never been treated properly, in my opinion. I believe I can promise you one thing if you make it possible for us to have the original. In our findings, we will be abundantly clear as to the important, even heroic role you've played in this matter.

Thank you, Tomáš muttered, wearying of the musicologist.

By the way, would you mind satisfying my curiosity about something?

If I can.

I was just wondering how our American friend, *slečna* Tavener, was able to find you. Your sister tells me that she never spoke with her.

Tomáš shrugged. Another American, a friend of hers, lives nearby on Jánská. Writer, a journalist, I think he said. He seems to have heard me playing—no, it was his piano teacher friend, an American who—

First it was the Germans, then the Soviets. Now it sounds as if the Americans have come to invade the republic, Kohout said, his uncomfortable laugh ignored by the others.

Yes, well.

And what would this other American's name be? Wittmann pressed, ignoring Kohout, not for a moment missing the possible reference to Gerrit.

If I remember right—

Marta had listened long enough and stepped out of the shadows, saying, I think that's about all the time we have, gentlemen. Dinner is ready and, as you can see, my father's not well and we don't want to cause him stress, do we?

Of course not, Kohout said, startled, rising from his chair. We were just leaving.

Wittmann rose more slowly, annoyed by her intervention. Not looking at Marta, taking Tomáš's hand in both of his own, he finished, Well, I do hope you'll give some thought to what we've said. It's been splendid seeing you again.

Once out of earshot, down in the elegant square that fronted the old Lobkowicz Palace, Wittmann cursed and seethed. Kohout stared at the cobbles, hands in his pockets, then looked skyward. A darkening doubt had come over him in the Langs' parlor about his role here. Wittmann still had the fire of ambition blazing in his belly, but Kohout had to ask himself whether the prize they sought hadn't already slipped away irretrievably. He didn't like the expression on Tomáš's daughter's face when she ushered them out of her house. The withering farewell she offered at the door made it as certain as death they would not be given another audience with her father. Mandelbaum, whom Karel Kohout respected, intended to look out for his protégée, putting the original doubly at a distance from them. Most aggravating was that this Taverner girl had played a far better chess match than he might have thought possible, given how nervous she'd seemed when they encountered her in Old Town Square, how diffident she appeared to be in his office, audaciously showing up with a homemade transcript of the original. Even at the time he had thought, How amateur can you get?

He now sensed it wasn't amateurism that informed her choices, but distrust. Had it been up to Kohout alone, he would have been inclined to concede checkmate. However, he'd known Petr Wittmann too long to believe that his colleague was going to let the matter drop so easily.

The two entered the first pub they saw and ordered pints. Wittmann's mood had changed. No longer rancorous, he now grew contemplative. As they drank a second round, he proved Kohout's prediction right by formulating, sotto voce, an idea that reached beyond what he had ever risked in the past. His prior scholarship may have involved subterfuge, a little restrained plagiarism, some occasional intrigue. Whose didn't? But what he asked struck Kohout as borderline mad.

First, did Kohout still have the phone number that Johana Langová said those two girls had left in her mailbox? Second, the journalist who came by the other day asking about puppet theater and the postrevolution resurfacing of cultural artifacts—wasn't it likely he was none other than this fellow living on Jánská? And third, while it was clear the sonata had been harbored by many caretakers, wasn't it time to take action and wrest it from the clutches of the unworthy?

MANDELBAUM EMERGED FROM CUSTOMS wearing his signature black pullover and wide-wale black corduroys, looking like a disheveled incarnation of the great conductor Karajan or maybe Bernstein in his white-thatched days, and wrapped his long arms around Meta. Whenever time passed without their seeing each other, she always forgot just how tall he was, how lean and graceful, what a larger-than-life figure. Holding her away from him and studying her smiling face, he said, "You look positively aglow. Who'd have thought that Prague soot and diesel exhaust could do such wonders for a girl's complexion?"

"Shameless flatterer. I'm pasty as a potato and you know it. Here, let me take your shoulder bag."

"I'm not a total cripple yet, little Sherpa girl. I can manage my own carry-on."

"Were you able to reach—"

"Yes, your mother's quite devoted, you know. She made it to the bank before they closed. I have it right here," he said, patting the side of his well-traveled bag.

They walked down the corridor, falling into old, easy rhythms. Meta hadn't realized how much she missed the man.

"Baggage claim's down this way," she said.

"I don't have anything to claim. I come with one spare shirt, a couple of pairs of socks, my toothbrush, heart meds, reflux meds, cholesterol meds, and whatever other dainties my dear wife said I couldn't live without. I had more to wrap up at home than I'd thought, and barely made the plane as it was."

"I'm sure we can find you whatever you need."

"Much more important than my picayune needs, tell me how your recital went. Is the movement a decided connect? Do you have a clear cycle coming together? You'll play it for me a hundred times as promised? How's Sam *et famille*? Catch me up on everything."

During the drive back from Ruzyně airport in Sam's crummy four-door Škoda, Meta told Mandelbaum, yes, there was a clear connect. Explained that the original was under lock and key at Gerrit's flat, where Irena's movement could now join it.

"And you absolutely trust him?"

"There are people here in Prague I don't trust. He's definitely not one of them."

Hard by the Municipal House on Náměstí Republiky, Mandelbaum checked into his hotel, whose lobby was ornately decorated with art nouveau murals, chandeliers straight out of a Klimt dream, windows incised with arum lilies on intertwining stems. He left his things with the concierge and gave the desk receptionist an unmarked package housing the manuscript, to be placed in the hotel safe until he returned from lunch. Meta was waiting for him in the restaurant bar.

"Too stuffy-sterile in here, and I want to stretch my legs. Is that little hole-in-the-wall Konvikt still in business?"

"You know Konvikt? That's where Sam and I first met."

"Do I know Konvikt. Please, a little respect for your elders. Who do you think turned Sam on to Konvikt in the first place?"

They walked, Mandelbaum admiring this and that in a city he knew more intimately than Meta might have guessed. She envied him his cosmopolitan ease and at the same time felt comforted, if a touch nervous, that he was here. If ever she could use a sounding board—a figure of speech she always loved because it turned people into pianos—now was that time.

Mandelbaum sighed with satisfaction as they entered the monolith of lush smoke that was Konvikt's interior and sat at a free table near an open courtyard window in the back room. "Ah, yes. This is more like it," he said, removing his coat and settling himself. When the waiter came, he ordered house beer for them both with his slow but serviceable Czech, and asked for a menu. "Sop," he explained to Meta with a wink. "I haven't eaten since they handed out dry mystery-meat sandwiches over the English Channel."

"Don't forget tonight's a dinner reunion with the Kettles, so save room."

"Yes, Mother," he said, and ordered grilled sausage and sauerkraut when the waiter returned with their pints.

"Feel good to be back?"

"As if I never left. I feel the same when I'm in Paris and Vienna. But now then," he continued, relishing his first swallow, savoring the inch of foamy head that banded the top of his pint glass. "Meta first, then music, then Mandelbaum after. Tell me what's up with this new love of yours."

"It's progressed since I spoke with you last."

"Which means it's a fast-moving storm."

"More like the rainbow that follows the storm."

Meta described how she'd quickly grown close to Gerrit, and how her relationship with Jonathan, which had been unraveling since the day Irena gave her the manuscript, finally fell apart. She faulted herself every step of the way, as the father figure across the wobbly round table gently defended her from herself.

"I happen to be a rare example of the lucky one who met the only person he'd ever want to be with first," he said. "But don't forget, my dear, you were not married. Apparently with good reason."

"Maybe so. Still, it's hard to feel good, given how it all ended. But it's not like I feel shattered either."

"I always thought Jonathan was a decent chap who, despite his good intentions, never really understood you. I also hoped you'd find somebody who, like my Annalise, loves music but doesn't need to breathe it every waking hour to stay alive."

"Gerrit's exactly that way. He really seems to get music but doesn't live or die for it."

"Perfect," Mandelbaum said.

"Well, no, he's not perfect. I mean, he has his own flaws and demons."

"Who doesn't?"

Meta took a sip from her glass, shrugged.

"Is he in love with you?"

So forthrightly asked, that one took Meta aback. She looked down at her hands, remembering how just that morning Gerrit had kissed them. "Yes, I think. I really hope so."

"Good man. When do I meet him?"

"We could meet tomorrow morning, I thought."

"I have business tomorrow morning. Can we do lunch, then afterward you play it? If the manuscript's at his place, I assume he has a piano. The movements can be reunited then."

"There's a decent Steingraeber downstairs in his landlady's front room," Meta said, figuring Mandelbaum must have a meeting scheduled with one or another of his musicologist colleagues. Wittmann was her guess, and she inwardly flinched as she thought this, recalling Jonathan's accusation. How was it she had never really asked herself just why Mandelbaum decided to drop whatever he was doing and rush four, five thousand miles to be at her side? A long way to go just to meet a former student, listen to her play an unknown manuscript. Though these thoughts made her uncomfortable, she trusted her mentor to fill her in when he felt she needed the information. The man was like a river, not to be pushed along.

Back at his hotel after leaving Konvikt, a reluctant Mandelbaum retrieved his package and handed her Irena's goatskin portfolio, which housed the manuscript.

"I still believe it belongs in the safe here, my dear."

"I know it's valuable, but we're not in some spy movie. It'll be fine at Gerrit's. Now get settled and I'll come pick you up for dinner tonight," she said, and gave him a hug before heading to the metro.

Clothes and hair still reeking of Konvikt smoke, Meta let herself into Gerrit's apartment, holding her coat close to her breast.

"What an excellent surprise," Gerrit said, getting up from his desk.

"I have a bigger one," she told him, out of breath from the hurried walk up Nerudova. "Look what I've got."

With that she pulled out Irena's scuffed burgundy-colored satchel.

"Is this it, in here?" marveling at how unassuming the thing looked. Nine out of ten people wouldn't bother stooping to pick it up off the sidewalk.

She went over to his desk, where she set it down, turned, and kissed him. "It sure is. The original of the second movement. What Irena gave me before she died. This is what started everything."

"Can I see?"

"I waited to open it until I got here so we could be together," she said, unstringing the thong wrapped around an ambered bone button and pulling out the manuscript.

"It's an honor," Gerrit said, and Meta could tell he meant it. "Shall I fetch the other movement?"

"Please," handing him the skeleton key.

He brought the dispatch case that housed Tomáš's brown envelope and stood by her side while she opened it and placed the movements together for the first time in sixty years. Both stood there awestruck. Not just by the significance of this small moment, but by the beauty of the physical scores, one tattered and soiled, the other remarkably fresh. Meta wanted nothing more than to sit down and examine every millimeter of what lay before her on Gerrit's desk, but she had promised Mandelbaum they'd do the comparative examination when all of them were together. "Since he's come all this way, a promise is a promise."

"Agreed. But this merits a toast," Gerrit said, heading for the kitchen. "Let me see what's in the cabinet while you put them away for safekeeping."

"So what are you writing?" she called out to him in the other room, as she locked the secretary.

"Take a look," he replied. "How's a glass of red sound?"

"Great, but just a finger's worth."

Sitting down in Gerrit's chair, Meta read what was on the laptop screen. Such a wonderful writer, she thought, as she casually browsed what was there and in the notebook that lay open next to the computer. She even loved his handwriting, the way he formed letters, the dark blue of his ink. When she glanced at another of the notebooks lying on the desk and opened it out of curiosity, she was taken aback by what she saw. She hastily turned a page, then another. Her recent life was here. Her struggle, her search. And what was this about Petr Wittmann? What was any of this doing in one of Gerrit's notebooks?

When Gerrit walked into the room with the wine, his smile faded. Meta looked up and said, as calmly as she could, "I'm sorry. I didn't mean to pry. But why didn't you tell me you were writing everything down?"

He set the glasses on a side table, nervous and embarrassed. "No, I'm the one who's sorry. Writing notes is just something I do, the same way your lifeline is music."

"You should have told me, shouldn't you? I can't tell if I should be flattered or weirded out. I mean, if I were a composer and decided to write songs about you behind your back, how would you feel?"

"I suppose if they were love songs—"

"But this isn't a love song," she said, closing the notebook and crossing her arms. "It's reportage. Notes and facts and lines of inquiry for I don't know what, an article, a book?"

His cheeks flushed. "The truth of it, Meta, is that it is a kind of love song. For you, what you're doing here. That doesn't excuse the fact that I've been writing it down without your knowing. I just didn't want you to think I was using you for your story."

Meta listened carefully and watched him while he spoke, then uncrossed her arms and stood. Looking away from Gerrit, running her eyes over his wall of photographs, she surprised him by saying, "And I was concerned about using you too much. Your time, your energy, your knowledge of Prague, your Czech. Your encouragement."

"No, please. My time, energy, all of it, is yours for the taking."

"What's that about Wittmann in there?"

Rubbing the back of his neck with a flattened palm, Gerrit said, "Another confession. I arranged to see him not long ago. Told him I wanted to discuss that story I was writing on Czech puppet theater."

"What?" Meta half-laughed, turning back to Gerrit. "What does Wittmann know about puppets?"

"More than you might imagine, actually. Point is, I really went there to see if he'd let his guard down about you and the manuscript. I got nothing out of him, as it happens. I thought I might try again, but things developed too quickly after that for him not to see through my ruse. So I left it alone."

"Understood," said Meta with a relieved sigh.

"I did make a call to an older colleague at the *Prague Post* and, without telling him why I was asking, got a little history on Wittmann. What kind of influence he had in the days before the revolution, what sway he has now."

"And?"

"To cut a long story short, he had sway then and still has, even if his star doesn't shine quite as bright."

"So Paul's right about him."

"Looks that way," Gerrit said, taking a step toward her. "More important, will you please accept my apology?"

"Any other confessions to make?"

"No, none. We're okay, then?"

"We were never not okay," she said, giving him a kiss. "Just you need to know you can tell me anything and everything."

"Fair enough."

"Now, what about that toast to the remarriage of the manuscripts?" she said, retrieving the wineglasses from the table and handing one to Gerrit.

THE ONLY WAY HE COULD LOOK MORE GUILTY, Mandelbaum mused when they shook hands in the hotel lobby, would be if his face were doubled, one in profile, the other with the same self-assured smile, and both displayed with a booking number beneath.

But that was ridiculous, and Mandelbaum knew it. Here were two of the more distinguished men in their esoteric field seeing each other after a long hiatus. And, as a matter of incontrovertible fact, there was a phase decades ago when Mandelbaum's own face might have appeared above a similar string of numbers. Besides, he had no evidence that his Czech colleague had done anything wrong other than put himself in the middle of things. The point of his trip to Prague at least in part was to allow his old friend a chance to rectify matters in person, get the scholarly process of this discovery on the right track. There was still some possibility Petr hadn't robbed Paul, or rather, Paul's student.

He erased the imaginary profile and perp numbers from his mind, warmly shook his friend's hand. "How good it is to see you after—what has it been?"

"Six years, no, maybe seven. Whose centenary were we at up in London? Annalise obviously keeps you stored in first-rate moth-balls. You haven't aged a day."

"Renata did her best by you to the last, I see. But it looks like she got some of your hair in the settlement."

"Ex-wives have a way of doing that. I think thinning hair gives one an air of greater authority."

Serious for a moment, Mandelbaum said, "I'm sorry about the divorce, Petr."

"Couldn't be helped," he responded, a bit subdued, before clapping his hands and returning to form. "Breakfast here at the hotel all right? I know you don't have starched white tablecloths and such heavy silverware back in the swamps of New Jersey."

"This place has always been a little too Alphonse Mucha for my taste, but I hear the kitchen's good. Let's do."

This was how they'd been from the very first. Mandelbaum had liked Petr Wittmann for his erudite humor, old-fashioned in its way but crisp. And Wittmann respected Paul for his depth of musical knowledge more than he was ever quite able to admit. Besides, they always enjoyed the amicable sparring. As they ordered smoked trout and scrambled eggs, and splurged on champagne with their orange juice, Mandelbaum allowed himself the luxury of some unguarded dialogue with his fellow musical obsessive-compulsive.

Wittmann wondered what Mandelbaum made of Philip Glass, who, as far as he could tell, composed "with a machine gun." He asked what it was about American culture that so many of its rock musicians died in their twenties while its classical composers—Aaron Copland, Elliott Carter, Milton Babbitt—lived into their nineties, even made it to a hundred? Was it a dietary difference or merely drugs? He speculated about how many classical composers' estates were suing this or that wealthy Hollywood composer for lifting some of the best passages for their movie scores.

Mandelbaum drew his eyebrows together in mock disapproval. "You spend too much time keynoting highbrow colloquia, my friend. The word's not 'lifting' anymore. It's called 'sampling' now, just ask your students. All acceptable in the rap world. Your beloved Wagner was one of the biggest 'samplers' of all time, so I see no need to make remarks about sturdy film composers who get a little honest inspiration from the classics."

"I stand corrected," Wittmann said with an amused cough, as the food arrived at their table. "How soon can we expect a learned monograph from you on the contrapuntal influences of neoclassical Stravinsky on Run-D.M.C. and Aerosmith?"

That they found themselves discussing the appropriation of other people's ideas hadn't escaped Mandelbaum's notice. He was still sharp, Wittmann was. Sharp as ever, despite the difficult divorce a year earlier. Which only confirmed for Mandelbaum that, after dismissing Meta's find to her face, Wittmann wasn't acting out of character when he reported to friends in the musicology community that he had examined a hitherto unrecorded eighteenth-century manuscript of potentially landmark importance. Though the through line from the manuscript to her was indisputable, Meta Taverner's name had been glaringly absent, it seemed, in his various correspondence. So nimble was Petr's disclosure, so agile his working of the small musicological grapevine, neither fully claiming pride of place in the discovery nor hinting that he had nothing to do with it, it was plain that he had poached or piggybacked on other scholars' work before. Paul had no intention of filling Meta in on the past he and Wittmann shared, but felt it imperative that he personally set things right.

His thoughts must have been easily readable on his face, as Wittmann now cut directly from their silly jousting to the chase itself.

"I know why you've come to Prague," he said, after wiping his lips with a napkin and dropping it back into his lap. "Under the circumstances, I can't say that I blame you. I'd probably do the same thing if our roles were reversed."

Mandelbaum laid his fork on the plate. "And what have I come to Prague for?"

"You've come to personally register a complaint that in my very delimited, very preliminary announcement to a handful of scholars about the sonata discovery I failed to mention your charming acolyte."

"That's one reason."

"On that count at least I could have saved you the trip. After you phoned to set up this little tête-à-tête, I realized what that tone in your voice was all about. I think you Americans have a phrase, *poker face*. Well, you have a bad *poker voice*. Your animosity came through loud and clear."

Mandelbaum smoothly pushed his plate away and folded his large hands on the table. "I don't feel animosity toward you, Petr. I feel confused by you."

"You'll be pleased to know that I intend to rectify any misconceptions I may have caused, inadvertent though they were, with those few colleagues in question, and will credit Miss Tavener and you yourself for making the initial find."

"Her name's Taverner, not Tavener."

"Another mistake for me to correct. I must have been thinking of that crazy Russian Orthodox Brit composer."

"I wouldn't call John Tavener crazy, but that's neither here nor there. Tell me, is it true you told her—having by your own admission announced its discovery and without, by the way, seeing the original—it was a forgery, a fake?"

"That was my considered first impression," Wittmann replied.

"You seem to have made quite the about-face on that count."

Wittmann leaned forward. "I have. Our friend Karel Kohout and I had dinner one evening a while ago and this business came up. Both of us have shown considerably more due diligence in the matter than you seem to give us credit for."

"I never said anything about Kohout one way or the other."

"Be that as it may, Kohout, despite his own negative impression of the manuscript, did some asking around, mostly about the narrative your Meta gave regarding its supposed Prague origins, and he happened to locate an emeritus from the department who recalled having heard an uncannily similar story. A brother and sister living in Josefov, neither of them particularly compos mentis, survivors from the Nazi occupation days, had made noises about an early sonata manuscript, divvied up into three parts as Caesar divided Gaul."

"And?"

"And so I began doing a little of my own research—let me repeat, my *own*—and I tracked down the sister. As supremely paranoid and unhelpful a person as you'd ever want to meet. It turns out they're both still alive, though the brother, whose house in Malá Strana seems to have been burned by Nazi arsonists on their way out of Prague, had moved back across the river after the revolution."

"Why didn't you contact Meta to let her know what you were doing?"

"Because I had nothing concrete to tell her. For all I knew I was wasting my own precious time. Why waste hers?"

Born politician, Mandelbaum thought, not without reluctant appreciation. No wonder he breezed through the Communist years. Everyone on the far side of the Iron Curtain had marveled at the freedom he enjoyed to travel abroad to conferences and do research in Western institutional repositories. Equally impressive was the ease with which he shed any taint of Party membership when the Reds were swept out of power and the new democratic Czechoslovak Federal Republic took its place. Their shared history, dating back to their earliest days, had in part been protected by this very survivor's genius Wittmann possessed.

Petr was certainly the braver, more brazen, and perhaps crazier of the two young men, Mandelbaum—senior by some years—had long since understood. Had Wittmann been searched by border guards at the frontier and discovered transporting antiquarian manuscript materials out of the country without Party authorization, he might not have seen the outside of a jail cell for the rest of his days. But then, as now, he seemed to have a taste for recklessness, especially if he'd convinced himself that his motives were ultimately right. He was speaking, though, and Mandelbaum snapped back into the present.

"Besides, the sister told me during my second or third visit that two young women were pressuring her, harassing her on her intercom, leaving notes. Not the subtlest approach for a field researcher, I wouldn't have thought."

"You should have contacted Meta, shared your findings," Mandelbaum asserted. "You wouldn't have a clue about this if I hadn't sent her to you for advice."

"Oh, don't worry. I was going to call her once I knew there was something to call her about. I have her phone number on my desk, and she has my card, for that matter. I must admit I was dismissive during our initial meeting, and it seemed only right that if I was to reverse my opinion, I ought to do so with a few hard facts filling my sails, no?"

Mandelbaum let out a sigh.

"Paul, stop it. You're trying to make me feel like a common criminal. If I didn't know you better, I'd start to resent all this."

"Relax, Petr. If I thought you were a criminal, I'd have to concede you're the most *distingué* of all criminals I've met," he said, easing up, even as he made subtle reference to their presumptuous past.

"So," Wittmann said, offering a provisional smile. "Friends and partners again?"

"I never said we were enemies. All I ask is that you put your time and energies into what I'd originally requested."

"Please remind me," the smile fading. "Just what was it you requested I do?"

"Confirm my opinion about the score's authenticity and value. Help point Meta toward leads that might connect her with the missing movements. Discuss possible provenance, since it was owned by a Czech. And if you were of a mind, offer her your thoughts on attribution."

"In other words, appraise it for you and do all her work for her?"

"It's called scholarly advisement, academic counsel, the interchange of ideas. Not to mention professional courtesy between colleagues."

"There was no reciprocity in her approach to me. She didn't trust me enough to show me the original. And now that you mention it, without seeing the original, how can I possibly comment on its potential value?"

Realizing that diners at nearby tables had turned their heads and were watching, Mandelbaum said, "Let's lower our voices, what say? Never know who's listening."

Wittmann glanced nonchalantly around, dropped his voice. "Let's just suppose this manuscript proves to be something on the order of what we handled back when—"

"Really? You're really going to say that here?"

"Well, let's be honest. Its ownership is murky at best—"

"We don't know that. The owner might still be alive."

"If it was quietly placed with a private collector," Wittmann glided on, "not only could we benefit, but your young protégée would be able to stop living hand to mouth for years to come. Productive years, I might imagine."

Mandelbaum started to speak but was again interrupted.

"Not that I'm saying this is a remotely feasible course of action—"

"You're out of order, Petr. Ownership before commerce."

Wittmann sat forward, placing his elbows on the table and folding his arms. "So you're all angelic now? Is that what I'm to understand? Such niceties didn't trouble you in days of yore. We were a superb team. Why walk away from this?"

"These aren't days of yore. My goal right now is to advise Meta."

"Are you telling me that you came here just to protect your Meta from me, with no other motive slightly in mind?"

"Such as?"

"Oh, I don't know. Such as keeping the manuscript for yourself, if a partnership doesn't interest you, perhaps making your own deal."

"Have you gone insane?"

"Glad to hear it," Wittmann said, ignoring the question. "Let me remind you of a few things, though."

Mandelbaum clasped his fingers into a knot on the starched tablecloth. He didn't want to give Wittmann the pleasure of a response.

"You made it abundantly clear to me when you bowed out of our arrangement that you questioned my motives in wanting those manuscripts out of Czechoslovakia. It wasn't always like that. Early on, you agreed that originals of Dvořák, Mozart, all these unique treasures that were being destroyed by damp and mildew and insects in nasty cellars, uncataloged, neglected, some of them fed to the fire by ignoramuses and ideologues, or stolen by thugs who wanted them for every wrong reason, all of them should be rescued, taken to a safe haven in the West."

Mandelbaum sat back in his chair.

"Did you or did you not?"

"I did."

"You also agreed at the time that since we couldn't risk donating the works to a Western institution for fear word would get out about our activities, and I at least would wind up in a very ugly, very solitary prison cell, the only solution was to put them into individuals' hands. Discreet individuals. Individuals who would take care of the materials, know their intrinsic value, appreciate the opportunity of custodianship."

"Yes, I agreed about that too."

"And you further agreed, since we had no way of financing all our travel and other expenses, which were not inconsiderable, when we were just getting started in our careers, that the only way to do it was to sell the manuscripts. And sell them below fair market value, with the promise that the buyers—we trusted only a few—would keep our secret, and keep the papers out of the public eye until such time as they could safely be made available to scholars. You agreed to that as well, didn't you?"

"All of this is basically true, yes. And so?"

"So, what we have here is a situation that runs the opposite of what was going on back in the late sixties, early seventies. Here's a manuscript that, in lieu of a living owner, must be repatriated, not in the possession of some eager thirty-year-old whose family never spilled a drop of blood in the cause of its survival. Our government, flawed as it may be, is not the culture-hating mob of Marxist morons that preceded it. There are collections here now that are more than capable of assuming responsibility."

Mandelbaum leaned forward. "That's a very pretty speech, Petr. But I have nothing to say on the subject." Seeing Wittmann shrug with irritation, he moved ahead. "What interests me at this moment is whether you have made enough progress in the interim that you'd be willing to confer with Meta."

"I have and I will," taking the hint and shifting the tone of his voice back to urbane cordiality.

"She deserves full credit for the discovery of the middle movement, and for setting the research in motion. Thereafter, all's fair in love and war. Even if it's just musical warfare."

"I'm no warrior, so don't worry about it." Wittmann waved the waiter to their table, passed him some crown notes after telling him they needed to settle.

"Let me charge that to my room," protested Mandelbaum.

"Nonsense, this is on me." As they left the restaurant, Wittmann took in a hearty deep breath outside and asked if Mandelbaum had as yet made his pilgrimage to the astronomical clock in Old Town Square. "I recall it's one of your favorite things here. If we walk a little faster we can be there for the eleven o'clock tolling and the grand procession of saints and devils."

"I'm only just in town, as I said. Haven't seen much beyond your handsome face."

They chatted about Petr's teaching and Paul's retirement as they ambled beneath the arched stonework of Powder Gate and past Celetná's elegant windows sparkling with glassware and jewelry, its high-end boutiques that displayed nary a hint of its earlier history of Eastern European deprivations or the drear of Red rule. Thanks to none other than Petr Wittmann, Mandelbaum had been allowed to visit Czechoslovakia for months at a time as a guest lecturer or scholar in residence in the days when frontiers here could be tricky for Westerners to negotiate. He remembered how colorless and tired this now-chic street had looked then. Never a fan of the Madison Avenues of the world, or what excesses they represented, Mandelbaum still had to admit this one was more palatable than before.

"So," he said before they entered the square to witness the mechanical pageant that had taken place every hour off and on since the fifteenth century. "When can Meta, you, and I sit together and discuss these manuscripts like proper scholars?"

"Manuscripts, plural?" Wittmann said, stopping.

Mandelbaum suppressed a cringe at his slip. "It sounded as if you located another movement of the sonata through this woman and her brother," he improvised.

"Nothing of the kind," Wittmann improvised back. "Has your Meta come up with anything more than what she first showed me and Karel?"

"I haven't talked with her about it. I wanted to speak with you first."

Each knew that the other wasn't telling the truth, and that they were now forced to hedge in order to keep a semblance of peace.

"When do you intend to see her?"

"This afternoon."

"Well, maybe it's best for all involved that you take your meeting with her. Convey my best regards. Tell her that I intend to give her credit for the work that's been done thus far. And then we can put our collective heads together."

Mandelbaum said, "That sounds like an excellent idea. By the way, there's no need to mention my name in any of your writings about this. Consider me an observer."

"As you please. Meantime, you'd better run or you're going to miss the tolling."

"You're off?"

"I realize I'm late for a student conference," stealing a glance at his watch. "Being emeritus, you've forgotten all about the endless obligations of academe."

Mandelbaum readily accepted the excuse. He had heard enough and needed time to think. They shook hands with an almost genuine amity. But as he turned to go, Wittmann added, "In all this splendid superfluity of determining acknowledgment, we haven't spent a single minute talking about attribution. If, just say, it does prove to be a lost Mozart—"

"You know it's not Mozart."

"P. D. Q. Bach, Muddy Waters, whoever—"

Mandelbaum couldn't help but chuckle before saying, "Neither of them is Czech."

"—it's a precious thing. The composer had a genius both for breaking rules of the period and for conforming to essential tropes."

Wittmann's statement was as simple and solid as one of the square cobbles beneath their feet. For all their joking and obfuscation—"muddy waters" pretty much summed things up—Mandelbaum suddenly wished he'd not acquiesced to Meta's request that he bring the original of the sonata's middle movement with him. She was the only person besides her mother who knew it was here. It had become essential that this remain their secret.

"See you soon, my friend," Wittmann said, jutting his chin. "I'm glad you're looking so well," and strode away across the square as the clock began to chime, launching its painted medieval characters into pirouetting action from behind their carved and decorated doors.

How strange it had been not to spend the night with Meta after she and Sam Kettle went out for dinner with their mentor Mandelbaum. Or rather, how strange that it was strange, given the newness of their relationship. She had stayed in Vinohrady, saying she didn't want to wake him if her dinner ran late, but his awareness of her absence made it difficult for him to fall asleep. He tried to calm himself with the memory that her body and his had intertwined right here, naked in these bedclothes the night before. But her scent and his own, the salty ocean scent of lovemaking, didn't calm him. Just the opposite.

Gerrit had always been welcome at the Hodeks' breakfast table, though he rarely availed himself of the standing invitation. Having gotten up at six after a few hours of vague dreams, he made coffee and sat at his desk working for a time, revising an article about the Czech Republic's evolving emergence into the European economy. When he heard muffled voices downstairs, he decided that his deadline was well in hand and company among friends might clear his head. He dressed, finger-combed his hair in the mirror, and walked down the interior staircase that led from his flat into the Hodeks' kitchen, knocking before he entered.

Mr. Hodek had left for work but Andrea and her mother were finishing breakfast.

"You not look very good" were the girl's words of greeting.

"Nice to see you too. I'm fine. Just didn't sleep much last night."

"Love is good thing," she continued, "but maybe not good for you."

"Andrea," her mother warned, and offered Gerrit toast and coffee before leaving the kitchen to get ready for the day.

"You're wrong," Gerrit said, sitting next to his young friend at the heavy refectory table. "Real love and I haven't kept company in a while, if ever, is all. It's very good for me. I just need to make sure it's something I'm good at myself."

A quizzical birdlike tip of her head preceded Andrea's question, in Czech, asking him to explain what he'd just said. Rather than telling her that one day when she was older she'd understand, he spoke in the familiar role of her English teacher.

The power of the preposition, he said in Czech. Remember I told you the little words are the ones that carry the biggest weight? Prepositions such as *for* and *at* are like strong ants. They haul around heavy words on their backs, pronouns like *me* and *it* that are a hundred times their size and weight.

But *me* and *it* are little words too.

Yes, except when you start thinking about what they stand for. *It* is love. *Me* is Gerrit. And I can't honestly tell you I fully understand either of those things, but I'm working on it.

He spoke in a tone meant to convey that they should change the subject, but Andrea wasn't finished. Is she going to live with you here now?

You're moving us along pretty fast, aren't you? Meta already has a place to stay, Gerrit said, sounding more like an exasperated parent than he meant to. She's probably going to be leaving Prague pretty soon to look for the other missing part of the music.

Where will she go?

I don't know. Maybe London. She needs to try to follow where the lady went who owned it many years ago.

Andrea's mother returned to the kitchen, asked Gerrit if he wanted more toast, maybe a pear or some grapes, then tapped her wristwatch, frowning at her daughter. Thanking the woman, he took an Anjou pear from the wooden bowl in the center of the table.

The girl switched to English when her mother turned away. "If she go, you leave Prague too?"

For all his thoughts about Meta, this simple question hadn't dawned on him. "I'm not sure. We haven't talked about it."

"I miss you bad."

"I'd miss you, too, Andrea. But I think it's premature to worry about such things," he said, knowing she probably didn't understand the word *premature* and hoping she wouldn't request a translation.

She didn't. Instead she plucked a purple grape from the bunch in the bowl, set it on the table before her, and meditatively rolled it back and forth from one forefinger to the other.

"When she come here next?" she asked in an abruptly tiny voice.

"I'm meeting her professor friend, Dr. Mandelbaum, for lunch. After that we're heading back here so he can see the manuscript."

Andrea didn't look up, but continued her finger-hockey game in contemplative silence. She wasn't herself this morning. First adolescent case of moonstruck jealousy?

"Andrea, you know what? You don't look so well either."

The girl sat unspeaking for another moment, then brightened. Smiling at Gerrit, she said, "No. I am very well, very, very," and popped the grape into her mouth, then left the kitchen to pack her things for school.

A few hours later, Gerrit himself left for the Indian restaurant where he had agreed to meet Meta and her mentor. He and Mandelbaum greeted each other with a kind of friendly awkwardness, but quickly found their way to warmer banter. Mandelbaum reminisced about Prague's fall skies leaden with "coal smoke and the cumuli of angst," and he and Gerrit compared notes on whether Mandelbaum happened to be in Prague when Gerrit was a boy.

This was, to Meta, a propitious start. Sitting close beside Gerrit, fingers interlocked with his, eyes lingering on his face whenever he spoke, she displayed a quiet, ardent affection the likes of which her mentor had never seen in her before. If nothing else, he thought, she's finally found happiness after a youth stunned by disappointment.

Lunch finished, Mandelbaum said, "That korma was delicious, but I've come a long way to see a certain manuscript. Shall we go or would you rather sit here and drink tea?"

Outside, the day was brisk but the coal-smoke-and-angst clouds had parted, so that the finials on all the spires in town twinkled in the sun like innumerable copper eyes. They decided to take a tram to the river and walk the rest of the way.

Despite his unsettling dialogue with Wittmann, Mandelbaum couldn't help feeling exhilarated at being here. Meta had discovered half of what she came looking for. Last night at dinner, Sam had struck Mandelbaum as a man enviably at peace with himself. And Gerrit seemed a strong match for Meta. Not a subject came up during lunch that the journalist didn't show himself informed about. Even when their talk turned to music, he was able to keep up. Mandelbaum couldn't put a satisfactorily defining word to it, but Gerrit seemed to be one whose spirit was senior to his years. During his own time overseas he had never once met an expatriate who didn't bear the cross of some turbulent, unfortunate past, but Gerrit, a survivor of the Prague Spring, seemed not to be your everyday American abroad.

On foot, passing by a rococo palace on Jánský vršek, Mandelbaum paused and said, "You know this joint, I assume."

Gerrit said, "Bretfeld Palace. It's called Summer and Winter, the pub is."

"Right you are. That's where we can toast the reunification of these movements this evening. I've always loved raising a glass where Josef von Bretfeld hosted Casanova and Mozart at his all-night bashes. The boozing and carousing were legendary."

"Mozart partied here?" Meta asked.

"If trompe l'oeil walls could speak, right?"

The group ambled uphill, turned onto Jánská, and Gerrit opened the door. They went upstairs, Meta leading, Gerrit behind her, Mandelbaum catching his breath on the landing.

"You all right?" Meta asked him.

"Fine, fine, my dear. I just forgot one needs a mountaineering license to get around this part of town."

When they entered Gerrit's flat, Meta felt a visceral thrill pass down her spine. Count von Bretfeld may have entertained his profligate Casanovas and prodigal Mozarts, but her needs were simpler. To now be able to play two of the sonata movements for both her lover and her mentor was beyond anything she'd imagined when she arrived in Prague.

The sun shone calmly on Gerrit's books and chattels. The room seemed so familiar to Meta, though she'd only been here for a matter of some sublime hours.

"Mind if I open it?" she asked, though she knew she needn't.

"You're the one with the key."

Meta pulled off her silver necklace, to which she'd attached the skeleton key, went to the secretary, let down the lid. She lifted out the handsome leather briefcase and removed it to Gerrit's desk. With Mandelbaum at her side, and Gerrit peering over her shoulder with a look of warm pride on his face, she opened the briefcase to discover there was nothing inside.

· 7 ·

WHEN JANE BURKE, FORMERLY DECKER, wrote back, wildly excited by the prospect of her wartime bosom buddy coming out to Texas to visit, maybe finding a job and a place to live, Otylie was torn. Mr. and Mrs. Sanders would want to let her go sometime soon. Their children were growing up, and though it had been home for more than seven years, she couldn't stay in the maid's room on East Eighty-Sixth Street forever. Yet despite having reached out to Jane, the prospect of pulling up roots and reinventing herself anew was a daunting, exhausting idea. She made a telephone call to her secretary friend in Manhattan and, in something resembling a final effort at making a go of it here, she agreed to attend the next dance at the club they'd spoken of in the bistro that night.

"Good for you, kiddo," her friend enthused.

The band was loud, the crooner creepy, the room smoky, the atmosphere desperately festive. Otylie was dressed to the nines, as her girlfriend put it, and threw herself into the dance with all the abandon she could muster. The problem was, she quickly understood, abandon wasn't a state one mustered. Either you gave yourself over to all the fun, fully and openly, or you faked it, which was far worse than sitting on the sidelines.

She was surprised by how many gentlemen found her attractive enough to invite her out onto the floor. She'd learned some of the dance steps popular with these Yankees when living in London, although there she only danced with other gals. But none of it meant anything to her. She went home more dejected than ever, feeling like a fraud. It was as if happiness was way over there, Otylie was way over here, and between them stretched an impervious membrane.

When she gave notice, Adele Sanders told her to take all the time she needed. Grace was more upset than Otylie might have expected. The poor girl promised to play Schubert every day, to spend more time with Otylie, to take her out with her girlfriends to the soda shoppe. *All of this*, Otylie wrote to Jakub in her diary, *only makes me miss you more.*

Late winter, 1955. Jane had scouted out a one-bedroom efficiency apartment that would become available for Otylie to rent on the first of May if she wanted it. None of the standard first and last months' rent would be required, since Jane's husband, Jim, was a childhood friend of the owner. There were all sorts of odd jobs available, Jane assured her, but if she wanted to pursue her music teaching, they could rent a piano and get her set up. She had a few acquaintances who had children of the right age to take lessons.

Otylie wrote back saying yes. Privately, she wasn't sure about the teaching scheme, recalling that she had been able to tutor Grace only so far before having to give her up to a seasoned piano teacher. If only she had learned to speak French or, God forbid, even German, some tongue these Americans might be interested in learning, she could have become a language instructor. She was sure nobody, but nobody, in Texas gave a hoot about learning Czech. Still, it was time she moved on, and if taking on music students was the best way for her to make ends meet, so be it. Besides, with practice, she could become more seasoned herself.

She had one final encounter in New York to live through, anyway, as fate would have it. One morning in April, the first that promised an end to the wintry snow and brash wind swirling down the city's corridors, Otylie saw Irena Svobodová walking on the opposite side of Park Avenue around Sixty-Fifth Street. She was wearing a red knee-length coat and a black fur hat, and she strode with Irena's unmistakable gait. The lights were against Otylie, so she paced along, parallel to her friend, on the west side of the avenue. She would have crossed, running through traffic to reach the island median, and darted again through uptown traffic to the other side, but the lanes were thick with cars and taxis. Careful not to lose sight of the woman, she became more convinced with each step that she was in fact following Irena. She even caught a distant glimpse of her familiar profile as the woman glanced to the left before crossing the street, continuing uptown.

The lights finally changed and Otylie ran, colliding with a man carrying a briefcase as she dashed across Park Avenue.

"I'm so sorry," she mumbled, reaching down to retrieve his fedora, which lay on the pavement. He reprimanded her for not looking where she was going, but she didn't hear his words. Running up the sidewalk past the Armory, she was frantic at having lost sight of Irena. She pushed her way past other pedestrians, apologizing as she threaded her way along. At the corner of Park and Seventy-Third she bounded into the crosswalk against the red light, barely dodging a car, brushing up against a bicyclist who shouted at her.

Then she saw that red coat again. Slow down, Irena, she thought. The figure was nearly two blocks ahead of her. Otylie broke into an open run now. To avoid jostling others on the sidewalk, she ran alongside the curb, stepping out into the gutter when necessary, hoping not to be struck from behind. She was within a block of her friend when a car honked. She swiveled about, jumped back on the curb, buffeted by the hard breeze of the vehicle as it swept past her barely a foot away. Her heart was thudding in her breast. When she turned, facing north again, Irena was nowhere to be seen.

Must have dropped down a side street, she thought, and continued to hurry uptown. For the next two hours, she walked up and down every cross street between Madison and Lexington Avenues, over to Third, from the Seventies up into the Nineties. Her search proved fruitless. No Irena was to be found. And though she went back to the same neighborhood day after day for the better part of the next month, having searched the telephone directory in vain for an Irena Svobodová, the woman in the red coat and black fur hat never turned up again. Desperate, she confided to Adele what had happened.

"Irena. Wasn't that your daughter's name?" she asked.

Otylie had nearly forgotten her pathetic little fabrication during that first interview with Mrs. Sanders. Her first impulse was to say, simply, that she'd named her daughter after this friend. Instead, she confessed.

"I have never lied to you or anybody in your family since," she said, holding back tears. "I hope you don't think I'm a bad woman."

"That's the last thing I'd ever think about you," Adele Sanders said, cupping her hand on Otylie's arm. "I do have to admit you had me completely convinced. But, you know, we all bend the truth now and then, and you meant no harm. So let's just let it go, all right?"

"Thank you, Mrs. Sanders."

"About your friend, Irena," she continued, and suggested they run a classified ad in the *Times* and other local newspapers.

It was a good idea but produced no results. As the days passed, Otylie began to doubt what she had seen. After all, she thought, it wasn't as if she recognized her old friend's face absolutely, without any shadow of a doubt. Grace and Billy's father offered to hire a private detective to search for her, but Otylie gratefully declined. She convinced herself that any investigator would be chasing a specter, a dead idea rather than a living woman.

The entire Sanders family accompanied Otylie to the Port Authority Terminal, where she caught her bus to Texas. Another departure, another schism. This time, however, was the first in which she experienced anything approaching feelings of joy, bittersweet as they were. Seeing Grace and Billy and their parents waving to her as she boarded the bus was utterly novel. Every other leave-taking in her life had been accomplished by herself. No one had ever said goodbye to her at a train station or ship pier. And in times past, whoever awaited her at the far end of her journey was someone she had never met before. The thought of Jane standing in an Austin bus station at the end of this long ride gave rise to a sense of wary hope. It fluttered in her body like a palpable, living thing. Like a rare little bird, or an exotic dragon whose wings were both vigorous and invisible.

III

Eternity depends on whether people are willing to take care of something.

—Werner Herzog

· 1 ·

JÁNSKÁ AT NIGHT is the darkest, most taciturn street in
Malá Strana. A few unshuttered amber windows look out over
the pitched cobblestone lane, but its feeble streetlamp has
little to offer. A boy or girl could skip down the narrow lane from
end to end in less than half a minute. Wide enough for just one
car to travel, and yet it's a world unto itself. In daylight, Jánská
is as beautiful as a film set—the set for an old movie about war,
love, loss, pursuit, betrayal, maybe hope. Or a classic Prague tale
by Jan Neruda himself. At night, though, it truly comes into its
own, flowering like some forbidden black orchid. Only the rarest
cinematographer could capture its spectral glow. Nerudova, one of
the quarter's busiest thoroughfares, may be just a block over, but
standing alone in front of Jánská 12 one might never suspect other
streets existed. And tonight, in a way, they didn't.

Petr Wittmann stood alone, an elegant ghost of sorts in his
dark gray herringbone greatcoat, before the Hodeks' door at that
very Jánská 12. In the purple dark he loitered, looking back down

the brief empty street. He took a few steps away from the house and saw that the windows on the top floor were still unillumi- nated. Furtive, his mind stretching in conflicted directions, he had spent his evening walking up and down the Jánská sidewalk of gray and white mosaic stone, and along neighboring streets, in silent negotiation with himself. The American who lived in the attic apartment showed no sign of life. Whereas others, moving behind their windows above the alley, had turned on lights, made dinner and eaten, sat before televisions or in favorite chairs to read before retiring, he had not. How Petr Wittmann wished he had not stopped smoking, on his doctor's recommendation, the year before. If he had an honest unfiltered cigarette and match on him, the hard work he had done to abstain would suddenly come to nothing, yes, but he would certainly feel better.

Did he really propose to push matters this far? Could he even pull it off? He could, surely. Nor did it hurt that he felt him- self to be fundamentally in the right. Should such an important manuscript be relegated to an inexperienced young lady and her sideshow smattering of half-cocked Nazi sympathizers, retired professors, earnest piano teachers, aspiring writers, and the rest of Miss Tavener's fond, foolish band? No way could he stand by and watch such amateurs proceed in ignorance of what they held in their hapless hands.

He caught himself chewing one of his fingernails. Ridiculous. He had maneuvered serenely through the riddlesome networks of Communist rule, staying above the fray and ahead of its bald and besotted gatekeepers at every pass, and now he was gnawing on his nails like a schoolgirl? He quietly cursed himself. He'd hesi- tated long enough. The time had come to make his move.

Earlier in the evening a woman had opened the door to Jánská 12 and disappeared inside the building. Wittmann, who'd nodded genially in the damp dusk as he pretended to stride with purpose past her, waited hidden in a recessed entryway to the next house up, then nimbly doubled back and caught the door just before it fully closed. He slipped a folded piece of paper into the bolt gap. Nobody had entered or left since.

Pocketing the paper as he opened the door, he found himself in a dimly lit corridor with a marble floor and plaster walls painted a dark butterscotch. Quiet, affecting nonchalance though no one was there to appreciate his performance, he climbed the staircase to the right of the ground-floor apartment door. He moved expeditiously, knowing the chances were slim he would actually be able to gain entrance to Gerrit's flat. If not, he hoped to depart Jánská without anybody's knowing he had been there.

When he reached the top landing, he saw there was no name beneath the bell by the door, so he rang. If Gerrit answered he could apologize for having disturbed him without an appointment, but say he happened to be in the neighborhood and wanted to add a few thoughts to his interview about postrevolution rediscovery of cultural materials, or some such malarkey. Thin excuse, he knew, but hardly thinner than Gerrit's for meeting with him in the first place. Wittmann blamed himself there—a scholar's fame tended to have a hasty half-life unless it was constantly tended to, and knowing that fame, like time or money, is power, he'd agreed to the extempore interview—but it gave him a convenient cover story now. Besides, he'd pulled off far more chancy situations with less. If worse came to worst and Gerrit was here, he might throw the journalist off balance by demanding, point-blank, why he'd come asking about puppet theater when what he really wanted to discuss was the sonata manuscript.

No sound from within. He tried the knob. Locked. Lifting the doormat, he looked under it for a key. None was there. Slid his fingers across the top of the lintel but found nothing. At the end of the hallway a vase of tired flowers stood at the center of a small table. Beneath the vase he found what he was looking for. Strange how a stirring of excitement and worry wove through him. Any minor illegalities—he'd already theorized about his statement to the authorities—might be overlooked in light of the significance of the find. More important, he had not forgotten to bring Tomáš Lang's copy with him to exchange for the original. Who could claim with any absolute assurance that old Lang hadn't given the wrong copies to his benefactors? There was considerable latitude here for muddying any legal waters. He unlocked the door.

Inside the room, a vague glow from the windows outlined the furniture. Some chairs, bookcases, a desk laden with what appeared to be careful stacks of books and papers. Being no burglar, Wittmann had neglected to bring a flashlight. He waited for his eyes to acclimate to the gloom, listening to himself breathe. A fluting wheeze, quick ins and outs, was what he heard, making him realize he was far more nervous than he had allowed himself to believe. After a minute, he decided there was no choice but to turn on one of Gerrit's lights. A floor lamp stood farthest from the windows against the back wall of the room. He found its switch and suddenly the study burst into view.

If the score was here, it could be in any number of hiding places. Rather than waste time pondering options, Wittmann started rifling through typescripts and notebooks on Gerrit's worktable. Busy scrivener, he thought. Drafts upon drafts of articles and essays on European, and in particular Czech, politics and culture. In an earlier decade, Wittmann might have had him arrested on suspicion of espionage. Would that he still could. How he sometimes missed those days when he had more leverage, more shrouded clout.

Feeling the pinch of time passing, he started looking behind volumes on the floor-to-ceiling shelves. As he pressed forward, he became less aware of the noise he was making. He dropped more than one stack of books on the floor, replacing some haphazardly before moving on to another row. He pulled up chair cushions and glanced beneath them, not seeing what he'd come for. He drew back the edges of the rugs, peering under them, stifling a sneeze. An antique secretary stood against the wall. Taking a penknife from the desk, he jimmied the lock until the lid fell open, revealing a leather brief and nondescript bric-a-brac. He rummaged through the brief, and, finding nothing, tossed it to the floor.

The bedroom, he thought. People hide money under their mattresses, why not an eighteenth-century music manuscript? When he stepped through a tulip-arched alcove—the architectural addition of a nouveau-loving former occupant, no doubt—he thought he heard a door open. Not the door he'd used to enter the flat, but another, back near the kitchen. He froze, his breath caught in his throat.

A little girl, her slender outline backlit by the overhead light she'd switched on in the kitchen. "*Kdo jste?*" she asked. Who are you?

"*A kdo jsi?*" was all Wittmann could think to say, a weak response that carried weight only because of the gruff authority of his voice.

"*Bydlím tady,*" Andrea responded, arms crossed. I live here.

Wittmann frowned. Had he made a mistake? Was this the wrong apartment?

Gerrit told me he lived here alone, he improvised, figuring that any fib he told her could later be denied.

You know Gerrit?

Of course. Why else would he have asked me to come here to get something for him.

Get what? Andrea pressed, suspicious.

Wittmann offered an ingratiating smile and spoke slowly, playing the patient adult to an irksome child, Now look. What did you say your name was?

Andrea hesitated before saying, Petra.

Yes, of course, Petra. Gerrit's mentioned you on a number of occasions. He said I might run into you and that you could help me find some music he needs.

A wave of fear burned through the girl. She had enough presence of mind not to let it show. She took a step back toward the downstairs door, asking, Where is Gerrit?

He's waiting for me with some others down on Karmelitská, he said, seeing her begin to retreat and standing his ground.

Why didn't he come here for it himself?

You ask an awful lot of questions, don't you? Instead of wasting his time and mine, why don't you help me find it? Did he show you where he kept it?

Before Wittmann had finished asking this third question, Petra had disappeared through the same door by which she'd entered. It wasn't until he heard her throw the dead bolt and clomp quickly down the stairs that Wittmann knew he had to leave, and fast. Clutching Lang's copy of the manuscript, he flew back out to Jánská. Hearing no one pursuing him, he walked, as swift as downhill water, over the echoing cobblestones. He had half a mind to double around to Šporkova and murder Tomáš Lang in his sleep, but he couldn't prove himself an effective thief, never mind a killer. He walked across the Charles Bridge toward his apartment on Týnská, not far from Saint James Church, where the mummified and scrawny hand of a thief has hung for centuries near the entrance to the nave. Turning the collar of his greatcoat up against the buffeting, snappy breezes off the Vltava, he felt defeated but defiant. His acts, he reminded himself, had been for a worthy cause. He had done nothing wrong. If Petra described him to the authorities, and if by some improbable stretch they came questioning, and if by an even more far-fetched stretch of the imagination he stood accused of entering the American's garret, nothing serious would come of it. He knew too many people and was, in turn, too well known for there to be consequences of any import. Times may have changed, he thought, but his influence had not.

He could almost talk himself into believing this narrative line. Certainly, it was the way things should be seen, were the world clear-eyed and just.

Not an hour after Wittmann had slipped away into the heavy Prague darkness, Meta and Gerrit stood before the same door at Jánská 12. A blue dismal fog had crept up from the river and lay in crevices and corners, chilling the air and blunting every stone that surrounded them. Mandelbaum's suggestion, after they discovered the manuscript was missing and the Hodeks knew nothing, was to drop in on all his contacts unannounced.

"Less time to concoct a story," he reasoned, "so maybe we'll get lucky."

They'd spent the rest of that day and the next not getting lucky. Together they traipsed from one address to another, looking for Wittmann, for Kohout, for Johana Langová, for Gretja Toplová, even for the curator at the Lobkowicz palace upriver, for anyone with whom Meta had discussed the sonata. Kohout claimed innocence of any such intrigue, and appeared genuinely rankled by the question. Who did they think they were, he groused, some sort of independent inquisition? None of the others they approached seemed suspect. They failed to locate Wittmann. He wasn't at home, nor was he in his office at Charles University.

Back in Mandelbaum's hotel room after a second long, distressing day, their emotions veered from muffled despair to abject defeat.

"Why don't we go to the embassy? We have to do something, don't we?"

Paul realized he could no longer withhold Wittmann's barely veiled admonitions. As Meta listened to his story, he saw a look on her face he had never seen before. Anger, worry, and contempt clouded her eyes.

"All those years studying theory," she said. "Heinrich Schenker. Meyer, Schoenberg, Lewin, Babbitt, all the rest of them. It was about music. Not criminal psychology. I know Wittmann's behind this. It's pure madness."

Mandelbaum shoved his hands into his pockets. "Madness?" he asked. "Gesualdo wrote some beautiful madrigals, but also murdered his wife. Donizetti was probably bipolar. Schumann, mad as a March hare. Even Bach spent a month in jail for breaking a contract with his Weimar patron. You can still see the lock from his cell in the Bach Museum in Eisenach. The list is long, Meta. Why should people who research their music and lives be any different?"

"For a thousand reasons. They don't work in the same boiling-hot cauldron, for one."

"Maybe. But they're often no more balanced than those who did and do."

"I know," she moaned, tucking her hair behind her ear, the old nervous tic, before covering her face with her hands. "It's just, people showed such courage over the years to keep the manuscript from being stolen and I lost it in a matter of days. I've totally failed them."

"No, you haven't," said Gerrit. "I did."

"Nobody's failed anybody except maybe me," Mandelbaum contradicted them, "for having sent you to Petr Wittmann in the first place. And for agreeing to bring the middle movement from New York, where it was safe. But that's all beside the point right now. We have to stay focused on finding it."

Having bade Mandelbaum good night, Gerrit and Meta took the metro back across the river to Malá Strana. Tired, depressed, distracted by the day, both looked forward to slipping into bed together and forgetting for a while the folly of not having deposited the score in a more secure place.

Their spirits only sank further when they discovered that the apartment door was ajar, the key from beneath the vase still in the lock. Stepping into the front room, they were sickened by the ransacking. Books splayed on the floor, reams of paper splashed onto the carpet. Why break in a second time if the single object of value here had already been taken? And why be tidy the first time only to wreak such havoc on a second foray?

"No matter what either of you say, this is all my doing," Meta apologized, no longer able to hold back tears. Stepping over to the window, she stared out at Petřín Hill, a great murky hunchback huddled under tiny stars. "You had a nice quiet life before I came crashing in, asking crazy questions, turning things upside down."

"That's not true," Gerrit countered, standing with a clutch of notebooks in his hands.

"I'm no better than my father, thinking only of myself and wrecking everything around me. Honestly, I should take a hint and get out of Prague before anything worse happens."

"No," he said, slapping the notebooks down on the table. He walked over and turned her to face him. The gloom in his eyes quickened into a hard resolve. "What you should do is help me straighten up. In the morning, I'll get a better lock and stop leaving the key on the hall table where any idiot can find it. Please," putting his arms around her, "stop now."

"I'm sorry. I guess I'm just at an end here. Not with you," she was quick to add. "With myself more like."

"That'll change."

They set about replacing volumes on shelves and typescripts in stacks on the worktable. Why was it, Meta wondered, gathering up an armful of scattered books, that burglars, would-be or not, couldn't resist vandalizing victims' homes? Was it written down in some manual of evil deeds?

Not wanting her to see the forlorn briefcase lying on the floor, Gerrit set it back inside the secretary and closed the lid. When they finally went to bed, agreeing they'd finish cleaning up the rest of the mess tomorrow, Meta, despite her fatigue, whispered to Gerrit that she had another idea about how to track down Wittmann. Whether he was willfully evading them when they'd gone to his flat on Týnská and his office at Charles University was anyone's guess. But, either way, she had noticed the professor's course list, with classroom hours and locations, posted beside his door. A class was scheduled for tomorrow afternoon. She would run him to ground in his academic lair.

Under a cobalt sky, a bite of autumn in the air, Gerrit accompanied Meta to the university the next day, where she asked him to wait outside. "Nothing may come of this, but it's my responsibility to confront him on my own," she told him, resolute.

From the notes on the chalkboard, Wittmann's lecture appeared to be about Arnold Dolmetsch's work on seventeeth- and eighteenth-century musical ornamention. Meta stood at the back of the hall, as yet unnoticed, half-wishing she could understand the professor's Czech. She was struck by how formal his delivery was, how precise and authoritative. Quietly, diligently taking notes, his students were attentive to every word he said.

When Wittmann glanced up from his lectern to see the American staring at him from some distance, he continued, seemingly unperturbed, to finish the point he was making and then dismissed the class for a break. Students pushed past her, opening packs of cigarettes and looking at mobile phones as they emptied the room. Meta took this as a sign to approach.

"What brings you here, Miss Tavener?" Wittmann asked when she reached the front of the lecture hall. "I would have thought you already knew Dolmetsch's work backward and forward."

"We tried calling you," she said, ignoring his remark, as well as his insistent mispronunciation of her name. "We even went to your flat."

"We? Who's we?"

"Gerrit and I, along with Professor Mandelbaum."

"All three of you? Whatever for? Has someone perished?"

Impatient with his sarcasm, she spoke bluntly. "Why did you break into Gerrit's apartment and steal those manuscripts? I'm here to ask that you give them back to me."

"Miss Tavener, how dare you disrupt my class in order to make such a ludicrous claim?" Wittmann rasped, his voice as razory as quills. "First, I have no idea what you're talking about. And second, you don't know me in the least. You come waltzing in here, accusing me of crimes that, even if they occurred, are probably a result of your own carelessness—"

"No, I—"

"—and rather than sharing the originals with me in a collegial manner, you tell me of their existence—*their* in plural, I hear—only when you've managed to lose them? *Egregious* is one word that comes to mind. Egregious, negligent, heedless in the extreme."

"Aren't those words equally applicable to a thief?"

"Young lady, let us be careful. I am not without resources. You'd best not be making unfounded accusations after seriously mishandling an historical document of potentially great significance."

Meta crossed her arms, upset yet holding her ground. "Professor Wittmann, twice you told me it was a fraud. Suddenly it's of 'great significance'? You're really going to stand there and say you had nothing to do with this theft?"

"I wish I did have those manuscripts. At least they'd be in good hands and properly cared for. Now, if you don't mind, I have a lecture to finish."

Seeing that some students had begun to filter back into the hall, Meta decided she had gotten all that she was going to get from him. She thanked Wittmann for his time, he bowed slightly, and she left. Most troubling, Meta thought as she rejoined Gerrit, was a nagging feeling that the professor was telling her the truth. Nor did it make her happy to know that some of his more pointed criticisms were not without merit.

Dejected, silent, the two walked back to Jánská to finish putting Gerrit's apartment back in order. As she went into the kitchen for water, Gerrit noticed that he had failed to completely shut the lid of his misbegotten secretary the night before. Reflexively, he lifted out the leather case to search it again, then stopped, astounded. Had they made a mistake when Mandelbaum was here, or when Gerrit had put it away after the second break-in? Impossible, unthinkable. Each of them in turn had searched the several compartments of the attaché. The score had vanished. Now it had reappeared.

"Meta?" he called, barely containing his confused excitement.

"What?" she said from the kitchen.

"You'd better have a look at this."

The original manuscript, every page of it, was in just the same condition as when Meta had first placed it inside the case.

"What the hell's going on?" Clutching the sheaf, she sat on the wooden chair by the secretary, feeling faint.

"No idea whatsoever."

Dizzy with relief, she carefully paged through both movements again, and again a third time. "You think Wittmann or some underling of his stole it, scanned and replaced it?"

"Anything's possible," Gerrit said, flushed with bafflement and doubt.

"All he had to do was ask me," Meta continued, thinking out loud, wondering if what she was about to say was fully true. "I'd have given him whatever he needed."

"But I thought Mandelbaum said it was imperative that your role in this—"

"Mandelbaum and especially Wittmann are way more worried about scholarly kudos than I am," she said, suddenly back on solid ground. "I'm not in this to build my résumé. Maybe I'm as naive as Wittmann and Kohout think. But this"—she held the pages up in both hands—"isn't *mine* any more than it's theirs or anybody else's. The only exception is Otylie and her heirs, if she has any."

"Not everybody's as idealistic as you, Meta."

"I'm not so idealistic. I'm not pure." She frowned, putting the sheaf into the briefcase, setting it on Gerrit's table. "It's not that I didn't daydream a little, early on, about getting my name in the paper," she admitted, continuing in a self-mocking voice, "Front-page headline in the *Times*, 'Young Musicologist Makes Historic Find, Awarded Nation's Highest Honor.'"

They both chuckled.

"But the more I learned about Jakub and all that he and his poor wife and friends went through to preserve this thing, the more foolish that felt." She reached into her pocket to retrieve her phone, saying she needed to let Paul know the manuscript had resurfaced. While the hotel number rang, she told Gerrit,

"This thing was put into my hands for a reason, and the reason is simple. To make it whole again. No more amateurism, no more mistakes."

Gerrit watched her as she called the hotel, occasionally glancing at the dispatch case and shaking her head with a frown. True, his affection for her colored his perceptions. But if he'd been swept away by her before, the commitment he felt toward her now, witnessing her fierce resolve, was even deeper.

Mandelbaum didn't pick up. As Meta left a message with the desk, Gerrit found himself wondering why anybody would want to burglarize an apartment in an attempt to steal this manuscript, which brought him back to Margery's query regarding attribution. There was no way he could ask Meta the question in absolute innocence, but it nonetheless needed asking. When she'd hung up, he continued their talk where it had left off.

"Making it whole is one thing. But I'm curious about who you think wrote it. If someone went to the length of stealing and replacing it, this music must be by an important composer."

Meta rose and stood looking at the photographs pinned to the wall. They reflected back the muted light of the overcast day. While it was true she hadn't known Gerrit very long—though it seemed like a long time—how was it possible she hadn't shared her speculations on this subject? The easy answer was that she hadn't revealed them to a soul. Not even Mandelbaum knew her deepest conjecture. She refused to share because, if she was wrong, it would be profoundly humiliating, another nasty bit of hubris.

"I have my suspicions, strong ones, about who composed it," straightening a photo whose pin had come loose. "I'll tell you what. I even have a feeling when, where, and possibly why."

"Okay. So who, when, where, why?"

She turned to him, shaking her head. "Suspicions aren't scholarship. Feelings aren't facts. I don't mean to be coy. But there's still work to be done before anyone worth her salt would throw names around for the record. Now that we've got these movements back from whoever took them, I think it's more important than ever to track down Otylie Bartošová as quickly as possible and pray she still has the opening part. It will tell me the rest of what I need to know. That's the hope, anyway."

Gerrit had been making mental notes about the day's events, that old and ingrained habit, but put them aside for the moment. Yes, this would make a good story, even a great story, he thought. Right now, though, what mattered was to help Meta get where she needed to go. "I have to ask the obvious. How do we locate Otylie Bartošová?"

"I'm not sure. London's the only other place where I know she lived and worked. If I can find somebody to buy my piano I'll have enough for the trip there and to get back home. Maybe I don't stand a chance of tracking down this woman, who'd be somewhere in her late eighties, early nineties now, but—" Here Meta fell silent and simply looked at Gerrit.

"Yes?"

"—will you come with me?"

"Do I have a choice?" he said, a smile breaking out on his face.

"I hope not."

That afternoon, an unusually subdued Andrea helped them set the apartment to rights, and after a spur-of-the-moment celebratory supper at the Kettles'—*"Fantastický!"* Sylvie shrieked when Meta called and explained what had happened—they fell asleep at home with the manuscript in its case under the bed, directly below their heads.

Gerrit woke first, out of a dream in which he and Andrea were playing a game of hide-and-seek in a park. She was swift as a fawn, peeking out from behind a huge oak, then dashing, in a lightning-quick blur, to conceal herself deep in a thicket of freestanding ivy. Without going through any conscious process of reflection, he began to piece together what might have happened over the past few days. That puzzling, impish look on the girl's face as she left the kitchen table, having batted her grape back and forth after grilling him about love, the unwonted shyness in her behavior yesterday—was it possible she opened the secretary with its token lock and took the score herself to delay his inevitable departure?

Rather than going down, he phoned to ask Andrea's mother if she wouldn't mind sending the girl upstairs, if she was free and had a minute. Best not to confront her with her mother present, he thought. When Andrea knocked on his door and sheepishly entered the room, he knew he'd guessed right. It didn't take much cajoling for her to confess to Gerrit and Meta, who was up by then.

"I not want you to go. Very stupid, very," she said, staring at the floor. "I very sorry."

Gerrit put his hand on her narrow shoulder. He thought to ask her how she knew the manuscript would be in his secretary, but realized she'd seen him store important things there in the past and knew how easy it was to jimmy the lock. Annoyed as he was, it was impossible not to say, "It's okay, Andrea. You put it back, didn't you? You told us the truth. Both were the right things to do."

The girl hesitated before making a further confession, eyes still fixed on her feet.

"I put back it because that man came here, your friend. I never saw him before. He not very nice."

"What man? Where was he?"

"In your room, here," looking up.

"I have no idea what you're talking about," he said, glancing at Meta.

Seeing alarm flash across his face, Andrea switched to Czech to be sure she was making herself clear.

A man who said you'd told him to come get a music manuscript. Said you were waiting for him on Karmelitská. He told me you were friends and that you mentioned me many times. But he got my name wrong, called me Petra. I got scared and ran away.

Gerrit was astonished at such brazenness. What did he look like?

She gave Gerrit an unmistakable description of Petr Wittmann.

"Did you understand any of that?" he asked Meta.

"Only a little," she answered. "What's going on?"

As Gerrit recounted Andrea's story, he watched Meta's face settle into angry disbelief. "He lied to me. Right to my face in his classroom. We have to report this to the police."

"The police, I'm sorry to say, will probably be inclined to believe a respected university professor over a young girl. If we point fingers at Wittmann, I'm afraid we'll end up being the suspect ones."

"How so?"

"Because, bottom line is, we have no incontestable proof he was here. What's more, he didn't actually steal anything." He and Meta looked helplessly at each other. Then, turning to Andrea, he asked if he could accompany her downstairs and say hello to her mother.

"You going to tell her?"

"I'm going to tell her what a fine young lady you are."

"But about me taking the music?"

"I don't see any music missing."

She shook her head, then walked straight over to Meta to hug her and offer another apology. It wasn't lost on Meta that the girl, with her childish act, had inadvertently saved the manuscript from really being stolen. Following Gerrit's lead, she smiled and said, in rudimentary Czech, Apology for what?

*

After Andrea left with Gerrit, Meta started coffee brewing, then sat at his desk. The question about attribution hadn't been posed in a vacuum or asked out of turn. Petr Wittmann's early slight— or perhaps sleight—his growing fixation and competitiveness, and now his unveiled threats made it impossible for Meta to ignore what she'd harbored as a theory from the first time she'd played this piece of unknown music. She had gotten so fully involved in her search for the physical manuscripts that this more purely scholarly issue had been set, at least a little, to one side.

Sure, she'd had those first conversations with Mandelbaum during which they dropped the names of minor and major composers with the alacrity of children tossing knives in a game of mumblety-peg. Well, no, she thought. They hadn't been that cavalier. But what lay behind Wittmann's inimical scheming was a possibility of such magnitude that she had to take it at least as seriously as Wittmann and Kohout clearly did. She owed it not only to Irena and Otylie but to the one who composed this work.

Holding pages of the paper up to the sunlight to view the watermarks once more, Meta murmured, "What's your story, troublemaker? You want to tell me who you are?" Backlit, a fleur-de-lis in a crowned shield was plainly visible. On another quadrant, letters and a number that had initially stumped her: MUI8 H. Turning the page in her hands and candling it in the morning light she saw what it really was: H BLUM. Paper from Germany or Austria? Maybe Basel, she speculated. Certainly not Holland or Italy. This would help with dating the manuscript, and further assist in proving or disproving the theory that was more and more taking hold in her head.

Hearing Gerrit reenter the apartment, she spoke while still peering at the illumined leaf. "There's coffee in the kitchen. Did it go okay?"

"Andrea's secret is safe," he said, pouring himself a cup. "Wittmann's another story."

"Let's talk about him later."

Her tone of voice had changed, deepened. He watched her studying the manuscript, serious and curiously serene, and waited for her to continue.

"Gerrit," she said, looking at him now, "since apologies seem to be in the air, I owe you one. I dodged your question last night but I realize you deserve to know why people other than Andrea may be breaking into your apartment."

"Lunacy is why," he said, pulling up a chair beside her.

"True enough, but"—Meta gestured toward the paper. "See this watermark? Enough of the letters look the same forward or backward—the 'H,' the 'U,' and 'M'—and even the 'B' and 'L' aren't that far from mirror images, they just seemed stylized. Hard to believe, but I've been misreading the watermark until just now."

Gerrit found a clear spot on the desk, far away from the sonata manuscript, where he set down his coffee. "Can I see? My hands aren't washed, so if you can just hold it up to the light for me—"

Meta, who handled the timeworn manuscript with a curator's care, showed Gerrit what she was referring to. "There in the middle? It's the name of the paper mill where these sheets were manufactured. Paper wasn't as cheap then as it is now. And different composers and copyists tended to buy from different paper makers and suppliers."

"Makes sense. So how do you determine exactly when this 'H Blum' fleur-de-lis mill was making paper?"

"That shouldn't be overly difficult," Meta assured him, setting the manuscript down. "Before I made up my mind to come to Prague, I spent weeks poring over all the standard texts about the quarter century or so when the piano sonata form crystallized. A lot of the books I already owned and had read. Stuff like William

Newman's *The Sonata in the Classic Era* and Charles Rosen's *The Classical Style* on Hadyn, Mozart, and Beethoven. Key biographies too. I read chapters in Jahn, Braunbehrens, Geiringer, zeroing in on the mid-1780s to the early 1790s. Wegeler and Ries, Schindler, Thayer, Lockwood, Solomon. You know any of these?"

Gerrit shook his head, bowled over by this avalanche of authors. "No. I mean, I've heard of Rosen, but I can't say I've read any of them."

"I'll be the first to admit that none of this was as methodical as it sounds. It was all hunches based on hopes, hopes based on hunches. To tell you the truth, I barely knew what I was doing, hadn't really gotten over the shock of this thing that came nosediving into my life. Anyway, listening to as many piano sonata recordings as I could manage, playing unrecorded scores from the period, I found myself doing exactly what a good musicologist, or any scientist for that matter, isn't supposed to do."

"And what's that?" Gerrit asked, filling the silence that followed her last words.

"Reaching toward a conclusion before having the evidence in place. Cardinal sin."

"That may be, but it's certainly understandable."

Meta glanced with a frown at Gerrit. "It's not how you'd ever go about investigating a piece of journalism, is it?"

"Well," he said, wincing invisibly, having no ready answer.

Gerrit knew the time was coming when he would either need to confess that he'd kept working on her story behind her back and risk the consequences, ask her forgiveness and permission to continue, or shelve his notebook once and for all. The closer Meta got to her quarry, the closer he got to his. And if she discovered treasure, a major composer, at the end of her search, he'd have the journalist's version of a royal flush. Music, war, heroism, politics, intrigue—the narrative moved on so many levels. Gerrit hadn't spoken about his dilemma to a soul since that night with Jiří, and he'd been more careful to keep his notebook out of sight after Meta had discovered it. Now that they spent their nights together, and most days, he could hardly take clandestine notes, but at this moment the desire was palpable. "So what's this conclusion you so sinfully arrived at?"

She said the name quite deliberately. "Beethoven."

After staring at Meta for slow silent moments, Gerrit said, "What?"

"I'm convinced this is a lost early Beethoven piano sonata."

"Talk about above-the-fold news."

"You understand I might be totally wrong. But what's more amazing," she added, "is there seems to be a decent chance my bastard conclusion has merit."

"Go on."

"Where to start," she said, although she'd covered this terrain in her head many times. "How much do you know about Beethoven?"

"Layman's knowledge. No more or less than most, I'd imagine."

She steepled her fingers under her chin, then braided them in her lap. "So his early life was a kaleidoscope of highs and lows. The highs, like giving his first performance in Cologne when he was seven, publishing his first work at eleven—the Dressler Variations it's called, and then heading off to Vienna to meet Mozart when he was sixteen. All very heady stuff. Mozart was the biggest rock star of the day and Beethoven wanted to move up the charts. But death had a way of trying to cut him down to size every time he was starting to get somewhere. His grandparents died when he was young, and he lost a sister when he was eight or nine, and a baby brother when he'd just got into his teens. When he was fifteen, composing away, working steadily as a court musician, his mother gave birth to another girl, Maria Margaretha. That would be around 1786. A year later, in the spring of 1787, he's off to

Vienna and Mozart, and it looks to him, aside from the setbacks, like the world's a pearl in his palm. But after just a few weeks in Vienna, you know what happens?"

Gerrit shook his head.

"He gets a message telling him to return to Bonn immediately, that his mother's dying of consumption."

"No lessons with Mozart?"

"Doubtful. There's a story that after Mozart heard Beethoven play, he told others to keep an eye on this young man, he's going places. Possibly apocryphal, but it's a mainstay in the lore. So his mother, whom he considered his best and dearest friend in the world, dies that summer, his one-year-old sister, Maria, dies that fall, his father becomes an even worse drunk than he was before. And in 1791, Beethoven's dream of studying with the greatest living composer in the greatest musical city in all of Europe goes up in smoke when Mozart dies too. What I find most interesting, just in terms of Otylie's sonata, is that during the period between 1787, when all this tragedy comes thundering down on him, and 1789, his composing grinds almost completely to a halt. Or, that is, we have almost no evidence he was writing."

"Maybe he was just too depressed."

"Could well be. In his earliest known personal letter he says as much. I've read it so many times I practically know it by heart. It was written around the middle of September 1787, to a lawyer named von Schaden, who Beethoven stayed with on his way back home from Vienna to be with his mother in Bonn. After she died in July, he wrote von Schaden that he was suffering from melancholia and asthma, and feared he himself might die of consumption like his mother. So, yeah, he moves into a dark, barren period—one of his biographers calls it a 'moratorium.' Plus, his father couldn't stay sober enough to earn a decent living, so Beethoven was forced to act as a kind of surrogate father and mother for his family. He had to grow up fast," she said, glancing down at the manuscript. "He fought a lot of demons over the course of his life, not just death. Ill health. His failure to find any kind of real relationship with women he loved. His own struggle with the bottle. His deafness. Even his political idealism caused him grief from time to time." Meta ticked them off on her fingers. "The list is long. But for all his frailties, he was really tough. The hardships he went through even while he was being furiously prolific make it difficult to believe—difficult for me, at least—that he just dropped composing, the one true love of his life, for such a long time even though he was only a teenager."

Gerrit himself now glanced at the manuscript where it lay in a soft trapezoid of sunlight, looking at the procession of notes and marveling at how this relatively primitive form of annotation could translate into such magnificence as music. "So, you're suggesting the Prague Sonata could be autobiographical—Irena's movement that goes from joy to grief—and maybe was written in this period when he was supposedly blocked?"

"I'm hardly alone in thinking he couldn't go completely dormant, no matter what the circumstances. He was young, a virtuoso, passionately committed to his work. It's known that he wanted to write a symphony in honor of his mother, in C minor, but all we have of it is a very unfinished draft written out on a couple of staves in his hand, almost definitely from this period I'm talking about." She suddenly interrupted herself and asked, "Bored yet? I'm throwing a lot at you."

Gerrit didn't try to hide his admiration. "Whatever's the opposite of bored, that's what I am, all right?"

"Okay," she said. "Just stop me if that changes. So Beethoven, as you probably know, wrote thirty-two sonatas for the pianoforte, and those sonatas made a profound impact on music history."

"That I do know."

"Not so many people are aware that he wrote three earlier piano sonatas, the 'Kurfürstensonaten,' published in 1783, when he was about twelve or thirteen, and dedicated to Maximilian Friedrich."

"Who was Friedrich?"

"The elector of Cologne and a powerful early supporter."

"Twelve or thirteen? I'll say he was an early supporter."

"I hear you. But they're almost never included in the boxed sets or featured in concerts. Beethoven himself essentially excluded those sonatas from his official canon by not assigning them opus numbers. Catalogers later gave them what's called a WoO designation, *Werk ohne Opuszahl*—"

"Work without an opus number."

"Right."

"This is all new to me."

"You're not the only one. Fact is, many Beethoven commentators generally don't waste time on these 'Electoral' sonatas, WoO 47, because—unlike Irena's central movement of the Prague Sonata, which is highly original, to say the least—they don't show much evidence of superbright burning genius. They're wonderful pieces for one so young, but at the end of the day they're well-crafted and mostly derivative."

There were exceptions to the "Electoral" sonata naysayers, naturally, of which Meta was aware. She knew, for instance, that Ludwig Schiedermair, in his 1925 *Der junge Beethoven*, had proposed that in Sonata in F Minor, WoO 47, no. 2, one could hear faint intimations of the "Pathétique," one of the master's later triumphs. She'd read of J.-G. Prod'homme's important 1937 study, *Les Sonates pour piano de Beethoven*, claiming that the third of these sonatas advanced a motif revived in the opening passage of the Seventh Symphony. There were other such suggested echoes; some of these resonated with her, others didn't.

As it happened, Meta knew these three earliest sonatas well. She had found herself after the accident playing them from time to time before audiences of schoolchildren. It never failed to give her young listeners a shock when she told them that the composer was hardly older than they were when he wrote them. That wasn't all, either, when it came to the adolescent Ludwig's early attempts at sonata writing. He left behind two movements of an incomplete sonata in F, WoO 50, dedicated to his friend Franz Wegeler. It dated from 1790–1792, just before he left his birthplace, Bonn, to head back to Vienna, where he studied with Haydn, whom he considered the next best thing to Mozart. The piece, an allegretto, wasn't published until after Beethoven died some thirty-five years later.

As for the Prague Sonata, if it proved to be Beethoven's composition, it would bridge aspects of his earliest piano works, which relied considerably on the received ideas of his contemporaries, to the vigorously original sonatas that were part of his cherished canon. "Even when he was most influenced by Mozart, Beethoven had his own sound and dynamic rigor, both of which are present in Irena's movement. The more I play it, the more I hear Beethoven."

"You said this is in a copyist's hand, right?" Gerrit asked. "That none of what's on these pages is written down by him?"

Nodding, Meta said, "Copyists made more legible and uniform versions of composers' original scores so they could be shared or preserved. If this were in Beethoven's hand—which I can assure you is far messier, bristling with more visual energy than what you see here—it would be an open-and-shut case. A find nobody could contest."

"Okay, so pardon me if I'm way off, but what would a teenager be doing hiring a copyist? Wouldn't that have been something more established, older, and, I have to think, richer composers would have done?"

"Yes and no, mostly yes. There are other manuscripts of his from before this that exist only in a copyist's hand. I'm thinking of the surviving score of the piano part from his earliest known piano concerto, in E-flat, when he was just twelve. That one does have corrections as well, in his own hand. My point is, he had access to copyists through his father, not to mention the musicians he played with and knew at court. I might add that there's a decent chance Beethoven himself did some transcriptions for the court orchestra when he was young. In other words, he was probably, at times, a copyist himself in his early career."

"You think that's what this is?" asked Gerrit, taking a sip of his coffee, which had gone lukewarm.

Meta paused. Had she gone too far? But no, she'd read on microfilm—a dissertation by Douglas Johnson—that the adolescent Beethoven's hand from this period sometimes resembled that of a copyist. Granted, there was a great paucity of manuscripts from the "moratorium" years, but a side-by-side analysis of what did survive might bear fruit.

She told Gerrit as much, concluding, "Again, no way to know yet what this is exactly, but it's actually unlikely. One thing I do know is that his dealings with copyists weren't always rosy. He had a famously confrontational relationship with a copyist named Ferdinand Wolanek, who was born right here in Prague. When Wolanek wrote Beethoven a letter in 1825, basically quitting as his copyist for the Ninth Symphony—if you can imagine quitting *that* particular gig, no matter how bad-tempered your employer was—Beethoven x'd out the letter and wrote nasty retorts all over it, things like 'Stupid, conceited, asinine Churl,' and complained about the idiotic transcription mistakes Wolanek was making, calling him a lousy, arrogant scribbler, and telling him that he'd already decided to fire Wolanek before receiving this letter of resignation, and so on. Beethoven didn't suffer fools lightly."

"Could this be Wolanek's hand then?"

"No, no. Poor Wolanek was probably a baby fast asleep in his crib when this sonata was composed," she said. "It's someone much earlier and in Bonn most likely. Researching the detailed history of Beethoven's earliest copyists is a task that lies ahead for me—talk about recherché, no?—but it's something I'm looking forward to. It'll be key to confirming this harebrained theory of mine, assuming I can actually prove it."

"'Harebrained' is not the word that comes to mind, Meta."

She smiled. "Well, you can see why I'm so desperate to find that first movement and sit in a quiet room to try to solve this puzzle."

"We'll find it. You'll solve it."

"From your lips to some kindly god's ear."

· 2 ·

WHEN SOBER, JAROMIR LÁSKA was a quiet, thoughtful man. He was a docile dreamer known to all as an exacting music teacher, a loving husband to his wife, Jana, and father to sweet Otylie, his only child. When in his cups—he was fond of mulled wine, often after his working day was done—he tended to lecture, invent, chase ideas across curious landscapes until both the ideas and he himself went off philosophical cliffs. He managed to balance these extremes for the most part and was generally well regarded, even admired, in the small city of Olomouc, where, as he liked to repeat, the first treatise on music written in Czech was published back in the sixteenth century and the great Dvořák composed for the city choir.

But there was a third man—a man both drunk and sober at the same time, one might say—who lived inside Jaromir's skin and spirit. This man was an obsessive collector of music manuscripts from earlier eras who made extravagant purchases when the mood struck, wise and foolish acquisitions from antiquarian dealers in several corners of Europe. This Jaromir was never averse to risking money he didn't have in order to obtain an autograph concerto by Rameau, a Bach keyboard fragment, a work for harpsichord by an unknown composer from the sixteenth century.

Some of these manuscripts were authentic. Many were not. He was assured by his suppliers that everything was bona fide, and they provided him with elaborate documentation to support the legitimacy of their materials. Some of these documents of provenance were authentic. Many were not. Most were not.

When he encountered what would nearly a century later become known as the Prague Sonata manuscript, he was neither sober nor drunk. Instead, he was unusually suspicious, certainly at first. One of the reasons he loved to collect music manuscripts was that he felt as if through the mystical medium of the score itself—its holy pages covered with notes and ligatures, tablatures and trills, progressions of chords and flights of arpeggios—he could almost touch the soul of the composer. So why, on that overcast afternoon in Vienna, did he have such doubts?

For one, he was never much drawn to acquiring works in a copyist's hand. The composer's original autograph score was what he prized. Such documents let him place his own mortal fingers on the very paper that had been touched by one whose genius was, he believed, immortal. A copyist, he scoffed, was no more a composer than a typesetter was a poet, or a bricklayer an architect. Copyists were as necessary as bricklayers, just as piano teachers such as he were necessary to society and the continuance of civilization. But the composer, the poet, the visionary architect?—they were blessed with a higher calling.

And what was being offered today, although with an abundance of ballyhoo, was a work for piano in the hand of a copyist.

How easy it would be, he thought, to fake a copyist's hand. He had a decent working knowledge of what any number of composers' scoring styles looked like, what their particular calligraphic eccentricities and telltale approaches to musical annotation were. The dense muscularity of Bach. The chromatic delicacy of Chopin. To look at original manuscripts by them or others opened a window, for a romantic collector like Otylie's father, onto the cauldron of composition itself. But the copyist had no connection to heroic volcanism, aesthetic passion. The copyist's job was to be legible and accurate.

Another reason for his suspicions was, ironically, also the strong motivation for this special trip from Olomouc to Vienna, which was roughly equidistant from Prague. And that was because the composer in question, Ludwig van Beethoven, was one master his collection lacked and the one he desired above all. The Viennese antiquarian who had offered Jaromir the manuscript was generally esteemed in the trade. His family had been in the business for several generations back to the mid-nineteenth century and had occupied the same shop for all that time. To Jaromir's mind, he had impeccable taste in both rarities and hand-tailored suits. Over the years, he had supplied Jaromir with handwritten scores by half a dozen important composers including Liszt, Brahms, and Rachmaninoff. Not the most valuable manuscripts available to collectors, but historically interesting artifacts.

The dealer explained that the sonata manuscript he'd come to inspect had been in the firm's possession since the 1860s, but until now had not been offered for sale. Before he was shown the item itself, Jaromir was invited to examine the ledger in which the purchase, made from Karl van Beethoven's only son, Ludwig, was noted. Jaromir knew that Karl, the master's nephew, whom he regarded as a son—the composer never married nor had any children of his own—was declared his "sole and universal heir" in

1827. He was also told that nephew Ludwig inherited Karl's estate in 1848, and the firm acquired this and several other rarities before Ludwig immigrated to the United States.

Between these two bequests and because Beethoven had always been generous with Karl during his lifetime, the dealer told Jaromir, he no doubt came into the possession of a considerable number of manuscript materials and memorabilia, some of which were passed on to Karl's own son.

Without a doubt, Jaromir agreed.

And this, the antiquarian continued, setting the manuscript before Otylie's father on a mahogany table whose ornate legs were carved to resemble griffins, is one of those manuscripts.

Jaromir gingerly turned the first two pages, still suspicious despite the alleged provenance and the credibility of the firm's ledger entry.

I don't see a signature, Jaromir commented, realizing that in saying as much he was already entering into a negotiation.

As I'm sure you know, many of Beethoven's manuscripts are not signed. And decidedly not those in copyists' hands.

Well, then, how can you be at all certain this work is by Beethoven and not another composer? Just because the manuscript came into your possession—

Into my exacting grandfather's possession.

—from a member of Beethoven's family—

The last among Beethoven's descendants to be baptized Ludwig.

—doesn't guarantee it isn't someone else's composition, does it?

The manuscript merchant calmly palmed the pomaded hair on the side of his head and told his potential and slightly annoying customer, Just keep turning the pages. I think you'll find something of paramount interest at the end of the first movement.

OTYLIE HAD NEVER SEEN SO MUCH SKY in her life. Its clouds were like roiling, mammoth castles drifting across the sun, casting shadows over the grasslands and limestone buttes below. The horizon was endless in every direction. Roads were broad as rivers. Fields wide as floods. Sage-green and pale brown rolling hills were oceanic. Even these Texan accents were broader than anything she had ever heard in London or Manhattan, let alone Prague. Jane told her the word for the way they drew out their vowels was *drawl*, a term she would remember because it rhymed with *tall* and *sprawl*.

All this sprawl tall drawl makes me feel small, she thought, pleased with her little joke in English. She added, *y'all*, another word she heard for the first time after stepping off the bus in Austin, handing her valise to Jim Burke, and sliding in next to Jane in the front seat of their Plymouth convertible. As the wind blew in her hair on the drive to her new home, Otylie remembered how frighteningly small she'd felt—a parentless, meaningless girl—on the train that carried her from Olomouc after her father's death. She recalled the nauseating sense of insignificance that had pressed in on her when she'd been forced to leave Prague and Jakub for exile in England. And though she'd experienced happy turns of fate in New York, Otylie, as she'd sat flanked by other immigrant nannies on their shared Central Park bench, often felt less consequential than the least child playing on the grass. Yet in strange sky-draped Texas, the smallness she felt was of a different order. Here her anonymity, her insignificance, proposed a kind of freedom. She was no longer looking for anybody or anything. If her fate had so far made her, to use one of Jakub's favorite words, a kind of *Schwindelkopf*—one with a spinning head and no constant view—the American West promised to still that motion. Here the spirit could stretch and steady, along with the eye.

So despite being dwarfed by her new surroundings, Otylie settled into the sparsely furnished apartment Jane and Jim had secured for her, and embraced this new frontier with a quiet vigor that surprised her wartime friend. She took on a dozen music students, teaching both piano and voice. Her pupils were mostly sweet, studious, and hopeless. One boy insisted on pronouncing Beethoven "Peethoven." An older girl said "Chopin" in the same way she might have referred to what one did to a tree with an ax.

The shortcomings and, to her, fascinating idiosyncrasies of her students only made Otylie more devoted to them. She sat through hours of scales that went flying off the tracks like derailed freight trains. She succumbed to four-handed "Chopsticks" when there seemed no better way to get a student to overcome his gremlin fear of the keyboard. She found that by first teaching her vocal pupils to sing a tune by Stephen Foster or a cowboy classic like "Streets of Laredo," she could better entice them to try Vivaldi's short and simple "Vieni, vieni, o mio diletto." A spinet that was included with the furnishings became the centerpiece of her world. She liked to place a fresh bouquet of wildflowers, picked during her morning walks, in a chipped yellow Fiestaware pitcher on top of the piano. Pupils who did an especially good job got a flower for their lapel or hair.

Otylie had never anticipated, back in Prague or London or New York, one day needing to know how to drive. But once she'd arrived in Texas she recognized quickly that, unless she were to ride a horse, a driver's license was nearly as necessary for survival as fresh drinking water and a wide-brimmed hat. The day she passed her driver's test was nowhere near as momentous as when she had become an American citizen in Manhattan, though she did feel a giddy pleasure knowing she could, if she so chose, climb into her rusted Chevrolet and drive to Mexico or Canada or California, and nobody could stop her.

Instead, she drove to her second job—or jobs—cleaning houses to make ends meet. This work she liked less than the hours spent with her children, as Otylie came to think of them. But she never complained, and she took silent pride in her ability to polish a copper pan or wax a linoleum floor. She liked discovering how these wealthy ranchers and bankers lived. Everything was a revelation. She had never before seen such fancy televisions in mahogany consoles, such efficient washing machines or gleaming electric stoves. Though some of her clients were "filthy rich"—Jane's phrase—she bore them and their wealth no malice, nor was she jealous. Her sole mission became to save enough money to one day buy her own small bungalow so that nobody could ever send her away from home again. Slowly, day by day, a deep peace came over her. She slept better at night to the chorus of crickets outside her window than she had even during the halcyon days on Wenceslas Square before the jackbooted thugs took over. The gratitude she felt toward her benefactors here was inexpressible in English, in Czech, in any language.

Jim worked long hours for a construction company while Jane had a part-time job at a local hospital. They spent as much time with Otylie as they could spare, and Jane met with her some evenings to continue their old moviegoing habit. Cary Grant was still Jane's idol, while Otylie developed a passion for Humphrey Bogart. *Casablanca* was her favorite movie because of the idealistic, fearless, handsome Paul Henreid, who played Victor, leader of the Czech underground. To be sure, his escape from a German death camp was as unlikely as his impeccably tailored, spotless white suit and his leisure to travel in Europe and North Africa, promoting the resistance while drinking champagne cocktails with his gorgeous wife at his side. If only Czechoslovak realities had been so elegant. Still, it made Otylie proud that a Czech stood at the center of what Bogey and Ingrid Bergman believed in beyond love itself.

Whenever Otylie had the Burkes over for dinner, Jim delighted in calling her curious cuisine of Bohemian dumplings and cabbage with Angus steak and pinto beans "Tex-Czech." Now and again, Jane invited an unattached gentleman friend to join the three of them for a backyard barbecue at the Burkes' two-bedroom suburban house. Otylie was still a handsome, youthful-looking woman. She had put on some needed weight while in New York, so the scarecrow slimness Jane had grown used to seeing in London was gone. She always had a modest flair for style, and wore bright silk scarves tied at her throat and dresses cinched at the waist with wide leather belts. Looking every bit the modern woman, Otylie Bartošová cut a striking, shy figure, rather more exotic than many of the neighborhood women at Jane and Jim's parties.

Otylie appreciated Jane's good intentions as a matchmaker, but none of her proposed gentlemen callers got anywhere with her. She was likable in the extreme, but closed to any intimacies beyond a Sunday drive in the country or attending a picture in downtown Austin. Try as some did now and then to encourage her to talk about her past, her family, what life was like for her during the war, she always politely changed the subject. She spoke longingly at times about Prague's magical palaces and the beautiful river that ran through the city. Czech culture—its Němcová, queen of fairy tales; its Dvořák of *New World Symphony* fame; even its beer-hall polkas—offered subjects about which she could be drawn out. But her personal biography was off-limits. If it came up and she was seated, she would stand and walk away. If she was standing, she would find a place to sit down.

One man, however, did manage to break through Otylie's reserve and become a close friend. Daniel Hajek, who had grown up in a small settlement an hour's drive southeast of Austin, was a second-generation Czech American whose family had emigrated from České Budějovice. He worked with Jane at the hospital. Tall, lanky but strong, with close-cropped black hair silvered at the temples, Daniel—or Danek, as friends called him—was a plainspoken man, who, according to Jane, had lost his wife to melanoma fairly early in their marriage. He continued to live alone through the rest of his thirties, and was now well into his forties. For Otylie, aside from his steel-blue kindly eyes and the fact that he pronounced her name properly, easily, with its accent on the first syllable, what made him stand out from other men was his speaking voice. His melodic baritone gave even the simplest phrase a quality that approached poetry. Something as unheroic and everyday as "Want to go down to the Lyric to see the new Gary Cooper?" was tinged with a kind of mild electricity and gravitas. But Danek showed no great initial interest in pressing her into any kind of romance. Delivering her to her doorstep after an evening out, he would warmly shake her hand and give her a friendly hug, but nothing more. He was a committed bachelor-widower.

"The kind of man every parent wants to have as a godfather," Jane confided, "since he's so generous and sweet to kids but never had one of his own."

"I like him very much," Otylie said.

"That's wonderful," exclaimed her friend. "Maybe you'll be the one to bring him out of his shell."

"Not like that."

"Not like what?"

"You know. That."

"Honey, hear me out," Jane continued one evening while the two were taking a stroll, the golden apple of sun flattening out into a bronze pear as it sank into the horizon. "You don't want to grow old alone, without love in your bed. Your Jakub wouldn't want you to, I'm sure of it. Not if he really loved you."

Jane, the only person with whom Otylie ever discussed Jakub, felt her friend withdraw into herself. She immediately felt sorry for having overstepped.

"I'm sorry, darling," she said. "I didn't mean to be pushy."

"That's all right."

"It's not. Please forgive me."

Jane hated to see Otylie's eyes well with tears which, from sheer willpower, did not spill.

"You know I love you."

"I love you too, Jane," Otylie said, taking her hands, voice cracking for the first time since Jane had known her. "I had a friend like a sister once. Irena, as you know. You're the only sister I have left. My only family. Can we talk about something else?"

Fifty miles southeast of Austin as the crow flies, down past hamlets with names like Rosanky and String Prairie, in the flats where Farm Road 1295 intersected with South Knezek, was an even tinier hamlet named Praha. Settled by a Bohemian immigrant, Mathias Novak, in the middle of the nineteenth century, Praha briefly boomed, its mostly Czech population swelling toward a thousand until the Southern Pacific Railroad laid tracks through the rival town, Flatonia, Daniel's birthplace and childhood home just north, drawing people away. In the new century, Praha became more and more a ghost town, as its schools, its businesses, and finally its post office closed. The population soon shrank to a couple of dozen stubborn, deep-rooted souls.

What kept little Praha on the map was a parish church with a single steeple rising over the local plain. Completed in 1892,

Saint Mary's had been, on every August 15 since 1855, the site of Pražská Pout, a popular festival celebrating the feast of the Assumption. On this day, upwards of five thousand people, many of Czech descent, converged on Praha to celebrate Mass, dance to live accordion music performed by Texas Czech musicians, and eat Moravian and Bohemian fare. Otylie asked Danek about the feast one evening while they had mint liqueurs after dinner on his porch overlooking a tangle of mulberry bushes sparkling in the moonlight.

"Praha's famous for more than just that annual festival."

"How so?" she asked.

"Sad story, but Praha lost more men per capita in the Second World War than any other town in America."

The idea that the little town gave so much blood to the cause of defeating the Reich galvanized her. "So, will you take me to the Mass there next month?"

"Sure, love to," he answered. "But I thought you weren't religious."

"I'm not," she assured him, wondering if that was still true, given how often she found herself saying a brief prayer of thanks when she woke in the morning or silently dialoguing with Jakub before she floated off to sleep at night.

During the drive to Praha, Otylie felt an unusual sense of excitement. The air rushing in through the open windows of the car was rich and soft. An all-night rain had greened the fields and raised the creeks that snaked through them. When they arrived at the festival, Danek parked among rows of cars and trucks lining the road, and they joined a steady stream of people making their way toward the village center.

Saint Mary's vaulted sky-blue ceiling, blue as the day outdoors, was painted with golden angels, as well as wondrous pelicans feeding their young, and the eerie floating eye of the Holy Ghost. It was different from any church Otylie had ever seen. In some inexplicable way, she found it more inspiring with its homespun modesty and clapboard quirkiness than the grand soaring cathedrals she'd seen in Prague and London. Danek, who sat close beside her in the pew, told her about the muralist, Godfrey Flury, a Swiss immigrant who made his living painting houses, signs, and county-road billboards, and who transformed this sanctuary into a folk art heaven.

"But, then, that's America for you." He craned his neck as he admiringly scanned the indoor firmament above them. "Settlers from everywhere just hankering to leave their fingerprints on the new homeland."

"Beautiful fingerprints," Otylie added, her spirit lighter than it had been for how many years? Many, too many years. At the same time, the throng of Czechs who spilled out across lawns surrounding Saint Mary's and beyond made her homesick. The pilsner was not as nutty or rich as what she drank back home. The famous *kolaches*, she laughed as she told her companion, were filled with such sticky-sweet, bee-drawing jelly that it made her teeth feel on fire while frozen in ice.

Yet what did it matter? She delighted in hearing the Czech-accented English at every vendor booth beneath the overarching shade trees that edged the parish cemetery, loved seeing Czech descendants playing country games—Danek excelled at the ring toss. Never a fan of polkas, she let herself be swept along with the dancing couples, some in traditional regalia. Doing the short steps and twirls with her enthusiastic partner, she sang "Roll Out the Barrel" with others in the broiling afternoon.

As Danek drove her home that night, she mused that, much as she liked Austin, it would be lovely to live where fellow immigrants from the homeland congregated. Those sugary *kolaches* must have gone to her head, she thought, and laughed. When Danek asked what was so funny, she told him what she'd been thinking. The

Texas Praha they'd just visited was all but a *nekropole*, a necropolis that rose to life like Lazarus but once a year. But she had to wonder whether, in a country as vast as this, there wasn't another Praha. One that hadn't died yet.

He nodded. "Minnesota, Oklahoma, Arkansas, Nebraska—we're here and there all over the place."

It needn't be, she told him, anything like her—their—shining jewel on the Vltava. Obviously it wouldn't be. No medieval castles and statuary in Oklahoma. No known alchemists in Arkansas. But why not look into it?

"I'd miss you terribly, Otylie," Danek said, surprising her as much because of the sentiment itself as because he had confessed it to her.

"You know you'll always be welcome in my house no matter where I end up," now surprising herself with how foolish and sentimental that sounded. More shocking was the realization of how much she would miss him too.

Maybe Daniel Hajek, who that evening kissed her good night on her doorstep for the first time, would come along with her, she mused. A long-shot fantasy. Besides, his job at the community hospital was steady, and most of his life had been spent in these parts. But who knew? They were birds of a similar feather. Maybe he would be willing someday to fly elsewhere with her, if there was a better place to nest. She adored Jane and really liked Jim. Her students were charming. She had some years to put in here in order to make her bank account grow, so unless something unforeseen happened, the idea that hatched on the Day of the Assumption would have to wait. That night, though, when Otylie put her head on her pillow, exhausted but wide awake, and watched the constellations trek across the pane of glass in her bedroom, she knew that this was not where her journey would end.

*

Some strategic long-distance telephone calls and discreet behind-the-scenes inquiries preceded Danek's showing up unannounced at Otylie's door on an early September morning following their Praha jaunt. She knew right away that something out of the ordinary lay behind his unexpected visit, given that Danek was even more formal than Otylie when it came to making appointments. "Starched shirt, starched blouse, you two're a perfect match," Jane once teased her friend. Unable to disagree, Otylie just shook her head with a wry grin.

"Danny," she said, using her personal nickname for him, as she pushed open the screen door, "what brings you here?"

"My day off, and I hoped to find you home." Hat removed, he asked as he stepped inside, "Anybody got a cup of black coffee around this place?"

"You bet," she said, amused by how many of these American-isms had crept into her once formal British locution.

"Good, thanks. I brought cinnamon buns from Brody's, hot out of the oven, as they say in the commercials." He presented her with a brown paper bag from the bakery, a couple of silver-dollar-size grease spots on its sides attesting to his claim.

Another scent besides cinnamon wafted in the air. Did he smell of extra aftershave this morning—sandalwood? And while Danek was always nicely groomed, this morning he seemed particularly natty in a deep blue dress shirt tucked into dress jeans, wearing black cowboy boots that had been polished earlier that day.

After trading small talk in the kitchen while Otylie poured their coffees and arranged the buns on a plate, they sat together, as they liked to do, out on her back porch shaded by cottonwood trees that were older than the two of them combined. Though it wasn't quite eleven, the late summer heat had quieted the song-birds. Cicadas droned away. A magpie squawked out at the edge of the gravelly yard, hopped twice, nonchalantly took wing.

"So, then," she said. "This pastry's delicious, but really, what brings you by this morning?"

"Well, I just had a very interesting conversation and thought you'd want to hear about it. You remember mentioning that you'd enjoy visiting other places where there were more folks who had settled from the old country?"

"I do."

"Well, wouldn't you know, I've been asked to interview for a job at a big hospital up in Lincoln, Nebraska."

"I'd need a map to know where that is," Otylie admitted.

"It's pretty much due north of here, up past Oklahoma and Kansas in the southeast part of the state. Now, I haven't said yes to anything and neither have they. But a friend of mine from school days married a girl originally from Lincoln, and they moved up there and really like it. It's the state capital, you know. Good university, considerable culture from what I understand, a music school. But here's another thing. Less than an hour farther north and west out in the farmland, there's a town called Prague."

"What? Really?"

"They pronounce it long so it rhymes with *hay* but it's still spelled P-r-a-g-u-e."

"That all sounds terribly exciting for you," Otylie said, feeling a sudden pang of abandonment.

"Hear me out. They've asked me if I would mind driving up to meet with them, see the facility, with the idea that if things worked out I would be given a better job there, more responsibility and higher pay, and what I'm wondering is if you might want to come along on the trip. I have vacation time I haven't taken, and if you could steal a week off from your piano lessons, maybe—"

"You know I'd love to go, see this American Prague town too, if we could—"

"That'd be half the point. Of course we'd visit there, to boot."

Otylie hesitated, feeling ridiculously prudish when she asked, "Would it be considered a little improper—is that the right word?—being that we're not married?"

Danek surprised her by laughing. "No, no, dear Otylie. We'll stay in separate rooms at the motels. Everything right and proper. Besides, it's not like we're not old enough to take a road trip together without a chaperone."

"It's a wonderful offer, Danny. And to get out of this Texas heat for a break—"

"Oh, they got their heat spells up there too. That's corn belt territory."

She wasn't exactly sure what *corn belt* meant, but rather than asking, she said, "Do you mind if I sleep on it?"

"Not at all. Only want you to come along if you'd find pleasure in doing so," he said, and they passed the rest of the morning chatting as they always did about politics—Danek liked this Nixon's chances; Otylie preferred Kennedy—friends, movies, weather, whatever came to mind.

When Otylie told Jane later that day, she wasn't surprised that her friend was madly enthusiastic to hear that things were, as she put it, "finally warming up" between the two. "I'm telling you flat out, girl. Nothing ventured, like they say."

"Like who says?"

"Oh, it's an old dusty attic of a phrase, 'Nothing ventured, nothing gained.' Forget that, though. The prairie's beautiful, what with its honey-gold fields and sandy-bottom rivers so shallow you can wade across barefoot. Go, live!" To underscore her enthusiasm, she pulled down one of her favorite books from childhood, *My Ántonia*, and gave it to Otylie. "This was written years ago, but the heartland of Nebraska and the Bohemians who settled there haven't changed all that much. Time kind of stands still on the prairie."

That night, reading in bed, Otylie found the prose of Willa Cather's novel simple enough to understand yet powerful, as if it had been written with her in mind. Skipping ahead to the final page, she read lines that especially moved her. They conjured a "road of Destiny" that

> had taken us to those early accidents of fortune which predetermined for us all that we can ever be. Now I understood that the same road was to bring us together again. Whatever we had missed, we possessed together the precious, the incommunicable past.

While Jakub could never travel any farther than he already had, Otylie realized that her road, no matter how it turned and twisted, no matter whether she traveled it alone or with a companion who possibly loved her—not as Jakub had, but in his own way—would surely reconnect with her husband's when she, like he, took ultimate residence in the forever past.

<h1 style="text-align: center;">· 3 ·</h1>

THE TEMPO OF EVENTS QUICKENED in the wake of Meta's revelation to Gerrit about the sonata's possible origins. And as the tempo sped up, the purpose of every day, every hour, intensified. More than once, Meta had to remind herself to stop and breathe. Now that the pages were back in her hands, she was galvanized. If she had been committed to bringing together the three sonata movements before, now she wouldn't rest until that came to pass.

When she finally got through to Mandelbaum in the morning, his tone was jarringly different than she might have expected. A flow of imperatives cascaded from the other end of the line, in a voice more clipped than she was used to hearing. Yes, he was relieved the manuscript had turned up, and yet, he continued, "Best not tell anyone you've found it. Too bad I was asleep when you called, but no matter. I'm meeting Wittmann again later on, and I don't want him to know that we've spoken."

"All right."

"Also, I want to examine both movements before I see him," he continued. "Is Sam free, you think?"

"I can ask, but I'm afraid I already told him I found it."

"That's fine. Sam's the exception," said Mandelbaum. "Call him and set it up, if you would. Do you have everything in order here in Prague?"

"What do you mean, 'in order'?"

"Any outstanding business left, any loose threads dangling?"

"Not really, I suppose."

"Good. Call Sam. Let's meet as soon as possible."

With that he hung up. In all her years of knowing Paul Mandelbaum, in the course of more than a hundred telephone conversations, he had never before hung up on Meta, nor had she ever heard him sound so agitated. That role had historically, if rarely, been hers. His had been that of the genial, teasing, methodical patriarch—her "old owl."

They convened midday at Sam's place. Mandelbaum was already there when Meta and Gerrit arrived, listening to Sam play the second movement, which he had nearly perfectly learned himself. When Meta heard the familiar music she felt the immediate equanimity of when she was a girl and their Saturday-morning apartment was filled with the warm sound of Jean-Pierre Rampal, her mother's favorite flutist, on the record player.

"Here," she said simply, handing Mandelbaum the leather attaché case.

The man withdrew the manuscript, and quietly studied the work, note by note. Seeing the two originals together for the first time made it clear to him, as it had been to Meta, that they were part of the same score. Dimensions were identical. Stitch holes large enough to accommodate cord or thin binding ribbons were punched down the fold at just the same places. A cursory glance was enough to let him see that both movements had been written by the same hand. The third movement was faded and its first and last leaves were damaged by unfortunate smearing, not to mention creasing and tears along the edges. On the first leaf, he noticed some faint words in Czech partly missing at the chipped top of the page. Neither Sylvie nor Gerrit could make them out. These disparities aside, the pair of movements had a similar, almost sibling-like, appearance. Their most conspicuous difference was plain as day. Irena's movement, however peripatetic its history after it left Otylie's possession, was in far better condition than Jakub's—as if the manuscripts themselves were biographical likenesses of those who had carried them.

Arms crossed, Mandelbaum stood by the studio window as Meta performed the work through twice more. Gerrit couldn't help but shoot furtive glances over at him, trying to get a measure of what he was thinking as the music unfolded, revealing itself like a formerly unknown species of avian life to an ornithologist whose whole world was birds. Though he presumed Mandelbaum was impressed by this lovely rondo, the professor's face—blank while Meta played, enigmatic afterward—betrayed little. If he felt moved or mesmerized or vexed by the music, it didn't show. It was as if he had left his body here in the studio with the rest of them while attending to more important business elsewhere.

The room went silent a second time as the last notes faded. A bittersweet wistfulness fell across the air, as weightless as a shadow. Not until this moment had the sonata seemed to Meta so destitute in its state of incompleteness. Was it possible for two ideas to actually yearn for a companion idea that might fulfill them? She, Paul, and Sam knew very well that a sonata need not by definition be in three movements. Nor were sonatas necessarily clear logical progressions from one movement to the next. Thesis, antithesis, synthesis—this was not the analytical morphology of the classical sonata. But what the three of them were hearing, each in a different way, was a story whose fountainhead of first notes was still wanting. The artist who wrote this music had an originating idea, a movement that had begun, like a life, with spontaneous energy. Surely, it was out there somewhere.

Unlike the gathering on Šporkova, the several run-throughs in Vinohrady lasted only an hour. No celebration followed Meta's performance. No dancing, no jubilant lifting of glasses. Instead, the manuscripts were collated and placed back inside Meta's leather briefcase, and the visitors took leave of the Kettles with hugs and handshakes all around. Sam read in Mandelbaum's pensive expression that he might not be seeing his old teacher again for a while. The idea made him unhappy but he understood. A break-in and the strange disappearance, then resurfacing of the movements—it was enough to make the most intrepid soul want to spirit the documents to a safer haven.

Once they were down in the streets, Mandelbaum's disquietude only grew. "My intuition tells me that you might want to leave Prague sooner rather than later."

"You don't think Wittmann's really going to escalate this, do you?" asked Meta. "We can put it in the safe at your hotel, like we should have in the first place."

"Let's deposit it there temporarily, since I don't have a better idea. But it may not do for long."

"Why?" she asked, perplexed.

Hearing the worry in Meta's voice, Mandelbaum said, "Please forgive me. I don't mean to be mysterious, but you don't know everything and I'm not sure there's time to catch you up. Let me talk with Petr and I'll answer your question afterward."

"Well," Meta said, as they continued to walk, "if it's all right with you, I think I'll just hang on to it myself after all. I'll feel better if I have it with me."

"I'm not sure" was all the professor managed.

Gerrit squeezed Meta's hand, an anticipatory gesture suggesting she might want to leave Mandelbaum to his own devices. He sensed there was much more to what the man was thinking about than the music they had heard.

Misinterpreting Gerrit's clasp as a simple sign of affection, she asked her mentor, "You remember when I first spoke with you about this and instead of taking it out to Princeton I insisted you come to New York to see it?"

"Of course."

"You laughed at me and said, 'Very Conan Doyle of you, Meta,' when I wouldn't tell you more. Who's being Conan Doyle now, Paul?"

A faint smile broke on Mandelbaum's lips. "I can't fairly disagree."

"What's wrong?" she pressed.

"After, I promise you. Besides, maybe I'm mistaken."

Gerrit, seeing their impasse, took this as his opportunity to alter the landscape. "Can I ask what you thought of the music?"

"I would have imagined my response to it would be clear as the noon Angelus bells in Rome. It's wonderful. But what's even more interesting is—"

Meta picked up Mandelbaum's sentence without missing a breath. "—that it's a bit immature? Brilliant but just a little unpolished, right?"

"Unpolished?" Gerrit asked, dumbfounded.

"Well, *unpolished* might not be the most courteous term," Mandelbaum agreed, brightening, the pedagogue in him rising to the fore now.

"Okay," Meta interjected. "Knotty, rough, unfettered. I mean, there are a lot of terms one might apply. Still learning, but at the same time vigorous as a hurricane and virtuosic as—"

"Meta's a better pianist than most, even after her injury," Mandelbaum told Gerrit. "But as a vigorous young musicologist who's still learning, she's a bit unfettered herself."

"Oh, please. We're thinking along the same lines, aren't we?" she countered, this time squeezing Gerrit's hand, signaling that a meeting of the minds, a disclosure, possibly loomed. "It's not Hummel or Hiller or somebody else who came later to the scene working in early Beethovenian modalities and voicings. Not to my mind, and not to yours either."

"Well, as far as minds go, I think we may well both be out of ours," Mandelbaum said, hurrying them along the cobblestone sidewalk as a less-than-gentle rain began to fall.

No one but Marta would ever know that Tomáš committed suicide the night after the musicologists Wittmann and Kohout paid the pianist a visit. His death was his decision alone. And Marta believed that his decision needed to be privately honored. After a lifetime of trying and often failing to live up to others' expectations and demands, he deserved not to be judged now.

She discovered him in bed the morning after the professors left Šporkova, the empty bottle of sedatives upright on the bedside table next to his bifocals. A volume of poems by Goethe that he had been reading was placed neatly beside the lamp. The look on his pale bluish face was serene, dignified. It was clear he hadn't taken the handful of pills for insomnia, accidentally overdosing. As she stroked his cool forehead, Marta understood that her father had reached a turn in his road where he felt at peace, or at least squared, with the life he'd lived, and he had chosen to leave the path.

Breathing hard, she disposed of the pill bottle before calling the authorities. She would insist he'd died of natural causes. If the coroner's office reached other conclusions, she would do her best to keep them confidential. She also secreted away the note Tomáš had written and left on the table. Curiously, it was not a letter of farewell or apology as Marta had expected when she first caught sight of it. The note, signed, stated that Tomáš intended to give the American girl Meta Taverner the two letters Otylie Bartošová had sent him so long ago. *She needs them more than I do* were the last words of the note, written in Czech in the old man's shaky script.

Marta was comforted to see that her father's final outward gesture was to help Meta in her quest to locate Otylie. If anything, she thought while seeing his body removed to the funeral home, it was Wittmann and Kohout, decorous and dignified with their nice suits and smooth urgency, who were to blame for this. Tomáš seemed to have aged a decade after their quietly terrorizing visit.

What's the matter? she'd asked him as they sat down to dinner after the two left.

Nothing, nothing.

Aren't you hungry? You haven't touched a thing on your plate.

At that, Tomáš gamely took a bite of roasted potato and absent-mindedly chewed.

What did those men want?

Nothing really.

That's just not true and you know it. I was listening and I didn't like what I heard. You want to discuss it?

No, he said, shaking his head as he reached for his cane to leave the table.

Fortunately, this was not their final exchange. When she took him his evening cup of steamed milk sprinkled with cinnamon, they spoke about how the weather was getting colder. Marta fetched a heavier goose-down comforter for his bed from a clothes press in the adjacent room, and filled the water decanter he kept on the same table where she would find the note the following morning.

"*Dobrou noc,*" she said, closing his door.

"*Dobrou noc,*" he answered, lifting his eyes from the page of Goethe bathed in lamplight. Good night, his last words.

Close friends in the neighborhood spent the morning with Marta, consoling her and one another, talking about funeral arrangements and reminiscing about how contented Tomáš had seemed since moving in with his widowed daughter. When Johana turned up from Josefov, however, the conversation took a darker turn.

If that American girl had never come here, my brother would still be alive, she said. The professor warned me she was nothing but trouble, and he was right. Ringing my bell at all hours, leaving me notes.

Aunt Johana, you're wrong. But it's not the time to—

She talked Tomáš into giving her our family's treasure, the woman interrupted, her white crepe-skinned face growing even more blanched.

She did nothing of the kind. I witnessed the whole thing. It was what Father wanted. Besides, I need to remind you it was never our family's treasure in the first place. It's been in our care for a long time, so it may feel like it's ours. But it belongs to the Bartošes.

Those ghosts? That Bartošová woman abandoned it years ago, just like her martyr husband. Left it to my brother to hide in my house, put us all at risk, and you a tiny baby, that thing hidden in my wall. Imagine. And now look. The strain of it finally killed him.

Marta glanced around the room apologetically, then said, If anyone caused him undue strain, it was your friend Professor Wittmann. Now we should talk of other things.

Johana looked down at the carpet in the parlor as if the truth were somehow written in its pattern, then up again, startled, oddly, to find everyone staring at her. Maybe you are right, maybe wrong. I'm just an old lady, so don't listen to me. He was my only brother, a fool sometimes. But I loved him from our earliest days and won't stop loving him now that he's gone.

With that, she began to weep. Marta heard insincerity in her aunt's words, but also confusion, and went over to put an arm around her. The shock of Tomáš's sudden death has overwhelmed her, she reminded herself. Grief takes many forms.

Only when she was finally alone in the house was Marta able to attend to Otylie's letters. She saw no reason to delay fulfilling Tomáš's last wish, sitting down to telephone the Hodeks, with whom she knew Meta was staying. The young woman, who in no way resembled the covetous interloper her aunt had described, deserved to know that her benefactor had died. In any case, now that everyone had left, Marta had to admit that she didn't want to be by herself this evening. The rooms were too quiet. The ticking clocks bothered her. The dripping kitchen faucet chipped away at any hope of sad calm. Her father was gone, and Meta would appreciate the fact that with him went part of an era.

Within the hour, Meta and Gerrit were at Marta's door, huddled under a wet umbrella. Handing her a bouquet of flowers, Meta said, "I can't believe it. We're both so sorry."

"Come in before you get pneumonia." Marta took the flowers, thanking them and giving each kisses on both cheeks. After they had hung up their coats in the foyer and stowed the sopping umbrella in a large amphora-shaped urn, she led them down the corridor to the kitchen. "The first time we met, we shared some brandy, I recall."

They sat at the table, shaking their heads at how unexpected Tomáš's death was given what fine form he had been in during the private recital. They made the small talk people at a loss for words, thrown together in mourning, must make.

"He was not a young man," Marta offered, tasting her brandy and staring at the lights reflected on its jostled surface as she set the snifter back on the table.

"We feel so fortunate to have met him," said Meta.

Thanking her, Marta switched to Czech, too exhausted to string together her thoughts in English, and relied on Gerrit to fill Meta in. "'Given that he survived not one but two oppressor regimes, it is a miracle that he didn't go permanently insane. Of course, he did lose some part of himself over time, but unlike most people when they get older, he was less, how should I describe this, less . . . *dementiaed* than when I was a young girl.'"

"I didn't really live here under the Party," Gerrit commented, "but I remember the euphoria in the air when I first moved back to Prague. He must have felt it like everybody else, that new sense of freedom."

I'm sure you're right, Marta agreed.

Meta had been listening intently to Gerrit's translation as Marta aired her thoughts. Now she spoke. "One thing I regret is that he'll never know if I was able to find Otylie."

Here Marta had to smile. A flat sort of smile that meant, even before she said it in so many words ahead of Gerrit's translation, "'I hate to dampen your optimism. You may one day find the missing part of the music, but the chances of Otylie Bartošová being alive? I'm sorry to tell you, Meta, but that will not happen.'"

Having held back her tears all day, Marta finally broke down.

Meta rose and stood behind her, placing both hands on the woman's shoulders, saying nothing. Gerrit looked at Meta as she remained there for a minute in a wordless tableau. What was there, finally, to say?

Marta apologized and left the room, telling her guests she would be right back. They assumed she wanted to dry her tears in private. Meta sat beside Gerrit again, took his hand into hers on her lap. Her mind was awash in crosscurrenting thoughts. On the one hand, she was grateful that she had managed to find Tomáš, talk with him, discuss the sonata, play it in his presence. On the other, Marta's blunt statement unsettled her. Everything seemed wrapped in death. Mere months ago, Irena had opened a steamer trunk and handed over a sheaf of music. Now she was gone. Only yesterday, Tomáš might have been sitting in the very chair where Meta herself now sat clutching Gerrit's warm hand, utterly unaware that the angel of death was perched on the roof of his house.

"Don't think like that," Gerrit whispered, interrupting the image of a thin, leathery black figure flexing his wings on the cornice somewhere above them.

There he went again, reading her mind. "Like what?"

"Like it's hopeless you'll find Otylie."

"I have to admit, she's probably right."

"You found Tomáš before he died, didn't you? You managed to meet Irena."

"Well, she found me, not the other way around."

"Doesn't matter who found whom. You'll get there, maybe not to Otylie herself, but at least to the other pages of the manuscript. I have faith in you—"

"So do I," Marta said, reemerging unexpectedly from the dark hallway to sit with them again. "Please, don't misunderstand. My father and I both think—or thought, I guess now for him—that you have the, how do you say this, the right passion in you. The will. The people who have the pages, they were just trying to survive and keep it safe, the manuscript. I never did know Otylie

Bartošová, but always I expect one day she might show up at our door. She didn't. That means for me she cannot."

"There might be other reasons, though. You said this house didn't exist here for a lot of years. That it was burned down. Maybe she came looking and saw it was destroyed and made some of the same assumptions you're making."

Instead of pursuing further speculation and counter-speculation, Marta laid Otylie's two letters on the table. "My father wanted you to have these. He said you needed them."

"You're sure?" Meta asked.

"He was sure. This was important to him."

"Thank you," said Meta, holding them before her as if they were paper amulets. "I'll keep them with the manuscript."

"He would like that. It is where he kept them too."

"How I wish I could thank him."

"Find that first movement. This is the way you can thank him."

Back at Jánská, Gerrit helped Meta go through the two missives sentence by sentence, as they hadn't had time to do when Tomáš first brought them out. The letter dating from 1978 especially touched Meta. *Do you have any idea what became of the sonata manuscript? I can't forgive myself for ever having broken it up.* Her words conveyed all the tragedy that Meta felt every time she played the second passage of the work's likely second movement, that dropping-into-the-abyss mood it proposed. One of the standard premises she had been taught about music and meaning was that it was a very tricky, iffy, slippery business to attribute literal story lines to the abstract, ineffable gestures of music. Mandelbaum had always been as strict as a penal code when it came to overinterpretation.

"More often than not, music means music" was what he'd told his students. "It's not a poem about a tree. It's not an essay about nematodes. It often stands for nothing greater or lesser than itself."

But she never believed him. Listeners' spirits soared or sank because of something the brain linked to story or portrayal or even landscape, no matter what Mandelbaum said. Interpretation logically assumed narrative framing in some degree and form. At any rate, the words in this letter were written by one who knew what the sonata meant in profounder ways than anyone else could possibly experience.

Having heard nothing from Mandelbaum, Meta tried to reach him at the hotel before going to bed. The rain had tapered off to a light drizzle and the wind had died down as she listened to the phone in his room ring a number of times before the receptionist came back on the line.

"I am sorry but no one is answering. You would like to leave a message?"

"Yes, could you say that Meta Taverner called." She spelled her name and gave the woman her cell number.

That night in bed with Gerrit, Meta found her thoughts flowing back and forth from Otylie's desperate words to the harsh reality of Marta's. The one glimmer in her musings, which were otherwise dark and chill as the night, was Otylie's mention of her friendship with a wonderful girl, and about having found a good man. This made her happy for the woman. But wasn't it also possible that the existence of this friend and lover meant she had a network, a coterie or circle, and was thereby just a little more traceable?

London. Meta had performed there. That there was no language barrier for her to hurdle would help. Still, London was a prodigious megalopolis compared with Prague's relatively compact medieval web. These were night thoughts, of course. In the morning she'd be able to embrace the fact that tracking a Czech who worked for the Beneš government in London during the war would surely be much easier than wandering streets with names like Veleslavínova or Žatecká using a compass without a needle.

UNEASY, AS FIDGETY AS THE NEGATIVE POLES of two magnets forced together, Wittmann and Mandelbaum huddled in a dark corner of Konvikt's rear room. Though they had arranged to meet earlier in the evening, Wittmann pushed the hour back with the excuse that something unavoidable had come up. Personal matter. Couldn't be helped. Sincere apologies.

The last person he felt like speaking with at the moment was Paul Mandelbaum. He hadn't enjoyed their conversation at the hotel any more than had his colleague. Sniping, however civilized, wasn't their forte. What was more in their wheelhouse was whether Jean-Yves Thibaudet's rethinking of the complete keyboard works of Ravel and Debussy merited all the attention it was getting—Paul thought yes, Petr no. They might have been closer comrades in musical arms had they lived on the same continent. Still and all, even with an ocean dividing them, snail mail, the occasional conference, and sporadic telephone marathons had kept the fire of friendship burning.

The problem of the sonata blanketed all this warmth in a layer of frosty dissension. Mandelbaum's position was, to Wittmann, parochial. He was unable to see beyond the immediate research of his acolyte. The resourceful, enterprising, risk-taking accomplice Wittmann once counted on was now as absent as were the low-level Communist curators who'd acted as his suppliers in exchange for modest remuneration and simple considerations such as a bottle of vodka or an hour with a genial prostitute.

Hadn't he for the most part spared Mandelbaum some of these more sordid details? All the American needed to know was that such trafficking was dangerous but ultimately in a just cause. Paul must have suspected that the manuscripts might never be repatriated even if the Reds did ever fall. But for reasons of his own, he never asked. Then, one day in Amsterdam, he'd told Wittmann that he would take this parcel to New York and deliver it to an address he had visited twice before, but that he was getting married and his role as courier had to come to an end. Too touch and go. And what with a tenure-track professorship offered at the same time, he simply had to get out.

Wittmann had almost felt sorry for the man back then, and in a way still did. Mandelbaum had wanted, in lieu of further payment for his role as wary mule, Wittmann's assurance of absolute confidence in the matter. He'd done his bit, and done it less for the money—though money had helped in those church-mouse-poor graduate-student days—than because he mostly believed he was in it for the common good.

Idealism unanchored by realism was something Wittmann never found terribly useful or effective. This was one of the several reasons he was here tonight. And the primary reason he found himself working against his old accomplice.

Never had they felt so uncomfortable with each other. The foam on their untouched pints settled toward flatness. The last-call supper they'd ordered, as a polite way of putting off the inevitable, would arrive at the table soon, though neither had much of an appetite. Mandelbaum, who had demanded his colleague meet him on neutral ground, broke the silence, if only because civility suggested he must.

"That was you, or somebody sent by you, who did a little illegal enter and search at Gerrit's, wasn't it," he asked, although the tone in which his question was posed didn't so much invite an answer as a confirmation.

"You make me smile," Wittmann said, unsmiling. He slowly flicked ash off his cigarette—he'd capitulated to the urge to start smoking again—into the tray.

They spoke in English, not only because Wittmann's English was better by far than Mandelbaum's Czech but to protect themselves from eavesdroppers at nearby tables such as those they had drawn during their breakfast in the hotel restaurant. It seemed probable that they would be revisiting unpleasant truths, and the Konvikt crowd of blue-collar locals sudsing away their day jobs were less likely to understand those truths—or lies, for that matter—if they weren't exchanged in the native tongue.

Satisfied he'd gotten one of the confessions he was looking for, Mandelbaum aimed for a second. "What did you have in mind to do with the score if you'd found it?"

Wittmann now did take a sip of beer. "Do you remember when you and I strove so beautifully together to do the necessary work that the larger international community could not effect? Like Maisky and Argerich playing one of the Bach gamba sonatas, so in sync with each other we were. So much on the same wavelength."

Taken aback by the outrageous analogy, Mandelbaum opened his mouth to comment, but Wittmann raised a warning hand, palm out.

"No, let me finish. I know you remember. What I'm wanting to ask, since it seems we're here to ask questions, is if you think what we did was good or bad."

"May I speak now?" Mandelbaum said, leaning back in his chair.

A brief flourish with the same hand, a go-right-ahead gesture.

"I doubt Mischa Maisky and Martha Argerich would appreciate your comparison, not to mention Bach. Ethics aside, what we did was against the law in at least one country, yours. That much we both know. Whether it was good or bad? With forty or so years of hindsight to bring to bear, I suppose you could make a pretty strong case either way."

"And you think I'd be the one making the case that it was good, while you'd advocate it wasn't. Am I right?"

"That may or may not be true. But you know what, Petr? It's water under the bridge, clean, dirty, or otherwise. We're not here to discuss the past. We're here to discuss Meta's sonata manuscript."

"Ah," Wittmann laughed, or sneered, or groaned—it sounded as if he'd managed all three with that single exhalation. "There you are. What do you mean, 'Meta's' sonata manuscript? Its ownership is Czech, about that there's no question. This woman, Otylie Bartošová, was the original owner, a Czech. Tomáš Lang—yes," he said, seeing Mandelbaum's raised eyebrows, "I told you I knew about the final movement being in his care—Tomáš Lang and his sister, both Czechs whose family hailed from Sudetenland. Irena Svobodová, pure Czech. Jakub Bartoš, a true Czech hero, it would seem."

"So I understand. But neither Irena nor Bartoš is alive, and it remains to be seen whether Bartoš's wife is. Until such time—"

"Until such time as her existence or demise is determined, it is our responsibility to see that this manuscript is handled as we both know it merits, and to consider all appropriate options. Failing acquisition by an institution here, the score must be placed in the private hands of a Czech who would be able to act as custodian and curator," he said, gazing coolly at Mandelbaum. "Several people come to mind."

"Needless to say, you deem yourself the most fitting of these several," said Mandelbaum, stomach churning. Despite the sophistry of Wittmann's claims, Mandelbaum knew this man was potentially as dangerous as he was striving to present himself, and might in fact be capable of having the manuscript seized. The situation would have to be handled with a surgeon's care.

"I never said that," Wittmann scoffed, as the aproned waiter suddenly appeared and set their plates of food before them. A roseate birthmark covered one side of his face, which Mandelbaum caught out of the corner of his eye. Stay focused, he scolded himself.

Need anything else? the waiter asked.

Both men ignored his question as if he weren't there. Impatient, he walked away.

"Last time we spoke about this, you were willing to work with Meta, help her. What happened?"

"What happened is she seduced that fool Lang into giving her the original, when in fact, in private, and with Karel Kohout as my witness, he expressed profound confusion about the matter. Frankly, I think he was so agitated by the whole thing that he either took his own life or died from worry about it."

"Tomáš Lang is dead?"

Wittmann frowned. "You didn't know? Part of the reason I delayed our meeting is that I had to pay a call on his grieving sister, Johana. She blames much of this upheaval in her family's lives on your obstinate Meta, and I can't say I disagree. Johana was too distraught to discuss it in depth, but my impression is that she'd be willing to press charges that the original score of the third movement was stolen, or at minimum taken without the full understanding or permission of its owners. I have friends in high places who would agree with me, I might add."

"Meta tells me she has written proof of ownership of the second movement, and Lang's daughter witnessed her father giving her the original of that outer movement. So in point of fact, who cares about your friends in high places?"

"Your Meta might want to care," Wittmann said, gazing at his dwindling cigarette nipped between long fingers. "I told her so when she barged in on my lecture."

"Please. This is all bluster on your part, and you know it. You're making me wish I'd never trusted you to help. I feel I've gone and thrown her to the wolves."

"Charming words coming from an old comrade in arms."

"Damn it, Petr. You're so good at what you do, one of the best. Why do you need to behave like this? Is there something I'm missing here?"

"What you're missing is your problem, I imagine," Wittmann sniffed. "What I'm missing is an old colleague who used to have some bone in his back."

"You sound less like a musicologist than a melodramatist," Mandelbaum said, shaking his head as calmly as he could. "Just what did Renata do to you on her way out? Is the divorce what's pushed you to this? Or do you miss the bad old days that much? Has simple academia gotten too dull?"

A rare flash of anger betrayed the open wound that Mandelbaum's barb had struck. "Renata has nothing to do with anything. You and I always used to speak between the lines, so how was I to know that you sent this document my way with any intentions other than to acquire and place it?"

Mandelbaum said nothing, waited.

"Listen, have you ever had a serious exchange with your Meta about the dialectic of that second movement, what's happening there musically? And I mean note for note, measure for measure? And how to interpret the jejune nature of that rondo?"

"Jejune shot through with exquisitely radical dynamics here and there, you mean."

"My point exactly. Does the girl really know what she may have here? Do you?"

"And what does she have here? That is, beyond two thirds of a lost score?"

Wittmann shook his head with disgust. "You want me to help her. But how can the wolf, as you so nicely put it, help the innocent lamb? It's against the wolf's nature. And, I might add, the lamb's."

Mandelbaum knew it was time to move in a different direction. "All right. Let's stop for a minute and think this through." He exhaled through pursed lips, smiled.

The abrupt change in tone, the unexpected visage his colleague now presented, did stop Wittmann in, as it were, his wolf's tracks.

"We're both good at theorizing, or we used to be. Correct?"

Wittmann nodded, a deep frown carved into the flesh of his lips.

"I've heard everything you've said, and while I might have differing opinions, I'm not deaf. Nor am I dumb. Dumb in any sense of the word."

"No one said you were—"

"Please, Petr. Your turn to listen. You might not hate what you're about to hear, so let me speak."

Wittmann lit another cigarette and snapped out the match flame with several quick flicks of the wrist, trying to betray nothing though his irritation now edged toward curiosity.

"Meta trusts me and listens to me," the American continued. "If—and this is a very theoretical *if*, mind you, the iffiest of ifs—if she fails to locate the initial owner, and if I were to tell her to give you the originals of both movements so they may be offered for sale to whatever collection you feel would be best suited for their preservation here, would you agree, privately but in writing, to two things in return?"

"One 'if' calls for another, though you've presented two. I will agree if I logically can."

"The caveats are easy enough to guess. One, Meta gets full credit for her discovery and you help her as originally requested with authentication and attribution. That much you already knew. Two, she benefits from the proceeds of the sale—"

"But—"

"Hear me out. She benefits together with the Lang family, assuming their partial ownership is proved. Details will remain, as in times past, confidential. I'm not saying you should be cut out, by the way. Whatever commissions, finder's fees, contractual arrangements, and all that, you should certainly be accorded."

"What about you?"

To Wittmann's surprise, Mandelbaum answered, "I will take twenty percent of your twenty percent. In the old days we shared far more equally, but you're left to do the heavier lifting this time."

Wittmann stared past his colleague into the smoky room. "Why the change of heart?" he then asked, abruptly fixing his eyes on Mandelbaum.

"I don't wish to see Meta or, for that matter, you, end up hurt. Not when there may be a compromise in which everyone gets what they want. Or mostly. You'll need to make peace with her for this to work, you know. At the moment she's not very pleased with you."

"Do you think your displeased devotee could find such terms acceptable? She seems more intransigent than you ever were, and that's saying something."

Mandelbaum let the jab go by. "Well, that's where more of the iffy part of this idea comes in. But I think if I tell her that you're considering going to the authorities—a risky proposition, given your own Achilles' heel in all this—it might soften her intransigence. Besides, she's borderline broke."

"Just what makes you think Johana Langová will agree to all this?"

"I'm sure you'll think of something," Mandelbaum said, with a faint forced smile.

"I already have," Wittmann retorted, his voice dry as flame, any hint of banter gone. "The score must be kept in neutral hands until such time as the widow Bartošová is found, a highly unlikely scenario, but there it is. I doubt you would trust me to hold it myself, and I don't particularly trust you or your young friend, no offense. Let us place it in the joint custody of Lang's sister and daughter. Get them a bank box and give them the key with the understanding no one's to have access until you and I both say so. Agreed?"

"Shall I broach the proposition to Meta then?" ignoring both question and proposal.

"You may," said Wittmann. "But also, if you would, tell her that I'm not absolutely convinced I want or need to proceed this way."

"Your friends in high places?" Mandelbaum frowned as he reached into his jacket pocket, pulled out his wallet, and said, "It would be best if I went to her with a more solid assurance than that."

"Well, see what she says and get in touch."

Each, as if on cue, placed on the table more than enough money to settle their bill.

"Let me know soon. Tomorrow would be good."

"Day after would be better," Mandelbaum countered. "I have to sit her down and talk all this through, give her time to think. As you yourself said, she can be obstinate and I don't imagine I'll have much luck persuading her to agree to any of this if I look like I'm forcing the issue."

Curiously, Wittmann seemed to stare at the money on the table and made no response.

"Always good to see you, Petr," Mandelbaum said as he got up. He pulled on his overcoat, which was hanging on a nearby peg next to others of various shapes, weights, and lengths, and slipped out of the cozy bar-restaurant into the wet Prague darkness.

· 4 ·

JANE AND HER HUSBAND threw a barbecue for Otylie and Danek the night before they headed to Nebraska. The Burkes loved their parties, and though their friends would be back in a week, this was still a welcome excuse. In Otylie's honor, Jim decided he would try to add something Czech to his standard baby back ribs, shell steaks, and chicken. His attempt to make fried cheese on the grill was a disaster, though, as it caught fire and dribbled into the bed of briquettes. The laughter this mishap provoked, he told his friends, was well worth the cost of the block of frozen Muenster. A self-appointed bartender poured highballs, and people helped themselves to bottles of beer from a big wash-tub filled with ice water. Frank Sinatra and Nat King Cole floated over the backyard gathering from the hi-fi in the family room that gave onto the patio. When the two women found themselves alone in the kitchen, Jane slipped Otylie a sealed envelope.

"Now, you have to promise me you won't open this until you get to Lincoln."

"What is it?" asked Otylie.

"Nothing much. Just wanted to make your trip a little extra special."

"Oh, Jane. You don't have to make more of this than there is to it. I'm just going along for the ride to keep Danek company."

"You never know," said Jane.

When she opened the envelope several days later, at the Cornhusker Hotel in downtown Lincoln, Otylie found fifteen dollars inside. Jane's note read, *Told you it wasn't much, hon, but please do me a favor and get yourself a dress with some pretty prairie flowers on it, promise me you will?*

A sweet gesture, typical of Jane, but Otylie hoped her friend wouldn't mind if instead she bought an inexpensive floral blouse and used the balance to help Danek with food and gas money. Since he'd allowed her to share some of the driving, which she loved to do, she felt it only fair that gas stations and eateries along the highway pocket her cash as well as his.

Riding in Danek's years-old Fairlane, windows down as they made their way north, Otylie didn't want to listen to any country-music radio stations, preferring Danny's voice as he commented on every curious sight they saw. Little seemed to escape his notice. He pointed out creeks with quaint names like Running Turkey, Little Emma, Smoky Hill. Where the soil was red in Oklahoma, he remarked, it was black in Kansas. Around Salina, a grain elevator looked to him like Goliath's tombstone.

"That crop there is sorghum, farther along it'll be corn," he said. And, "Look at all those redwing blackbirds, not usually a flocking type, and those white egrets fishing the aqueduct there." Otylie listened with delight.

True to Danek's word, they stayed in separate motel rooms, after dinner at a roadhouse or Mexican joint—Otylie had a weakness for sopaipillas and honey—and a twilight walk to stretch their legs before bed. For the first time since her younger days, she found herself wondering what it might be like to fall asleep in a man's arms, or rather Danek's arms, nestled next to him for the night. Which raised conflicted feelings about loyalty to Jakub, her *Kocourek*, her little tomcat, gone all these years. There was also this—it was well and good to carry on her inner dialogue, but what if Danek intended to maintain nothing greater than a close friendship with her?

Even if it all came to naught, Danek had helped open her more to the world. Like him, she was in her mid-forties—well, forty-seven, to be honest—but could pass for years younger. Friends said she looked good, and she knew she was in robust health, for all the devilments of her earlier years. She fell asleep on her first night in Nebraska fully aware that she might have half a lifetime ahead yet to live, not squander.

Next morning, after breakfast, Danek went off to meet his potential new employers at the hospital while Otylie explored the city, really more a spread-out town. She visited the capitol with its colorful mosaics and murals and rather amusingly bawdy, to her mind, statue of a man sowing seeds atop the golden dome of its phallic-shaped tower. She wandered the grounds of the university, reminding herself that the novel Jane had given her to read was written by the same Willa Cather who went to school here. The blocks of unpretentious houses with their brick walks; the downtown barbershops and five-and-dimes and, yes, movie theaters with handsome marquees; the plaintive wail of steam engines rolling into or out of the busy rail yard; the singing meadowlarks—all that she saw and heard made Otylie feel oddly at home. And look, she thought, as she returned to the hotel to meet her companion, she hadn't yet visited the namesake Prague! The Prague of the plains nestled in a small valley notch—they called it a "bottom" here—due north.

Danek liked what he saw at the hospital, the facility itself, the people he met. "More modern than I expected," he told her over drinks in the Cornhusker bar. He weighed a palmful of salted peanuts he'd taken from a bowl on the counter, selected one and placed it in his mouth, the look on his face more contemplative than this trivial gesture might merit.

Otylie didn't know whether to be excited or worried. "What's the next step?"

"They want to see me again the day after tomorrow," he said. "Peanuts?"

She shook her head. "And you're going, right?"

As if waking up from a dream of sitting in another bar, speaking with another Otylie, eating other peanuts, Danek looked up from his palm and said, "Oh yes, absolutely."

"That means we can drive up to Prague tomorrow?" She was careful to pronounce the name with a long *a*, *Prāgue*.

"Sure does. One of the interns gave me the name of a man there, Kliment, very nice I'm told, family goes way back in Saunders County. A wonderful musician, he said."

"Music or polka?" Otylie teased.

"Guess we'll find out soon enough."

Danek fell serious again, finished the last of his peanuts, and took a sip of Scotch.

"Did they tell you more about Prague?" she encouraged, wondering what was troubling him.

"Well, if we were looking for a settlement of Czech immigrants, this is the right place. Vavra, Janáček, Wirka, Rak—I'm only remembering a few names he told me," Danek said. Then, out of the blue, "Otylie, they offered me the job—"

"I knew they would," she exclaimed.

"—I'm not the most suave man," he continued. "I've been a widower for a long time and I've been so grateful to have your friendship. What I want to say is, I don't really want to accept their offer unless you'd consider coming with me. I mean, we've only just got here and tomorrow we'll go up to Prague and give it a look-see. But I would only be interested in moving if you came too."

Stunned, Otylie reached over and took both of Danek's hands in hers.

"Look," he said, lightly clearing his throat, "whether we move here, stay in Texas, or live on the moon, I'm wondering if you would marry me."

She didn't want to cry but did despite herself, nodding her head yes. "I will be honored to be your wife, dear Danek."

Waking the next morning for the first time ever beside a man not Jakub Bartoš, Otylie experienced a cluster of emotions. She was grateful to have a fresh chance, she who'd rarely hoped for such a thing. Nervous, daunted, as well. Would she, who had so settled into a life of solitude and self-sufficiency, be able to make a good wife for Danek, a solitary and self-sufficient man? As he stirred her to life from a deep sleep, Otylie made a silent farewell to Jakub, whom she would or wouldn't rejoin after death—she retained her doubts about the existence of hell and heaven beyond this world—telling him that she would always love him but now she had to live fully with her husband-to-be.

The drive from Lincoln up to Prague began in dense fog, under a pewter sky thick with low-running clouds, and ended in steady soaking rain. The metal roofs of barns caught the spare light and glimmered like square jewels in the distance. A small swift fox, wet and muddy, looking for all the world like a mysterious denizen of some secret underworld, crossed the raised road as they approached Valparaiso. All along, tatters of mist-clouds chased across their path like sails of ghost schooners that had come detached from their masts.

Hardly the popular vision of romance, Otylie thought, as the heavier rain let up and gave over to drizzle, but this was a day in her life she would never forget. Had the prairie sun been shining bright gold in a sky unblemished by a single cloud, it would have been the same to her. She felt feather-light and certain of the rightness of what she was doing.

The farther north they drove, the more the landscape rolled, hillier than they might have expected. After they'd crested a long rise that gave onto another long, shallow bowl of land, Prague finally came into view. The drizzly fog beginning to lift, they turned off the county road, crossed a bridge over a small stream, and soon enough found themselves driving alongside one of the grain elevators ubiquitous in this part of the world until they reached the foot of the town's modest main street, where they parked.

"Place seems deserted," Danek commented.

"I love it," said Otylie, wondering what it must be like for an American of Czech descent to go to the homeland for the first time, stand on the Karlův most, gaze up at the castle, the Pražský hrad, and marvel at its centuries of history. Here, in this midwestern Prague, the centuries of history had nothing to do with citadels and statues, and everything to do with the earth and sky. It reminded her of childhood, and day trips she used to take with her parents into the countryside before the First World War, when her mother was strong.

They left the car and umbrella behind and walked the quiet streets of Prague, some of which simply dead-ended at the edge of a cornfield. Up behind the town rose a hill where there was a small cemetery near the town's water tower, the tallest structure they saw aside from the grain elevator and church steeple. Hand in hand, they watched the last clouds break apart, in layers upon layers, allowing blue to emerge and an intermittent sun to shine on the wet trees and roofs of perhaps a hundred houses, a dozen commercial buildings, not many more, and unbounded farmlands. Otylie could only wonder if some folks who settled these fields and made a livelihood here so distant from Czechoslovakia had family or friends who had known any of her family and friends. The odds seemed small, but that didn't stop her from turning to Danek and saying, "This may sound silly, but I feel more at home here than I've felt since I was exiled from Praha all those years ago."

"Not silly at all. Shall we walk down, see about finding this Mr. Kliment and having lunch?"

The whole village, it seemed, or at least its farming men, were huddled in a small bar-restaurant on the main street. Weather had kept them from their soggy fields, and the grain elevator was silenced as well. When the couple entered, the air was dense with cigarette smoke; and taciturn camaraderie of the sort that comes from having grown up together in a tiny settlement where parents and grandparents had been raised. The visitors sat on stools since all the tables were already occupied by men, young and old, in overalls. Though welcomed by a brightly smiling waitress who passed them menus across the counter, Otylie for a moment wondered if this Prague was such a tight-knit community that outsiders might find it hard to fit in. As she and Danek ordered the daily special of duck and cabbage, most of the dialogue she heard was spoken in flat midwestern American accents although now and then she overheard snippets in Czenglish, which she found embarrassingly heartening. Nearly everything they said had to do with forecasts.

Finding Mr. Kliment wasn't hard. They asked their waitress and, as it happened, her uncle, Josef Kliment, known to everyone in town as Joe, was a few stools down, nursing a cup of coffee and biding his time along with everyone else. Danek got up and introduced himself to Joe, whose unshaven face broke into a smile as friendly as that of his niece. After a few minutes of back-and-forth, Danek brought him over to meet Otylie.

"Joe, my fiancée. Otylie, Josef."

"*Těší mě,*" tried Otylie, not knowing whether he would understand her or not.

Joe said, "*Potěšení je na mé straně*"—The pleasure is mine—with a clear American accent but in otherwise perfect Czech. "Your man tells me you're from the old country."

"Praha," she nodded.

"Well," said Joe, planting a pair of large hands on his narrow hips, "our Prague ain't so grand as the original. But we like it here. Except for when it rains too much. Grinds the local industry to a halt, like you see." He sat next to the couple as his niece brought his cup, set it down, refilled it. "So you could be moving up to these parts, Daniel here told me."

"We haven't worked out the details, but that's the general idea," Danek said, sitting again. "Through the hospital in Lincoln we'll have subsidized housing to get started. But Otylie thinks one day she'd like to put down roots right here in Prague."

"People here are friendly. Honest working folks. Just keep in mind there ain't much to do unless you farm or raise a hive of kids."

"Otylie's a music teacher," Danek said. "Is there much interest in music here? I was told you're a musician yourself."

"Me, I'm polka. But there's all kinds of music out in the country."

After lunch, promising to come back and get a guided tour of the town—"It don't take long"—they were given Joe's telephone number. During the drive back to Lincoln, Otylie basked in the warmth of their visit. Because Prague was a little farther away from Lincoln than she'd imagined when looking at it on a map back in Texas, she settled in with the idea that they might live in Lincoln, visiting Prague often, attending its recitals and dances, then one day retire there if fate allowed. She even floored Danek by saying, "You know, I think I might try to get myself to like the polka. What's to lose?"

Back at the Cornhusker, they gave up their individual rooms and moved into a slightly larger suite that had a nice view of the sower atop the capitol dome. "Newlyweds," Danek white-lied to the hotel manager, who obliged by sending up a dozen red roses.

· 5 ·

FOR EVERY FOOL THERE IS A FOLLOWER. So Wittmann silently sneered as he exited Konvikt in Mandelbaum's wake. For every dunce, a devotee. Mandelbaum himself, pacing along the narrow echoing streets, struggled with the raw threat his old friend, once his partner, posed to Meta and her project. Each man, assuming the other had walked back to his home or hotel, in fact strode with deliberate haste toward another destination.

Kohout was in bed when the door buzzer woke him. His wife stirred, rolled over, and went back to sleep while Kohout semiconsciously tried to do the same. Given it was past midnight, he assumed some damnable fool down in the street had made a mistake or maybe was pulling an unfunny prank. A third and then fourth insistent buzz forced him to climb out of bed, cursing, and in pajamas the professor made his way to the front-room foyer. Standing in the dark, annoyed, he pressed the intercom button and asked, What the hell is it?

Let me in, Karel.

Who is this?

Karel, it's Petr and it's urgent we speak.

Are you injured, dying? Otherwise, can't this wait until morning?

A pause before Wittmann shot back, It's a matter of urgency.

That damned sonata, Kohout grumbled, reluctant to let his colleague come bursting into the apartment.

Yes, to be sure. Let's talk. I won't be long.

Huffing with indignation, Kohout pressed the button that unlocked the downstairs door. He returned to the bedroom, put on his bathrobe and wool slippers, quietly closed the door behind him so as not to disturb his snoring wife, and turned on floor lamps in the living room. Their old mica shades cast a golden glow over a pair of club chairs and a sofa that were in need of reupholstering and a large Kazak rug that had been passed down from his grandparents, once bright with a thick nap underfoot but now sun-faded and worn thin. It occurred to him, as he waited for Wittmann to ascend the stairs, that this once dignified parlor had, like its occupant, seen better days. Still, it was home. A sanctuary he didn't want to risk losing.

This really must be the end of it, Kohout thought. I am too old, too tired for this kind of thing. I can't allow Wittmann to count me in on whatever he's scheming any further.

But antagonizing or disappointing the not uninfluential Wittmann wasn't what Kohout, or anybody else, wanted to do either. He was in a lamentable bind, he realized, as he opened his door to a very wide-awake Petr Wittmann.

At about the same time, on the other side of the inky Vltava, Gerrit went downstairs to answer his door. Unlike Kohout, he and Meta were still up, discussing Otylie's letters. Neither was prepared for Mandelbaum's words when he followed Gerrit into the room and, without the slightest preliminary, asked Meta, "You have the manuscripts, right?"

"Of course, Paul—"

"Okay, good. Listen to me. It's time for you to leave Prague. Even tonight, if there's a train."

"What the hell?" Meta protested, as Gerrit answered, "At this hour, I doubt it."

"Or, Gerrit, do you have a car?"

"No," and for a moment all three were talking at once, Mandelbaum asking about ways to depart, Gerrit trying to find out what had prompted this upheaval, Meta objecting that she had every right to be here, insisting this made no sense at all.

Finally she placed her hands on Mandelbaum's shoulders and said, "Wait, Paul, stop. Stop. What's going on, what's this about?"

Catching his breath, he apologized, "I'm so sorry, Meta, so sorry. I don't think you could have come here without talking to Petr, but I'm angry with myself for not having thought it through more carefully. Too late now. It's crucial you get the originals not just out of Prague but out of the country, quickly and quietly."

"I still don't understand."

"My dear colleague has threatened to go to 'friends in high places' and accuse you of theft of national cultural property."

"That's totally crazy. It was given to me. I have written proof," Meta said, backing away, clenching her fists at her sides.

"He doesn't give a damn one way or the other."

"But the law's on my side."

"Not if it's on his," said Gerrit, watching Mandelbaum with a growing sense that the man knew Wittmann's complexities far better than he'd ever let on. No time to worry about that, he thought, then added, "I have an idea. My friend Jiří Pelc—Meta's met him—has a car. He can get us to Germany, I'm sure of it, and from there we can go to England like we'd planned anyway."

"He'd just drop everything and do that?" she asked.

"Heart of gold and soul of a firebrand. During the revolution we did far crazier things than this. Knowing Jiří, I'd say he'll consider it a lark."

Mandelbaum said, "A lark it isn't, but if you think he'd be willing, give him a call first thing in the morning."

"I'll call him right now. Guy never sleeps anyway."

"Good. I can stall Petr for a couple of days. All I want is to see that Meta, and you, and the manuscript are beyond whatever immediate reach he's got."

Meta clamped both hands over her eyes. "This is all so insane. What does any of it have to do with Otylie Bartošová's wishes? What does it have to do with music?"

Picking up his phone to call Jiří, Gerrit answered her as calmly as he possibly could. "It's clear that Wittmann wants it for something beyond music and cultural integrity and national pride and all that bullshit. It's valuable, as in money valuable."

Hearing this, Mandelbaum realized that Wittmann might be playing with more dangerous fire than he thought. To his credit in some ways, to his detriment in others, the man had gotten away with a lot over the years, had successfully walked razor-thin lines, manipulating authority for personal gain. But Gerrit was no doughy operative looking for quid pro quos. And he was in love with Wittmann's possible prey.

"Jiří's on," said Gerrit.

"Just like that?" asked Meta.

"Just like that. He picks us up at the end of Jánská in an hour."

*

Before Wittmann departed Kohout's apartment about half an hour after making his impromptu appearance, his reluctant accomplice had consented to stand by the complaint that Petr proposed to take to the cultural ministry the next day. While it would be up to Wittmann to present the matter, Kohout agreed to second his opinion that the musical documents Meta Taverner possessed were very likely not her property, were possibly stolen from a Czech citizen, and were above all of signal cultural import.

The more Kohout had listened to his pontificating, however, the more he believed Wittmann, for all his reputation, would be shown the door. Hadn't another faculty member at Charles University only the day before privately whispered that she worried a little about Wittmann's stability? A few students had complained to the department chair about his lateness to classes, the fellow music professor shared. As meticulous as ever with his lectures, but leaving seminars early too. Acting odd, curt. Not himself.

Kohout defended Wittmann by saying, He's just finished this Mahler book and he always gets edgy when he turns in a big project like that. Postpartum anxiety, I rather think.

Postpartum? Let him ask for maternity leave next time, I say.

Karel Kohout didn't disagree that Petr seemed unbalanced. Despite any differences they may have had in times past, he felt a bit sorry for his colleague. This sonata business had become a toxic obsession, and it was Kohout's hope, in fact, as he hung his robe on the back of the bathroom door and returned to bed, that the ministry would dismiss Wittmann's claims as baseless hearsay unworthy of investigation. Petr could use a healthy reality check. And a vacation. Spend a week in Greece over the holidays. Start a new book. Go on a date. Listen to some damn music.

Kohout's thoughts weren't all that far from those of Mandelbaum, who was ready to leave Jánská to return for a few hours' sleep at the hotel now that contingency plans were in place. A few minutes before Jiří was to arrive, he said his goodbyes to Meta after shaking Gerrit's hand.

"I'm sorry this didn't go according to plan in any way conceivable."

"Not to worry, old owl," she said, giving him a hug. "I never expected things to go as well as they have, frankly. Didn't think skulking out of town would be my exit strategy, but what's a woman to do?"

"You shouldn't underestimate Wittmann," he warned.

"He shouldn't underestimate me."

Mandelbaum looked her in the eye. "All right, so go find that other movement."

"And restore it to its rightful owner."

"That's vital because that's what defangs Wittmann."

"Then the musicology can begin," she said.

"Then the musicology can begin." And with that Mandelbaum left.

Meta placed a call to tell her mother that she was leaving Prague and, echoing her mentor, asked her not to discuss her daughter, the manuscript, her departure from the Czech Republic, or anything else with a soul. Much as Mandelbaum had done, she told her that she would explain everything later.

"Are you all right? Can you tell me that much?" her mother asked.

"I'm very much all right. Better than all right. Believe me."

"Well, I always have," her mother said. "No reason to stop now."

While she was on the phone, Gerrit sat down to write the Hodeks a letter apologizing for his abrupt departure and to let them know he would be back soon. Impromptu holiday, he fibbed, in case Wittmann or others inquired. He enclosed two months' rent inside the envelope. In a second letter, he wrote a note to Andrea. Keep studying your English, keep practicing the piano, little platitudes at which he could picture her scoffing with a good-natured laugh. To her too, he gave assurance that he would be back. And if anybody dared to tell her that Meta was guilty of anything bad, she shouldn't believe it. If Meta was guilty of anything, it was conscience.

This was, he thought as he sealed the envelope, in many ways a wonderful trait, in others an onerous burden. In Meta's case, both.

True to form, Jiří was decked out in his worn black leather bomber jacket as he sat behind the wheel of his car, caffeinated and jazzed to participate in anything that undermined oppressor authority. Headlights off, engine idling. As they had hoped, no one was about. It was too late for the last of the pub-crawlers and too early for the work-at-dawners.

"Thanks for this, Jiří," Gerrit told his friend.

"Please, man. No sweat."

Recalling that Meta loved heavy metal, Jiří offered to play a mixtape of Darkthrone, Mayhem, and Burzum he'd brought along.

"Believe it or not, I don't want to hear any music right now, metal, classical, or otherwise. Just wind on the windows."

"No problema." Jiří knew the road well, having driven many a time past Pilsen into Bavaria on vacation. Careful not to exceed the speed limit, he drove like "a saint," as he put it with a laugh.

Although Gerrit's and Meta's minds were racing, both remained silent. Without saying as much to one another, they found themselves wondering if running off like this on the spur of the moment, in the middle of the night, might not undermine Meta's case. In urging them to flee had Mandelbaum been operating under the influence of a mind-set that would have been valid a decade ago but was no longer justifiable?

Meta wasn't in the habit of doubting her mentor. She had always placed faith in his every small pronouncement, every idea, no matter how outré it happened to be, about life, music, anything. Even when they disagreed, she respected his position, knew it was well considered. But this fear of Petr Wittmann, what fostered it?

Wittmann was a complex bundle of impulses, some good, some not. Was he such a towering figure that skittering away like cockroaches startled by a suddenly switched-on overhead light made real sense?

A crescent moon shed little radiance as the car moved swiftly toward the German border, taking a less traveled road through the heavy woodlands of Český Les. Meta couldn't help but think of Jakub Bartoš hiding in tall forested isolation like this when the Nazis drove him into the underground. Which meant, of course, that part of the manuscript she clutched in her lap had been out there in similar cold and pitch-darkness. Once more she was reminded how far the Prague Sonata had come—now leaving its titular home again—and had yet to go.

The tiny border crossing at Eslam, to their surprise, appeared deserted. Lights in the small guard station were on. A radio was faintly playing. But there was no sign of life.

"Do we wait?" asked Meta.

"Does the nest build the bird?" Jiří said, dropping the clutch into first gear and crossing the frontier.

Their collective sigh, once the travelers had entered Germany, was audible. For all his threats and bluster, Wittmann had failed to stop them from exiting the country with the manuscript in hand. They drove for a time in silence, Meta fitfully dozing off as the engine hummed and breezes whistled.

When she woke, dawn had broken on the eastern horizon and Gerrit was at the wheel.

"If life were a more reasonable beast," she said with a yawn, "I'd love for us to go first to Bonn, Bonngasse 20. We're only a few hours from the place where maybe this all began." Even as the words came out, she knew this was not the time to rest on the laurels of an unresolved hypothesis. A side trip to pay homage to Beethoven would be an unnecessary caprice, a whim that would only slow them down.

"We talked about it while you were asleep," said Gerrit. "Subject to your approval, we think it's going to be best to head straight up to the coast."

"It's not too long," Jiří added. "Nuremberg, Frankfurt, Köln, then the ring road around Brussels after Aachen and Liège. Will take all day into evening. On to Ostend and Dunkirk, where I can drop you off. Or Calais."

"The ferries run regularly out of Calais. It's a crossing I've made many a time."

Meta took a deep breath. They were right. Life was not a reasonable beast.

Their passage across the English Channel seemed somehow imaginary. The French shoreline shrouded in sea mist, the light gray-green chop of the Channel waters and hypnotic cries of gulls trailing the ferry, the British coast also carpeted in fog—it all only added to the dreamlike quality of the trip. Meta and Gerrit sat close together on a sternward bench out of the salt breeze. During this leg of the journey it was Gerrit who napped, his head resting heavily on Meta's shoulder, while their shared duffel, which housed spare clothes, his laptop, the manuscript, lay across her lap. Things had changed so much since Otylie made this crossing, Meta knew, but a part of her urgently tried to imagine what the woman's experience might have been like. More nightmare than dream.

Not far from Paddington Station they set themselves up in a nondescript, inexpensive hotel. They registered under Gerrit's name, aware it wasn't much cover. The thin mattress on their bed sagged like a hammock, and the plumbing clanked and banged. Still, after a pub dinner and pints of Guinness, the sorry state of the hotel bed didn't stop them from making love. "I adore you," Gerrit whispered, still inside her, as Meta shuddered in the wake of her orgasm. Before she slipped toward unconsciousness, she repeated his words, a whisper of warm breath against his cheek.

In the morning, at Gerrit's suggestion, Meta phoned Sam to tell him they had arrived in London without incident, and to ask him to pass the word along to Mandelbaum. If Wittmann was as much of a threat as Mandelbaum seemed to believe, best not to have him receiving transnational calls from her via a hotel desk.

"We miss you already," Sam said before they rang off.

"Miss you too. Maybe I'm being overly hopeful, but I promise you we'll be seeing each other again sooner rather than later. And it won't be through jail bars."

Gerrit had helped her do some on-the-fly research about the Czech government in exile just days before she found herself exiled from Prague. They had discovered that many of the main offices in London proper had been housed in Fursecroft, a large building on George Street in Marylebone. Otylie might well have worked there herself, Meta began to think, maybe in the support staff or secretarial pool, or possibly as an assistant to someone in the middling ranks. None of the wartime offices would still be around, so, as when Meta first arrived in Prague, the search would be one of going from door to door.

Other possibilities loomed as well, including Buckinghamshire, in the south of England, where exiled Czech president Beneš was forced to move for safety's sake after the Park Street building in which he'd first set up shop had been leveled by German bombs. Meta learned that all the staffers, Otylie undoubtedly among them, had been situated in London during the devastating worst of the Blitz. After that, there was a slim chance the woman had moved to the safety of Aston Abbotts, out in the countryside, with Beneš's close circle, so that area would also have to be checked out.

With these destinations ahead, Meta felt a new resolve and a stirring excitement that put Prague in the background, along with Wittmann. At least somewhat.

They spent their first couple of days tracking people whose movements were known to history. They'd read that in October 1938 President Beneš had first moved to the Putney district of London, where he lived for a time with his wife, Hana, and their nieces. This was as good as any other starting place, if only to rule it out. As Meta and Gerrit wandered along Gwendolen Avenue, and up and down side streets, she was reminded of her first days with him in Malá Strana, blind-knocking on doors and asking questions of strangers. But other than finding a handsome circular blue plaque that read "Dr. Edvard Benes 1884–1948 President of Czechoslovakia lived here," they came up empty.

"Poor Beneš," Gerrit commented. "Lost his presidency twice, first in '38 when the Germans annexed the Sudetenland and forced him to resign, then again a decade later, after returning triumphant to Prague, when the Communists pulled a coup on his three-year-old government. Talk about not catching a break. And look here. Man doesn't even get the courtesy of a háček over the *s* in his name on this plaque."

"He didn't live very long," Meta noticed.

"Well, sixty-four isn't exactly a short life. He did manage to oversee arrangements for assassinating Heydrich. That alone is a life well lived. And given how many enemies he faced, it's sort of amazing he made it as long as he did."

Having located a copy of a document called the "Czechoslovak List," which had been published by the ministry of foreign affairs during the war and which noted addresses in London where the exile government operated, Meta and Gerrit found themselves canvassing Grosvenor Place and Wilton Crescent, Princes Gate and Keswick Road. They were met with a wide variety of responses, from the usual "I'm terribly sorry I can't help you, but good luck" to the rare if always deflating "I don't have time for this."

"Why don't you go to the Czech embassy and ask if there are records there?" one man suggested. It was an obvious question, but they couldn't admit that their uneasiness about Wittmann kept them away, so thanked him and moved on.

Near the hotel they found a kiosk that sold an array of international newspapers, many of which Gerrit knew well and several for which he wrote now and again. As Gerrit—who was more multilingual than Meta had realized—pored over the pages from front to back, she found herself most worried that Mandelbaum's name would turn up. Arrested, she feared. Or else deported. Discredited, either way. But his name never appeared in the British, German, French, or even Czech papers, nor did anything having to do with them or the manuscript.

The most heartening response they got was from an elderly woman who lived near Fursecroft. Standing hesitantly at her front door, she knitted her brow and said, "Bartoš?"

"Yes, Otylie Bartošová—her husband's name was Bartoš."

Meta's pulse doubled when the woman turned to face inside, still holding the heavy oak door half-open, and called to someone unseen, "Wasn't there an Alfréd Bartoš who lived around here somewhere during the war?"

There was, yes. When Meta and Gerrit were invited in, they were introduced to a man in his late seventies seated sleepily in a wheelchair. He wore a cardigan sweater and dark green corduroy pants. A display of medals, citations, and period photographs of an aviator, surely this very gentleman, was proudly laid out on a mahogany secretary in the corner. At the far end of the room a television was tuned to a cricket match with the sound so low as to be inaudible. Despite his being elderly, the man's memory was unimpaired, and he briefly told these strangers the story of a

First Lieutenant Alfréd Bartoš, a war hero, as it happened, who had been in London but was dispatched to operate undercover in the Czech homeland, helping covert paratroopers infiltrate Prague and its suburbs.

"Nice man, quite handsome, tall forehead, strong noble nose," he related, as if he'd seen Bartoš just yesterday. "I heard he shot himself in the head before the Gestapo could catch him. That was back in June of 1942. True hero, and like so many he didn't live to see he'd won the war."

Having finished his story, the man turned, somewhat wistful, to Meta and apologized that, alas, he was afraid he had no knowledge of any Otylie Bartoš.

For a moment, silence hung like a clapperless bell in the room. Only the tinny cheers of the stadium crowd were heard. Gerrit couldn't help thinking of what Jiří would assert, that the Czechs, unlike the Brits, had only temporarily won their war.

Meta finally said, "Thanks so much for your time. You've been very kind."

"I'm sorry. I think we're keeping you from your match," Gerrit added, but as he and Meta were about to leave, the man's wife spoke up.

"Henry, wasn't there a lovely Czech girl who roomed for a time near here who went by the name of Tilly? Didn't she work for the Czech government during the war?"

"The one who had that American friend who worked at the hospital?"

"They might both have done. But yes, that's her. I wonder if she might possibly be your Otylie."

"Tilly, Otylie," Meta said. She could hear it.

"Those two young ladies were inseparable," the woman told Meta and Gerrit, who stood waiting for more, doubtful yet dumbfounded by the possibility.

"I don't recollect the American's name, do you?" the man went on.

His wife couldn't, she admitted, but a friend who used to go out with them during the war, a woman with the memorable name of Max, might. "Let me see if I can ring her up. Lives not far from here, with her son and daughter-in-law. She's not young, mind you—"

"None of us are," her husband said.

"—but who knows?"

Max was asleep, it turned out, not feeling well, and couldn't come to the phone. But after hearing the reason for the call, her daughter-in-law said that she would get back to them if Max happened to remember anything about this Tilly and her American friend. Did they have a hotel exchange they could pass along? Meta and Gerrit thanked the couple, leaving their phone and room numbers.

"I'm sorry Henry and I weren't able to be of more help," the woman told her visitors as she showed them out.

"Sorry?" said Meta, shaking her fragile extended hand. "You've given us more than we could've hoped for."

A trip out to visit Aylesbury Vale the following crisp autumn day, to see where the exiled president and those closest to him lived and worked, turned up another couple of Bartošes, men who served in the presidential guard. But again, no one recalled an Otylie Bartošová. Bartošes had been everywhere, it seemed, but not the one they sought. A woman they met at a local pub, the Royal Oak, a place that had been serving stout and fare for centuries, did know a bit about the exile government days, having been born in nearby Cublington and grown up here during the war. She insisted that when they finished lunch they had best return to the city to look further into the Fursecroft offices. "Unless your Otylie worked for the president or his closest advisers, she most likely worked there. Many of the Czech refugee secretaries at the time did."

"If she was right, then it's not like we've been so wrong," said Meta on the train from Aylesbury back to London.

"True," Gerrit agreed. "Problem is, we've already asked around the Fursecroft block. We can do it again, but I think we have to admit that this is a way bigger haystack than what we were dealing with in my little neighborhood in Prague. Twenty thousand Czechs, give or take, fled here during the war. Trying to find a specific one of twenty thousand needles, especially half a century later—well, I think we may want to take a different approach."

Meta remembered worrying over the same problem in the middle of the night not so long ago, after paying respects to Tomáš at Marta's place. "But what would that be?" She tucked her hair, which had grown longer than she usually wore it, behind her ear.

"When we were crossing the Channel, I gave this some thought."

"When we were crossing the Channel you were mostly asleep, babe," she reminded him with a grin.

"Dozing, daydreaming. But weighing options too. I'm more convinced than ever that the only way to do this right is for me to go to my paper's bureau here and contact Margery in New York," he said. "She'll have resources that can potentially help move things along."

Meta's smile flattened. "Aren't you afraid of drawing attention? I mean, I don't know whether Mandelbaum was being paranoid or not, but he was flat-out explicit in telling us to stay under the radar. You really think it's a good idea to risk exposing ourselves to a major newspaper editor?"

"I hear you," Gerrit said. "But Margery's never sold me down so much as a stream, let alone a river."

"And I hear you, but there's so much at stake. We fled Prague in the middle of the night. I'm being accused of things that aren't true. I'm a trusting person. But right now, other than you, I hardly trust a soul."

"If you trust me, then let me trust Margery."

"She's going to ask you what you're doing, right?"

"Point-blank. She hasn't heard from me in a while and I imagine I'll get it in the neck for being so off the grid."

Meta gazed past Gerrit at the Chiltern Hills countryside flying by outside the train's windows. She caught a flickering image of herself reflected in the glass, backgrounded by the wintry blur of Chorleywood. What was her hesitation? and wondered, What was there to lose? Look at how many people had risked so much when this manuscript had come into their lives. Her eyes refocused on the man looking at her.

"I'm the one being paranoid, probably. You should follow your instinct, go to the bureau, make the call."

Gerrit kissed her and said, "No guarantee she'll be able or willing to help, but you never know unless you ask."

"While you're doing that, I want to follow up on an instinct of my own."

"Something you've told me about?"

"I'm heading to the library. Like you said, there's a whole lot of haystack here. I want to try approaching this from a different angle. You'll be the first to know if I come up with anything."

"All right, deal. Tomorrow morning we part company."

"Just for a little while."

"For a very little while," he said.

MANDELBAUM AGREED TO MEET WITTMANN for what he knew would be their final meal in the hotel restaurant where they'd shared their reunion breakfast. From Wittmann's perspective, all might yet be well if he could persuade his old colleague not to squander this opportunity. From Mandelbaum's, it was a matter of subtly forcing a delay, biding and buying time. He had to play a bit of the fool to do this, but pride was a luxury at the moment. Perhaps he could be proud later, if Meta succeeded in finding what she was looking for rather than becoming the center of an international scandal in the rarefied classical music world.

Caviar pie, asparagus with hollandaise, and, *bien sûr*, champagne, Wittmann told the waiter, after Mandelbaum settled a napkin on his lap and insisted his friend order a king's meal, his treat. Rather than appearing distressed this morning, Wittmann was upbeat.

Mandelbaum felt upbeat too, having heard from Sam that Meta and Gerrit were in England. Clearly, his colleague didn't realize the two had eluded him. Had he known they'd left the country, a gourmet breakfast would be the last thing he would want.

"Caviar pie. You'd think we were celebrating," Mandelbaum said.

"Maybe we are, who knows? Now tell me what your acolyte thinks about the proposals we discussed day before yesterday."

"I will. But first," taking a sip from the sparkling flute, "tell me if what we talked about has remained between us. Your 'friends in high places' made me uncomfortable."

"Well, they were meant to, I admit." Wittmann went on to report that he had phoned a close contact inside the culture ministry. "Kept everything obscure, no names, just inquired whether certain authorities would be interested if I was unable to resolve the matter myself."

Cloaking his anger behind as cool an image of nonchalance as he could muster, Mandelbaum asked, "And what did this culture vulture say, may I ask?"

Wittmann hesitated for several beats. "He told me, in essence, that if I required any help from the ministry, for me to call him—*right* away."

That sounded off. Mandelbaum had a good ear for the operatic, and interpreted the pause and inflected *right* to mean that Wittmann may have encountered problems with his upper-echelon connection. Assuming he'd even had such a conversation.

"Good of you not to unleash the dogs, Petr."

"Am I detecting some cynicism? You think the dogs don't exist?"

"I said nothing of the kind."

What Mandelbaum didn't know was that Wittmann had placed not one but several calls to officials he had worked with over the years. With some he had encountered frustrating apathy, even mild antagonism—this was a matter for the justice department, not for culture. But others were not so dismissive, and suggested he stay in touch if he needed advice about potential recourse.

"You never answered my question, Paul. How did your Meta respond to our idea?"

No choice but to lie. "She wasn't closed to it."

"That's all?" Wittmann said, coloring. "She wasn't closed to it?"

"I don't think you understand how central this is to her life, Petr. For you, for me, even for the Lang family the manuscript has a certain significance. And, fine, maybe for the Ministry of Culture. But it's more than a project to Meta. It's practically become her reason for living. Give her a couple of days to think things through."

"This sentimentality is really awful, Paul. Wax sentimental about our divine beluga, not eighteenth-century manuscript material, and a hopeful girl who doesn't know what she's doing or whom she's dealing with. Please."

Mandelbaum just said, "You're not mistaken about this caviar pie. It's delicious."

"Delighted you like it. So, where is the manuscript now?"

"In a safe place, trust me."

"I want to trust you, Paul, but I'd rather see the score for myself. Also, I think it would be best if it was kept here in the hotel safe, where both of us know its location."

"I'll see what I can do," Mandelbaum responded.

His face abruptly brightening, Wittmann changed the subject. "I made another call that's worth discussing. Again, no need to give you names, but I spoke with a gentleman of considerable means with homes in Manhattan, Paris, Geneva, as well as here in Prague."

"He collects more than houses, I gather."

"Indeed, he does."

"And he's willing to pay a small fortune for the sonata?"

"Let us say his interest is piqued. Especially when I mentioned Beethoven as a strong probability."

"Probability?" Mandelbaum chuckled. "I'd say possibility at best. There's a great deal of work to do before any such claim can openly be made. Hell, you know that."

"I do know that. But this collector is vastly wealthy for a reason. He's a speculator. We would not, mind you, price the manuscript at what one might estimate its full retail value would be were it definitively attributed to Beethoven. Instead, give it a valuation somewhere between that of a lesser composer and the master himself. I didn't even discuss price with him anyway. Just his interest."

"Don't you think you're getting a little ahead of yourself, Petr?" Mandelbaum asked, hardly knowing what else to say.

Ignoring the interruption, Wittmann finished, "The best part about this, should it come to pass, is that even though he's not Czech, he'll be willing to loan it indefinitely to the proper institute here in Prague for limited-access study."

"You mean for yourself to study."

"Yes, of course. And," as if waking up, "your Meta Tavener, as well."

"She's not *my* Meta, Petr. She's her own Meta Taverner, not mine." How sorely Mandelbaum wanted to tell him that not only was Meta not his ward, she was no longer even in the Czech Republic, and might soon leave Europe, for all he knew. But he held his tongue. The farther away Meta could get from this man who couldn't, or wouldn't, get her name right, the better. Petr would find out eventually that she and Gerrit had left. Maybe tomorrow, maybe the next day, maybe later that afternoon. When that did happen, Paul thought, he might want to be out of the Czech Republic himself.

Wittmann was speaking. "—never meant that as derogatory. The opposite, my friend. Anyone can plainly see how fond she is of you and vice versa."

"On that point I have no argument."

"Well. This collector is in Barcelona on business but will be here in Prague at the top of next week and would like to examine the score."

Four and a half, five days, thought Mandelbaum. At least there was a timetable now.

"That sounds fine," he said, in as placating a voice as he could manage. "Now, old boy, shall we set all this business aside for a moment and enjoy our breakfast? What do you say we order more of this excellent Louis Roederer and talk about fine champagne, the price of eggs—hen's or sturgeon's, I don't care—anything other than that damned manuscript."

THE PHONE WOKE THEM BOTH. Its ring was loud, an insistent, atonal double pulse. Coming fully awake, they blinked at the late morning light that streamed in a chalky column through the sheer window curtains. Meta glanced at the bedside clock and realized that, exhausted from all the travel and turmoil, they had overslept. Her first jolting thought was that Wittmann had found them.

She cleared her throat, picked up the receiver. "Hello?"

"Is this Meta Taverner?" a woman asked.

"Yes?" she said, wondering why she'd pronounced the word as a question.

"You were the one inquiring about Tilly Bartošová?" The surname was pronounced as an English speaker would say it, with the stress on the third rather than the first syllable.

"Yes," she said, this time with no hint of a question.

"My mother-in-law, Maxine Kendrick, isn't feeling up to speaking with you directly, but she did want me to convey that she knew your relative or friend."

By now Meta considered Otylie, or Tilly, both relative and friend, so she didn't contradict the caller. "Oh!" was all she could manage.

"And Tilly's friend Jane too."

"Jane?"

"Yes, I gather from Mum that Jane was Tilly's closest friend here during the war."

"Does your mother-in-law know where Otylie—Tilly, I mean—is now?"

"Well, I'm sorry but after the war she went back to Czechoslovakia to find her husband. I gather he was in the underground."

"And Jane?"

"Jane went back to Texas to marry her soldier fiancé."

"What was Jane's last name, or the name of the soldier? Does your mother-in-law remember?"

"I thought you might want to know that. But I'm afraid she says it was so long ago that all she remembers are their first names, how supportive they were of each other, how much they liked going to the picture shows. She tried to think of others who might have known them, but I'm sorry, Miss Taverner, she just couldn't."

Meta thanked the woman and hung up. Wide awake now, she told Gerrit what she'd learned. While the information wasn't specific enough to lead them to her door, Otylie Bartošová had suddenly become more real than ever. Their trip to London, haphazard as it was, had borne fruit.

After a quick breakfast, they each got down to their separate agendas. Rather than taking the tube, Meta walked along Marylebone Road for a brisk three quarters of an hour to the British Library. The sky above London was overcast, with clouds running low and swift, and though it wasn't too chilly, the pearly light had a deep autumnal cast. She couldn't help thinking, as she made her way through the morning crowd, that the odds were against her.

The reading rooms were busy, but a hush blanketed the air. She sat at a long table and looked over a well-used atlas of England and another of continental Europe—this time giving in to using the index—in the hope of locating a city or town named Prague other than the Czech Republic's capital, Praha. There was a Rome in upstate New York, a Versailles in Kentucky, a Manhattan in Kansas. A British or Irish or Welsh or Scottish Prague didn't seem out of the question. Was looking for a place in Europe any different from searching for one woman in Prague or in London? At least places, unlike people, generally stayed put.

The idea had occurred to her back in Malá Strana, when she'd first noticed something in one of Otylie's letters to Tomáš Lang. She'd meant to mention it to Gerrit at the time—the inconsistency of Otylie's having written *Prague, 1978* on her second letter to the pianist, rather than *Praha*—but with everything else going on neglected to bring it up. Later, after reflecting on it a little, she'd shrugged off her initial perplexity and dismissed the matter. This morning, though, when Gerrit set off for the newspaper bureau, Meta pulled the letter out again. There it was in Otylie's sure and steady hand. *Prague*. Probably meant nothing. She might simply have gotten used to saying *Prague* while living in London. Yet in the earlier 1946 letter, she did use *Praha*. Why the switch?

Either way, there wasn't a town called Prague in all the British commonwealth. Nor did it take longer than an hour to conclude that she'd come here on a fool's errand.

But maybe not. She pondered for another moment, then pulled down a detailed atlas of the United States. This is probably wrong too, she thought as she turned to the index. Breathing unevenly, she ran her finger down the columns past the Petersburgs and Pleasant Valleys, the Pittsburgs and Plainviews, until it hovered next to what she sought.

"Eureka," she whispered, blinking in disbelief.

Way out in the flat, sparse heartland states of Arkansas, Oklahoma, and Nebraska, there were not just one or two but three Pragues. What was more, she soon discovered that Texas boasted a Prague of its own, one that used the original Czech spelling, Praha. Was it possible Otylie Bartošová, having fled two wars in her native Europe, might burn all her bridges to the past and migrate to the middle of America, and from there write her old acquaintance Tomáš Lang one last letter?

Sure, Meta and Gerrit could continue to trace gossamer threads around London. But she had to wonder if a road trip in a rented car from Prague, Arkansas, over to Praha, Texas, then straight north to Prague, Oklahoma, and from there along exactly the same longitude line to Prague, Nebraska, might not be as good a plan, if not a better one. There was even a New Prague, Minnesota, farther north and east, though Otylie's letter bore only the single word.

She made notes and left the library in a hurry to meet Gerrit in Regent's Park. They could fly to New York, crash at her place—hard to believe she still had an apartment of her own—and do some Internet research at Gillie's, or at a bare minimum check out the white pages. But had Otylie changed her name by now? She'd made mention of a man in her life. Maybe she had remarried. Unless Gerrit had a eureka moment of his own, this seemed like the best, the last, and the only way to proceed. As with everything in her life these days, she was ready to, for want of a better phrase, go for it. One of the many reasons she loved Gerrit was that this seemed to be his modus operandi too.

Meta reached the park first and sat on a bench where they'd agreed to meet. The clouds had dispersed to form a filigree, leaving a rich blue dome over the city. Enough of a breeze remained to hoist several kites above the trees, and jacketed children played on the grass, kicking a ball about, or chasing one another as mothers and nannies looked on. It couldn't have been a more bucolic setting, even surrounded as it was by the incessant drone of double-decker buses, taxis, scooters.

As she waited, thoughts drifting, she wondered how things would be at home with Gerrit by her side rather than Jonathan. Would Gillian like Gerrit? Would her mother? Would Gerrit's family approve of her? And what of her students? Would they have moved on or would she be able to teach lessons again to help pay for all this travel?

Would, would, would—and all at once Meta understood that going to New York, no matter how briefly, was not the best course. She had more miles to travel before she could face all the comforts and difficulties of homecoming and risk slowing her momentum, scattering her focus. No, unless Gerrit strongly disagreed, they should fly from Heathrow on as direct a flight to Arkansas as they could afford, rent a car, and take a drive that would connect the Prague dots. These Pragues looked to be relatively small towns— from barely a few hundred people to barely a few thousand— where, she imagined, most everybody knew everybody and history was a thing of the present. Even if Otylie had changed her name a dozen times, they could ask around, Meta figured, and locate her through her story and the sonata itself.

"Penny for your thoughts," said Gerrit, slipping onto the bench beside her.

Meta started. "Hey, not fair to frighten a person like that. Anyway, how do you know my thoughts might not be worth pence instead of just a penny?"

"Really now. Tell me."

"First, what did you learn?"

"Well, for one," said Gerrit, hoping not to betray the nervousness he felt, "I learned that my exasperated editor says I may still have a job if I behave myself. I had to tell her what's been going on, get her up to speed, in order to ask for help."

"That's wonderful about the job, but how much did you tell her?"

Here he hesitated. "Pretty much everything."

"What does 'everything' mean?"

"It means I told her you have two of three movements, that you believe it's a lost Beethoven sonata. She knows about Wittmann, that we're together in London."

"Gerrit, I don't—"

"I know what you're going to say, but hear me out. Margery thinks it's a great story—"

"When did this go from a love song to a news story?"

"—maybe as big as that front-page article you once fantasized about. And honestly, so do I."

"But that was a fantasy I rejected, Gerrit. Have you forgotten why we're here, what Paul told us? We're practically in hiding. And you go and tell your editor everything?"

When she looked at him, hurt and confused, he took her hand and said, "Meta. Listen. Margery gets it that you're not ready to go public yet and that if any of this was published prematurely it would cause more harm than good."

"That's really thoughtful, but I'm surprised you're talking about publication. Have you still been taking notes behind my back? You never stopped, did you." She gently removed her hand from his, stood, and, crossing her arms, looked across the park toward two boys trying to launch their kite.

Gerrit got up from the bench and embraced her from behind. Resting his chin on her shoulder, he said, "I'm sorry. This is what I was afraid of all along, that you wouldn't understand. That you'd think I was using you as fodder for a story."

"And you're telling me that's wrong."

"I'm telling you what you're doing is important, Meta," he said, moving around to face her, "and at some point people will want to know about what happened from the first moment this sonata entered your life. I can't help writing it down, asking questions and following threads, and I can't help loving you. Whatever you think, if I'm able to use what I do to help you, well, I can't help that either. That's why I talked to Margery. And there was a dividend at the end of our conversation."

"I'm not so sure about all of this, Gerrit," she said, but knew in truth that if he fully trusted Margery, she'd be wrong not to follow his lead. They were, after all, in it together. Swallowing her anger, she continued, "So what's this dividend?"

"First, we're all right?"

"I understand your motivations are good."

Drawing her down beside him on the bench, Gerrit said, "Margery had an intern look into it while I was at the bureau. Turns out there was an Otylie Bartosova, no accent marks, naturalized as an American citizen in the early '50s, not that many years after our Otylie disappeared from the timeline."

"I knew it," Meta burst out. "This couldn't be more perfect. Everything fits."

Now he was startled. "What do you mean? Did you find something at the library?"

As she filled him in, Meta could hear how preposterous her proposed next step might sound, but as she realized Gerrit was not going to think her out of her mind, some of her upset began to drain away. He did wonder whether it might be more efficient to, in the good old Yellow Pages' advertising phrase, let their fingers do the walking, or ask Margery for another hour of her intern's time. Meta shook her head.

"This is how I've done it all along. Phone books and interns don't lead to memories, or personal recollections, or private networks. I'm thrilled Margery came up with that information, assuming it's the same person, but Irena didn't find me through a database. We didn't find Tomáš that way, either. Or each other."

"Can't disagree with a word you're saying."

"If we go to these Pragues personally and don't find her, or at least a gravestone, a death certificate, then I'll know I did everything I could. I hope that doesn't sound fanatical."

"It sounds like good investigative journalism, oddly enough," Gerrit said, taking her hand as they left Regent's Park. "One thing's for sure. Wittmann won't be looking for us in Arkansas."

"Who knows? The man's complicated."

"Dangerous and harmless. Brilliant and stupid. Powerful and strangely weak."

"There but not all there," added Meta, and Gerrit was relieved to see a real smile.

"At least he's not here."

When they reached the hotel to make travel arrangements, Meta said, "By the way, if there turns out to be a story to write— big *if* since an important part of the sonata's still missing—I wouldn't want anyone else to write it."

"You know," pulling her to him and kissing her, "despite the fact that Venus de Milo is missing her arms, she still represents classic beauty, and you can find her in enough art history books to fill a library. Your incomplete sonata is also a thing of classic beauty, and it's already a story of real interest. Everything about you is, as I see it."

"Yes, but you're blind."

"So was Homer, and it didn't stop him."

Given that Meta was mollified enough to chuckle at his little joke, Gerrit hadn't the heart to tell her that the first thing he had done at the office wasn't to place that call to Margery but to check the wire service, see what was being reported out of the Czech Republic. A small piece surfaced in which a noted Czech music scholar had claimed that an eighteenth-century music manuscript of considerable import, the property of an unidentified Czech family who had survived the Holocaust, had gone missing and was possibly stolen. Gerrit had smirked at that reference since the Lang family Wittmann was trying to claim it for were anything but Holocaust survivors. It came as a relief to note that in the single sentence mentioning Meta, either the reporter or Wittmann himself had misspelled her last name as "Tavener," and she wasn't outright accused of the theft. The information offered was simply that this young American musicologist had brought the manuscript to Wittmann's attention and was working with the original when it disappeared. Why Wittmann's name wasn't specified in the brief piece was unclear. There was no mention of Paul Mandelbaum or, for that matter, Gerrit Mills. Gerrit's assumption was that Wittmann was testing the waters, making his first public accusations without setting himself up for a slander suit.

Gerrit didn't much relish the idea of keeping this from Meta. But it was a pathetic squib, misinformed, and hadn't apparently been picked up by other news outlets. He and Meta needed to move forward, take their journey to America, and tend to neither the distraction nor the threat that was Wittmann.

· 6 ·

OTYLIE HAJEK, formerly Otylie Bartošová, settled into the newest phase of her life with the transparent joy of a lapsed believer who had once again found God's path. Which was not to say she ever finally embraced organized religion. That would always be for others, though her wedding in Texas was officiated by the groom's favorite minister, Reverend Pursel Moore, in the First Methodist Church where Danek had been a congregant since childhood. The ceremony took place on a sunny Saturday afternoon, with colorful jewels of light dappling the sanctuary from the stained-glass windows, before a surprisingly large group of friends, cousins, colleagues, and others. Otylie nearly fainted when, just as the minister was about to begin, her onetime charge, Grace Sanders, all grown up and more radiant than ever, appeared as a surprise guest. Grace, a college graduate now with a fiancé of her own accompanying her, had never lost touch with Otylie over the years. They always spoke by phone on their birthdays, caught up on each other's doings as if they were contemporaries rather than decades apart. With both Jane and Grace present, impromptu flower girls beside her near the altar, Otylie felt represented by true family. This was what faith was all about, she thought as she said her vows.

Jane had promised the newlyweds a reception back at her house that would not soon be forgotten, a shindig so festive it might be deemed sinful, and she made good on her word.

"You've invited the whole county, Jane," Otylie gushed, seeing her soon-to-be-former piano students running around the backyard while many of Danek's coworkers from the local hospital milled near the bowl of spiked punch, dancing and laughing, and told the couple how much they were going to be missed.

"We're not moving to another planet, mind you," Danek assured his closest friend from the congregation. "Just a couple of states away. Besides, we'll be visiting and you're always welcome up in Nebraska."

In Lincoln, whenever Danek attended Sunday services throughout the course of what would evolve into a long, close marriage, he not only didn't begrudge his wife her resistance to church religion but took it as a matter of honor that she followed her heart as she saw fit. He reminded himself that neither did she grouse when, on a perfect Sunday morning in early June, he passed an hour listening to a sermon about the stormy weather of the soul before they got in the car and drove out to Branched Oak Lake for a buttermilk-fried-chicken picnic or over to Prague to visit newfound friends for a hand or two of bridge. Once, when he asked Otylie more about her upbringing, especially her religious upbringing, she told him she'd grown up in a household where music was the religion and composers were its saints. Cantatas were chapels. Pavanes were prayer. Fugues were the firmament and God existed in every note. Just as Jakub had before him, Danek loved Otylie more than theology, more than Judaism or Christianity. And like

Jakub, Danek made peace with this single schism in their otherwise unusually harmonious life together.

Work at the hospital was more rewarding, but also more grueling, than what Danek had been used to at the Texas facility. Never
much of a complainer, he rolled up his sleeves and threw himself
into his job with zeal. Otylie noticed that, in part because of the
hospital's seniority system and in part because her husband had
a habit of volunteering to take on duties others might not, Danek
was often called in for shifts at odd hours.

"They are working you hard," she once remarked when she'd
gotten out of bed to make him bacon and eggs in the middle of
the night because he was called in to cover the short-staffed emergency room.

"Any other job, I might consider it hard work," he said, washing down his toast with black coffee. "But where there are people,
there are sick people, hurt people. I just happen to be one who
knows how to help them."

"You're a good man, Daniel Hajek."

One thing he kept from Otylie was how many patients, an inordinately high number, he felt, were admitted to the emergency
room because of injuries to their hands, injuries so horrific he
didn't dare tell her what he'd seen. Mangled or lost hands in particular bothered him, as he knew how essential hands were to a
farmer's work, any laborer's, not to mention a musician such as
Otylie. And he adored his wife's hands. After they'd settled here,
she had taken on a number of students, voice and piano, and was
well loved by the Lincoln kids who studied with her. When he
glimpsed her demonstrating arpeggios for them on the piano, or
making a three-bean salad for lunch after lessons, or gesticulat-
ing wildly as she spat furious curses at the 1968 Soviet invasion
of Czechoslovakia on their black-and-white television, he always
loved those hands. Her fingers had thickened over the years, but

what Danek saw were intricate instruments, skilled and delicate, always alive. The veins that made such strong mosaics on the tops of them and flowed their way past her prominent, elegant knuckles into her fingers. When she confessed to him that for a long time she had renounced music altogether, he found it hard to imagine.

"I'm glad those days are over," he said.

"So am I," she admitted, marveling at how much her horizons had expanded beyond European music of the nineteenth century and before. If early in her American life Otylie had been told that a day would come when she'd love upbeat swing music, weepy cowboy ballads, the music of Woody Guthrie and other American folksingers, she would have dismissed the notion as an insult. But as it turned out, many were the Saturday nights when she and Danek dressed up in the appropriate outfits and joined others at dances in a regional Grange hall, in the church basement, even out under the stars during summer gatherings before a park band shell with live music. Music grew to be central to her and Danek's lives. Twice a month, Otylie hosted a potluck dinner recital at their home, inviting anyone who owned an instrument—accordion, guitar, clarinet, washboard—to come on over and play after a smorgasbord meal of macaroni and cheese, meat loaf, cole slaw, and all the rest. She and Danek invested in a turntable and speakers, and made biweekly trips to their favorite record stores to add LPs to their collection. From classical to bluegrass, their tastes were eclectic, and music emanated from their windows from morning to night.

On occasion, though less frequently over the years, when Danek was on his shift and no pupils were scheduled to come to their modest bungalow in Woods Park for a lesson, Otylie pulled out the sonata manuscript and played the first movement. Sometimes tears welled in her eyes as she did so, tears of remembrance, tears of frustration, but also tears of joy—or something akin to joy. She had long since dismissed her father's drunken theory, from their last night together, that war is music and music is war. This passage of music had survived its share of wars and more often than not offered Otylie peace. At other times she simply marveled at what she was playing and wondered if her father's speculations about who composed this actually did have merit or were, as she had always feared, fanciful illusions.

The man had been a dreamer, but also a true musician. And this fragment of unknown paternity—illusions be damned—proved without a doubt that his taste in music was unerring. She regretted not having made copies of the other movements so that she would have the work in its entirety, but reminded herself how brutal were those hours in which she was forced to make so many life-and-death decisions. Her focus had been on Jakub, his abrupt disappearance into the resistance, and when she looked back she began to realize that she'd chosen to break up the manuscript not only in an attempt to make it worthless to the Nazis but as an act of solidarity with Jakub himself. If the sheaf had finally made it from that gaunt boy—wasn't his name Marek? it was so long ago—to her first husband, then at least he'd had something of hers to comfort him, maybe, in the darkest hours.

Though the photograph of her parents, its details now somewhat sun faded, hung in the guest bedroom, and she occasionally reread randomly from the clutch of unsent letters she had written to Jakub, Otylie tried not to dwell in the past. When, one evening during dinner, Danek mentioned out of the blue that a colleague at the hospital had a brother who worked as a private detective and had, as he was told, "a hunting dog's nose for tracking down anyone and anything, anywhere," he asked Otylie if she'd like him to discuss locating Irena Svobodová. "Or maybe see about finding the lost parts of your father's manuscript."

Otylie stared at her glass of water. Saying nothing, she took a drink from it, set it down. Finally, with the saddest smile on her face Danek had ever seen and with her eyes averted, she thanked him and said, "I think this is not what I want to do."

"You're sure now? We can afford to have him look for you. Our savings are good. It wouldn't cost too terribly much."

"You are so dear to offer this," she said, a firm weight of finality in her voice. "But I think no."

Danek asked, "Can you tell me why? I know Irena was your best friend."

"She will always be."

"So then?"

Otylie confessed, "It's selfish of me. I hope you won't think I'm a bad person."

"Never," he said.

"I just don't want to risk disappointment, I cannot. Any hopes about that are over and it is better they are. I am here now. With you. It is enough, more than I ever dreamed possible."

He reached over and pressed her hand, which was neither cold nor trembling, and knew never to broach the subject again. Nor did he once during the twenty-three rich and affectionate years that followed, during which time the Hajeks grew old together, retiring as planned from Lincoln to the hamlet of Prague where, after his usual stroll up to the cemetery hill and back before supper on a perfect summer's evening, Danek collapsed while taking off his jacket in the hallway of their house.

Otylie, having heard an odd muffled cry and soft dull sound, came rushing from the kitchen in the back, expecting to find that a neighbor's child had wandered in—no one locked doors in Prague—and maybe tripped and fallen. Expecting it was her imagination playing tricks on her. Expecting anything other than her husband lying there inert and unresponsive. She tried to revive him, tears spilling onto his face and shirt as she pushed her palms against his chest, thinking he'd suffered a heart attack. Seeing that her efforts were failing, she rushed to the phone and called the local doctor, a fishing buddy of Danek's, who came immediately. But there was nothing for it. An unsuspected aneurysm in the brain had burst and her husband was gone. Otylie began to shiver as she watched him taken away, and though a neighbor placed the heavy crocheted afghan from the sofa around her shoulders, she felt she would never be warm again.

Jane and Jim Burke as well as several others made the trip up from Texas to attend the funeral, along with former colleagues from the hospital, friends from Lincoln days, and a host of Praguers. The small hillside prairie cemetery rarely saw so many people gathered at once from such different walks of life— doctors, farmers, pupils, the local pharmacist, the village banker, the mechanic who only the week before had installed new brakes in the Hajeks' Chevy. Some were Czech Americans, some not. Some knew Danek well, others in passing along the sidewalks of town. More than a few showed up to support his widow, who had taught them to play music, which, along with family and church, was one thing that deeply bound this community.

As she listened to the eulogies, Otylie couldn't help but admit to herself that she had always quietly hoped it would be she who went first. Danek would have missed her, she knew, just as she was now fated to miss him, but he was always so resilient. He would have survived, even thrived. Not that she herself wasn't a proven survivor, but being a survivor meant that you lived to some degree in a chronic state of mourning, like a low-level fever that waxes and wanes but is never truly eliminated.

While the minister read a psalm from scripture, Otylie strayed from his words and found herself wondering if she would ever fathom life, ever understand herself. Was that what we were here to do? Fathom life? Understand ourselves? Even if it were possible, she mused as the last prayers were uttered and the funeral drew toward a close, what then? Understanding was a fluid thing because, like music, it flows and shifts and reinvents itself with every passing moment. Worthy of reaching toward, yes, always. But finally beyond our human grasp. It was too mercurial, too capricious, too unstable to rely on as a sturdy truth.

She had friends here, some of whom would stick by her for a little while, she knew, and others whom she could count on as her own life moved forward. So she determined to set aside her darker thoughts about mortality and understanding and try her level best to be heartened by the outpouring of kindness and condolences shown to her following Danek's interment. The wildflowers that grew in abundance on this hushed hill nodded as if in assent.

Still, though, when everyone left—including darling Jane, who stayed with her for three whole weeks after the burial—there she was, alone again. This time, she believed, for good. Her life would now be a matter of sheer routine. Rising, going through the day, sleeping, dreaming. Rising, going through the day. Nothing more of importance would ever happen to her. Rather than being depressed by this thought, Otylie Bartošová Hajek accepted it. For all of the storms in her life, she believed she had been more fortunate than many.

· 7 ·

WITH TIME TIGHT and resources getting tighter, the side excursion from their starting point in Prague, Arkansas, to the all but nonexistent community of Praha, Texas, was an admitted indulgence. But what was one more day on the road?

"Besides," said Meta, "we're just following your philosophy of life."

"Really now." Gerrit raised his eyebrows. "And what philosophy of life is that?"

"You don't remember what you said on our first date, do you."

"I don't remember that we officially had a first date."

"Sure, up at that open-air café in Hradčany near the castle? You told me you didn't believe that anything is finally a waste of time. I thought you were just trying to cheer me up. But now I think you're exactly right."

Having struck out completely on their first stop—no Bartošovás in municipal records, nursing homes, cemetery logs—they decided that an afternoon in tiny Praha was all they needed to determine that Otylie was not there. Very few people from the past or present were. There was no town hall, so they asked at the parish church, where a man in bib overalls who appeared to be the custodian told them, in a mix of Spanish and English, he knew nothing that would be of help. Nor did a nearby antiques, or rather junk and funky knickknacks, dealer have any ideas. They checked the cemetery, smaller than the one in Arkansas, but found no sign of Otylie.

For all that, as they drove up I-35 North together in the silver Accord they'd rented in Little Rock, they felt closer to each other than at any moment in the past. After phoning Gerrit's family to say he'd be visiting New York soon with someone he wanted them to meet, as well as Meta's mother to let her know they'd landed in Arkansas and were on their way to Nebraska—"You're what?" she'd exclaimed—they took turns at the wheel. They stopped for take-out cheeseburgers and chatted about sights along the way during their seven hours' drive up from Texas to Oklahoma City, just another couple, in love, on the second leg of their first road trip together.

From the moment they stepped off the plane in Little Rock, each of them had felt the strangeness of being back in America. In her performing days, besides playing on both coasts, Meta had taken the stage at festivals in the Midwest and West—Chicago and Minneapolis, Aspen and Santa Fe. But this part of the country was new to her, exhilarating and exotic in its way—the impossibly theatrical sky, the only partly tamed wildlands—if disconcerting. And while Gerrit had visited these parts before, simply having been away from America for so long left him in a bit of culture shock.

Throughout the drive east from Oklahoma City to their next Prague, a heavy wind buffeted the car, propelling bits of debris and the occasional tumbleweed across the highway. In distinct contrast to the travelers, the weather had a bad-tempered cast

to it, with gray and old-bone-white clouds snaking around themselves, and with spitting rain blowing sideways in gusts.

"I'd say we're not in Kansas anymore," Gerrit joked.

"And we haven't even gotten to Kansas yet." Gesturing at the
landscape, she said, "I know there are people who would totally
hate spending five minutes in Manhattan, and I get it, but I doubt
I could make it out here. You really need to have a pioneer heart to
live under a sky like this, knowing it can drop down and erase you
and your town whenever it likes."

"For what it's worth, I'm not predicting a tornado in our near
future. Don't think it's the season."

"Hope your meteorology's up to speed. But I guess I'm wondering how Otylie managed the transitions from Prague to London
and then out here, assuming that's what she did. My sense is that
if anybody could handle it, she could."

The car was buffeted again. Silence settled for a time between
them as another mile clicked by, and then Meta exhaled hard,
slapped her palms against the steering wheel, and said, "Damn it,
Gerrit. I hope to God she's still alive."

"I'm with you on that," he said, surprised by her sudden stridency.

"But for personal reasons. It's crazy, but I feel so bonded to her.
It's like I actually *miss* her."

A highway sign and an auto-shop billboard that read "Czech Us
Out!" made it plain they were near. When they turned off the highway and drove into town, the wind was whipping worse than before.
They parked on Jim Thorpe Boulevard—named after the great ath-
lete who was the town's most famous native son—and entered the
chamber of commerce building. A birdlike woman in a brown wor-
sted suit was eager to help, and together they went through town records and more contemporary census accountings on the chamber's
computer, but without luck. When she said, "The Historical Museum is open this afternoon if you'd like to try there," they thanked

her and, undeterred, walked over to Broadway, a street wider than the highway so that farm equipment drawn by teams of horses could make U-turns in the days before Thorpe was born. The museum, a squat squarish brick affair, proved to be a treasure chest of Bohemian memorabilia. Two women volunteers assisted them as they read handwritten ledgers and historical records, looking for an Otylie or a Tilly or anyone named Bartoš or Bartošová who might have lived in Prague during the last fifty years. But again, they were forced to concede they had come up empty.

"You've been so helpful," Meta said, trying to hide her sense of defeat, especially in light of how deep-rooted this community's investment was in its Czech legacy.

"Wish we could have found what you're looking for," one of the volunteers replied. "There's three cemeteries. The Prague cemetery on the road out toward Paden, the Catholic cemetery, and the Czech cemetery. But I misdoubt she'd be resting in any of them if there's no record of her here."

The day was getting old and dark, the sky and wind no less ugly. They left this most recent Prague in time to make it back to Oklahoma City for the night, and checked into the first motel they spotted just before the daylong winds finally ushered in cold rain. In the morning, drinking from Styrofoam cups the thin coffee they brewed in their room, they spread out the maps they'd picked up at a gas station and plotted their next move. The skies had mostly cleared overnight. A sunrise of frosty pinks and silvers was reflected in puddles in the parking lot outside.

"Well, our last and least Prague is about four hundred and sixty miles north of here. Should take us seven, maybe eight hours."

"Why do you say 'least'?" asked Gerrit. He had awakened before Meta and lain in bed worrying about how she was going to handle not finding the first movement of the sonata. Her brief outburst in the car had startled him into the realization that if this third and final American Prague didn't turn up Otylie Bartošová, Meta could easily make the mistake of considering her quest a failure.

"Oh, I don't mean it derogatorily. The opposite. Just it's the smallest of the three Pragues and pretty much my last chance. If we drive straight through and the weather stays nice, by tomorrow sometime we'll have been able to knock on every door in town. Then we'll know."

"Meta. Remember Venus de Milo, hear me?"

She nodded at him without saying anything, but he could see the worry there.

"Besides, it's not your last chance. We'll go back to New York and regroup. We haven't checked national census records yet, and there are other ways to find people. We're not out of options."

He weighed whether to share with Meta the information he'd learned about Wittmann when they were in London. It had been quite a stretch since then—four days? Five? The travel from Prague to Pragues began to blur. He decided to wait until after the trip north. "Some breakfast first?" he asked, breaking the silence.

"I'm famished," she agreed. "Shall we just grab something and eat it on the road?"

"Sounds like a plan."

They packed their few belongings after a quick shower and set off for, as Gerrit had taken to spelling it in his notebook, having learned how the name was pronounced out here, *Praygue*.

UNNERVED BUT UNBOWED, WITTMANN lit the first of many cigarettes he would smoke that day, then tossed his match into the gutter as he stood looking up and down the street in front of

Mandelbaum's hotel. Not that he expected to see the man's back as he disappeared around a corner like some tawdry rat. Mandelbaum was neither tawdry nor a rat, he knew, but rather had become someone who no longer seemed to understand how the world worked.

To think he, Wittmann, had been naive enough to believe he had formed a collegial pact with his American friend. Not collaborative, no. Not symbiotic. But, at minimum, the beginnings of a civilized negotiation. Moving uneasily together toward a common goal, improvising their way as they had done in times past. For him to have checked out like this without the common courtesy of a forewarning, a simple call? And where precisely were his acolyte and the goddamn manuscript? He couldn't remember feeling such a combination of disgust, chagrin, even dread—of not being in firm control of his corner of the world.

Now here he stood with nothing more than a note on hotel stationery, sealed in an envelope with its fancy engraved coat of arms, which the desk clerk handed him while they exchanged a few cordial unpleasantries of their own.

Please, Wittmann had tried, offering the younger man in his somewhat military-style hotel uniform a gracious smile. I've been trying to call him since yesterday. I expect that if you dial him from the front desk, you'll have better luck getting through.

I can assure you, sir, that no one will answer the phone. There is no one in the room.

Can you confirm he has checked out? Or would it be possible for you to let me see for myself?

Sir, as much as I would like to accommodate—

I'm concerned he left something behind in the room that is our joint property.

The housekeeper, who has already made up the room for our next guests, would have brought it to my attention if she found the gentleman had forgotten anything.

What about the hotel safe?

Shall I get my manager for you?

That won't be necessary, Wittmann said, certain that the clerk was right and Mandelbaum had in fact left nothing behind.

Then I'm afraid there's little else I can do. Perhaps your friend will have notified you of his plans in the letter he left. You'll excuse me, sir.

With those words he turned gratefully to a couple trailed by a luggage-laden bellhop, and set about checking them in.

Outside, Wittmann was tempted to tear the envelope to pieces and toss it into the gutter beside his spent match. But though there was a time before the revolution—not so long ago, a mere decade—when he might have made some calls and had Mandelbaum detained at the gate before his flight took off, those days were over.

For as long as it took him to slide his forefinger under the flap, open the square blue envelope, and pull out Mandelbaum's note, hesitating before reading, Wittmann experienced a numb, even paralytic, minute in which he regretted ever getting involved with this sonata manuscript. Of its importance, historically and musicologically, he was long since convinced.

The movement Meta had brought to his attention, unlike the concluding rondo that had been in the Langs' possession, did not resemble the work of anyone from the period in which it was evidently composed. Except, that is, Beethoven, who alone was capable of such unique bravura combined with what Wittmann discerned as the profound spiritual conscience that informed the more meditative, lachrymose passage, a harbinger in some ways of full-blown romanticism. Though he hadn't physically handled Meta's original, he was sure, on the basis of Mandelbaum's assessment if nothing else, that the paper on which its companion rondo was written was from the same period, as the central movement.

Yes, he might have approached things differently. Rather than attempting to finesse her to gain access to the original, he might have sincerely apologized to the young lady that night when he and Karel ran into her in Old Town Square. Could have really tried to assist rather than thwart her, hoping to discredit her with both Johana Langová, who was willing to see Meta discredited if there was any advantage to it, and Tomáš, who wasn't. Some of the claim to the discovery might have been his, had he played by the rules. But he hadn't done any of that, and whether he liked it or not, he now paced in front of this elegant hotel with a letter in his hands and an unshakable determination to follow through on his decisions. There had to be some logical means whereby he would come out on top.

Finally unfolding the paper, his cigarette clipped loosely in his lips, he forced himself to peruse Mandelbaum's handwritten note.

Petr, it read, *I have not given up on you, but neither can I allow you to ruin yourself and others over this matter. The score is in a safe place. Meta has left the country together with her companion. As you can surmise, so have I. Let her track down the lost movement, if she can, without interference. Myself, if you wish to contact me, I'll be home, easy to find. There was nothing left for me to do in Prague. I'd have preferred more gemütlichkeit between us, but maybe next time. I continue to admire you, Petr, and hope your actions will allow us to remain friends. S pozdravem, Paul*

While he had anticipated everything in Mandelbaum's letter, it stung to see matters laid out in so many flat words. And as Kohout had fallen by the wayside, an aging man more concerned with retirement than discovery, Wittmann was on his own now. By the same token, he realized, when had he not been?

Having walked swiftly back to his office, the note tossed into a trash receptacle along the way, Wittmann sat on his swivel chair and looked at the framed book jackets, awards, and degrees, both earned and honorary, arrayed on his wall in French-parlor style. He pressed his palms together, elbows on his desk, and, as a ribbon of blue cigarette smoke curled from his ashtray, deliberated how to proceed. As Mandelbaum had written, there was nothing left to do in Prague. He stared for a moment at his phone, then lifted the handset and made three calls.

The first was to his travel agent. Round-trip ticket to New York, business class, with an open date for the return flight.

The second was to a personal assistant of Charles Castell, the collector who was more avid to acquire the manuscript than the Czech musicologist had implied over breakfast with his American counterpart. Shaven headed and lean as a vegan ascetic, with warm, gray eyes and a disarming, soft voice that navigated a number of languages, he was a businessman who, as Wittmann had told Mandelbaum without sharing the man's name, liked to speculate in things other than just stocks, gold, consumer commodities.

Castell's assistant transferred the call and, after a brief silence, an amicable voice said, "Hello, Petr. Good of you to call. So where do we meet in Prague?"

"I'm afraid there's been a change of plan, Charles," Wittmann said, hoping not to convey anxiety.

"News of the opening movement?"

"Not yet," he said, then admitted that the score had been removed from the country, and proceeded to inform Castell of what he knew, leaving out elements he sensed were neither integral to their dealings nor favorable to himself as broker.

Not one to be perturbed, Castell asked, "What's the next move?"

"I just booked a flight to New York, leaving tomorrow. I need to track down the person who first brought it to me for authentication and advice."

"Meta? The one who was mentioned in that little article?"

Knowing he shouldn't appear caught off guard by Charles Castell's attentiveness and reach, he was caught off guard nonetheless. Best to respond with the truth. "Yes. I planted that hoping to generate a response."

"Makes sense. That's what I would do. No results, I gather."

"Not yet."

"All right, I was going through Prague on my way back to the city"—spoken like a true New Yorker, Wittmann thought—"but since you're leaving, we'll just catch up in the States. You have my private number. Get in touch when you have something?"

"Will do."

"And, oh, Petr," said Charles Castell just before hanging up. "The woman's name is spelled 'Taverner.' I think you'll find she lives in the East Village and her mother is over in Chelsea. Look forward to hearing from you."

Embarrassing, Wittmann thought. He had planted that squib through an insider at the paper in the hope of flushing out information about Meta's whereabouts. And he had succeeded not because she contacted him to complain but because Castell's people were ahead of him. Well, at least it proved that Charles Castell still depended on him to obtain the manuscript rather than independently approaching Meta. But this was as it always had been in earlier dealings. Anonymity was a priority. The man cherished privacy and revealed the treasures in his collections only when he so desired, whether to lend, donate, or sell.

Wittmann's third call was a long shot, but he wasn't in a frame of mind that proposed capitulation or defeat. Yes, his highest contact in the ministry of culture had expressed interest but offered little help when Wittmann first approached him regarding the sonata—its ownership in question, its provenance murky, its cultural importance not fully established. Now that the material had been taken out of the Czech Republic, he was emboldened to inform the ministry that his fears had come to pass. Trying not to sound the acerbic notes of *I told you so*, he reached out again to his old comrade who'd weathered the revolution as a mid-level bureaucrat and parlayed his experience into increasingly responsible government positions.

Well, it happened, Wittmann said, exhaling to add a little dramatic spice.

And what is that?

You know what I'm referring to.

This purported Beethoven manuscript.

It's gone, left the country. And that's a crime in more ways than one.

Ah. Well, Petr, I do understand the depth of your concern. I've had an opportunity to reflect on our last conversation and have even discussed it with others here at the ministry. We collectively feel that you should simply file a lawsuit, or help the putative owners do so. I don't know how far you will get with such an action, however, since there is no clear evidence a crime has in fact been committed.

The suspicion of transporting stolen property across national boundaries—

I in no way wish to minimize this, but your news only complicates things. Please understand that we can't approach the American embassy about the matter without firm evidence of wrongdoing, and we just don't have enough to make an international case of it.

Stymied, Wittmann said nothing.

I'm afraid this is all I can do for you, Petr. Get an attorney, level charges, as you please. But the ministry cannot assist.

There was a time—, Wittmann started to say, but hung up. From hotel clerks to government functionaries to erstwhile colleagues here and abroad, he got neither advocacy nor respect, as he saw it. This was not how Wittmann was accustomed to being treated and he didn't like it. The disgust and chagrin he had felt earlier were joined by new sensations, ones he had experienced the night Marta had turned him and Kohout out onto the streets of Malá Strana, terminating his plea to Tomáš to give him the original of the rondo movement. Bald, scalding indignation. Indignation and, of all things, helplessness.

THE SUN ON THE SNOW outside her windows was filtered, its light gaunt. Occasional stray flakes corkscrewed down from a sky the color of a house wren's breast. Though her front room was warm, she would rather have liked to burn a fire in the corner potbellied stove, but she only lit it when it was storming hard and she needed the extra heat, or when the electric power went out. Otherwise it would be bad for the piano, a baby grand, the treasured gift from her late husband. She had known from youth that dry heat and pianos with their taut strings and exquisite woods were not friends. Her father taught her that way back when. She made sure to refill the two baking pans that sat on the radiators near the piano with fresh water every morning. They weren't lovely to look at, but they worked nicely as humidifiers.

If only pans of heated water could make her knees feel better on wintry days like this, she thought. How many more winters would she have? Her doctor and friends marveled at her health. Good genes, they all agreed, although she had no way of proving it, since both her parents died young through no fault in their gene pool. Otylie felt lucky that she wasn't afflicted with arthritis in her fingers like most friends of her age. Only her neighbor Anna, a quilter who at eighty-seven was still producing colorful Pride of Nebraskas, crazy quilts, and log cabins that won prizes at the local county fair, was as nimble.

Like many others in tiny Prague, she tended to eat her main meal of the day not in the evening but in early afternoon. That day's dinner was chicken casserole and frozen peas cooked in broth and butter. Her habits and chores around the small house were not unlike what others of her generation and even a generation younger would be doing on a nippy, gray day like this. Perhaps the only difference was that on her hi-fi she was listening to Mozart's *Die Zauberflöte*, conducted by Sir Colin Davis in Dresden in 1984, with Margaret Price, one of her favorite sopranos, singing the role of Pamina.

The doorbell startled her. Who would be out in this weather? Otylie had just put on the first record of her box set to listen to while she ate, so she was only at act one, scene two. Papageno, playing his panpipe and singing, had come down the path carrying on his back a cage housing all sorts of birds. Tamino, performed by another of her favorite opera stars, the tenor Peter Schreier, had asked Papageno, "*Sag mir, du lustiger Freund, wer du bist?*"—Tell me, my cheerful friend, who are you?—to which Papageno responded, A man like you! What if I were to ask you who you are?

She knew every word of the libretto and continued to hum Tamino's next lines, that he was a man of princely blood whose father ruled over many lands and peoples, as she reached for her metal cane, rose from the kitchen table, and made her way to the front door.

Peering through one of the three small door windows that let light into the foyer, she saw a young couple who were clearly from elsewhere. She pulled her shawl closer around her shoulders and opened the door.

"How can I help you?" Otylie asked, a little nervous in front of these strangers.

The young woman gulped a deep breath of cold prairie air and said, "Excuse us for bothering you. But we're looking for Otylie Bartošová, and some nice people down in the local café said she lives here. Or Otylie Hajek?"

"And who is looking for her, may I ask?"

"My name is Meta Taverner," she said, feeling her pulse quicken. "And this is Gerrit Mills. We've come a very long way looking for her because I have something, a music manuscript, that I believe is hers."

Otylie looked hard at Meta, then at Gerrit, and then past them over the leafless trees toward the snowy horizon. Meta stared in wonderment at her pale, wrinkled face framed by silver hair pulled back into a bun. Finally, in a voice abruptly hoarse and small, the woman said, "*Pojd'te dál*," reverting unawares to Czech. Do come in.

Still unsure what to think, but sensing that this was a moment in her life she would never want to forget, Meta said, "*Děkuji*—I mean, *Děkujeme*," switching to the plural to include Gerrit, and they stepped over the doorsill into the entry hall and warm living room. Hearing *The Magic Flute*, seeing the piano with sheet music propped open, and above all watching the woman's eyes as they searched her own—Meta knew, she knew this had to be right, this had to be her.

When Otylie said, "Let me turn this down," Meta said, "No, please. This is where Tamino sings, 'I doubt if you are human,' right?"

Otylie nodded, said nothing, her mind racing, bewildered, and yet trusting this girl who was so earnest, clearly, and led them back into her kitchen. When she walked into the room, Meta was overwhelmed by the memory of Irena's kitchen, every bit as tidy,

old-fashioned, and marvelous as this one. Instead of canned tomato soup, here the room was redolent of baked chicken. Meta
and Gerrit sat, waiting for this woman to utter the next words.

"I am Otylie Bartošová," she confirmed, a tentative smile working at her lips. "You have some of the manuscript that I broke up,
what, fifty, sixty years ago? Is that what you are saying?"

"A piano sonata. Eighteenth century?"

Rather than appearing happy, Otylie seemed disoriented. "It
cannot be true."

Meta looked at Gerrit, speechless.

"It is true, *Paní* Bartošová," he assured her.

"How, how is this possible?" Otylie had never liked to cry but
she was struggling.

"We have stories to share, but—" and Meta reached into the
leather briefcase Gerrit had given her, pulled out Irena's burgundy
goatskin portfolio, then carefully withdrew the manuscript pages
of the second and third movements of the Prague Sonata. With
both hands she passed the manuscript to Otylie, who slowly
looked it through before setting it on the table, placing both palms
on top as if to keep it from blowing away in some phantom wind.

"Forgive me," she said, her eyes wet. "I have thought for so
many years these pages were lost forever. That this part of my life
was closed and done," she managed, her voice cracking.

Meta and Gerrit glanced at each other, remained quiet, each
realizing that for weeks, months they'd thought of Otylie's pages
as the lost ones.

"Two times, kind people offered to pay for private investigators to
go searching for Irena, who I knew might still have the part I gave
her. I was too scared to risk bad news. But here, look. You made the
search and—" She pressed her lips together, shook her head.

Meta softly asked, "We didn't make a mistake, did we, bringing
them back to you?"

Otylie brushed away tears. "No. No, not at all." After taking a moment to collect herself, she went more carefully through the manuscript. When she turned to the third movement, Meta pointed to the faint handwriting at the top of the leaf.

"Gerrit says this is written in Czech, but we can't make it out."

Otylie squinted, raising the page closer to her eyes. She read what was there and looked at the young woman, smiling. "I wrote these words for Jakub when I gave the movement to a boy—I can still see his face; I think his name was Marek—to pass along to him in hiding."

With her fingertips, she lightly touched the paper.

"Many times I scolded myself for doing what I did," she went on. "I had to think too fast. I didn't mean to put such a burden on my poor husband and friend, who had their own lives to save, not some piece of music."

"If you don't mind me saying so, I believe it might have given them a reason to live, or at least a tangible connection to you, whom they loved," Meta said, and described in detail how she'd met Irena Svobodová through her friend Gillian, how she'd visited Irena at her home in Queens, how she listened to Irena's account of the harrowing events of 1939, and how the sonata manuscript came into her possession.

At this mention of Irena, Otylie's eyes brightened. "Is she well?"

Meta gently broke the news to her. "I only really talked with her that once, but I can assure you she felt it was urgent that the manuscript get back into your hands."

"Queens," mused Otylie with a sigh. "You know, I lived in Manhattan for a time and I swear one day I saw her walking along Park Avenue. I chased her but couldn't catch up. And there was no Irena Svobodová in the phone book, so I assumed it was my mind playing tricks. I loved her, you know."

"She loved you too," Meta said, imagining how bittersweet this all must be for Otylie, a coil of unexpected elation and melancholy. "I have the phone number of one of her friends in New York. I met her at the funeral and took it down, not really knowing why at the time. Now I do."

As Meta described her journey from that first afternoon on Kalmia Avenue, Queens, to this one on Danube Street, Prague, Nebraska, Otylie marveled at her young benefactor's perseverance and was taken aback that Meta had no patrons, no grants, to support her work. Gerrit, noting that Otylie had picked up some good midwestern practicality along the way, said, "Meta's a classic idealist to a fault, Mrs. Bartošová-Hajek."

"I have known such people," said Otylie. "I can see you are devoted to her. This is why?"

"One of the reasons," he said, charmed by her frankness.

"I'm sure there are many others." With a smile, she looked down at her wrinkled hands with their pale knobby knuckles folded on the tablecloth. "I think it's time you see what you have been searching for, no?"

"Nothing would make me happier," Meta answered.

Leaning on her cane, Otylie retrieved the first movement from her bedroom and, reentering the kitchen, offered a worse-for-wear hart-skin satchel to Meta, who asked, "May I wash my hands first?"

"Please," said Otylie.

Afterward, Meta sat down again at the kitchen table, and with the same care as if she were handling a newborn, she turned the leaves one by one and began to read the music.

The only word on the first leaf besides Otylie's father's tender inscription to her in German was *Sonate*, and it appeared to be in a different hand, probably nineteenth century. Might have been written there by a manuscript dealer rather than a musician, Meta speculated. To her delight, although exultation was more what she was feeling, the key was just as she and Mandelbaum had conjectured months ago. Sonata allegro, first-movement form in the key of E-flat major. Running her eye across the staves, turning the first page, she began to get a clearer sense of the composer's artistic universe. Seeing its progression, the way the movement unfolded in classic tripartite form—exposition, development, recapitulation—Meta could tell at once that this music was unquestionably related to the other two movements. Plus, the physical evidence bore it out. The hand was the same. The paper, while discolored from being housed inside the acidic deerskin, was in better shape than the movement Jakub had carried before passing it along to Tomáš, and both in turn had aged differently from Irena's. But it didn't take a musicologist's or conservator's eye to see they were all of a piece.

"I would love to hear you play it," she told Otylie, impatient to experience the music off the page and set free in the air. "That is, if you were willing."

Otylie had been watching as Meta read the first few pages of the score, and noticed the silent, involuntary movement of the young woman's lips and fingers.

"You are a real musician, I can see. Maybe you should play instead."

Meta hesitated. "Oh, well. I could sight-read my way through it, and it'd be an honor to do that. But my guess is, much the same way I know the other movements by heart at this point, you must know the first. You know how it should sound."

"I have an idea," said Gerrit. "Otylie plays the first movement and then Meta plays the others. How's that?"

They moved into the living room, where the piano awaited them. Outside, the snow had picked up a little. Large flakes drifted downward and reminded Gerrit of the napkin Meta had, in quiet nervousness, torn to shreds while they shared their first coffee together up in Hradčany. She'd improvised that it was confetti to toss in celebration when they found what she was looking for. He would tell her later that her confetti had reappeared in the form of snowflakes on the other side of the world.

"Do you need the manuscript?" Meta asked Otylie.

"No, you have it right. The music is all inside me."

"Will it be okay if I follow the score while you play?"

"Of course," said Otylie, as Meta set the manuscript on the wooden music stand that Otylie used when teaching, and for a long moment the room was filled with rich silence as the world outside its windows was shrouded in an even deeper, denser quiet.

What was wanting in technical prowess—Otylie's fingers walked rather than ran, and her dynamics were flattened somewhat to an evenness, a plateau of attack—was compensated with feeling, Meta thought, as the woman began to play. The kind of feeling that comes only from a familiarity and complexity of experience interwoven with the work itself. Otylie was, in essence, living these musical notes.

Half in rapture, half in a state of fervent attentiveness, Meta listened. Turning the pages, she saw the music unfold before her eyes and she clearly heard how this first movement was part of the whole composition. Goose bumps on her arms, she continued to listen, immersed. But when she turned the penultimate page and saw the last leaf, on which the first sonata movement ended just past midway down, her breath stopped. Everything for her stopped. On the bottom of the page were two heavily corrected staves of dissimilar music scrawled hastily, furiously, in yet another hand, nearly illegible and in much darker ink.

"That was beautiful," she managed.

Gerrit agreed, noting Meta's expression had shifted from plea-sure to incredulity.

Meta lifted the manuscript from the stand and held it closer to her face, studying the unanticipated autograph musical sketch, a dozen measures or so, feverishly scored.

Gerrit hesitated before saying, "Are you all right?"

"There's more here," she said, looking over at him, eyes opened wide, then back at the messy notes that bristled with visual energy on the page.

"Yes, the other movements," Otylie said. "May I hear you play them? So many years have gone by, and I've tried to remember. But I can only do small parts and even then I'm not sure whether I am making it up."

"I'm sorry, yes, happily," Meta said, collecting herself. "But, first, may I ask you about this writing at the bottom here?"

She'd taken the manuscript over to the piano and sat on the bench next to Otylie, whose perfume, she noticed, was the scent of gardenias.

"Oh, this." Otylie squinted at it as she might have done many times before, and shrugged. "This I never understood. I tried play-ing it, but could never really make it out."

"Do you have any idea what it is?"

"Probably nothing, just some foolish child from centuries ago making a mess."

Meta eyed Gerrit, who tilted his head, conveying a silent, What's up?

"Mrs. Bartošová, you only just met me. You don't know me at all, but if you believe what I've told you about Irena, going to Prague and finding Tomáš Lang, going to London, and all the rest of what it's taken to get us together, you need to believe me when I tell you I think this manuscript may be very valuable, not just to the history of late-eighteenth-century music but valuable in every way conceivable."

"I believe all you have said, yes," said Otylie.

"Let me show you the letter Irena gave me," Meta continued, retrieving it from the leather briefcase and handing it to the woman.

This manuscript now the property of Meta Taverner until such time she is able to return this to Otylie Bartošová or heir, with agreement that she try to recover entire manuscript as were Otylie Bartošová's stated wishes.

When the older woman finished reading, Meta said, "'Such time as I am able to return it to you' is what Irena wrote, and now I am returning it to you."

Stunned, without thinking, Otylie looked at the reverse side of Irena's note and saw her own handwriting in Czech from six decades and a year earlier, giving custodianship of the manuscript to Irena. She gazed up at Meta and—modestly, simply—said, "Thank you. I thank you and I thank dearest Irena. How I wish she was here with us."

"She is, you know, in a way."

"I spent so many years trying to get away from Prague, and those hard, hard days, and ended up here in a simpler Prague. But to see her handwriting, and my own to her, and hold these pages my husband protected—well, I can almost feel them alive again."

Seeing that Meta had no words, Gerrit said, "I'm a pretty secular person myself. But if I had to imagine a worthy moment when the spirits of the dead might be allowed to reconvene, this would certainly qualify."

The three sat in communion made the more silent by the settling snow, which dampened any sounds outside the house. Then Otylie placed the letter on the music stand above the piano keys and said, "Now, unless you have another question, may I hear the rest of the sonata, dear?"

"Of course."

"I'll play the first movement once more, then move aside so you can finish the rest."

Their tempi were different, as were their dynamics. They'd grown up listening to different pianists from different eras. One was an aged yet skilled amateur, the other an injured yet all but professional keyboardist. Meta marveled while watching Otylie bring to life the opening of a musical narrative by a young composer expressing his grief, yearning, and stubborn will to survive in the face of eminent loss. Then the woman shifted to the end of the long bench. As she watched Meta's fingers attack the same middle movement that she had heard her father play so often when she was a girl, an unexpected feeling of contentment rose within her. Music, she thought, had a magical way of collapsing years and bridging distances. Meta's interpretation varied from the way Otylie's father had approached this bright ascent to a trill or that mournful descending scale, but the music itself maintained its integrity, its character. Otylie was, she supposed, the last person to believe in miracles, but as the middle movement came to a close and Meta began the third, with its delightful melody as fresh now as it'd been when she heard it as a child in faraway Olomouc, it occurred to her that what she was experiencing here, now, bordered on the miraculous.

When the last notes of the rondo were struck and vanished, the living room, whose windows were filled by the soft motion of falling snowflakes, was overwhelmed by silence once more, none of its occupants knowing quite what to say. For the first time in well over half a century, the complete Prague Sonata had been played, and the two women along with Gerrit, their rapt audience of one, felt the weight and history of this private shared moment. What had been purposely dispersed, lost in order to save this piece of cultural history, had finally been brought together. Otylie reached over, took Meta by the hands, and shook her head in disbelief.

"Thank you, Meta," Otylie said again, after another while, "and thank you, Gerrit," as she reached for and found her cane, then rose from the bench. "It is as beautiful, even more beautiful, than I remembered. Maybe we can play it again in a bit?"

"As many times as you like," Meta said, inhaling deeply, realizing she'd been half-holding her breath these last minutes. "And then you can relearn it and play it whenever you want to. It's yours again."

"But what about you?" Otylie suddenly said, looking at Meta. "I must share this with you, otherwise all you have done—it is not fair."

Meta glanced at Gerrit, down at her hands momentarily, then at Otylie, saying, "Mrs. Bartošová, Mrs. Hajek, I did little compared with what you and your first husband and many others did."

"I am an old woman. No heirs, no one to pass it on to. You have given me back a precious part of my past, but I can give it no future."

"Let's not think about that right now," Meta replied, her words emerging slowly as she imagined what Wittmann's response to Otylie's comment would have been. "You can decide what to do with it later. As for me, all I want to do is study it. Especially now that there's this other handwritten music at the bottom of the page here."

"You think these scribbles are important?"

"I think yes, extremely. But that's one of a hundred things about this piece of music, and the manuscript itself, that I want to understand."

Otylie sat for a minute, watching snow gather on the sill. Hadn't it snowed the day the Nazis marched into Prague and turned her life, and the lives of all those closest to her, into a nightmare? But this was a different snow, calm and white, covering the earth for its winter slumber.

Meta's voice broke the brief pause. "I have another question. I'm wondering, did your father ever tell you the story about how the manuscript came to be in his possession? I know it was long ago, but any scrap of information you can recall might be very useful."

"I do remember that he bought it from a manuscript dealer in Vienna."

"Do you remember who and when?"

The old woman tipped her head to the side with a slight frown. "If he told me, I have forgotten, I'm afraid. I was nine when he died. The one thing I do recall is that when he made his embarrassing claims that this was written by Beethoven—"

"Not so embarrassing," Meta interjected.

"—the dealer told him it had been a gift to a girl, an inamorata whose name I do remember because it was so beautiful. Maria Anna von Westerwold. I even told my poor papa that when I grew up I wanted to change my name to Maria Anna von Westerwold."

Meta shot another glance at Gerrit. "I feel guilty asking you, but would you mind making a note of that name?"

He smiled, pulled out his pocket notebook, and began to write.

"Anything more?" Meta gently prodded.

"My father always said that war is music and music is war. This I never understood. But if you think of war as more than just nations fighting each other, think of it as all the demons we wrestle with, all our pain, then I can understand how this composer, whether or not it was Beethoven, brought music to life out of war. Personal war and disappointment, yes. And also the joy of life."

Meta was awed by what she had just heard. Again she looked over at Gerrit, who said, "Every word."

"Otylie," Meta said. "Anything more you can tell me about the sonata, your father, even the smallest details, could be helpful."

"I have many questions for you as well. But first, let me ask, were you two able to eat something when you were down at the Kolach Korner Café? That is where you were, right? The only one in Prague."

"We didn't, actually," said Gerrit. "Once we discovered that an Otylie from old Prague was living a few blocks up the way, we were too excited to eat one of the square fish sandwiches we saw on the menu."

"Mrs. Paul's," Otylie said with a winking frown. "Bad for digestion. Let's go into the kitchen and have some of my nice chicken casserole. I made more than enough for all of us. And I want to hear more about old Prague. What it's like these days."

"Gerrit's Czech American and he's lived there for years, so he'll be able to tell you better how it's changed since the revolution."

"And more about your trip, about so much."

The afternoon stretched into evening. Otylie pulled out her best bottle of vintage wine, one that Danek himself had told his wife he was saving for a special occasion. While she made no mention of it, sharing the bottle with this young couple was her way of including him in the festivities too, along with Jakub and Irena. Her cheeks warmed and reddened with the second glass Gerrit poured, and she felt ardently serene, surrounded by ghosts of the past and these angels, as she thought of Meta and Gerrit, of the present.

"Where were you planning to stay tonight?" she asked, noticing the hour. Nine thirty, a little after her usual bedtime.

"Honestly, we just assumed we'd be driving back to Lincoln," Gerrit answered.

Meta added, "I guess we never believed we would actually find you."

"No driving back to Lincoln in this weather. You can spend the night right here with me. I have a guest bedroom where you can stay."

"Are you sure? We can find a place here in town if it's an imposition."

"No imposition. Besides, there is no place in town. The thing is, I'm afraid I have twin beds in there, so you'll probably have to sleep apart."

"I doubt I'm going to be able to sleep tonight anyway," said Meta.

But she was wrong. The couple stayed up for only an hour after Otylie retired, having set out fresh towels for them. Over the last of the wine, Gerrit asked Meta what that look was in her eyes when she noticed the two staves of scrawled music at the bottom of the last page of Otylie's movement. Meta took a deep breath and said, "I'm not infallible. No, strike that. I'm fallible. All right?"

"I don't understand."

"I'm all but certain that so-called scrawl is in Beethoven's autograph. The system braces are vertical lines without slashes at top and bottom, and the treble clef has a central dot, which he abandoned for the most part in later years. Not to mention the dynamic signs, going from pianissimo to fortissimo just like that? Very Beethovenian. I can't be sure of any of this, but I'm more and more convinced this sonata is a lost piece of juvenilia. Whenever this sketch was made, he might have incorporated some version of it into another composition. He did that all the time, borrowed from himself."

Gerrit understood at once. "My God, this means your work hasn't even begun."

"That's just what it means."

Rather than sleep apart, they nestled together in one of the twin beds. Wound up though she was, Meta slumbered deeply until a brilliant morning sun, reflected by sparkling fresh snow, came pouring through the lace-curtained window. Gerrit had slipped out of bed earlier, she realized as she gradually awakened, stretched, and swung her feet onto the rug. She could hear his voice and Otylie's in the kitchen, and smelled coffee and sausage. Peering down at the faded cotton nightgown Otylie had lent her, she was enchanted by the old-fashioned pattern of small flower garlands. She looked around the room and noticed an old photograph, a silver print perhaps, of a newlywed couple posed stiffly, although emanating a nervous happiness, before a painted mountain scene. The bride was seated and the groom standing just behind to her left, his forearm resting on a carved wooden pedestal. Otylie's parents? She would have to ask, she told herself, as she changed back into her jeans and black wool sweater. She glanced at the bed where she and Gerrit had spent the night, tucked her hair behind her ear, and left the bedroom, following Otylie's distinctive and already familiar voice down the hallway.

A DIFFERENT GENUS OF SNOW from that in Prague, Nebraska, a sparse, urban snow, sootier than its prairie counterpart, filtered down from the drab skies over New York. It collected on parked cars and garbage bins, on streetlamps and bikes chained to wrought-iron fences, and on the overcoat of a man who stood in the East Village, blinking up at the tenement where Meta lived. Any passerby who didn't know Petr Wittmann might have thought he was weeping. He was not. Rather, he was frowning, awed by the ugliness, to his snow-wet eyes, of this run-down edifice with its fire escape zigzagging up the brick facade, its paint flaking, some plastic flowerpots perched on rickety landings where dead and leafless plants were glazed by hoary slush.

Having arrived by taxi from his midtown hotel, he now climbed the worn cement steps, entered the dim foyer, and pressed the buzzer for Taverner, noting the spelling with a shrug. Given the distressed state of the building and, for that matter, the neighborhood itself, he wondered why she, or anyone else, would choose to live here. Realizing that nobody was at home, or at least that no one was inclined to speak on the intercom, he crossed to the other side of the street and scanned the top-floor windows, hoping to see her furtive face there, or some sign of life. Instead, the dirty windows dully stared back at him.

Wittmann felt a sudden twinge of pity for Meta Taverner. He now believed he understood why she was so committed to the sonata manuscript. How else would she be able to escape this slum? Her life was a dreary dead end—subsistence in this ramshackle building, living hand to mouth, a concert career shattered as Mandelbaum had explained, and little to look forward to in the rebound pursuit of musicology. The sonata was her meal ticket. Her search wasn't the altruistic act of an idealist. It wasn't a leap of faith into the pristine air of pure discovery and research. It was her way to get ahead.

As more snow drifted onto his face, he grimaced and looked down at his elegant brown shoes, remembering that the last time he stood staring up at a set of windows was on Jánská, before breaking into Gerrit's apartment. He drove his hands into the pockets of his coat, shivered from both the cold and the memory, and silently walked away in a westward direction in search of a restaurant where he could have a quiet lunch, a drink or two, and think, before seeking out Meta's mother farther west of Fifth Avenue.

For all his keen skills of observation, his talent for scrutinizing works of music and subtleties of performance, for all his past savvy in convincing others above and below him to capitulate to his ideas, his will, his wants, Wittmann had to admit to himself that he'd never been accomplished at self-scrutiny. He'd always been too busy to bother. It wasn't as if, over the course of his notable career, he'd had a lot of time to sit down, fist to chin like that pensive Rodin, and think much beyond present exigencies. Maybe he should have. Maybe if he had, he'd be a still-married man collaborating on a once-in-a-lifetime discovery rather than thousands of miles from Prague, nursing a bowl of French onion soup and a glass of cabernet.

Reluctantly, Wittmann realized how nostalgic he was for the times when Mandelbaum and he had worked hand in glove. Heady days, those, when his books were doing well and he was manipulating a system that was itself masterfully manipulative of comrades who stepped outside politburo policies. The income from his complicated transactions never hurt either.

That Mandelbaum had gone to seed, shunning any such pursuits, was his choice. But Wittmann, now, here, for all his second thoughts, was in it deep. His return ticket was open, he mused, after a second glass. He could get a good night's sleep at the hotel, call Charles Castell in the morning with profound regrets at having failed to procure the score, catch his flight back to Prague, and start making notes toward his next book. He had been thinking about Leonard Bernstein, a natural outgrowth of his Mahler research. The composer of *West Side Story*, like his forebear, was a celebrated conductor, one who championed Mahler's once neglected, even Nazi-banned symphonies and brought them to the wider public. Bernstein was a man of his time. A political activist, he gave parties attended by Black Panthers. A married man, he also slept with men. A dashing globe-trotter, he was classical music's world ambassador. A born showman, he was balletic on the maestro's podium. Yes, Leonard Bernstein was a terrific subject. One his publishers would love, a project he could deliver in two years without any problem.

After a calvados, Wittmann paid his tab and left the restaurant. Snow had tapered off and the sun had come out. The city was sparkling and winking. He hadn't settled on what he would say to Meta's mother if he succeeded in locating her, but those drinks had dissolved his brief ambivalence. The air was bracing as he made his march up Sixth Avenue to Twenty-Third Street and took a left toward the Hudson River.

The opposite of Meta's down-at-the-heels brownstone, London Terrace was a classic prewar apartment building that took up an entire city block between Ninth and Tenth Avenues. Wittmann entered the lobby and asked to see Mrs. Taverner, telling the doorman he was a musicologist colleague of her daughter's in from overseas. When asked for his name, he said simply, "Petr," having no idea whether or not the girl had been in touch with her mother about him or anyone else in her travels.

"And your last name?"

"Wittmann," he said, reluctantly.

To his surprise, Meta's mother was in and Wittmann was invited up. Before walking to the elevator, he asked the doorman, "I'm sorry, but could you remind me what Mrs. Taverner's first name is? Her daughter mentioned it on more than one occasion, but the old memory, you know," and tapped two fingers on his forehead, offering an appealing grin.

"I know what you mean," the doorman said. "Her name's Kate."

"That's right—Kate, of course. Much obliged."

During the ride up, Wittmann forged his story. He needed to contact Meta directly to let her know he was sorry things had gotten off on the wrong foot. He now understood how consequential this manuscript was, and she would need help finding the lost pages and then deciding what would be best for its proper preservation. He knew a gentleman who would be more than willing to act as a kind of patron to fund all this, and he, Wittmann, was ready to serve as intermediary on her behalf. As he rehearsed this narrative in his head, it all sounded believable because, for the most part, it wasn't far from the truth.

When Kate Taverner opened the door, she didn't ask him in at first, saying instead, "You're friends with Meta?"

"We're acquaintances, yes. She's said many nice things about you, Kate. I hope you don't mind my dropping in unannounced." He identified himself as one of the musicologists her daughter came to Prague to consult, a longtime colleague of Mandelbaum, and explained he was in New York on unrelated business. "I thought I'd try to contact your daughter about something important that came up after she left the Czech Republic."

"About the manuscript, you mean?"

"Exactly. I've been approached by someone who is interested in her project and, if I'm not mistaken, might be willing to help her."

Still clearly wary but curious, she said, "Please, come in," and led him into a sparsely decorated, light-filled living room that doubled as a design studio.

"Graphic arts, interior design?" he asked, nodding at her drafting board and large computer monitor. Despite his focus on other matters, he couldn't help being impressed by this woman's style, her silk blouse and loose-fitting trousers that flowed with her as she turned and offered him a seat on a club chair covered with beige cloque.

"So, tell me more about this," taking a seat on a facing sofa and ignoring his question.

He decided to keep things vague. Describing an unnamed Castell as self-made, committed to the arts, a collector and lay scholar with whom he'd worked successfully in the past and deeply trusted, Wittmann explained he'd been asked to pass along the man's interest in the manuscript and see if some arrangement could be made.

"He wants to buy it, in other words?"

"He certainly has the means, if that's what Meta would want. Do you happen to know where I can reach her about this?"

"She doesn't have a cell phone in this country. Last time I heard she was in Texas. Or, no, maybe Oklahoma. I'm a little unclear, just that she was on the road."

Wittmann was unable to disguise how much this threw him. He stared at Meta's mother openmouthed before recovering his composure. "I naturally thought she would have returned to New York, or maybe gone to some other city with a research institution. I'm not even sure where Oklahoma is," he said, raising his eyebrows. "The only reference to it I know, besides the Rodgers and Hammerstein musical, is in Kafka's *The Castle*. And I'm positive Kafka never visited Oklahoma."

"That makes two of us."

"Did she say what she was doing there?"

"She's doing the same thing she has been doing for months, chasing down—" and here she halted, remembering too late her daughter's warning not to discuss these things with anyone. If this man, surely the expert who gave Meta so much grief, didn't know about her theory that Otylie might be residing in a Prague right here in America, then Kate was not about to reveal the information. Not wanting to hurt Meta's prospects, but reading a strange blend of eagerness and discomfort in Wittmann's face, she said, "Professor Wittmann, I have no idea exactly where she is, and since she's on the road, I have no way to reach her."

"Well," he finished, deciding not to push further, "do please let me give you my hotel information, in case she gets in touch. I'd be delighted to fill her in on the details."

On his way out, he asked, for no pointed or scheming reason, "Is this where your daughter grew up? I couldn't help but notice the piano over there."

"It is. That piano was her entire life. I can still see her playing it."

His eyes swept around the room, as if its details might some-how help him figure out what he should do next. Normally when he found himself in New York with no schedule to adhere to, he would find out who was playing Carnegie or Avery Fisher or down-town at the Blue Note and go listen to music. But just now, as he found himself back on the chill and slushy streets of Chelsea, another glass of something strong seemed more in order.

All Mandelbaum could manage to say to Kate Taverner, after his wife called him to the phone, was, "You've got to be kidding."

"I'm telling you, he left here five minutes ago."

"How did he find you? What did he want?"

She gave him as close to a verbatim account of the visit as she could, then added, "I'm not sure what to do. He did sound very serious about this collector being interested."

Mandelbaum sat on a stool at the long butcher-block counter in his kitchen and looked out the window at a family of chicka-dees on the bird feeder. "Like him or hate him, that's a part of the musical universe he knows well. Fact is, there's little about music he doesn't know to some degree, and that's why I proposed Meta meet with him in the first place."

"She knows your intentions were good, Paul."

"What's that line about the road to hell being paved with good intentions? Meta and Gerrit are on a different road, though. Did she give you any idea when she might touch base next?"

"She wasn't specific, but it sounded like they were close. I'm so mad at myself for mentioning Oklahoma to him. At least I didn't say anything about Nebraska."

"What on earth's in Nebraska besides corn and sandhill cranes?"

"With luck, Otylie Bartošová."

"Well, Godspeed to them, wherever they find themselves," Mandelbaum said. "Your daughter's a force of nature."

"What about Gerrit?" Kate couldn't help but ask. Watching from afar Meta's long-distance breakup and new relationship with someone Kate had yet to meet was like squinting at something important that wasn't quite in focus. "Did you get to know him a little when you were there?"

Hearing the concern in her voice, Mandelbaum assured her, "A good man." He rose to go tap on the window to ward off a raucous blue jay that had scattered the chickadees. "I'm no authority on romance, far from it, but from what I can see he's madly in love with her, and vice versa."

"Music to a mother's ears," said Kate Taverner.

After she gave him Wittmann's hotel number—"Not sure what I'd say to him that I haven't already said," Mandelbaum told her—he returned to his study, where he lit a rare cigar and paced up and down the wide floorboards that creaked comfortingly with every step. Wittmann's tenacity was jolting, if not entirely surprising. Mandelbaum had to admit to himself that he'd been wrong. Disappearing from Prague, tacitly recanting any deal they'd flirted with, was not enough to convince his colleague that an endgame had been reached and it was time to move on. Just as the sonata had assumed control of Meta's life, so had it seized Petr's. Mandelbaum wondered in passing if the moneyman Wittmann had in tow was somebody they could work with toward a favorable solution. But he knew that either Meta's idealism or Petr's avidity, or both, would be likely to rule it out.

For his part, Wittmann, emboldened by yet another calvados in a nondescript if noisy bar on Ninth Avenue and then, back in the tastefully oak-paneled and quiet hotel bar, a split of chardonnay, decided to proceed with the plan he'd set in place before leaving Prague. The time had come to call his newspaper contact and tell him to publish the full story. Was there risk in going public with his claim of discovering the final rondo movement of an unknown piano sonata attributable to Beethoven? Yes, but the time line was murky in his favor, he felt, and Johana Langová would stand by him if push came to shove. Was there further risk in asserting that he himself had first identified the central movement, brought to him by an American student for examination, as being by the great composer? Of course, but his scholarly reputation and popularity in various circles made it a practicable risk. Besides, unlike the girl, he was on record with several Beethoven experts as having proposed such a possibility very early in the game. He might have preferred to avoid directly accusing Meta of committing a crime by smuggling original copies of the manuscript out of the country, but the time for that was past. She herself would have to explain her actions and others could make up their minds.

As he had tried to tell Mandelbaum more than once, he'd been willing to share. Share credit, share whatever benefits might come from the salvaging of such a treasure. But he had been blocked, tricked, dismissed. And it was now clear from Kate Taverner that Meta was more lost in the woods than ever, running around Oklahoma—*where the wind comes sweepin' down the plain*. He smirked. Enough was enough.

After breakfast, Meta asked Otylie if it would be possible to make two long-distance collect calls, to her mother and her mentor.

"Anything you need," Otylie said.

Meta walked to the front room and sat at a small desk, which displayed framed photographs from Otylie's life. In one that caught

Meta's eye, Otylie, in her sixties probably, was standing knee-deep in a calm river wearing waders, with a bamboo rod in one hand and holding high in the other a trout she had caught. A handsome man, surely her second husband, stood next to her mugging for the camera with both palms extended outward, shoulders hunched in jesting dismay, rod tucked under one arm but no fish to brag about. A touching image, Meta thought. Such a path Otylie had followed, and now to have this moment that wove part of her past into her present? Once in a rare while life veered—or erred—toward perfection.

Her mother accepted the reverse charges.

Without preliminaries, Meta said in as calm a voice as she could muster, "I have the best news a daughter could tell her mother—"

"What!"

"—Oh, no, it's not that, but just as good."

Catching her breath, Kate Taverner quickly understood. She hated to cut in on her daughter's triumph, but she had to let Meta know about Petr Wittmann's unexpected visit.

"If he wants to help, fine," Meta interrupted. "If he wants to hinder, fine. It doesn't matter, not anymore. The fact is, I've put the sonata back into the hands of its uncontested, rightful owner, Otylie Bartošová Hajek, and nobody can dispute that."

"Meta. Listen to me. I've been getting calls since then from reporters looking for you to comment about a story that seems to have broken in a Prague newspaper. They're saying you may have fled the country with a stolen score, cultural treasure, all that."

Stomach tightening, Meta said, "That's crazy, totally backward. If I fled from anything, it was a potential thief named Petr Wittmann. I've got to call Paul right away, and Gerrit has to be in touch with his editor to get her the true story, so I'm sorry but I need to sign off now."

Mandelbaum, it turned out, had also received calls from several news organizations and had refrained from commenting. "But tell me first," he said. "You actually found her? The manuscript's intact? It all matches, aligns, musically fits? What does it sound like?"

When Meta, after briefly answering his yes-or-no questions, told him about the music written, she was as sure as sunrise, in Beethoven's hand, Mandelbaum's end of the line went quiet.

"An autograph sketch," he finally said.

"Yes, trust me."

"Christ almighty. Anything you recognize?"

"Paul, I found it less than twenty-four hours ago. I haven't had time for any kind of analysis. That said, I'd be surprised if it didn't find its way, revised probably, into the canon. You know how he worked."

"Do I. This brings the business into a whole new realm."

"I can say this. The sketch is definitely not a part of the sonata itself, at least this sonata. That much is indisputable. Feels later, more mature, more sui generis."

Mandelbaum hummed three random descending notes and asked, "So do they have a decent hotel in—where are you again?"

"Heartland America," she said. "Prague, Nebraska."

"Nearest city being?"

"Lincoln. You coming?"

"Immediately. And as far as dealing with this bad reporting coming out of Europe, don't complain and don't explain. It's all bee stings, and we're neither one of us allergic to bees. The truth will take care of everything."

He was right, of course. "One more thing," she said. "Have you ever heard of a girl named Maria Anna von Westerwold?"

"Can't say as I have. Why?"

She told him what Otylie had said, adding, "I obviously don't have access to any reference books—"

"Got it," said Mandelbaum. "I have the principal biographies here. If there's time before I head to the airport, I'll see if she turns up anywhere." Before hanging up, he said sternly, "Please assure me that Prague, Nebraska, has a bank with safe-deposit boxes?"

"Yes, Father."

Otylie agreed to everything Meta and, through her, Mandelbaum proposed. "I never had need for a deposit box. But Danek was friends with the man down at the Bank of Prague. I'm sure he will help."

"I know it's cold out, but if you could see your way clear to coming with me to the bank—where is it?"

"Across the street from the café and post office."

While Meta and Otylie drove to the hamlet's tiny business district, where the bank did have a vault and a scanner—and to pay a visit to the local photographer to arrange a spur-of-the-moment shoot—Gerrit telephoned New York to give Margery an update.

"How quickly can you get corroboration, airtight authentication?" were her first words, and, in the same breath, "And how fast can you get me the story?"

"Story's essentially written. I just need to sit down at the keyboard—"

"Keyboard? Listen to you. You've obviously been hanging around with musicians too much."

"Laptop," he said with a laugh. "As to authentication, the musicologist Paul Mandelbaum is flying out here immediately to examine it."

"What about one of the Czech musicologists who saw it?"

"Wittmann is a lost cause, but there was another man named Kohout, who, though he had initial reservations, might be a possibility."

"Find him, ask him. Meantime, Mandelbaum and Taverner may be enough to go with preliminarily, worded gingerly. My bottom line? Bring it back to New York, where a group of experts can evaluate it and make as absolute an adjudication as possible. And—"

"And?"

"You're not going to want to hear this, but you're in the middle of this story now, and I'm not sure it should have your byline. Certainly not exclusively."

"I've been in the middle of stories before and reported on them without problem."

"True," she agreed. "But when you were covering the Velvet Revolution, if Václav Havel were Václava and you'd fallen in love with her, we would have had a serious problem on our hands. You know memoir isn't journalism."

"And we both know history is subjective. Just ask Herodotus."

"Herodotus, thank God, is not one of my reporters. File your draft and let me get one of our classical-music people from Arts to work on it."

"Understood," Gerrit said, a little deflated by her words even as he recognized the ethics and propriety that prompted them.

"Meantime let's pursue redundant authentication. Anybody who's wedded to there being only a certain number of Beethoven sonatas is going to push back, look for holes, all the usual contrarian activity. I believe in this story, but prove it to me again."

After looking up Kohout's phone number in his notes, he glanced at his watch. It wasn't that late in Prague, he thought, so why not? At worst he'd get through and Kohout would hang up on him. This was known as "declined to comment" among many in the journalism world. In that event, Gerrit would simply leave the man out of his story.

"*Ano*," a voice answered, to Gerrit's surprise.

Is this Professor Karel Kohout? he said in Czech.

Who is asking?

Now was not the moment to mince words, to hedge in any way. Gerrit identified who he was, including his relationship to Meta Taverner, and why he was calling. When the line didn't go dead, he proceeded to tell Kohout about what had been discovered in Prague, Nebraska, and confirmed that the sonata's original owner was alive and her property had been restored to her. He then stated that the first movement appeared to include a brief autograph sketch by Beethoven, and that it seemed increasingly likely the work was by this composer, a sonata not part of the known canon.

I am aware, Gerrit said, that you had an opportunity to examine the other two movements, and was wondering if you might be willing to state your impression for the record.

Kohout audibly inhaled before saying, My impression was inconclusive when Meta Taverner first approached me. My impression will have to remain inconclusive until I have had a chance to examine the entire work. I know the controversy surrounding its ownership. I know the principals involved. I think there is a chance that great confusion has unnecessarily caused great problems.

Do you think there is a possibility, sir, that this sonata might have been written by Ludwig van Beethoven?

I think, despite all the odds against such a thing, that there is a possibility, yes.

A strong possibility? Faint possibility?

A good possibility, Kohout said.

Thank you, sir.

Oh, and I would very much like to scrutinize the original, should the opportunity ever be offered.

I will convey that.

Good night.

After assuring Otylie that his newspaper would pay her phone bill, Gerrit began writing a full-length article. Knowing that some material would be cut, some added, he left himself out of the story except to stipulate, as disclosure, that the writer had traveled with Ms. Taverner from Prague to Prague. Nor did he have any qualms about discounting his participation in the quest, since he had committed early on to letting Meta follow her own instincts and intuitions. She was the prime mover, he the encouraging companion.

When the two women returned from downtown Prague, hours later, Meta told him how cooperative and friendly everybody had been.

"They were impressed by you and how serious you are," Otylie ventured.

"Thanks for saying so, but don't listen to her, Gerrit. This woman is loved here, by one and all. I think if I asked them to repaint the bank in neon pink to make her happy, they'd go outside, snow and all, and do it."

Gerrit chuckled. "Pink bank? No doubt you're right. Did you rent the safe-deposit box?"

"The original and three CDs of the scans are there tonight," Meta said, telling him how the manuscript had been carefully scanned at the bank and, afterward, shot from above leaf by leaf, in the home studio of a baffled but skilled local photographer who was used to taking baby, graduation, and wedding pictures.

"Very nice lady," said Otylie. "She promised to develop a set of prints by tomorrow morning."

"Sounds like everything's safe."

"I doubt it'll disappear this time, though I was tempted to get a box where we could hide the key to the other safe-deposit box," Meta said, half serious.

Gerrit told them about the conversation he'd had with his editor and the need to work swiftly. "Margery also suggested we consider flying with the manuscript to New York, where it can be analyzed by others as well."

"Would that be all right with you, Otylie?" asked Meta, knowing the weight of her request.

"This must be done," Otylie concurred.

"Would you be able to come with us, do you think? I know this is all sudden. We've kind of blown into your life like a blizzard."

Otylie couldn't help shaking her head in wonder. "A welcome blizzard. I must admit to you that when my Danek died, I thought nothing would ever happen to me again. But I was wrong. You have given me back a part of my life that I believed was gone for good. So, yes, yes. This kind of travel won't be easy for me but, yes, I would like to go."

"Wonderful," said Meta, beaming.

"Don't forget, I was once a New Yorker. I can maybe stay with my old family there. I'll call to let them know I am coming. They would love to meet you."

For the second time in a matter of weeks, Meta picked her mentor up at the airport, this time in snow-covered Lincoln, on a blindingly bright sunshiny day. "Short time no see," he said, kissing her on both cheeks and adjusting his shoulder bag.

"I should tell you," she replied, leading him out to the parking lot, "we're going to be right back here at the airport tomorrow on a flight to New York."

"In that case, I guess I need not adjust my watch to local time?"

As they drove to downtown Lincoln, Meta caught him up on what had happened and why, using the last of their resources and with Otylie's help, she had booked them all into the Cornhusker and reserved economy seats for the next day. The Prague Sonata original was with them as well—this was necessary for its authentication—and the negatives and photographs were stored safely in Otylie's deposit box along with one of the CDs. Meta had another in her bag and had mailed the third to her mother for triple redundancy.

"We only have photographs of several paintings by van Gogh to corroborate their existence and for art historians to study," Gerrit had pointed out. "I'm not feeling fatalistic about this, though. This sonata, at least as a work of music, will never be lost again."

Mandelbaum was as emotional as Meta had ever seen him when, at the hotel, she introduced him to Otylie and Otylie presented him with the score.

"In the life of someone devoted to music, as I understand you are as well, this is one of those moments never forgotten," he said. "Do you mind if we pass over preliminaries and get straight to the manuscript?"

"Of course. You've come for this purpose," the old woman said.

He put on his glasses, examined the top leaf, read Otylie's father's inscription to her from another era and commented, "'*Engelsmusik für mein Engelchen.*' Beautiful words. Your father loved you."

"Yes, it is true."

"'*Sonate*' in a later hand, but not your father's."

"How do you know this?"

"Script is mid-nineteenth century or thereabouts. We'll have to figure out who wrote that, if possible. Could be important."

"Maybe the seller that Otylie's father bought it from, or even a Beethoven family member," Meta suggested.

"Could be. By the bye," Mandelbaum went on, "I was able to look into your Maria Anna von Westerwold back in Lawrenceville. Meta mentioned to me that your father told you that at one point this may have belonged to her."

"Yes?" said Otylie and Meta at almost the same time.

"As it happens, she turns up in Wegeler and Ries."

Puzzled, Otylie asked, "Wegeler?"

"Franz Gerhard Wegeler and Ferdinand Ries," Meta explained. "Close friends of Beethoven's. They wrote one of the earliest memoirs about him."

"Do you have any written evidence about this?" Mandelbaum asked. "Did your father keep a receipt or have any documentation besides the manuscript itself?"

The woman shook her head. "I'm afraid all I have are patchy memories."

"Not so patchy," Meta interjected. "You remembered Maria Anna's name and it turns up in early source material? That's meaningful. This is potentially another piece of the puzzle we can put in place."

Gerrit jotted notes on this exchange, as grateful to hear its conjecture and knowledge as he was to be able to openly transcribe it in Meta's presence.

"She's right," Mandelbaum added. "And it would appear that our Maria Anna knew Beethoven more or less exactly when this piece seems to have been composed. There's plenty of research ahead. But now, let's look at this supposed Beethoven autograph sketch material at the end of the first movement," gazing over his glasses at Meta, eyebrows gnarled.

"Supposed? Owl, careful." She took the manuscript from his hands, set it back down on the table in the concierge room where they had gathered, and turned to the folio leaf in question. "You tell me otherwise."

He pushed up his glasses from the bridge of his nose. "Please, Meta, could you get me one of those protective sheets from my briefcase." Gently placing the clear plastic on the page, he told Otylie, "We don't need an aging professor to drip sweat on this now, do we."

She nodded, but looked on in disbelief, thinking how often, many decades ago, she had handled the score as a child with hands unwashed after eating porridge or soft-boiled eggs. How many times her father had done so, drunk with his mulled wine, smoking and singing and speechifying. How many times in later years she had wept while leafing through the pages, ruing her fate as an orphan of the First World War, and then, in a most different but equally horrific way, of the Second. And now, here was this scholar, his face inches away from a chaos of ink that she'd always considered a child's scrawl, an energetic but worthless doodle at the end of the first movement of her father's—her—manuscript.

"I'm damned if it's not," whispered Mandelbaum, so quietly none of them made out his words.

"What," said Meta.

He craned his neck, looked her in the eye, and repeated more articulately, "I said, 'I'm damned if it's not.'"

Meta's eyes traveled from Mandelbaum's to Gerrit's to Otylie's. She couldn't speak.

Otylie did. "If I understand you, my father was not so crazy? This is important? I was right to listen to him and to Jakub, to Tomáš?"

"You were more right than anybody knew, including yourself, Otylie," said Meta, as she embraced the woman—a granddaughter's embrace, as Otylie sensed it—then wrapped her arm around Gerrit's waist.

"Dinner tonight is on me, ladies and gent. A celebration is very much in order," said Mandelbaum. "Meantime, you'll excuse us, but Meta and I need to put our heads together about convening some musicologists to examine this marvel. Beethoven's own hand on the score complicates matters in the most delicious way."

As Mandelbaum meticulously collated the manuscript and Gerrit excused himself to complete and file the article, Meta asked Otylie, "What would you like to do with the rest of the afternoon?"

A moment of melancholy coursed through the woman as she remembered that the one person she would so wish to share the extraordinary news with, Jane Burke, had died a few years back, not long after Grace Sanders had called to share the news that her mother, Adele, was gone. Otylie sometimes wondered how she had outlasted everyone. Wasn't her time to join the vast community of the dead soon to come? Perhaps, but not just yet.

"A nice long nap before dinner," she said. "This old lady will need all her courage tomorrow."

"Courage?"

"Courage, yes, Meta. I've been on trains, boats, autobuses, even on a horse. But this is my first time up in the air," she said, with a calm if furtive wink.

TWO STORIES AS CONTRADICTORY as yes and no, each announcing the discovery of a hitherto unknown early piano composition purported to be by Ludwig van Beethoven, were published within days of each other. To the casual reader, these articles disagreed on all but two facts. The importance of the score and its miraculous survival.

Those who had authored or informed each news narrative read the other and found fault, of course, in what had been reported. But for Petr Wittmann, who, in his hotel room, read Gerrit's story, one detail in particular took the breath out of him. That Otylie Bartošová had been located, alive and hale, a widow living alone in a Czech immigrant community of three hundred or so townsfolk, was one thing. That Meta Taverner had assembled the complete score this widow had dispersed sixty years before—*dismembered* being one of the less savory but technically accurate terms used for what had occurred—was one thing more. That there was an original sketch probably in the hand of the composer himself, not yet fully confirmed or dated, was yet another tantalizing and devastating detail. One that, if proved to be authentic, Charles Castell would find irresistible.

But when Wittmann saw another, more fatal discrepancy between his copy of the final movement and the one now in Otylie's hands, he knew any pretext of disputing ownership on behalf of Johana Langová had evaporated like so much piss on a very hot stone. When Tomáš made his otherwise admirable transcription years ago—yes, personal animosities aside, he had to admit the job seemed precisely done—the pianist had omitted Otylie's inscription to her husband, an inscription that Wittmann might consider an act of vandalism but that conclusively proved Otylie's prior ownership.

He needed to make calls, he thought, rubbing his furrowed forehead. But to whom? And what to say?

Anxious as he was over what had just happened, his distress was countered by a sense of exhausted relief. It was as if he glimpsed, however vaguely, a course back toward the life he had been living before this obsession infected him. Perhaps there was a way to save face, to make things right. He went into the bathroom and poured himself a glass of tap water, drank it, poured another. Back at the desk, he looked up Charles Castell's private number in his pocket address book. By then, he knew, Castell would have read the same article he had, and probably expected to hear from his contact. He tried and failed to picture Meta's face as the phone rang.

"Yes." No intermediary, no private secretary; it was Castell himself on the other end of the line.

"Charles, Petr. You've no doubt read the piece in today's paper."

"Are you in touch with Ms. Taverner about the manuscript?"

Never one to mince words, Wittmann mused. Castell's tone didn't project frustration, displeasure, chagrin, defeat, any of the feelings Wittmann had been suffering. If anything, he heard encouragement, even hope, like the last sprite to fly out of Pandora's mythic box.

"I did pay a visit to the mother and she knew Meta was somewhere out in Oklahoma, but hadn't any idea where. That gave me little to work with."

"So you tried to draw her out with an accusation in the press."

Wittmann didn't know how to respond. Castell's observation was undeniable, but was it an accusation itself?

"Yes, Charles. I did."

The collector paused before saying, "I'm not sure I would have proceeded that way. But I'm not sure I wouldn't have either. In point of fact, procedural issues aside, it worked."

"Insofar as it's prompted this counter-article by her loyal boyfriend."

"You're right," Castell said. "Let's be careful, though, not to denigrate those we would prefer to befriend to reach our objective. I thought the article was, from what I know, accurate. My main point is this, Petr. I am still interested in making sure the manuscript is never lost again, and while I might have enjoyed owning it for a time, the tides have changed. What can you do to get me, still indirectly, still anonymously, if that's possible, in touch with Ms. Taverner? Or even Mrs. Hajek?"

Wittmann stared at his wristwatch on the bedside table and said, "I'm pretty sure this can be accomplished through my Princeton person."

"Mandelbaum. All right. You'll notice I'm not abandoning you. At all. Not every transaction goes the way we conceived it. Platitude, yes, but platitudes have muscle. Comes from the French for *plate*, but also *rectitude*. Look, you've always been resourceful and have helped me acquire some remarkable things over the years. Let's get this score, and if not, I would at least like to fund its scholarship, in which case we will go through my foundation. If I can't possess it, I'd like to be associated with it. Can you make that happen?"

"I'll do my best, Charles."

"Good, thanks. I have to take another call now. Look forward to hearing," and he hung up.

Wittmann didn't know whether to scream, laugh, curse, or throw the phone at the wall. Charles Castell had offered him a way out, sure, right. But to pursue it he would have to face truths— another platitude; how they proliferate, he thought, grimacing— he didn't want to face. One of which was that this sonata was more powerful than those who came into contact with it, possessed or didn't possess it, played it, died preserving it.

WHEN META AND HER COMPANIONS arrived in New York, Gerrit bought a copy of his newspaper in the first airport kiosk he could find and saw the article listed at the bottom of the front page, sending readers to the Arts section, where its opening was printed above the fold along with a cropped photograph of the score. Turning a few pages inside the section, he continued reading and he saw that less had been excised from his text than he'd expected. Interesting new material had been added, material that gave the sonata richer historical background and made mention— necessary, if annoying, Gerrit realized—of the conflicting accounts about how the manuscript ended up in the United States.

The byline was, as promised, shared. He was overall pleased with his first reporting on the Prague Sonata, knowing more lay ahead in the immediate future, especially after Meta and Mandelbaum met that very afternoon with the other musicologists who had agreed on short notice, setting aside busy schedules, to gather and analyze it.

"Reading something and having lived through it are such different experiences," Meta told Gerrit, after handing the paper to Otylie, who, still in a happy daze from the flight, sat on her other side in the backseat of the cab they shared going into town from La Guardia. "Thank God you were taking notes all along. Not that it didn't ruffle my feathers. But you couldn't have written this otherwise."

"Not as factually, at least," he said.

Meta squeezed his hand.

"I don't think it's fully sunk in what you have managed to do, dear," offered Otylie. "It does not seem entirely real to me, either."

"It's real all right," Mandelbaum said, reaching over from the front seat to take the paper she handed him. "But, lest euphoria get in the way of less pleasant realities, we'll need to contact Wittmann the moment we get to the city."

Unbeknownst to Petr, Mandelbaum had booked a room for himself in the same hotel where his disquieted colleague was staying. They needed to come to some resolution about all this, and face-to-face would be best, he felt. He had consulted with Meta the day before, the two of them alone in the lounge of the Cornhusker, and once they'd determined who among the most respected authorities on the period and the composer should be invited first to inspect the discovery, the subject of Wittmann— "Bête noire extraordinaire," groaned Paul—naturally came up.

"Sure he might have acted more collegial. But you did send me to him because you trusted his erudition and his opinion. In a weird way, I think his competitiveness, or whatever it was or is, spurred me on rather than defeated me," Meta said.

"Remember that old palindrome, *Able was I ere I saw Elba*?"

"Right, you did say he'd either be my Canaan or my Elba. Well, I was more provoked, even challenged, by Petr 'Elba' Wittmann. You know what, though. This isn't over yet. He could still help us and maybe himself at the same time."

Mandelbaum saw where she was headed. "A formal statement of retraction?"

"It might allay some of the confusion he's caused," she said, looking past her mentor out the high-floor window and over the snow-covered buildings of Lincoln.

"I'd suggest we consider inviting him to get over himself already and put his very seasoned eyes objectively on the score, but part of me wonders if he hasn't rendered himself an irrelevancy."

Her gaze returned to Mandelbaum, who was studying her carefully. "Getting knowledgeable, seasoned, objective eyes on the score is exactly what is most important now," she went on, her expression firm and open. "Its composer deserves no less."

"You're sure you'd be willing to do that?"

"Paul, he'll never be a friend of mine. Never someone I would personally trust. But something professional from him on this might clear his smoke and mirrors, make it so all the light is focused on the one thing here that matters most."

"And what about this collector contact of his?"

"The manuscript's not mine to sell, give away, or anything else," she said. "Right now I see that as more a blessing than not. But if this man can help somehow, I'm not in the business of turning away help."

A hastily arranged colloquy of three prominent outside experts— American, British, and German, the latter two living and teaching in the city—met in Mandelbaum's old digs at Columbia's music department. All agreed that it was imperative to widen the field and bring in authorities from Europe and elsewhere in America to weigh in on the discovery as soon as possible. Petr Wittmann was not a member of this first group, but after a tense conversation with Mandelbaum, it was agreed that he would extend his stay in Manhattan for another few days in order to examine the complete score. He also agreed to telephone Charles Castell, who was amenable to funding research on the manuscript as well as insuring it until an institution might be identified in which it could find a permanent home. Wittmann considered this his best and only course of action, knowing from past experience that though such arrangements would not result in a commission, Castell was generous with reimbursement of expenses and honoraria. This was his sole path and he took it with grudging consolation.

Having gone over the wording with Paul, Wittmann released a statement to the Prague journalist he had been working with, and provided it as well to Gerrit Mills for publication in his paper and anywhere else he deemed appropriate.

"On learning that Mrs. Bartošová is alive and in receipt of the sonata manuscript whose provenance and sole proprietorship have been firmly established based on internal evidence in the document itself, I wish to convey that Johana Langová, of Prague, Czech Republic, is delighted that the score has been returned to its rightful owner notwithstanding the means of its delivery, and in light of this new information she relinquishes any claim of ownership. As for my own involvement in this matter, my concerns and actions were solely based on ensuring proper handling of a unique cultural artifact. I look forward to working with the American team, along with an international collective of musicologists, on the further study of the document and will assist them in any way I can. On a personal note, I congratulate Ms. Meta Taverner on the discovery and diligent work involved in reunifying such a remarkable document."

Gerrit commented, "Well, I wouldn't consider that a particularly salient example of eating humble pie, but the bastard did the best he could manage."

"Caviar pie is more to his taste than humble," said Mandelbaum.

Meta asked to see the statement herself. She read it through, word by word. After tucking her hair behind her ear, she turned to Otylie, sitting next to her on the couch in Kate Taverner's apartment, and explained, as briefly as she could, what had happened and what Wittmann's admission meant. "Sometimes in life what's broken can't be put back together," she said. "Other times, like this time, what's broken refuses to remain so."

"This is right," Otylie agreed, a smile illuminating her wrinkled face, not thinking at all about Petr Wittmann. "Or maybe it was never truly broken at all."

NOT ONE TO BE RUSHED, OTYLIE'S FATHER continued to leaf through the score at his own pace, although the music dealer's tantalizing hint that something of great consequence was to be found at the end of the first movement prodded him on. When Jaromir did finally come upon two staves of music hurriedly written in a very different hand at the bottom of the specified page, his heart leaped.

Is this—?

Yes, we were guaranteed by Karl's son, Ludwig, that these measures, a brief sketch, are in the hand of his great-uncle and namesake. We believe it incontrovertibly proves that the sonata is by none other than Beethoven himself.

All this incontrovertible proof only served to renew Jaromir's suspicions. If, as you're claiming, this is a previously unknown Beethoven sonata, why haven't you sold it before now?

With a look an adult might set on his face before gently rebuking a wayward child, the antiquarian said, My friend, you ask an interesting question. The answer is that my father, recently deceased, never offered it for purchase because he preferred to keep it for himself. As for me, I believe one cannot be a seller and collector both. Conflict of interest, bad for business. So I have decided to place it on the market along with other materials my father stashed away in order to do what any merchant must do. Pay bills and stock more inventory.

Why me rather than a museum or library? Jaromir prodded.

The man quietly coughed, looking over his shoulder, then back. We prefer to deal with individuals, as a rule. Museum directors and librarians are, believe it or not, less than expeditious when it comes to fulfilling their financial obligations. That, at least, has been our experience over the course of three generations.

Jaromir couldn't contradict anything the seller told him, although that cough seemed manufactured. But then, people do cough. He continued to peruse the rest of the manuscript, feeling increasingly light-headed. The paper, ink, and stitching thread looked very much like those of other eighteenth-century manuscripts he already owned. The provenance was, it seemed, impeccable. The seller was established. And while the master hadn't affixed his signature to the work, the sketch at the end of the first movement could serve as something better. It might be viewed as a bonus, in fact. Beethoven was famous for writing quick musical notes on any piece of paper that happened to be handy, to be returned to later for possible incorporation into another work.

One other thing, sir, if it might have any bearing on your decision, the merchant said, seeing that his customer was now seriously weighing the purchase.

Yes?

Karl's son told my grandfather that he believed young Beethoven had given this manuscript to a student he'd fallen in love with, a Fräulein Maria Anna von Westerwold. And that when she broke off with him, he asked for its return. It is our working theory that the master had a fair score written out for her. This is all anecdotal, mind you, and we offer it to you with the understanding that its value doesn't depend on the validity or accuracy of this little story. We have no way to prove or disprove it.

That would explain why it is in a copyist's hand.

Even so.

But then, where is the original?

Precious few of Beethoven's early manuscripts have survived, alas.

Did Ludwig, Karl's boy Ludwig, say why it was never published?

Again, conjecture. And conjecture is not necessarily fact, but he believed that his granduncle was so upset by the breakup with this pupil and the tragic family circumstances surrounding its composition that he put it away and never returned to it.

Jaromir Láska knew that it now came down to a question of money. He had been circumspect lately, had he not? Had added nothing to his precious collection in nearly a year, instead saving a little here and there behind his wife's back, against the day when he might be offered something very rare—no, something unique. Something that would be the crown jewel in his collection. This sonata manuscript, were he to buy it, would be just that.

The asking price he was quoted, while steep by his usual standards, didn't seem unreasonable. He asked for a ten percent discount, given that he had been an occasional but steady customer, and also for terms. An invoice was drawn up, a down payment was tendered, and Jaromir left Vienna for Olomouc in a state of shock, of bliss, of blind triumph. He wanted to tell every passerby in the street and every fellow traveler in the coach that the neatly wrapped parcel tied with navy blue ribbon he carried under his arm was a manuscript by the greatest composer of all time. Nothing he would ever own would mean more to him than this. And if his beloved daughter never inherited anything else from him, this sonata manuscript would be a legacy, he surmised, that would afford her endless joy.

* * *

THE FIRST KNOWN PUBLIC PERFORMANCE of the Prague Sonata coincided with the 230th anniversary of Beethoven's birthday on December 16, the same year the sonata manuscript was reunited. Mandelbaum had hastily managed to secure Alice Tully Hall at Lincoln Center for a short-notice midday performance in New York City. The program included two other works, those that had been played by Tomáš Lang on Šporkova decades before—Haydn's Sonata in E-flat Major and Beethoven's first sonata in F minor—as performed by Samuel Kettle, in his first concert appearance in the United States in many years. The performance, underwritten by Charles Castell, who sat in anonymity at the back of the hall, was free and open to the public. Besides Gerrit and the Mandelbaums, Otylie Bartošová Hajek was in the audience of a hundred or so, as were Kate Taverner and Gerrit's parents. Near them, toward the front of the auditorium, sat Meta's friend Gillian, for whom the sonata performance was, as promised, a birthday present, just as

Meta's original introduction to Irena—the gesture that had set all this in motion—had been Gillie's gift for her thirtieth.

Dualing prezzies, wrote Meta in her inscription to Gillie on the program. *Always better than dueling ones.*

Sylvie and the two Kettle children were there. Marta Hašková had flown in. Grace Sanders was in attendance with her husband, two grown children of her own, and her brother and his boyfriend. Jiří had scraped together funds to make the trek, saying, "You came to my opening, I'm here for yours." All these friends were in attendance, together with a number of fellow musicians and musicologists, as well as Margery and other colleagues of Gerrit's, and a nattily if datedly outfitted hairdresser from Queens who had become fast friends with Otylie in the days before the recital.

As Sam Kettle launched into the Beethoven, opus 2, no. 1, Meta sat offstage, listening in nervous ecstasy. His presence here with his family, who were all staying at her apartment in the East Village, was the fulfillment of a promise she'd made to herself in Prague to do something special for the Kettles. And that they were living under Meta's roof—the kids camped out under her piano, just as she'd slept under Sam's—through Christmas and the New Year only made that fulfillment richer.

She did finally have to break down and borrow money from Mandelbaum to make it happen, but going into debt to her mentor was made easier by Otylie's insistence that any money that would come from publishing rights or a sale to Beethoven-Haus in Bonn or any other of a number of institutions that might preserve it must be shared. Offers from the unnamed Castell, as well as several institutions, to purchase the artifact were on the table, but at this moment nothing was settled, nothing ruled out. For the time being and the immediate future, everything was focused on the sonata itself. It was real; it was not unscathed but safe. It was, in a word, beautiful.

Meta understood that there was much yet to explore, including the historical terrain in which the sonata traveled from one custodian to another and ultimately ended up in the hands of Otylie Bartošová's father. She understood that some critics would deny Beethoven credit for this youthful music, created centuries ago at a time when he was otherwise silenced by grief for his lost mother. No matter. Even at this somewhat early juncture, after months of searching, Meta and other colleagues now had better than rudimentary ideas, solid ones indeed, to prove any naysayers wrong, knowing it would be the labor of years.

"But what are years for?" Gerrit asked her when she shared her worries with him.

Applause from the theater. Enthusiastic applause, cheering. And Sam smiling to her offstage before going back out to take another bow. Using meditative techniques she'd learned from youth, Meta cleared her mind of all things musicological and speculatively historical, and became again a pianist. A pianist at one with this sonata whose outer movements were lovely and very much of their era, but whose center movement foreshadowed, in both its light and its darkness, the compositions of a revolutionary.

A Note on Czech
Pronunciation and Usage

Unlike English, in which the pronunciation of letters may vary
from one word to another, Czech letters are reliably pronounced
just as they are written. Some are voiced differently when they
carry a diacritic, and there are no silent letters. Additionally,
words in Czech are nearly always stressed on the first syllable.
Thus, "Otylie" is pronounced "*Oh*-til-i-eh," and "Jakub," whose
first letter takes the soft "J" sound, has the phonetic spelling of
"*Ya*-koob." The háček (pronounced "*ha*-chek") in Tomáš's name
changes the sound of the s from "s" to "sh," so "*Tō*-mahsh." Jiří's
name, which ends with a long i, contains the Czech letter perhaps most difficult to pronounce—"ř," which, loosely speaking,
combines a rolled "r" with a "zh" sound (like the "s" in "pleasure"):
"*Yih*-rzhee."

The suffix "-ová" that indicates a feminine surname in Czech
(Bartošová, Svobodová, Kettlová) has been retained, but I have
taken the liberty of omitting the accent that usually appears over
the "y" in the Czech name "Otylie." This is already an unfamiliar

name to American and English readers, and, at any rate, Otylie herself drops the accent when she adopts the United States as her home. Finally, the term *"antikva,"* used to describe Jakub's shop, is not the word Czech speakers would typically use ("antique shop" is the rather gnarly *starožitnictví*) but because this novel was written in English, I preferred *antikva* as a term that would roll more comfortably off an English-speaking tongue.

Acknowledgments

I am enormously grateful to the Guggenheim Foundation for a fellowship that helped make much of the writing of this novel possible. Gratitude as well to my colleagues at Bard College who have been supportive while I worked on the project.

Also, in Prague: Thanks to Tomáš Joanidis for his wise and generous counsel while I explored Prague for insights into the Czech World War II resistance and the Velvet Revolution, for his interpreting, and for his knowledge of Czech culture and history and pubs. To Andrea Bartošová, who walked the streets of Prague with me, offering ideas and answering questions about her city. To Soňa Černocká, head librarian at the Lobkowicz Library, Nela-hozeves Castle, north of Prague, who allowed me to handle rare music manuscripts from the same period as the Prague Sonata. My gratitude also to the anonymous resident at Jánská 12 who answered his door and kindly allowed me, an inquisitive stranger working on a novel, into his building and his flat, then showed the way out via a courtyard to Nerodova.

In New York: My deep gratitude to pianist and friend Jeff Goldstein, and to my Bard colleague, the superb musicologist Christopher Gibbs, who brought a wealth of knowledge to bear on this work. A fraternal hug to Douglas Moore, who traveled with me from New York to two of the American Pragues, in Oklahoma and Nebraska. Thanks to Martine Bellen, who joined me on my first visit to Prague, Czech Republic, in the 1990s, and to Barbara Grossman, for her early encouragement. To Nicole Nyhan, Nicholas Wetherell, Tom Johnson, Beth Herstein, Hy Abady, and Jay Hanus, who read and commented on aspects of the book—thank you. A fanfare to fellow novelists Andrew Ervin and Eli Gottlieb, who each gave the manuscript a close reading and offered advice, and to Pat Sims, who provided a sage preliminary edit. George (Jiří) Huraj, Laura Arten, and Christopher Harwood helped with Czech phrasing, as did Tomáš Kotik, who was an art student in Prague during the Velvet revolution.

In London: To Beethoven expert Jonathan Del Mar, who offered crucial advice about music, composers, the sonata, and all manner of other matters I am greatly indebted. Thanks to Neil Rees of the Czechoslovak Government in Exile Research Society, who provided information regarding details about life in Edvard Beneš's exile government in London and the Aylesbury Vale during the Second World War.

In Prague, Nebraska: Warm thanks to Adolph Nemec, town historian and polka bandleader, who sat with me in the Kolache Korner Café on two separate visits, and answered questions about life in his community. The square fish sandwich was delicious.

In Los Angeles: I am grateful to Carolina Miranda, cultural staff writer for the *Los Angeles Times*, for her invaluable comments regarding the life of a stringer working overseas.

In Italy: To Maria Teresa Delpiano and the whole Delpiano

family, I owe thanks for their support and love over the years while this book was being written, and long before.

Huge gratitude to the wonderful people at Grove Atlantic for bringing this book into the light. To Morgan Entrekin for his belief in my work, and to Allison Malecha, whose keen editorial insights and knowledge of all things Czech made their mark throughout these pages. Warmest thanks also to Judy Hottensen, Amy Hundley, Deb Seager, Justina Batchelor, Gretchen Mergenthaler, Sal Destro, Julia Berner-Tobin, Susan Gamer, and everyone else at Grove. And to Kimberly Burns, whose energy and enthusiasm know no bounds, my own boundless appreciation for helping to get this novel out into the world.

I am truly grateful to my agent and friend, Henry Dunow, who took me and *The Prague Sonata* on years ago, and patiently represented other books of fiction in the interim while I continued to write this one. His persistence, guidance, and wise editorial perceptions played a critical role as he encouraged me to see this quest to fruition.

Finally, my thanks to the brilliant, indefatigable Cara Schlesinger, who read the many drafts of this novel and brought her razor-sharp literary sensibilities, her personal knowledge of the Czech Republic, and her generous imagination to this novel. My gratitude to her is beyond words.